ANOTHER MAN'S DREAM

Andrew Roth

COPYRIGHT NOTICE

Cover and Interior Design: Derinda Babcock, Deb Haggerty
Editor(s): Cristel Phelps, Deb Haggerty

PUBLISHED BY: Elk Lake Publishing, Inc., 35 Dogwood Drive, Plymouth, MA 02360, 2023

Library Cataloging Data
Names: Roth, Andrew (Andrew Roth)
Another Man's Dream / Andrew Roth

378 p. 23cm × 15cm (9in × 6 in.)
ISBN-13: 9798891340749 (paperback) | 9798891340756 (trade paperback) | 9798891340763 (e-book)
Key Words: Christian western; Santa Fe Trail; Civil War; spiritual growth; historical romance; Old West; Great Plains

Library of Congress Control Number: 2023948159 Fiction

DEDICATION

To those persistent men and women who risked everything and moved onto the Great Plains, into the high mountains, and carved a home from the wilderness. Sometimes they failed, often they succeeded, yet always the results provided the flavor of life.

CHAPTER ONE

The first canister round whistled harmlessly over the heads of the marching men, but the second took out almost a third of the company. Danny Mason staggered with the blast as the concussion swept through the ranks, the roar of the explosion filling his ears. Bodies in blue uniforms tumbled around him, falling like ninepins. He lifted his feet, stepping over the fallen, hastening to touch shoulders with the soldier nearest him.

He realized abruptly he could no longer hear the beat of the drums. The young drummer boys were behind the advancing regiment now, in safety, nowhere near his company. A high-pitched ring vibrated in his head, and he blinked, searching across the battlefield for waving flags or mounted officers to indicate which way to go. Only the unfamiliar lieutenant ahead of the shattered regiment gave any clue, waving a gleaming sword high as he urged the men on.

As Danny's hearing cleared, another roar to his left mowed men down, a few actually flying through the air. Knots tightening in his gut, he marched on, gripping his Springfield rifle until his knuckles whitened.

Danny turned at a *thwack* beside him. The man nearest him whimpered, dropped his rifle, and reached for his bloody face with both hands. Danny kept moving forward.

Jacobs, Mitchell, Thornton, Cassidy, and Leinsdorf were down, among others he barely knew. They were not his friends, he'd known them for only a brief time. The haphazardly refitted unit of men died all around him, but Danny felt no surprise. He gritted his teeth and refused to glance over his shoulder, afraid what he might find. *How many of his company remained?*

Danny sensed Bellows close the gap beside him, stepping over the body of the man with the crushed face. He felt reassured with his position in the middle rank, shielded by the ragged line of men in front of him. Despite the confusion and screams around him, a comforting familiarity swept over him as he brushed shoulders with Bellows. Perhaps the close order drilling did have a purpose after all, he mused as another shell exploded behind him. Danny's eyes held steady on the tree line ahead where the rebels hunkered behind a low stone wall.

"Keep moving, men. Stay in your ranks," the fresh lieutenant called from ahead of the disintegrating company.

The young officer had stepped up only moments before the battle. Danny didn't even know his name. No matter, he thought as another soldier fell farther down the line, the remaining men adjusting positions. The regiment exchanged fallen officers for green ones more often than Danny changed his socks.

He ducked as a mortar whined overhead. But Bellows still walked forward, and Danny straightened again. Bellows had the right idea. Don't stop.

You'll probably die today, so just keep moving. You don't want to be like those who turn and run. That would never do for you, Danny boy, he coached himself, stepping over a dead soldier.

When another blast from the rebel cannon landed behind his regiment, relief filled him. The rebs hadn't adjusted their artillery. He grimaced, knowing they would not make the same mistake twice. Smoke drifted across the field, forcing him to squint through the dark cloud.

Someone shrieked ahead of him, and Danny recognized Hallowell, the recruit who'd bragged about the new Henry rifle he'd purchased with his enlistment bonus. The boy wailed above the din of the battle. Danny reached to steady the hesitating youth when another blast showered him with blood. Blinking through the red smear, he saw Hallowell's head was gone.

He wiped a sleeve across his face, stepping over the dead man while lining on Bellows. Few soldiers remained in the front rank, but Danny pushed on, resolved.

Suddenly, men were thrown against him, and smoke enveloped the shrinking regiment. His hearing was gone again, only a dim buzz filling his confused mind. Danny staggered as his gaze riveted on the unnamed lieutenant that lay sprawled before the company, his body blown in half.

As Danny stared dumbly at the dead officer, another canister round ripped into the hesitating soldiers, and he knew the artillery had found their range. A huge gaping space opened as the men disappeared or fell before the blast.

The force of the round knocked Bellows into Danny's shoulder, spinning him to the ground. He landed atop crumpled bodies.

Something pinned him to the ground, and Danny shoved, needing to free himself from the heavy weight.

Making his escape, he glanced at the perpetrator, eyes widening when he recognized Bellows peering back at him with unseeing eyes. For an instant, Danny studied the dead soldier's face before pushing the man aside.

Thick smoke hung low over the battlefield like a concealing canopy. Beneath this cloud, Danny watched uniformed legs run and limp past him, heading for the rear. Were they retreating Union soldiers or pursuing rebels? At this late stage of the war, Confederate soldiers often stripped the dead for clothing, weapons, and food.

The screams of the wounded and dying filled the air, and he knew he could hear again. Where was his rifle? He glanced around, but no one near him moved.

The boom of cannon made him duck and cover with both hands. Rifle fire sounded close at hand, and he peered through the haze. The rebs had left the protection of the low wall and were in long ranks, marching toward his devastated company.

Danny kicked his legs free from Bellows' limp form. He couldn't feel any wounds yet, but he knew shock would soon wear off and might prevent him from fighting. *I must fight*, he reminded himself. *Danny Mason would fight.*

More shouts drew his gaze. He wasn't trusting his eyesight in the hovering smoke, but when a flag fluttered before the oncoming soldiers, Danny could see the tattered banner wasn't Old Glory. With sickening dread, he saw the stars and crossed bars herald the advancing Confederate line.

Danny snaked over a man on his left, desperately searching for a weapon. Hallowell's fancy gun caught his eye, and he reached for the Henry rifle. He gripped the slimy wooden stock. Blood stained his hand, and he smeared the sticky red stuff across his woolen jacket.

The unfamiliar weapon felt awkward in his hands, and for an instant, Danny considered replacing it with a more common military issue, single shot muzzleloader. But no, the Henry rifle could shoot seventeen times before reloading. He'd seen it done, marveling at its rapid fire, when Hallowell proudly demonstrated the weapon's capabilities before the entire company.

Danny wormed his way to Hallowell and stripped the cartridge belt from the dead man's body. A quick check of Hallowell's pockets resulted in handfuls of the precious bullets. With a tremendous push, Danny shoved the limp body on top of another dead soldier and squirmed behind the improvised breastwork.

He arched an eyebrow at the cowardly thought that came to him. He could just lay behind this wall of lifeless men and feign death. He might be overlooked or perhaps captured, but he would live. Or he could take his chances and run for the rear.

With a grunt, he gripped the rifle tighter and peered around the shoes of the blue-clad wall. Nope, he signed up to fight. Danny Mason was no quitter. No coward. His pride demanded bravery. He had nothing else.

Courage surged, and he grabbed Bellows by the collar and dragged him into place, improving his position. Danny closed one eye and took aim.

He had a clear field of fire. To fall into Confederate hands was almost worse than death. President Lincoln had stopped prisoner exchanges early in the war. A prisoner of war camp and starvation were all that awaited him if he was captured now. He'd heard sickening tales of Andersonville.

He grinned as he sighted down the barrel of the prized repeating rifle. Only the wealthy could afford such fancy guns. And yet an orphan boy from Philadelphia now possessed the remarkable weapon.

He glanced at the approaching rebels and his grin faded. Of course, he might not have this rifle for long.

The noise of the battle raged around him, and yet the hullabaloo seemed far away, as if he were alone, as if this moment were just for him. Wounded horses screamed, mortars shrieked, and men shouted as the clash of armies ebbed and flowed across the littered field. Yet Danny drew a deep breath as an unaccountable calm settled over him.

As the ragtag line of rebels advanced, Danny could make out the Confederate artillery battery posted within the distant tree line. Through the smoke, he saw the swift movements of the soldiers working the big gun. He hoped his fallen comrades would conceal his presence from Confederate sharpshooters hidden in the trees.

Danny held his breath and took up the slack on the trigger, the weapon leaping in his hands as he fired. A man in the front rank of the closest rebel line stumbled and fell as Danny moved the barrel an inch and fired again.

After six shots, the front rank had crumbled, men sprawling beneath their comrades. Soldiers hesitated to continue, but Danny peered past them to the cannon poised along the far trees. His next shot took out the man loading the big gun. His next took out the officer urging the artillery squad to fire.

Over Bellows' head, Danny sighted a gray-clad force moving forward under cover of the drifting smoke. He hefted the rifle and placed four quick rounds among the thickest part of the group. Three men fell and the fourth had to be carried back toward the Confederate lines.

He glanced along the black barrel before taking sight once more. With this gun, the Union Army could take the whole South in no time at all. Sherman himself might slap Danny on the back.

Three gray platoons moved forward on Danny's left. The piled wall of dead bodies would not allow him to fire at this target unless he moved. Leaving the relative safety he'd found behind Hallowell's body, Danny wriggled swiftly to another position. He leveled three shots into the front rank of the nearest platoon before he turned and fired into the next platoon, causing more men to fall and interfere with the advance of the men behind.

A rebel officer shouted orders. A few men took kneeling positions and lifted their rifles in Danny's direction. Without hesitating, he shot each of the four men before they fired a single round. For good measure, Danny shot the officer too.

The rest of the platoon began to fall back. Their orderly retreat quickly dissolved into headlong flight from the field. Danny alternated between the two platoons, hitting several more men before he was forced to load again.

The barrel heated, but Danny hurriedly reloaded. Might as well inflict as much damage as possible before he was discovered, and his position was riddled with bullets. Or a cannon barrage tore him to pieces. *No one would miss an orphan*, he thought bitterly.

The platoon nearest him had broken and run. The other platoon merged into the ranks of another company. Danny concentrated his fire power upon those slowly marching men. His quick and accurate shooting soon melted the platoon into a faltering mess. He rarely missed his targets, and many soldiers broke ranks and fled to the rear rather than face his crushing fire.

Danny praised the zealous Hallowell for the excessive amount of ammunition he carried into battle. Most men only carried forty rounds for their barrel loaders, but Hallowell easily had over a hundred.

Another cannon moved forward on his right and Danny just as quickly took out its gunners. Four more men with sharpshooter stances were systematically taken out of action. Firing with precision and patience, Danny held his ground.

For the better part of an hour, Danny Mason kept Confederate movement to a minimum along his sector of the battlefield. Finally, reserve units were brought forward behind Danny. Union forces claimed the field and pushed the rebels farther back. By nightfall, the tree line was secured.

No one noticed Danny Mason when he suddenly stood from behind a low wall of dead bodies. Black powder marred his face, and his red-rimmed eyes glowed a haunting white from beneath his blue cap. He wandered among the tired troops of the day's battle, searching for familiar faces. He found none. Once again, he was alone.

"Hey, soldier, where is your regiment?"

Danny faced the approaching officer. "Captain, my regiment is gone, I think." He wiped a grimy hand across his jaw. "I can't find anyone else from my company."

The young captain frowned. "That's a common enough story today, private." He hooked a thumb over his shoulder. "Report to the rear. You'll be reassigned to another regiment."

Danny drew a deep breath as he watched the officer stride away. He glanced over the recent battlefield and narrowed his eyes. *That could be me out there*, he thought as he surveyed the scattered bodies, blue and gray alike. So what? Who would care?

Slowly, he turned to make his way to the rear, still carrying the Henry rifle.

CHAPTER TWO

Firelight flickered dully on the faces of the sixteen soldiers who sat with Danny, strangers lounging silently beneath the pines. No one spoke, knowing they would soon be dispersed to other companies.

He glanced at the nearest soldiers, nonchalant stoicism etched into tired, powder-smudged faces. Familiar masks of the afraid and anxious, Danny thought as his gaze pivoted up, between the towering trees to the stars plastered thickly across the sky. He would not reveal his own fear and concerns. *Danny Mason's a rock, an island*, he reminded himself.

After today's battle, the division occupied a ridgetop, and now various regiments filled sections of the stretched front line. Dead horses and broken cannons littered the forest floor, but no one took notice of them. Danny wrinkled his nose when the pungent scent of dead animal drifted on the evening breeze.

Above, he glimpsed the broad belt of closely packed stars he'd seen back in Philadelphia, the light brightening the dark expanse. Where did they come from? In comparison to the twinkling orbs, men were such insignificant bugs.

And the strangeness of life could not be measured. He'd accepted his fate, expected to die in battle earlier today, only to now sit near a fire and wait to be reassigned to another unit.

He tilted his head. Accepting death and fighting courageously didn't seem to go hand in hand. Although resigned, he'd survived to fight another day. What end awaited him?

A sigh escaped him as he pondered his purpose. His musings were cut short when rapid footsteps sounded beneath the trees, approaching the campfire.

A tall, thin soldier, wearing the blue uniform of the Union, entered the circle of firelight. Danny read the stripes on his jacket. Without introductions, the sergeant pointed to the quiet group.

"All right. Let's go. Grab your gear," he ordered. Without looking to see if the men followed, he strode once more into the darkness.

Danny stood quickly with the other soldiers and bent to retrieve his pack. With a final glance at the dying fire, he took the last place in line. He knew from before they would be attached to platoons that needed replacements. Soon, he would be placed in a group of new strangers.

In the distance, he heard the low hum of voices and a somber tune played on a harmonica. He hurried to keep up with the men in front of him, surprised at how swiftly the sergeant led the line of soldiers through the gloom. They passed clusters of soldiers as they followed the ridge crest, fire rings revealing haggard faces around the leaping flames. Danny didn't even care which company he'd be attached to. *What did it matter? More strangers, lonelier.* The discouraging thought came to him, and just as swiftly, fled his mind. *Keep moving.*

He'd seen too much death, too many replacements. Rarely would soldiers of fractured regiments take the time to get acquainted with replacements. Too many gaps appeared in the ranks after every battle. There were always new soldiers added to Sherman's Army.

Danny knew how these things worked. He expected nothing else. Besides, he was here to do a job, to accomplish something. Friends and companions were entanglements he could do without. His life would be over soon enough, he figured. The war had intensified with General Sherman's march to the sea but could not go on indefinitely.

Up ahead, a large campfire blazed. The sergeant stopped in the circle of light and said something to the officer standing near a soiled canvas tent. Danny halted, watching the proceedings with little interest. His reassignment meant nothing, simply an unfamiliar group of men he would fight beside tomorrow, men he vowed not to know.

The officer gestured to a place beside the fire, and seven of the lead soldiers peeled from the line, dropping their packs as the remaining men continued after the thin sergeant.

As they left the firelight and plunged into the dark forest once more, the man ahead of him stumbled. He righted himself quickly, but Danny noticed he favored his left leg.

Another fire in the distance drew Danny's attention. Would he be left at this platoon? Fatigue dragged at him, and he longed to stretch in his blankets, to try and forget the day's battle and why he carried a new repeating rifle.

At the next camp, the tall sergeant said something to an officer seated on a stool. The line of men halted while the officer in charge related his replacement needs. The man didn't even rise from his place beside the warm blaze.

"We'll be needing seven men, Sergeant," the officer said in an indifferent tone.

Danny stared as seven men disengaged from the line of replacements, a cold knot forming in his guts. The officer considered these men as faceless fillers, fodder for the cannons, with no names or identity. So long as they could fight.

The tall sergeant threw a quick salute to the seated officer before moving once more into the night. Only Danny and the limping soldier remained.

The three soldiers melted into the deep shadows of the tall pines. A sentry challenged their progress, but at a word from the thin sergeant, they passed down the spine of the ridge. Danny could feel the thick carpet of pine needles under his worn shoes. With only the pair tagging behind the sergeant, he slowed, and Danny wondered if he'd seen the limping soldier. A glance skyward revealed the stars were no longer visible through the thick canopy of branches.

Ahead, the limping soldier gasped, having difficulty keeping pace with the sergeant. Just when Danny thought the struggling man would call for a halt, a fire gleamed between the trees. The three soldiers stepped into the firelight. The limping man dropped his heavy pack, but Danny stood ready to continue if this was not to be his new assignment.

A fellow sergeant rose from the ground near the bright fire. Danny appreciated his height, taller than the man leading them through the woods. His face seemed darkly tanned and creases lined his rugged features, yet his youth wasn't veiled. The lack of facial hair surprised Danny. Most men didn't take the time to shave, not making the effort to boil water and locate a razor.

"Blair," the thin sergeant greeted. "I've only got two left. Need replacements?"

Blair nodded, peering at the limping soldier with an evaluative eye before he glanced at Danny.

"What's your name, soldier?" Blair asked without the usual hostility a new recruit could expect from his platoon sergeant.

Danny hesitated only an instant. "Mason." He hoped this would be his placement.

"And you?" Blair turned to the man with the hurting leg.

"Roland."

Blair nodded again before turning to the thin sergeant. "I requested eight replacements. The scout platoon has seen a lot of action. Any chance more men are arriving soon?" Danny could hear the hopefulness in the man's words. All the platoons needed more men.

"Sorry. This is all we can give you for now." He gestured at Danny. "But this one carries one of those new Henry rifles. Be ready to move in the morning." Without another word, he left the circle of light and disappeared into the darkness, his retreating steps fading in the night.

In the twinkling firelight, Danny studied Sergeant Blair. Not remarkable looking, not distinguished in any way, except for a scar across one cheek. Yet a sense of confidence surrounding him made Danny immediately trust him. He'd seen the same leadership in other men.

The sergeant's short cropped brown hair perched above his gray eyes, but it was the scar marring his cheek that drew Danny's appraisal. Everyone had scars who'd endured the war, seen or unseen.

Despite his nondescript appearance, Danny sensed something different about the young soldier before him. And not just that he'd asked their names.

For another long moment, the pair of replacements endured Blair's appraising gaze before Danny shifted.

Although exhausted, he waited, knowing what Blair wondered as he considered the two untested men. Would they fight or flee, obey commands or freeze? Would they stand in battle?

Danny couldn't answer for Roland, but this wasn't his first go around. He'd been in countless skirmishes. He'd stick. He needed to stick.

He shrugged off his unaccountable curiosity of Sergeant Blair. This was just another regiment, another bunch of men to fight beside. The war continued, and Danny had a job to perform. A job to achieve.

Blair drew a deep breath. "You must be tired. I'm Blair, platoon sergeant. All the replacement officers have been killed, so you're stuck with me." He paused and then gave a halfhearted grin, but Danny read the gravity in his eyes.

"I need to check on my men but get some rest. I'll post you tomorrow." Blair turned and followed the ridge before he passed from view, the darkness swallowing him.

"We're lucky we don't have guard duty tonight," Roland muttered when he caught Danny's inquisitive gaze. "Plenty of others would've placed the new boys on guard, regardless of rest. This Sergeant Blair seems all right to me," he added as he bent to drag blankets from his pack.

Danny didn't respond. He would hold his assessment until later, see how the young sergeant performed under fire. He walked a short distance from the glowing fire before tossing his blankets beneath a huge pine. He leaned his pack against the trunk, peering into the gloom. Away from the warm fire, he could feel the chill of the late hour. Roland had followed him and leaned his pack against another tree before lying down in the shadows.

November in Georgia was cold at night. The days had been blue and beautiful, with some low clouds drifting from the east. Danny wondered how far they were from the sea. He had to admit he enjoyed these temperate days. His own Philadelphia could have snow by this time of year.

It took only a minute to remove his shoes and roll in his blankets. He didn't consider taking off his woolen trousers or jacket. This position on the ridge was the forward arm of Sherman's Army. He must be ready for an attack at any time, though night fighting had not been common these past three years, he reminded himself. And now the Confederates were almost whipped, they rarely attempted an offensive against Union defensive positions.

Without a word to his new partner, Danny stretched, allowing his muscles to relax. He listened to the moan of a gentle breeze overhead in the pine boughs. The sound comforted him—foreign before the war when he'd known only the hubbub of the city.

He sighed, remembering. The war was all he knew now. Blood and death. Fighting and ammunition and enough food to keep moving on, these were the things that concerned him daily. He reached for the Henry rifle, his fingers tracing along the barrel. The touch reassured him somehow.

Once, Philadelphia had been all Danny knew. Would he ever see the city again? Did he really care?

CHAPTER THREE

Danny blinked awake, staring up through the branches to the incredibly bright starlit night sky.

He'd been so many places in the last three years— Tennessee, Pennsylvania, Mississippi,—he couldn't think where he was at this moment. Then he remembered. Georgia. He blinked again, rubbing the sleep from his eyes. He could never sleep for long, although often desperately tired. Especially after a forced road march. His exhaustion seemed less significant beside his active, restless mind.

Danny sat up, knowing the futility of resistance. He doubted he would sleep more tonight. He needed to think, wrestle with his emotions. The pattern had become second nature.

As he tugged on his shoes, he shivered in the early morning gloom. Dawn was hours away, yet perhaps a coffeepot simmered on a sentry's fire somewhere. He retrieved his tin cup from his pack. Picking up his rifle, he glanced to where Roland still slept peacefully. Danny tried to make little sound as he made his way along the crest of the ridge.

He'd gone only a short distance when he saw the glowing embers of Blair's fire. A blackened pot rested on the edge of the coals, steam rising from the spout.

As Danny filled his cup, a low voice spoke from the shadows. "Still hot." He almost spilled when he jumped at the unexpected words.

Blair chuckled, and Danny squinted into the gloom. The sergeant sat leaning against a tree, a blanket spread across his legs. Danny moved to a nearby pine, making sure he'd stepped from the ring of firelight. Rebel sharpshooters could kill a man outlined near a fire.

"Can't sleep?" Blair's question made Danny snort. He hadn't slept well in years.

"Usually I can sleep anywhere, day or night, but never for long," he explained. He lifted his cup and blew on the hot drink, surprised he felt relaxed with the noncommissioned officer. Rarely did he make the effort to be sociable with the other soldiers.

Blair chuckled again. "You always have to be ready for battle or death, right?"

His casual manner made Danny prickle with curiosity. Every soldier had to be ready for battle or death, but no one ever spoke of the grim expectancy of the latter. Had the young sergeant guessed his secret? Again, he sensed something different about this man.

"I sure thought I was a goner at Shiloh," Blair went on. In the dim light, Danny saw him point to his cheek. "That's where I got this cut on my face. Rebel bayonet."

"I was at Shiloh," Danny volunteered softly.

"Ah? Then you were there when the rebs came at us before we set up proper defenses. Near overrun our positions. Hand to hand, men screaming all around. I'll never forget."

Danny stared into the coals, his coffee forgotten. "How can a man forget?" His whispered query surprised him further. Why was he speaking to this stranger? The grief and sorrow that Danny carried seemed to be a weight only he understood. Sure, other soldiers kept their distance and chose not to discuss past exploits, but he'd fenced himself off from everyone, not willing to get close to the other men. All his companions from his first posting were gone now, and, like the orphanage, he regretted their friendship, allowing them to get close. He didn't want to get close to anyone ever again. Only courage in battle remained. He would die soon—they all would. But self-respect, bravery, and a sense of pride in his adopted name still mattered. These ideas gave him something to believe in, something to fight for.

"I can pick up the Eastern accent in your speech. Not New York or Boston," Blair probed.

Danny shook his head. "Philadelphia."

"Born there?"

Danny tensed, unsure how much to share. "I think so. I was raised in an orphanage. No family."

Blair pushed his blanket aside and scooted to the fire. The low flames flared when he shoved more wood into the coals, sparks fluttering skyward. He offered Danny a refill before filling his own cup and moving back to his tree. "I've got a sister. Parents dead. But I have countless family."

Danny frowned, not understanding. "What does that mean?"

"I belong to the family of God. I'm ready for battle or death. No matter, eventually I'll be with Jesus in heaven."

Danny felt an icy chill snake down his spine before he drained his cup and stood. "Good for you," he called over his shoulder as he left the fire-lit ring and made his way to his bedroll once more. Roland's gentle snores drifted across the small clearing, and Danny stared up at the stars.

He cursed himself for a fool and tugged his covers higher. Never let your guard down, Danny had reasoned after the first few weeks in the army. With all his companions dead, life had proven precarious. Only his pride remained. Pride in his name, his ability, and his resolve. Danny Mason would fight. There was nothing else.

He listened to the sighing in the pines, agreeing with Sergeant Blair that everyone died eventually. But heaven? He'd heard of such fancies, but never believed. Could there be a heaven for men like him, who'd done the things Danny had done?

He remembered the cold winters at the orphanage, the bitter winds gusting off the nearby Delaware River, and the blistering hot summers in the attic where the boys slept. He remembered the malnutrition, lice, rats, threadbare clothing, and poor hygiene. When the war broke out, he'd considered running away and attempting to join up, even though fifteen was too young. He'd been dropped off at the orphanage just after birth, a crumpled piece of butcher paper tucked into a dirty blanket with one word scrawled across the page. *Danny*. Mr. Tate, the headmaster, figured he was born around the first of March, so Danny had to wait until the second year of the war to enlist. At sixteen, he was young but allowed to go to war—just in time for the Battle of Shiloh.

Eager to have his own things for the first time in his life, he reveled in the blue uniform and the gear issued to him, including the long Springfield rifle. Fed every day, he gloried in the way the army took care of him, paying him monthly for his service.

Danny hoarded the small allotment, not knowing what else to do with the unfamiliar pay. He detested the wasteful way many of the soldiers drank their earnings or gambled them away in games of chance. Although he didn't expect to make it through the conflict, he saved his money, reluctant to part with the unfamiliar cash.

Again, Danny slipped a hand from under his blankets to touch his rifle stock. Yes, the weapon was still there. The Henry rifle was not a common weapon, yet he, Danny Mason, now owned one of the superior rifles. He glanced up at the brilliant stars twinkling overhead. Was someone looking out for him? Sergeant Blair's talk sounded like wishful thinking, like a man could conjure family with simple declarations and thoughts. Danny scoffed at the religious ideas. Yet the sergeant's confidence bothered him.

★★★

A rough kick brought Danny awake. "Get up," a voice growled.

Danny peered up at the soldier towering over him, a pair of stripes on his blue tunic. "I'm Corporal Hewitt. Sergeant Blair told me you joined late last night." He shifted his gaze to where Roland leaped to his feet.

"That's right." Hewitt nodded slowly. "Jump when I bark and be ready when I say to move." He hooked a thumb toward the rear of the ridge. "Mess hall thataway. Get some grub and get back to the sergeant's fire. Double time," he ordered before he turned to make his way along the defensive line.

Danny and Roland hurriedly packed their gear, making sure all was ready for their return from breakfast. Other soldiers joined them as they streamed down the hill, rifles slung over their shoulders, mess kits in hand.

Lines of hungry men formed, and Danny watched the camp stir as the sun lifted over the eastern hills. Black cooks scooped potatoes and hash onto his plate. Another man handed him a hard biscuit. Danny dunked his tin cup into a huge vat of steaming coffee, drops falling as he walked from the line.

Roland seemed to attach himself to Danny, but he ignored the soldier limping after him. They found seats beneath a pine tree and sat cross legged to eat breakfast. Across the clearing, columns of refugees in ragged clothes shambled up the road to the north where the army had already been. Black men, women, and children moved in shuffling columns. Former slaves freed by the advancing army, they wished only to depart their farms, no real destination in mind. Many carried bundles on their backs or on their heads. Many carried nothing.

When a big cook at the grub line broke into song, some of the refugees joined in, their voices filling the air with plaintive, mournful strains. Danny listened as he ate, pondering the uncertainty of life. He and Roland cleaned their dishes in a nearby stream before tramping back up the ridge to their packs.

"What should we do?" Roland grabbed a strap on his pack, but then looked at Danny, waiting for instructions.

Sergeant Blair appeared, freshly shaven and uniform neatly brushed with his Springfield rifle slung over one shoulder. Danny had pegged him as an intelligent albeit religious man, not a dandy. Yet the sergeant seemed to value his personal appearance. But, Danny gave him points for preparedness.

"Good morning," Blair called as he halted beside their packs. "Have you eaten?"

The two newcomers nodded. "Corporal Hewitt told us to eat," Roland volunteered as he pointed down the hill toward the open-air mess area.

"Good, good," Blair muttered, peering down the hill. "Here comes Hewitt now."

Huffing, the corporal trudged into camp, his face red from the climb. Ignoring the two replacements, he gave his report to Sergeant Blair about the night guard, fighting readiness of his men, and who from the platoon had already eaten.

While he spoke, Danny studied the landscape to the front of the ridge. Trampled and burned fields stretched as far as the eye could see. The Southerners destroyed anything of value, wanting nothing left for the invading Yankees. Only silent houses and outbuildings showed untouched. Danny knew these structures would be burned to the ground when the army advanced.

Finally, Blair turned to face Roland and Danny. "After yesterday's defeat, we expect the rebels to be in full flight, and General Sherman aims to pursue. But we cannot be certain they have not left behind sharpshooters to slow us down. We've been given the honor of leading the army's forward progress. We have point, while other platoons are to fan out from here, destroying everything the rebs can use to fortify their troops. We leave within the hour. Grab your gear and move down to the road below the ridge."

They muttered their assent and reached for their packs as Blair strode down the ridge. Danny watched him go, a mixture of intrigue and anxiety filling him as he considered the day's mission.

"Well? What do you think of Sergeant Blair?" Hewitt stepped closer as they slung their packs over their shoulders.

Danny shrugged, unsure how to respond, but Roland laughed. "He seems the finest sergeant I've ever met."

"You think that's funny, don't you, private? Well, Sergeant Blair *is* the finest sergeant anyone has ever met," Hewitt snapped, his face clouding. "But he's more than that. He's our good luck charm. Don't mind any of his odd ways or his peculiar ideas. Just do whatever he says and do it quickly."

The corporal paused and rubbed a hand across his chin, as if wanting to add more, then lowered his voice. "What I mean is, he's important, you are not. There's something about him, something lucky, see?"

Roland nodded eagerly and dug into his trouser pocket. "Yes, Corporal, I understand. I carry a rabbit's foot." He held the amputated leg for inspection.

A scowl creased Hewitt's features. "Put that away. Blair doesn't hold with old wives tales and superstitions." He squinted at the two replacements. "Something about him, I say. You'll see."

Danny drew his pack to one shoulder. "I heard him last night. He said some things."

"I know, I know." Hewitt waved a hand dismissively. "Don't worry about that. He's different, that's all. But take care of him. Watch his back. He's our good luck charm, see?"

Roland and Danny exchanged skeptical glances.

Hewitt went on. "Don't think you're significant. You'll be replaced soon enough, if I don't miss my guess. But listen to Blair. He's our ticket out of here."

A knot formed in Danny's gut. He had his own ideas to follow. His name meant something too. He would never disgrace his name. A good luck charm meant nothing to him.

"I'll do what I can," Danny allowed quietly. "But I have my own notions."

"Not in this platoon, you don't," a gruff voice spoke from behind him, and Danny glanced over his shoulder. A trio of soldiers stood, arms crossed over their chests.

Hewitt chuckled without humor. "You see? We follow Blair. Do as he says or deal with us." He glowered at Danny. "Understand, private?"

Danny licked his lips, then nodded. He could already tell he wasn't going to like Corporal Hewitt.

"All right, men," Hewitt shouted as he stepped toward the road. "Get your gear and meet on the road. We're moving out."

CHAPTER FOUR

Danny stared at the three soldiers who faced him until they each turned to comply with Hewitt's order. Grabbing their packs, the entire platoon descended the slope toward the road. Danny kept a wary eye on the soldiers who'd confronted him, surprised at their willingness to defend a sergeant with unorthodox views. Yet the power of a talisman in battle could not be denied. If these men believed Blair possessed some kind of charm, he was worth their support.

The platoon gathered around Sergeant Blair where he stood in the center of the road. In the east, the sun peeked over the hills, casting a ruddy glow on the red dirt of the narrow path. Countless prints showed in the dust, revealing the troops fleeing from Atlanta.

The soldiers leaned rifles on the toe of their shoes or slung weapons over shoulders as Blair faced the clustered men.

"Well, boys, we've been selected to lead again," he began with a grim smile, no humor reflected in his gray eyes. His short speech was met with groans and low mutterings, but Hewitt hushed the men, allowing Blair to continue.

"We're the eyes of this army and are to scout this road for possible ambush. As the rebs fled from Atlanta, they might've left men too hurt to travel."

A soldier cleared his throat. "Are these men regular troops or militia?"

Blair nodded. "Most of the regulars went to join Lee at Petersburg or into the Carolinas, joining stronger forces. We're told to expect minimal resistance, but Sherman's Army needs this road for troop advancement and the supply train."

"Why not use the railroad?" a short soldier wanted to know. "Wouldn't that be quicker for both?"

The sergeant nodded again. "Yes, but unreliable. We don't know if the rebs tore up their tracks or not. We're to secure this road for safe travel."

"But we were in battle just yesterday," another man grumbled.

Blair held up a hand as others took up the complaint. "We have a job to do, gentlemen, and we'll do it to the best of our ability." Men lowered their protests until silence reigned. Blair went on. "It's no accident we've been chosen to lead this mission. You've proven yourselves capable, with valuable skills. Because of you, this army advances. Every effort you make will shorten the duration of this war. You are important. What we do here today is important."

Danny watched as men nodded, gripping rifles tighter in readiness. He'd never heard such an inspiring speech before.

"Sergeant," an older man spoke up. "Why not wait for more replacements? With yesterday's battle, every regiment needs more men." His nasal, New England voice grated on Danny's nerves, but he listened attentively, startled at the sergeant's willingness to hear his men's concerns.

"The generals have determined that to wait is to miss an opportunity to advance while the enemy is unprepared. Generals Grant and Sherman believe the Confederates are in full retreat, no longer attempting to defend the railroad hub at Atlanta. Now is the time to move forward." Blair paused and then grinned. "On to Savannah."

The men cheered as they shuffled into columns on either side of the road.

"Corporal Hewitt," Blair called, searching the crowd for his second in command. "Ten feet between men and get them moving."

Hewitt stepped to the center of the dirt track. "You heard the man, get some distance from the man in front of you. Line up, both sides of the road, weapons pointed out." He turned to Danny while the soldiers spread out. "You—in front. Let's see if that fancy rifle is any good."

As the soldiers split into two columns along either side of the road, Danny strode to the head of the platoon, scowling with resignation. He knew how units treated the new men, pushing them to the front, fodder for snipers.

He peered over his shoulder, seeing Roland had blended into the middle of the regiment, clearly not making any attempt to station himself near Danny. But Danny lifted his chin, determined, and held the Henry rifle across his chest, prepared to move out.

Hewitt grabbed the barrel and pointed the muzzle to the front. "Rifle ready," the corporal snarled. "If we're ambushed, you won't have time to aim your weapon. Be ready to point and shoot."

Danny nodded, unused to this style of warfare. Previously, he'd been with the infantry, dug into a defensive position or charging one. Now, as part of a scout platoon, he'd have to develop new skills.

Corporal Hewitt took a small notebook from his jacket pocket, flipped open to a clean page, and lifted a stub of pencil. "What's your name? I'll need to know for the death list."

Danny smirked, not afraid. "Danny Mason."

Hewitt scribbled the name into the book, then glanced at Blair where the sergeant stood in the center of his men. Blair nodded and Hewitt motioned forward. "Move out," he called. Danny peered down the road and started walking. Behind him, the sounds of the jostling platoon quieted as the scouts moved out.

"Eyes out," Sergeant Blair said in a low voice to his now silent men. "Stay alert. Expect the unexpected."

Danny felt a sense of anticipation fill him, the same way he felt before marching into battle. Yet the eerie silence around him made the short hair prickle along his neck, so different from the raucous clamor of the battlefield. This mission assuredly would be dangerous. Perhaps Corporal Hewitt would have cause to know his name by the end of the day. The list of those killed in action appeared often in the major newspapers.

He gritted his teeth and studied the timbered hillsides on both sides of the road. A sniper's bullet was no way for him to go out. No glory in that.

For a long while, the platoon filed down the road, two rows of blue-clad soldiers in enemy territory, no one speaking. How far to Savannah? Danny didn't know. When would he have another chance to display his bravery?

Across the road, an old man headed the column. A long gray beard touched his chest, and Danny wondered why Hewitt had put the geezer at the front.

"Hold," Blair called softly, lifting a hand. The twin columns stopped, eyes peering into the dense forest on either side of the road. The sergeant was twenty paces behind Danny, yet he clearly heard the whispered order.

"There's a plantation ahead," Blair told them. "Stay alert."

Danny didn't see a signal pass between the sergeant and Hewitt, but it was the corporal who instructed the platoon forward with a gesture.

Danny's nerves stretched taut as he crept along the red path. Ahead, he saw the clearing that indicated a house or village carved from the undergrowth and trees. For weeks, Danny's regiment had fired such houses, burning every structure they could. He wondered if Sergeant Blair's platoon would burn this place too.

Slowly, quietly, the soldiers came from the tree-lined road into the wide glade, a huge mansion nestled against the far end of an immense clearing. Empty fields showed where successful harvest had taken place before the Yankees arrival. Silence met the approaching platoon. Nothing stirred, the place abandoned.

"Watch the upper floor windows," the old man whispered from across the road.

Danny surveyed the distant barns, corrals, and pig sheds. A corn crib drew his attention, lifting his hopes, but the stalls seemed empty.

"Second story," the old man hissed again.

Danny turned as the soldiers slipped from view or dropped to one knee, all rifles pointed toward the quiet house.

A rifle cracked from the house and Danny felt the whiz of a bullet pass overhead. He dropped to the ground as another shot fired, this one from across the road.

"Got him," the old man stated calmly, slowly getting to his feet. Danny had never seen the old soldier drop to one knee.

"Good shot, Nelson," Blair called as he rushed forward in a crouch. All around him, soldiers zigzagged across the yard, sweeping toward the house while others took up a defensive position, peering behind them.

"You all right, boy?" The old man with the beard knelt beside Danny.

Scowling, he rose. "Fine," he muttered before racing forward, wanting to be one of the first to reach the wide veranda surrounding the stately mansion.

But Corporal Hewitt and another soldier stormed through the front doors before Danny could catch up. The rest of the platoon took up positions nearby, everyone watching and listening as boots thudded up the inner staircase. A minute later, Hewitt waved from the sniper's window.

"Just a boy," he announced. "Nelson, you squirrel hunters from Kentucky don't miss much."

As the platoon moved back to the road, the old man walked beside Danny. "You got to keep your wits, boy. I saw that rifle barrel just as he fired." He glanced at the Henry rifle Danny carried. "I dearly wish to see you open up with that thing. Really don't have to reload to fire again?"

"Nope." Danny took his place at the head of the regiment as Nelson returned to his position across the road, the other men lining behind them.

"Keep watch," Blair advised before the double columns moved on.

At noon, the sergeant called a break to their progress, moving the platoon into a circle amid a small grove of immense oak trees. A hundred yards distant, a well showed in the shadows beside a small cottage. They had come to no other homes or buildings since the plantation house.

Blair dispatched a team to fetch water while the rest of the men slumped to the ground or leaned against trees and dug into packs for food. Hardtack and extra biscuits taken from morning mess appeared plentiful.

Danny shrugged when Roland found a seat with other soldiers, letting him to eat alone. The familiar feeling of isolation surged, but he shook off the sensation, telling himself he preferred being alone.

When Nelson sauntered over and dropped his pack beside Danny, the younger man shifted, giving the old man room. Nelson sighed as he lowered to the ground.

"I'm too old for this," he mumbled as he bit into a biscuit.

"You were quick with that sniper," Danny said softly, hoping the old man understood his gratitude. Although he expected to die in battle, he didn't want to get killed by an unseen sniper. He shuddered, grimacing at the death without glory.

Nelson gestured to the Henry rifle lying on the grass. "Any good with that?"

"I hit what I aim at." Danny bit into a biscuit, angry with himself for engaging in conversation with the old man. Danny Mason needed no one, he reminded himself.

Nelson eyed Danny as he pushed his blue cap back. "Rich man's gun. I hear some of the regiments are being issued these rifles, but none around here."

"Took it off a fellow yesterday who bought the gun with his enlistment pay." Danny wondered why he made the effort to explain. Besides, he didn't want to recall the endless shooting he'd endured in the previous day's battle. Yet, he was thankful for the newfangled weapon.

"Yesterday?" Nelson arched a bushy eyebrow. "And you feel comfortable with it today?"

Danny lifted the rifle, studying the dull gleam of the wooden stock as he rested the butt on his leg. A dark red stain marred the stock, and he thought of Hallowell. "I've had a lot of practice since then."

Nelson chuckled, a glint in his eyes. "Tough day yesterday. The rebs have less men, less guns, and they still manage to put up a fierce fight."

About to grin at the old man's assessment, Danny squinted when he caught sight of Blair seated nearby, the thick boughs of a pine tree casting the sergeant in shadow. In his hands, he held a leather-bound book. Danny nodded toward the silent sergeant and glanced at Nelson, keeping his voice low.

"Probably reading the Bible. He said something odd to me last night. Said he belongs to the family of God." Danny grinned at the ridiculous comment, but Nelson shook his head.

"That's not a Bible. That's his journal, where he writes his dreams for after the war."

Danny blinked. "After?" He never considered anything beyond the war.

"And"—Nelson reached into his jacket and pulled out a black book—"this is what a Bible looks like." He held the book up for Danny's inspection. "And I belong to the family of God too. Because of the Lord, you can expect Blair will always try and do the right thing."

Danny snorted. "They put me in front of the column first thing, trying to get rid of me."

Nelson shook his head again, his beard swaying. "You got it wrong, sonny. Hewitt might've done that if he doesn't like you, but Sergeant Blair would never allow it. He does the right thing, puts men where they fit best. He knows I can see like a hawk." He motioned to the Henry rifle. "He must've thought that thing was best put in front."

Danny glanced at the prized weapon before laying the rifle on the ground beside him. "I don't move as quietly as the rest of you men. You're scouts. Do you think I'm here only because of this rifle?"

The old man grinned before he held out a hand. "I'm Nelson."

For only an instant, Danny hesitated, reluctant to know the old soldier. What's the point? Surely, he wouldn't last long. But then he gripped Nelson's hand. "Mason."

Hewitt called the men back to the road, and Danny and his new companion packed up their stuff and stood.

As the platoon lined the ditches, Blair spoke. "Cavalry should be our eyes and ears. We will go only a few more miles before we turn around and head back. Be careful."

Again, Nelson and Danny took point.

CHAPTER FIVE

The next day after morning chow, Hewitt called the platoon together. They gathered beneath the tall pine where Blair's little fire blazed in the frosty morning air, crackling merrily, as if death did not wait around every bend in the road. Late November in Georgia was cold, but nothing like Philadelphia this time of year, and Danny vowed not to complain.

As the men huddled shoulder to shoulder, Sergeant Blair kicked dirt over his fire and hoisted his pack to one shoulder. "We've been ordered to head directly east. Dispatch riders will follow our advance, taking scouting reports to the generals as we move toward Savannah. With the cavalry roaming far afield and us clearing the road, the army will follow tomorrow."

He nodded at Hewitt, and the corporal pointed toward the road at the bottom of the ridge. "You heard him, men. Assemble in two columns on the road. Double time," he barked as he herded the platoon down the slope.

Danny wasn't surprised when he and Nelson were placed on point again. He glanced to the top of the knoll where other soldiers still held their positions, watching as Blair's men lined both sides of the road, ten-foot intervals between each man. With a wave, Blair motioned the advance.

Today, the scout platoon went another way, taking a different road than the one they'd traveled yesterday. How far were they from Savannah? Danny had no idea, southern geography not being one of his strong suits. At the orphanage, he'd been taught to read and write and basic sums, but little else.

Dull sunlight accompanied the silent scouts as they moved up the road, passing quiet farms where the occupants had fled the Yankee advance or hidden in the woods until Sherman's Army moved on to the sea. At one house, a dog barked, but no one appeared.

Multicolored leaves adorned the maple, hickory, and oak trees. But the tall pines were evergreen, standing stately on the knolls and hills where the uneven land could not be cultivated.

At noon, Hewitt called a break. The platoon filed off the road, forming a relaxed perimeter around an outcropping of granite boulders. Danny was surprised when Sergeant Blair took a seat nearby, digging in his pack for food. As the hungry men nibbled hardtack and cold biscuits, Danny stole sidelong glances at the sergeant.

"What are you looking at, Mason?" Blair's tone was curious, not reprimanding, when he caught Danny's perusal. He chewed slowly, his bright gaze inviting Danny's response.

He settled his back against a large gray stone. "I'm surprised how young you are, Sergeant."

Blair smiled. "Do not let anyone look down on you for your youth." At Danny's obvious confusion, the sergeant continued. "From the Bible. A young man named Timothy was to lead a church, and St. Paul encourages him to be hard working and not let his young age interfere with his mission."

"His mission?" Danny's ears pricked at the familiar military term.

The sergeant nodded. "His mission was to lead a church while ours is to take Savannah. Still, I hope to be an example to my men."

Blair's attention to detail and the way his men looked up to him had not gone unnoticed by Danny. But the easy way the sergeant mentioned the mysterious book made him tense. Church had been an inconvenience at the orphanage where the boys were expected to complete endless tasks and the various jobs Mr. Tate hired them out for. The boys never had free time.

Blair gestured to where Nelson dozed in the weak sunlight. The day felt chilled, and a cool breeze ruffled the branches overhead, but still Nelson seemed relaxed.

"Nelson's the best point man I've ever seen. Trust him, and watch how he works, where he looks as he walks."

Danny recalled what an old soldier had told him when he joined his first regiment, so long ago. "Always rest when you can, sleep when you can, eat when you can."

Blair glanced around, checking his men before continuing. "You have the Henry rifle. The two of you make a good team should anything come our way."

"Do you expect trouble?"

Blair smiled grimly. "Always. To tell the truth, I think the regular reb army has fled to the coast. We'll find the real fight there. But between here and there, we'll find truly desperate folks afraid of losing what little they have. Either way, I expect trouble at all times."

Hewitt called Danny to replace one of the guards, and he nodded at Blair as he hurried to relieve the hungry sentry.

He felt surprised how much he'd enjoyed his short talk with the sergeant, never one to relish any acquaintance. Still, Danny cautioned himself from getting too familiar with any of the soldiers in the scout platoon.

As the break drew to a close, Danny kept one eye on the surrounding hills and forests while he pondered the young sergeant. Blair's confidence, his manner, his insight, all these traits intrigued Danny. Even his Christian remarks seemed to gnaw at him, as if Danny had not considered every aspect of a situation. He didn't doubt his own bravery, but could he be wise like Sergeant Blair?

After the platoon left their secluded resting spot, the afternoon dragged by slowly. For hours, no one spoke as the twin columns made slow advance to the east, ever vigilant. Occasionally, messengers on horseback raced far to the rear, carrying Blair's hastily scrawled notes to the officers who made important tactical decisions. So far, the scout platoon had encountered no resistance from locals and no discoveries of entrenched Confederate troops.

As shadows stretched across the red dirt road, Danny felt his eyes grow weary of the constant readiness as he scanned every thicket, every vacant house, every wooded knoll. His arms ached from carrying the rifle, the heavy pack digging into his shoulders. The chilled autumn air enveloped him, and he craved a hot cup of coffee.

Behind him, the faded red sun hung low in the sky. *When would Blair call a halt for the night?* Danny was about to whisper his inquiry to Nelson when the bullet shrieked past his ear. A rifle barked, and Danny threw himself to the ground, scrambling into the ditch for cover. Glancing over his shoulder, he saw his comrades followed suit, only a few faces peering from the foliage alongside the road to search for the attackers. He locked eyes with Corporal Hewitt where the man crouched beneath a thicket.

Danny turned his gaze when shoes crunched gravel as Sergeant Blair moved toward the front of the column.

"Amsted, Mason, come with me," he whispered loud enough for Danny to hear before darting into the brush. Danny shot a hurried glance to where Nelson had dropped to the ground, but the old man had vanished. Danny hastened to stay low and follow the sergeant.

"Look out for him," Hewitt hissed in his ear as Danny passed the corporal and plunged into the forest on a run.

Another shot rang out, but Danny had no idea where the round came from. Return fire blasted from the pinned platoon as staccato booms filled the evening, but Danny couldn't focus on the skirmish behind him. Branches slapped his face, and he struggled to keep up with Blair, the sergeant weaving through the undergrowth like a deer. Another shot rang out from the unseen attackers, and Blair corrected his course but didn't slow. Danny felt hard pushed to keep pace with him. Behind him, Amsted panted loudly, clearly struggling as well. Danny gripped his rifle tighter. The headlong race through the forest seemed faster than he cared to go toward an unseen enemy, yet a thrill coursed through his veins, and he knew the excitement of the dangerous assault consumed him. Regardless of the risk, he vowed to hang on Blair's heels. Ahead, a shot roared, and the trio slowed. Danny wiped damp hands on his pants as they drew closer.

Abruptly, Blair halted and held up a hand, his head poised like a listening wolf. Amsted stumbled noisily behind Danny, and he turned to glare at the clumsy soldier.

Not looking at his men, Blair gestured in the direction of the random rifle fire. Then he motioned to advance.

Spreading out, the three soldiers slipped through the forest, moving silently as they searched for the snipers. Danny gripped the Henry rifle, ready for a quick shot if one was needed. His heart seemed to swell in his chest, and he tensed with eager anticipation. At another signal from Blair, Danny located the enemy position on a nearby slope, a wonderful view of the road spreading below. Behind Danny, Amsted stumbled again.

"Look out," Blair warned as one of the snipers turned and fired. With a shove, the sergeant pushed Danny aside and returned fire. Danny bounced up, angry to be shoved from the fight, and aimed at the cluster of snipers.

At Blair's shot, Danny pulled the trigger and hurriedly slammed another round into the chamber, firing again and again until he was the only one shooting. The rifles in the firing pit stilled.

"Cease fire!" Blair shouted so the men below could hear him.

Danny advanced cautiously on the position, his rifle already reloaded, Blair and Amsted following. The trio of Union soldiers peered down into the shallowly dug trench where three Confederate men lay crumpled in the dirt. One of the men had only one leg. Another soldier had to be over sixty.

Blair pointed at one of the dead men and glanced at Danny. "This one had a bead on you." He paused. "Amsted, tell the platoon the threat is over."

Amsted shot Danny an apologetic glance before he ran down the slope. The sergeant spoke again. "You almost died today. Amsted is noisy in the woods, and I won't use him again for a flanking maneuver." He gestured to the rifle Danny held. "But that fancy gun makes all the difference. Thanks, Mason. You'll do."

Danny studied the three men sprawled in the mud, then turned to head back to the platoon.

Below the knoll, he could see men peering warily from their hiding places, then slowly assembling once more on the road. When he sensed the sergeant wasn't following, Danny glanced over his shoulder. He tensed anew when he saw Blair on the edge of the narrow trench, looking down at the dead snipers, his lips moving silently.

CHAPTER SIX

Flames licked hungrily at the wood Danny tossed into the blaze, the light leaping to reveal the small clearing where only the corporal and Danny waited, tending the fire until the sergeant returned. Quietly, the pair had kept their vigil, the others of the platoon bedded in pairs along a loose defensive perimeter. No one expected a reprisal, but the Confederates had surprised them more than once.

He glanced across the blaze to where Hewitt sat cleaning his rifle. They had nothing to say to one another, and Danny preferred the silence. Still, the corporal's taciturn nature grated on his nerves, and he thought of Nelson and the old man's easy conversation.

Soon Sergeant Blair appeared from the darkness, his haggard face etched with fatigue and worry as he accepted the cup of coffee Hewitt handed him.

The day's reconnaissance and minor skirmish had put the platoon on edge. Every man feared the shadowed forests lining the roads and the distant hills, any place that might conceal a sniper's lair. The wounded and aged Confederates were charged with slowing the Union advance, giving the enemy time to join other, stronger regiments. With the burning of Atlanta, the Southern spine had snapped. The greatest hub of Confederate rails was now in the hands of Union forces.

A foreboding hung thick in the air, as if everyone knew the end was in sight. How much longer could the rebels hold out? Starving, shoeless, dressed in tatters, the gray lines fought bravely, but they no longer had the needed supplies to continue a lengthy campaign. December loomed, and most agreed this would be the final Christmas of the war. Yet, they'd thought these same ideas before and were wrong—the tenacity of the Southern troops surprising everyone.

Blair settled himself against a tree and blew on the hot mug as he stared into the fire. Danny wondered about the officers' meeting at the headquarters tent the sergeant had attended. He glanced at Hewitt, impatient for the corporal to interrogate the tired Blair.

As if sensing his companion's unspoken inquiry, Blair nodded. "The generals are pleased with the advance. They think the rebs are moving to reorganize along the sea or have moved north to join Lee's forces. Either way, we are to march to the sea, take Savannah, and continue to whittle down Southern territory. They haven't got much land left to maneuver."

Hewitt licked his lips. "They can't hold out, right? Surely, the war is almost over."

A snort came from the sergeant, but he didn't turn from the fire. "We've had this same discussion a hundred times. We have a job to do. Stay diligent, wary, cautious. The Lord wants us to do our best, whatever is asked of us."

Hewitt shot Danny a thoughtful glance, and he read the apology in the corporal's look. Did he think Blair had lost his mind? Danny had seen countless men struggle to grasp reason after so many cruel battles and overwhelming deaths. Life felt so fleeting, so precarious. The somber thought didn't frighten Danny, but it did others.

No matter, he reminded himself doggedly. *Mason would fight gallantly, courageously. Danny Mason is a brave man.*

Blair shifted. "Corporal, tell the men we move out at dawn. We are not to allow the rebs to get comfortable. We will strike for the sea while the main body of the army follows our route, burns houses, and strips the land of provisions. Anything that might aid the Confederacy is to be confiscated or destroyed."

"But Christmas is in a month," Hewitt grumbled as he scrambled to his feet. "You'd think they'd let us off for a while, take a much-needed break."

The sergeant grinned a humorless smile. "We're not here for rest. We follow orders, do as we're told, and hope our efforts prove effective. God knows what he's doing. Trust the Lord."

Again, Hewitt glanced at Danny, his brows bunched at Blair's stoic speech. "Yes, Sergeant," he muttered, then shuffled into the darkness to spread the news.

Blair lifted his gaze from the fire. "Mason, you did good today. I predict that rifle will carry much weight in this war."

Danny said nothing, detecting his response was unnecessary. Blair drained his cup and tugged two small books from his jacket pocket. He closed his eyes for a moment before thumbing the thicker book open.

Watching from the corner of his eye, Danny sat motionless as the sergeant read silently. After a few minutes, he thrust the book into an inner pocket and settled back against the tree, opening the second, his leather-bound journal.

Leaning forward to toss more wood on the fire, Danny tried to get a better look at this second book. He assumed the first was the Bible. But where Blair had held the first book with a sense of reverence, he seemed to relax as he gripped the leather journal.

As if reading Danny's curiosity, Blair faced him. "Interested? The men know I read the Scriptures every chance I get, almost every night. The Bible helps me stay connected to the Lord. Jesus knows my heart, knows my grief. Only through knowing Christ can I navigate the challenges of this war. But this"—he shook the book in his hand with a grin—"this is for after the war. I think God has a plan for me to begin a stage station in the desert."

This man spoke of God as he would speak about others in the platoon. As if the Almighty were real and personal, moving among them. Did Blair believe God interacted with people?

At a chuckle from Danny, Blair's smile broadened. "You don't believe? That's all right. Not my job to make men into Christians. I'm to walk faithfully with Jesus, and the Holy Spirit is responsible for the rest."

"I have no idea what you're talking about," Danny confessed. "But thanks for the laughter. I can't remember the last time I laughed."

Blair reached for the coffeepot simmering in the coals and refilled his cup before hefting the pot toward Danny. Danny nodded, watching the sergeant through the rising steam as Blair poured.

"You seem awful sure of God's presence, as if he sits on your shoulder."

A low chortle escaped Blair as he settled against the tree once more. He gripped the hot mug in one hand, the black journal in the other. "There's little else I'm sure of," he agreed as he sipped his drink. "You're not so certain?"

Danny narrowed his eyes. "As best I can tell, there is no rhyme or reason as to who dies in this war. Christians don't seem to have any special protection that I've noticed."

"Not true. God's protection is very real. But he sees more of what's going on than the rest of us. He knows his purpose while we cannot see the whole of a thing. Whether we like it or not, God is involved in everything—life and death."

"Then what's the point?" Danny felt his scowl deepen, confused at this man's relaxed manner. "The men think you're a good luck charm. That somehow your zeal for Christ has spilled over to surround them, protect them. Yet you admit God knows what will happen, who will live and who will die."

Blair nodded, his smile fading. "From birth, our days are numbered. The Lord knows when each of us is to die. The ways of God are mysterious, yet I believe Jesus has a plan for each of us. We can trust he loves us, is always with us. An adventure awaits each of us, if we're willing to embark on the journey. But only Jesus knows where our journey will end."

Danny snorted derisively. "I'm on no journey. I joined the army to have food and clothing, a small income. I care nothing for North or South, slave or free. I doubt if I will live out the war, but my belly is full."

The sergeant eyed him closely, pondering Danny's words. "You see?" He gestured to the rifle across Danny's knees and the campfire they sat beside. "Our journey has brought us here. Warm food and monthly pay, yet God has more in store for us. He wants to teach us something while we're here. I am learning patience and obedience. I long to return home to begin my life again, but for now, I am here, serving in the army. My soul is in his hands."

He paused, peering at Danny over the rim of his cup as he sipped. "But you, Mason? What are you here to learn?"

"I've learned all I want to learn. Men are cruel, war is terrible, and God is silent. You may hope in him, but I hope in this." Danny hefted the Henry rifle.

Blair chuckled, the firelight dancing in his eyes. "Ah? So you trust in your own understanding. You have not heard God? I understand. Not everyone knows the Lord. Like I said, not my job. I am to share Jesus. Only the Holy Spirit can open a man to hear God."

He sipped more coffee while Danny squirmed. "I will pray for you, Mason, but unless the Spirit prepares your heart, I'm afraid I waste my breath. In the meantime, I'm also here to protect the platoon."

Danny waved a dismissive hand. "Please don't waste your prayer on me. I'm certain I don't want to know God."

Blair feigned shock, a grin creasing his features. "I'm wasting my time telling you about heaven and hell? Redemption that can only be found in Christ? Forgiveness of sins? What else matters in life?"

Danny grinned, liking the sergeant's easy manner. "Thanks, but no thanks. I'll pass."

Blair shrugged. "Suit yourself." He reached for a blanket behind him and pulled the woolen cover around his shoulders. "But God does not make mistakes. It's no accident you've been placed in my platoon. Surely, the Lord has a plan for you."

He paused again as he slid the journal into his pack and snuggled near the fire, tugging the blanket more securely around him. A sharp chill permeated the air, and Danny wondered if there'd be ice on the creek's edge by morning.

"But mark my words, Mason. Jesus put you in my path for a purpose. I don't know what it is yet, but in his perfect timing, the Lord will reveal his hand."

Danny stared as Blair drifted off to sleep, the hard lines in his face easing as the muscles relaxed. Soon, light snores lifted from the huddled sergeant.

Despite his great fatigue, Danny sat for another hour beside the little blaze. Occasionally, his gaze would lift to the star-studded night sky and then to the crumpled man who slept near the fire.

He glanced at his newly acquired rifle, comprehending the incredible power the weapon represented, then studied the sergeant in the fading firelight. Was there another power, one he knew nothing about? His gaze lifted once again to the canopy of stars above.

Danny shook his head, clearing his weary thoughts. He felt so tired. There was nothing more than this war, this night. A warm fire, a tin plate full of food, and a job to continue when the sun rose in the morning. It all seemed so simple, so easy to understand. Keep moving, keep fighting. *Danny Mason is a brave man, there is nothing more*, he told himself until his eyelids drooped.

CHAPTER SEVEN

The column moved steadily through the chilled morning sunlight. Again, Danny noted with pleasure the mild Georgia winter. While getting food at chow times, he'd heard soldiers share about cold weather up north, letters from home reporting storms already covering much of the land in snow. Danny imagined the filthy snow pushed to the sides of narrow alleys and cobblestone streets, the slush thawing during the day only to freeze in rigid mounds at night. Philadelphia looked so filthy only a few hours after every snowfall.

He pretended not to care when other men received such letters. Danny Mason wasn't soft, not saddened by the lack of friends or loved ones, he reminded himself. He was a tough man, right?

Danny recalled the night he and a few boys slipped out of the orphanage to sneak into the huge canvas tent. The carnival would leave town soon, but for tonight, Slugger Mason would take on any comers from the local audience. One by one, the muscular fighter vanquished every attempt the crowd made to beat the traveling pugilist, to no avail.

At the end of the night, Danny recalled how the referee had lifted Slugger Mason's gloved hand, declaring him undefeated. The fighter stood silent, grim faced with bruises puffing one eye and a cut on one cheek. He seemed solid, like a stone, tough and unbeatable.

That was how Danny had chosen to live life.

For a week after the carnival left town, the exploits of the boxer were told and retold around the orphanage. So much so, that Danny quietly assumed the invincible man's last name. Slugger Mason was brave, courageous, and resilient. So would Danny Mason be.

He looked over his shoulder now to where Nelson walked across the road and a little behind him. The old man peered into the dense forest, his gaze searching and restless. Danny turned and mimicked him, his gaze seeking an enemy.

At noon, a brief halt was called. Danny moved to the shadows under a pine thicket alongside the road. A little hardtack and water would have to suffice until supper. Sherman's Army was on the move, and it was expected to move slowly but steadily on its way to Savannah. Like him, Danny thought. Relentless and unbeatable.

He watched as Nelson moved to rest in the shadows farther in the woods, finding a seat with another soldier. Danny pretended not to be bothered at being left alone. He reminded himself he preferred to be alone. He didn't need friends, he thought as he ate his meager fare.

When Nelson stood and moved across the road, Danny tensed as the old man approached, an unfamiliar anticipation filling him. With a sigh, the hunter leaned his rifle against a nearby tree and lowered himself, resting against the rough bark. He studied Danny while the younger man nibbled hardtack.

For a long moment, silence enveloped the glade where the scout platoon had taken a break. A crow called from a high branch, and a gentle breeze chilled the crisp air. Danny hated how he waited for Nelson to speak, to acknowledge Danny's presence.

"Blair says we're making good time, except for the refugees tagging along," the old man finally announced. Occasionally, groups of the dispossessed followed the platoon until they couldn't keep pace and fell back with the slower moving troops that took time to burn plantations and destroy railroad lines. "At this rate, we should be in Savannah by Christmas."

Danny nodded, liking the sound of someone speaking to him. He didn't want to admit his loneliness, but Blair's frank talk of the other night made him think. Although he didn't agree with the sergeant's assessment, the ideas of future and after the war made him uneasy, and he wanted to hear what the old hunter had to say.

He squinted at Nelson. "Now, I know why Blair uses me and you in front. Where did you learn to move so quietly?"

Nelson grinned, the old man's gray beard parting to reveal stained teeth. "I trapped with Kit Carson and Bridger. I walked the high up Rocky Mountains in winter and summer, when the Indians watched for ways to take our scalps. That's how I know where Blair is from. We've talked of the mountains a time or two."

Danny listened, suddenly curious about the sergeant and irritated at his interest. To keep a safe distance from the other men was prudent. Danny had discovered that to get too close was to become vulnerable. Yet he couldn't contain his question.

"Where is Blair from?"

"East of the Sangre de Cristo's, along the old Santa Fe Trail. A little town has sprung up there. Name of Trinidad. Coal miners, some ranching, and a stage stop." Nelson shook his head. "Who could've guessed? While I searched for beaver, the land lay atop coal. Seems to be booming too," he reported with a look of disbelief.

A clatter of hooves sounded down the road, and all the men grabbed rifles before dropping into firing positions. Danny glanced over his shoulder to see a few muzzles aimed toward the approaching horses but only a couple of men presenting themselves as targets. Most of the scouts blended into the scant foliage.

The long column of Union cavalry passed along the road with barely a glance toward the soldiers hiding among the underbrush. In another moment, the mounted troopers had passed on, no doubt carrying scouting reports to the generals in the rear.

"He reckons to go back after the war and build a stage stop."

Danny frowned as he rose from his belly. Nelson had already moved to his tree, resting once more with his back to the tall pine. "Who? What are you talking about?"

Nelson pushed his cap back, his eyes glinting in the dull afternoon sunlight. "Blair. I'm talking about Sergeant Blair and his plans after the war. Here he comes."

The old hunter scrambled to his feet and hefted his rifle as the sergeant approached. Danny rubbed crumbs from his fingers and hurriedly stood. With a practiced swing, he threw his pack to one shoulder and lifted the Henry rifle.

Blair walked rapidly to the pair, glancing all around with his rifle ready for action. The platoon had met with no resistance today, but Danny knew that could change in an instant.

Blair halted beside them. "Howdy, men," he greeted. His gaze swept to the empty road ahead where the cavalry patrol had come from, always searching for snipers.

"Sergeant, what's the news?" Nelson wanted to know. Although the old man stood in a slouch, he seemed prepared for anything, and his rifle appeared an extension of his arm. The only Indians Danny had known were tame, of the east coast, who had adopted White ways long ago. No doubt the trapper had been made wary by his traipsing the far western mountains and being chased by hostile Indians inhabiting the high peaks. Danny would be wise to learn all he could from this cautious and experienced hunter.

"Cavalry reports not much ahead. Seems the rebs pulled out after we burned Atlanta and rejoined forces in the Carolinas. We should have little difficulty on our way to Milledgeville. That means we should expect anything. Be ready and keep your eyes open. We'll move out in a few minutes." With an encouraging grin at Danny, Sergeant Blair walked back toward the rear of the platoon.

Danny felt unaccountably bolstered by the sergeant's quick smile and Nelson's presence, as if he were becoming one of the platoon. Despite his wish to keep his distance and remain aloof, he was coming to know these men.

Quiet and empty were the grand plantations they passed that day. The orders were to destroy any property that could be used to aid the Confederacy, but Blair kept the scout platoon on task, clearing the army's route free of ambush. Broken and rotted fence rails indicated old farmhouses along the road. Their fields waved full of weeds, and only an occasional woman or old man peered at the passing Union Army from dark windows. The impoverished countryside had already been foraged clean by retreating Confederate troops.

Behind them, boisterous and eager men from other regiments torched these grand homes full of solitude and sadness. Most of their slaves had run away long ago.

Huge billows of dark smoke rose above these austere houses as they burned. Danny grew tired of the unnecessary raids upon hapless people. He turned away from the senseless destruction, continuing to walk ahead of his platoon, always hunting opposition.

He wondered how Nelson dealt with the mindless violence but chose not to pursue with questions. Danny knew Corporal Hewitt would support and even encourage the vicious reprisals against unfortunate civilians.

Soldiers in blue ransacked the properties for anything of value, including animals the army cooks could use. Danny felt a pity for these noncombatants he hadn't felt before, annoyed his defenses had weakened since joining the scouts. Was Blair having an effect on him?

Railroad lines were upended, tugged from their moorings before the rails were heated over immense fires and wrapped around telegraph poles. "Sherman's neckties," as these bent and twisted metal beams became called, littered the path from Atlanta to Savannah.

Danny thought of these things as the afternoon waned, the weak sun listing far west. Soon, the platoon would find a clearing to bed down, warm fires heating the evening coffee and rations.

Danny had almost relaxed too much as he thought about getting off his feet for the day when a bullet whizzed past his head, and he threw himself to the ground. The sickening thud of the speeding missile striking flesh sounded behind him, but Danny faced forward, searching for the ambusher's position.

After scanning the vicinity ahead, but seeing nothing, he glanced over his shoulder, looking for the wounded man. Not even a single man showed, the entire platoon melting into the thick foliage after the unexpected sniper's bullet. Danny peered ahead again. This time, far ahead, he glimpsed a man partially concealed behind a tree, hurrying to reload his gun. With careful aim, Danny sighted along his own weapon and fired.

The man jerked but did not fall. A second shot from Danny made the man crumple to the ground, his weapon clattering dully upon the thick mat of pine needles.

Danny rose cautiously and moved forward, knowing Nelson covered his advance. By now, he'd come to trust the old man's methods and abilities.

With slow tread, Danny stalked closer to the fallen man, ever alert for a trick. But the man dressed in homespun cotton trousers lay dead, two bullet holes in his open coat revealing Danny's true aim.

He knelt beside the old farmer, studying him in the fading afternoon light. The tattered clothes, the worn-down shoes, and the ancient musket all spoke of hard use. Danny suddenly felt sorry for the dead man, and seeing the enemy's privation touched him somehow.

Disgusted, Danny turned and walked back to the platoon. The other men rose from their positions and gathered around Sergeant Blair and Corporal Hewitt— where the pair stood near the sniper's victim.

Danny caught Nelson's inquisitive glance. "Another civilian sniper," Danny reported quietly, not wishing to disturb the silent aura around the soldier struck by the unexpected bullet. "Almost as old as you, Nelson."

The old hunter shook his head, his gray beard swaying. "Probably trying to protect his farm from Yankee liberators."

Danny walked on to where Blair prayed quietly over the fallen soldier. Ignoring him, Danny turned to the corporal. "Only another civilian sniper. They sure don't like us in Georgia," he reported sourly.

Corporal Hewitt said nothing at first, his eyes upon the sergeant praying over the dead soldier. Finally, he looked at Danny. "Can't blame them. It's their land. But they should know when they're beaten."

Hewitt bent to help drag the dead man from the road, and Danny recognized Amsted. His gaze darted to Sergeant Blair. The other soldiers watched as their comrade was dragged into the forest, but Danny couldn't tear his eyes from the silent sergeant. Blair was kind, yet his compassion seemed out of place somehow. Most soldiers had quickly lost a sense of sympathy long ago when the war began or when they watched their friends die. Danny wondered if he'd ever possessed such an attitude. Had he ever cared about another person? And yet now unfamiliar emotions stirred within him, feelings he couldn't identify.

He walked to the head of the column, resuming point. No doubt, Blair would soon call the halt for the night. But his inner turmoil would not leave him alone. Blair and Nelson had both mentioned spiritual matters, a Christian faith. Neither man had beaten him over the head with their personal beliefs. Nonetheless, for the first time he felt curious. Danny had always ridiculed or ignored the religious soldiers he'd met. They didn't seem to live any longer than other men in battle. But now, here in Georgia, he seemed intrigued by things he couldn't comprehend. He'd always been so hard, callous even. Now he longed to understand the sergeant's sympathy and considerations.

Irritated with these unexpected ideas, he blinked, trying to clear his troubled thoughts. However, a nagging question remained. Did Jesus make a difference in a man's life?

CHAPTER EIGHT

The progress of the advancing Union troops was only briefly slowed by a stopover at Milledgeville. The capital of Georgia offered little resistance to Sherman's forceful march to the sea. They reached Savannah the week before Christmas.

The city quickly agreed to the surrender demanded by General Sherman, and the Union conqueror passed the victory on to President Lincoln as an early Christmas gift. The year of 1864 ended with Grant stalled outside Richmond and Sherman making headway across the heartland of the South. Lincoln's reelection assured the war would go on, possibly to end soon, with the flailing Confederacy barely hanging on.

Despite Danny's efforts to remain detached from Blair's platoon, he soon found himself accepted by the other soldiers, although Corporal Hewitt maintained a gruff reserve. If his assimilation was because of Blair's posting him at the head of the column or Nelson's evident friendliness, Danny couldn't tell. Regardless, the other men regarded him indifferently or with a small measure of comradery. Only Hewitt refused to relent, holding Blair as a personal charm that he clearly didn't want to share with Danny.

"You're not important," he told Danny one day at mealtime, blocking Danny's approach to the campfire he shared with Nelson. "You'll be dead soon enough, no matter to me. But I don't want you getting Blair killed. He's kept so many of us alive. Use your fancy rifle to protect Sergeant Blair but keep out of my way."

As Hewitt stalked into the darkness, Danny glanced at the rifle slung over his shoulder. The Henry repeating rifle seemed like any other weapon, yet Danny knew its true potency lay concealed beneath this false front. Every day, he used this weapon to vanquish foe, to clear a route the scout platoon could follow. Or Nelson's unerring aim took out a sniper, backed by Danny's volley of bullets. Together, the pair made a formidable team.

More often than not, these small attacks were the feeble attempts of local militia groups, commonly made up of old men or very young boys.

"What did Hewitt say to you?" Nelson looked up from his plate as Danny entered the circle of firelight from the small blaze. The scout platoon did not carry tents, electing to roll into blankets rather than carry the cumbersome shelters. But tonight, a tent of abandoned ship's canvas formed a relief from the chill wind blowing from the nearby sea. Across the harbor, a ship's lantern glowed, revealing the Union blockade that guarded Savannah from Confederate blockade runners.

Danny lowered to the ground, carefully balancing his hot cup and the loaded tin plate he held. He met the old trapper's gaze across the fire with a shrug, unwilling to disclose Hewitt's ongoing animosity.

"Corporal Hewitt can be mean," Roland confessed in a low whisper. The talkative soldier had joined the platoon the same day as Danny, but he'd quickly made himself agreeable to the reticent unit. Within days, his limp had vanished. Eager to please, he'd formed friendships swiftly, often fetching firewood or taking guard duty that wasn't his responsibility. But Danny had to admit his efforts had proven successful. Where he'd become an accepted member of the platoon, Roland had become a favorite.

Nelson scowled at Danny across the yellow flames, as if sensing his reluctance to say too much.

Danny avoided his gaze and shoved his ration of meat around before dropping his plate for the thick slice of bread. He dunked the coarse bread in his coffee, allowing the dead weevils to float to the top where he skimmed them away before devouring the sodden hunk. Leaning back on his haunches, he drank the bitter coffee.

Conversely, Roland ate his dinner with relish, oblivious of the overcooked pork peppered excessively to conceal the ancient meat's true flavor. The farm boy from Ohio seemed content to eat what was served, pleased to have plenty.

"Hamilton, you have guard tonight?" Nelson's inquiry made another soldier lean into the firelight, revealing his pale, thin face. A newer recruit, he'd only been with the platoon since August, a few months before Sherman's onslaught of Atlanta. Blair had placed him last in the twin columns that lined the roads the platoon scouted. Haggard, with sunken eyes, his countenance still reflected the fear and worry the boy from Maine never forgot.

"Yup," Hamilton replied softly. "Not much to guard, I'm relieved to report."

Roland chuckled, and even Nelson grinned. Since occupying Savannah, the army had little work to perform. Scouting reports indicated the Confederacy knew the end was in sight. With only the Carolinas and Virginia remaining in Southern control, the Union noose was tightening.

Richmond, the Confederate capitol, was still free from Union occupation. But Grant's Army had Lee pinned down at Petersburg. Lee could only stay in his trenches and hope he could wait Grant out.

Sherman, on the other hand, had taken Atlanta, leaving him free to advance on Savannah. Five weeks of forced marching and raiding had delivered Sherman's men to Savannah and the port city into Yankee hands.

Now, with Christmas on the coast, Danny was reminded of former winters in Philadelphia. Cold and gray and wet became the norm again. Although no snow fell, the army suffered from the intense cold, hunkering down for rest and protection from the elements. Ships arrived often to keep Sherman's Army well fed and supplied.

Rumors flew daily through the ranks about impending movements northward toward Lee's backside. If the Union Army could invade Virginia and attack Richmond from behind, the war would be over.

Hamilton gathered his gear and moved into the darkness to locate his guard post. Danny watched him go, wondering again about Hewitt's comments. Was Blair truly some kind of good luck charm? He'd known several soldiers who carried likely charms, only to help bury them in a shallow grave. Charms held no real power, yet Blair still lived. And his men revered him, trusted him with their lives. Still, men of the scout platoon continued to die.

Danny leaned away from the small fire to peer through a rent in the canvas and study the night sky. He'd hoped to see countless stars, but a thick cloud cover concealed any of the tiny lights that hovered in the heavens. Heavens? Was there such a place? A relentless drizzle misted, forcing the trio of soldiers to huddle beneath the drooping tent. The fire sputtered but struggled on, fed occasionally from the woodpile stacked in a protected corner.

"Keep the coffee hot," Nelson ordered as he pushed another log into the hissing blaze. "The boys will appreciate the drink."

Tugging a blanket around his shoulders, Danny peered across the nearby harbor before staring at the reflection of orange flames on a nearby anchor chain. A frigate bobbed gently on the sea, the massive battleship guarding the port from a possible rebel attempt at recapture. Danny doubted the Confederate Navy retained the ability for such an attack.

Sloshing footsteps sounded outside, and Danny made out Sergeant Blair's form in the murky darkness.

Blair splashed through puddles before bending to peer beneath the sagging edge of the canvas covering. Around the quiet harbor, other such hastily fabricated shelters lined the walk, revealing the rest of the scout platoon's positions.

The dancing fire cast a dull glow upon the sergeant, and Danny marveled at the man's smile as he looked into the relative dry of Nelson's tent. "Evening, boys," he called.

"Happy New Year, Sergeant. May 1865 be a better year," Nelson replied with a snort.

Danny blinked, forgetting for a moment another year had passed. Then he shrugged. What did it matter?

"May it be so," Blair mumbled as he accepted the steaming cup from Nelson. "Oh, now this is a welcome thing." He blew on the hot mug as drops cascaded from his cap. He stood to survey the silent harbor before crouching to peer into the tent again.

"Well, men, I've finally received definitive word. We'll be moving out in two days. As we expected. We're to move north against Lee's flank. General Johnston is between us and Richmond, but no one seems to know exactly where. I'm sure we'll find him, no doubt," Blair reported with his typical acceptance of rough situations. Nothing seemed to fluster him or make him anxious. Danny surmised this was probably why the men trusted him so implicitly.

"Mason, the army is to advance in two parts. We are to be in the left column. Your Henry rifle and Nelson will lead our platoon. The generals have chosen the path we take. I trust you are up to this task?" Blair sipped his coffee while he waited for Danny's response.

"Why wouldn't I be?" Danny squirmed, sensing something deeper in the innocent sounding question.

"Well," Blair hesitated, glancing at Nelson before continuing. "Well, the point man is first target for the enemy. A man on point should be resolved, know his limitations and abilities." He paused to wipe water from his face, the cold mist dribbling down his cheeks.

Danny scowled, hoping the shadows hid his sudden irritation from Blair. "Haven't I proven myself? Haven't I walked point with Nelson?"

Roland coughed and then grabbed his rifle as he lunged for the opening. "My shift will begin soon," he muttered as he walked into the night. Danny sensed Roland wanted to avoid the brewing debate with Blair. He felt his blood boil, waiting for the sergeant to explain himself.

Nelson cleared his throat. "The sergeant only wants to make sure you're ready for real action. Until now, we've been finding militia snipers, old men left behind to slow our advance. From here, we will find regulars, Confederate soldiers who have endured many battles. Veterans."

"So?" Danny demanded, turning on the old hunter. "I've been in battles. I can handle myself."

Blair sipped his cup, eyeing Danny over the rim. Faint light from a partial moon glowed pale against the black canopy, but enough light showed the sergeant's doubts, making Danny angrier still.

"You have something to say, Sergeant," he blustered. "Spit it out."

For a long moment, no one spoke. Danny glared at Nelson, the old trapper going suddenly silent. But Blair shifted, drawing Danny's gaze once more.

"You mentioned you didn't think you'd make the end of the war. You're not a Christian. You do not have heaven waiting. I worry you might not try as hard as you might, given a tough situation. I told you I'm here to protect my men. The platoon is in your hands. I need every man to perform to their best, to hope, to give a hundred percent."

Danny grunted. "That's ridiculous. Every day, every battle, men hope, and men die. Having a positive attitude does not guarantee we'll make it through the next fight."

Blair nodded. "I agree. But you seem almost fatalistic, as if you expect to die. God willing, we'll make it through this war and live life to its utmost. But we might die in the next skirmish. I'm not afraid for me, for I know my Savior. Jesus promises to welcome me into heaven. A room has been prepared for me. But you might die, expect to die, and I'm not sure I want you leading the platoon into battle. The men deserve a leader who will give his best, fight to live."

"I will give my best," Danny snapped, his tension mounting. "Danny Mason will always give his best. I've heard the Irish sing songs of such men, men of valor."

Blair pursed his lips. "Is that your goal? To have men sing songs of you?"

"No, my goal is to be remembered as a man who died courageously. I have nothing else. You hope for a future. I have no future. I am nobody. I don't even deserve heaven."

"None of us deserve heaven," Nelson said quietly as he leaned away from the fire, as if giving Danny space. "Only by Christ's blood covering our sin do we enter heaven."

At Danny's silence, Blair's eyes widened. "Ah? Do you yearn for more? Any man can have eternal life. The Lord promises to never leave or forsake his people. Are you ready to know Jesus?"

"No," Danny said in a clipped voice as he kicked a burning log in the blaze, sparks fluttering. "I am no Christian. Yet I vow to meet my end with a rifle in my hands, fighting the only way I know." He paused before going on, sitting up straighter. "You can count on me."

Blair glanced at Nelson and then nodded once. He handed his empty mug to the old hunter and turned, disappearing into the night, his boots splashing softly in the puddles.

"He only wants what is best for the platoon," Nelson explained in the silence left by the sergeant's departure. "And you."

Danny held up a hand, anger heating his guts. "I don't want to hear it," he whispered as his gaze darted to the bobbing ships on the harbor, the rain falling steadily. Although his resolve was intact, he hated how the sergeant's words weighed on his mind.

Nelson shrugged. "We have a responsibility to share our faith, the redeeming work of Christ, but we are not responsible for your salvation."

Danny lifted his hand higher. "Enough, old timer," he begged, startled how much their argument had shaken him.

CHAPTER NINE

Danny awoke in the predawn of a clear day. Despite his belief the wet weather would continue, the rain of the past three days had passed. Only sporadic raindrops falling from the canvas overhead and the occasional cry of a seagull disturbed the silence of the ramshackle shanty.

His anger at Blair and Nelson had eased. He still felt annoyed the pair of Christians had questioned his courage, his bravery in battle. Danny Mason was no coward. He would happily give his life to prove his mettle.

Danny frowned, realizing this was precisely what Blair had been afraid of. But how could Danny explain his lack of anything else? No future awaited him. Only his adopted name and a brief legacy mattered. They were all he had, all he'd ever had. He had no family, no land, nothing to pass on to someone else. He felt alone, *was* alone. But he would fight fiercely to the end, so his name never carried shame.

But Blair and Nelson still irritated him. Those self-righteous Christians threw it in his face he wouldn't go to heaven. It rankled him, but what more could an orphan boy from Philadelphia hope for?

Danny cleaned his rifle, the weapon many envied. Perhaps he wasn't nobody. He owned the Henry rifle. When

Nelson returned to the tent, Danny ignored him. He didn't even offer the cold hunter a cup of coffee.

Nelson eyed him sternly as he poured his own mug, the steam lifting like ghosts above the mug's rim. "Last cup," he muttered, placing the pot where it could cool. Then he looked at Danny again. "You're still out of sorts, boy. I don't know what's got you in such a stew but shake it off. We move out tomorrow."

Danny chuckled without humor. "You don't know, huh? You and the sergeant tell me I'm not good enough to lead the men into battle." He eyed Nelson over the fire. "Maybe I'm not nobody. I have this." He indicated his prized weapon.

The old trapper sighed as he settled beside the low blaze, laying his rifle across his knees while Danny ran an oiled rag over the Henry rifle. "I know that, Mason. You have a good weapon, no one denies that. And you're a brave man. But Sergeant Blair worries you might be willing to take risks, take chances to prove your bravery rather than make the right choice in leading the platoon. Anything can happen in battle, and the mission comes first, not your reputation."

A scowl etched Danny's features. Yet something Nelson said resonated within him, and he drew a deep breath. "All right, all right, I know what you mean. I get my back up and can't see straight. To live well, to die well, it's all I have. Except for this." He patted the repeating rifle, "It makes me sick, but courage is all I have to give."

"Nonsense," Nelson muttered and took another sip.

A cold wind blustered off the bay, making the canvas tarp tremble in the breeze. In the sky, a dull gray hovered, like the ashes of a dead fire. Danny's scowl deepened with Nelson's rebuttal, and he kicked the old man's boot, bringing the hunter's gaze up from the fire.

"It's not nonsense to me," he bristled, ready to argue. But Nelson nodded.

"No one doubts your grit. But there's more you don't see. Blair is concerned for the men, the platoon. Your personal feelings don't count as much as their hope to survive the next battle. You must get your head right, fix your mind to do what is right."

"Isn't courage the right thing?" Danny huffed, exasperated by Nelson's remarks. He dragged the cleaning rag over the weapon's stock.

"Courage, yes, but for what reason? So you are remembered fondly? Who do you serve, Mason? It sounds as if you serve yourself."

"Who else is there? My name, my honor, what else is there?" Danny held his hands wide, appealing for insight.

Nelson shook his head. "Blair told me you're not interested in things above, things about God."

Danny snorted, his hands stilling on the Henry rifle. "Indeed, I'm not," he agreed. He placed the cleaned weapon aside and squinted at the old hunter. "But if I were, what does that have to do with this?"

For a long moment, silence filled the canvas shelter. Nelson poured water into the battered coffeepot and shoved the container into the coals before peering at Danny across the low flames. "God created everything around us. Our land, the ocean, each of us. But he is holy, completely good, while we are sinners, consumed with selfish desires like greed and pride."

Danny waved a hand. "I've heard this before. So what?"

"Our soul yearns for connection with God," the hunter continued, pretending not to notice Danny's interruption. "But with our wicked hearts, we cannot come close to him. So Jesus, God's Son, came to die for us, to pay our debt before a perfect God. Now we can know the Lord because of Jesus's sacrifice on the cross."

"Whatever," Danny hissed angrily. "This has nothing to do with me and the platoon."

Nelson chuckled. "It has everything to do with this, with you. Do you want personal glory for dying in battle? Do you need to prove your courage to someone? Or will you submit to God and serve him? Fight for others, not yourself. Serve the Lord and think beyond yourself."

Danny stiffened, seeing Nelson's point for the first time. "But there's always only been me. I'm alone. I don't—"

He was going to say he didn't care about others, but held his tongue, too shocked at this brutal truth than he wanted to share. Nelson's laughter made his head jerk, and he stared at the old trapper.

"I know what you're thinking. Are you ashamed of what you feel? I felt the same way once, thinking only of myself. But Jesus has shown me another way."

"Enough," Danny said wearily. "I will take this responsibility seriously, trying hard to consider what is best for the platoon, the rest of the men. Blair can count on me. But let's hear no more about God or his expectations of me."

He paused, remembering his resolve, the creed that had carried him across many battlefields. "I am Danny Mason. I will always fight bravely, willing to risk all to be remembered well. But now I will think of the men."

The hunter nodded. "It's a beginning. But I sense something more, something deeper within you."

Danny shook his head. "There is nothing more. All I have is this fancy gun and my name."

"You're wrong, boy," Nelson whispered as he poured ground coffee into the boiling pot. "The Lord is working on you. Today, you have taken a major step toward understanding."

"Understanding what?" Danny sneered.

"A life beyond yourself. A purpose for your life that stretches beyond you."

Danny said nothing for a moment, stunned at the depth of this talk. He wanted only to fight well, to be remembered well. Could there be anything more?

Finally, Danny laughed, liking the old man's cryptic message. "Whatever you say, old timer. But I trust in my Henry rifle and little else."

Yet he stored up Nelson's words to ponder later.

★★★

That night, as Danny stood guard duty, he watched the stars glitter between slowly drifting clouds, wondering anew. He'd thought he was wise when he chose something paramount to live for, to die for. Could there be something more? Courage had seemed so noble. Yet, he sensed something deeper, a nameless shadow lurking at the edges of his mind. He felt a nagging doubt for the first time in years. Perhaps Sergeant Blair and Nelson knew of another way, a destiny filled with unimaginable potency.

He shrugged deeper into his blue coat, warding off the cold and the misgivings that threatened. He'd believed wholeheartedly in valor, never questioning his resolve. What could be more significant than honor? He believed this was his destiny, to die in a grand cause. No matter that he didn't care which side won, only that he fought with all his ability.

Like a lightning bolt sent from above, an intense awareness struck him, shattering what he'd thought. Keeping his distance from others had not allowed men to get to know him. Who would care how he died? Who would speak kind words at his burial?

Angrily, Danny realized his carefully devised plans had been empty, built upon a soft foundation of unrealistic goals. Even if he died carrying the flag, died protecting a general, or was killed surrounded by countless foes, who would remember a brave stranger?

Slowly, he exhaled, deflating. Was he a fool?

He drew a deep breath and shook his head. No, he would die gallant, because Danny Mason was an honorable man. He must be true to himself, right? Other men's perspective didn't matter. Danny had to do what he felt was correct.

Yet, abruptly, his resolve felt shaken. What if he were wrong? What if his destiny lay in another direction, one he'd never considered? All the God talk had unnerved him. He'd never considered heaven and hell, his eternal resting place. What happened to a man after death? Was there something more?

And future? He'd never thought of a future—the war consuming him, giving him the opportunity he thought he longed for. The war gave him purpose. Could there be something for him after this terrible conflict? With a shudder, he realized he might live beyond the battlefield.

He glanced at the bright stars, still only seen in part as they played peek-a-boo behind the dark clouds. An unfamiliar yearning filled him. He wanted to know more, but he feared his carefully crafted ideas might suffer.

"You're teasing me, like the stars," he muttered, wondering if God were real. "I can't see you, can't touch you, yet you taunt me. Are you speaking?"

He'd never gone to church before, never thought of God—the orphanage never being a place where spirituality was mentioned. He had no land, no heritage, no great money, but if he survived the war, what would he do? He'd never thought of a future, his future.

With a chuckle, his gaze shifted, and he looked out over the nearby harbor. What was he doing? God didn't call to him. Danny Mason, orphan from Philadelphia, using a borrowed name. He was nobody, he reminded himself bitterly. God wouldn't care about him.

With a grunt, he patted his rifle affectionately. This fancy gun gave him purpose. Gave him a place in this world. And that was all he needed for now.

Boots crunched on gravel, and Danny swung the rifle from his shoulder. He narrowed his eyes and watched as a figure loomed from the darkness. Recognizing Sergeant Blair, he relaxed.

"Mason? When did you go on duty?" Blair stuffed his hands into his pockets and hunched his shoulders against the rising breeze off the water.

"Around three, I think. Should be dawn soon," Danny said in a low voice. Sound carried easily on the chilled wind, and he didn't want to disturb the sleeping men around him.

Blair nodded. "Let them sleep," he said, as if comprehending Danny's need for quiet. "We'll be moving out soon, moving north. Somewhere ahead, Johnston's Army is waiting, or perhaps we'll strike Lee's flank. Regardless, the end is near. The Confederacy is shrinking. Not much left."

He paused, as if considering something. "We're to scout in advance. You and Nelson will lead our platoon on the road. We're to go inland, search for defensive rebel positions. Another column will follow the shore. Tomorrow, we head north into South Carolina. Be ready."

Danny felt anticipation bubble, and he wanted to crow. He would lead with Nelson, despite his apparent spiritual shortcomings. They needed him, they needed his rifle. The Henry repeating rifle made him special.

A grin split his cold face, but Blair shifted, calming Danny's elation. "Don't think I haven't forgotten our conversation," the young sergeant said softly. "But after much prayer, I believe you and Nelson are the right pair for point."

Danny nodded, unable to speak as he struggled to contain his excitement. With a grunt, Blair walked into the darkness.

Danny's grin widened. He wasn't wrong. Courage, honor, bravery would mark the Mason name. Through the massed clouds, he glimpsed a bright star, one even brighter than the others. "You have nothing for me," he whispered gleefully as he watched the clouds slowly conceal the glittering stars. "This war is almost over, and I'll lead into battle. Honor awaits me."

CHAPTER TEN

Despite winter storms haunting the Carolina coast, making occasional appearances, Sherman's Army moved northward. Danny and Nelson led the scout platoon, sometimes discovering small outposts of wounded guerrillas attempting to slow the Yankee advance. But nothing seemed to slow Sherman's troops.

Through bitter cold rain and blustering squalls, Sergeant Blair's scout platoon directed the army north. Across desolate roads and barren pastures, through frozen woods filled with leafless trees, the army wound like an unquenchable snake. Ever pressing forward, the Union Army moved through South Carolina and into North Carolina. Ahead, Lee's Army held Richmond.

The days passed with supplies from the nearby sea, allowing quick delivery to the front. Food, ammunition, and clothing were brought in abundance to the marching army while the Confederates did without. Starving and unkempt, dressed in rags and barefoot, the rebels Danny met were little better than scarecrows. Yet, they fought bravely as they attempted to repulse the invading army that conquered their lands.

Jefferson Davis was reported to still be in Richmond, still holding the Confederate presidency. Soldiers debated his fate upon the Southerner's imminent defeat.

General Joe Johnston's Army had not been located. Cavalry patrols discovered nothing to indicate where the main body of rebel defenders were positioned. The next day dawned with the two columns already on the move. February in the Carolinas was cold, but at least there was no snow on the ground.

Underfed and poorly equipped local militia groups proved ineffective in slowing Sherman's advance. More days passed, the army progressed, the Confederacy continued to shrink.

At night, around the campfire, Danny attempted to get to know as many of the men as possible. Where before he'd been aloof and standoffish, now he made every effort to appear friendly. He wanted everyone to know him, to remember him when he fell.

Each night, as he worked to kindle connection with the platoon, Danny noticed Blair studied his Bible and then the little black journal that housed his dreams. What would it be like to have thoughts of a future? Danny wouldn't think of that now, so committed was he to his path. There was no chance a luckless orphan from the slums would survive the war. His only choice was heroism.

The Ides of March came and went, and Danny pretended he understood the reference men made to Caesar. He'd heard of Shakespeare but had never read any of his works.

Tall pine forests covered most of the land, and the red soil stuck like clay to everything when wet. Smell of the salt air drifted on the breeze from the distant sea. Inland from the coast, Blair's scout platoon covered miles a day, passing quiet farms or burned houses, reminders of former battles or Southern attempts to thwart the advancing Union Army. Regardless, Sherman's troops marched ever northward.

Near the small town of Four Oaks, bullets rained upon Blair's men. Hastily, Danny threw himself aside, glancing over his shoulder to where Nelson had vanished behind a thicket. After the initial noisy volley, the chilled spring day stretched quietly. Nothing stirred. Minutes passed.

Finally, Nelson appeared in the middle of the road, waving for the platoon to follow. Men scrambled from hiding places and joined Danny and Sergeant Blair near the old hunter.

"Must've been an outpost. I rounded their flank and caught sight of them hightailing it to yonder hills. They know we're here." Nelson pointed to a low ridge where, even at this distance, defensive positions could be observed. All along the extensive ridgeline, flags fluttered above trenches behind earthen breastworks. The long sought Confederate Army had been discovered. Excitement passed through the gathered platoon as Blair pulled a telescope from his jacket and studied the distant ramparts.

"Rebel soldiers. Regulars, not militia, no doubt about it," Blair muttered.

Danny felt a thrill worm through him, as if something noteworthy had been achieved. Here at last was his long-awaited opportunity at significance.

Behind them, the sound of marching feet sounded. A portly officer mounted on a bay gelding rode beside columns of approaching Union soldiers. The officer called for a halt as Blair stepped forward.

He saluted before giving his report. "Rebel defenses are on that ridge, Major. My scouts determine they are regulars, probably Johnston's forces."

"Where is your ranking officer, Sergeant?" The overweight major peered past Blair's shoulder.

Blair shifted. "I'm afraid we haven't had an officer in months, sir. I lead the scout platoon."

"Most irregular," the fat major mumbled. He held a gloved hand out to an aid who quickly handed him a telescope. For a long moment, only the impatient horse broke the silence with loud snorts as the officer studied the rebel positions on the ridge.

"Yes, yes," he murmured. Lowering the glass, he shoved the instrument short before returning it to the aid. "We will attack immediately."

Danny watched as Nelson and Sergeant Blair exchanged worried glances. "Begging your pardon, sir," Blair began. "We're ordered to locate enemy positions and report to the rear. We're not to engage unless attacked, and then we're to break off and retreat."

"Sounds cowardly, Sergeant," the major boomed as he signaled his troops forward.

"Sir, we're scouts, not regular infantry."

"Nonsense. Today is a day of glory. You have discovered the enemy and will join the attack. They are reduced to rabble. Reports indicate they are low on ammunition and food supplies. We should take them easily."

"No one will take Old Joe's men easily," Blair said in an icy tone. "Perhaps we should wait for reinforcements or artillery support." But the major only waved dismissively as his men assembled into battle formations.

"You will lead the attack, Sergeant," the major ordered. "Have your men join ranks with my regiment and prepare for advance." At Blair's hesitation, the major glowered from his perch on his high horse. "That is an order, Sergeant. Obey me at once."

Blair turned and whispered to his men, "Follow their lead. Join the infantry and prepare for attack." His men hesitated as he had, and Blair barked, "Follow me, men."

With purposeful strides, Blair raced to line up with another regiment, pointing his men to positions in the front rank. Danny watched Nelson frown, but Corporal Hewitt bellowed at the scout platoon to follow Sergeant Blair. Soon, the scouts stood in two ranks at the head of a lead regiment.

"What are we doing here?" Danny's anxious whisper made Nelson frown even deeper, but both men formed into line, shoulder to shoulder with one another.

Hewitt thundered, "Quiet in the ranks. Line with your neighbor. Steady, men."

Sergeant Blair walked along the front of the twin ranks, offering encouragement as drums sounded behind the forming regiments. Danny glanced behind him, past the third rank of men to where cannon formed into a long line of big guns under the edge of the nearby forest. Everywhere about them, men in blue uniforms gathered into battle lines, forming ranks of men prepared to march against the Confederate defenses.

"This isn't bravery," Danny scoffed as the order was given and the lead ranks began to march across the open fields below the high ramparts. "This is suicide."

"Quiet," Hewitt snarled over his shoulder as he and Blair walked ahead of the regiment.

The scout platoon blended with another unit of infantry, lieutenants leading each regiment with a drawn sword. Before their knot of men, Blair marched, holding his rifle ready. Danny studied his profile, surprised to not detect any fear on the sergeant's features, only a grim acceptance. Perhaps they were alike, Danny marveled. Perhaps the sergeant valued gallantry and honor also.

A tremor of anticipation shivered down his back, and Danny realized he was exactly where he'd hoped to be. Although the circumstances were not to his liking, the result would be the same. They were going into battle. With the rebel guns pointed down at them from the ridge, the outcome left in little doubt.

Not since Atlanta had he marched in battle formation. The scout platoon had moved silently and quickly, flushing resistance from the countryside as the army pushed to the north. Now he was posted with the infantry once more, fodder for the big guns that crowned the distant crest. As if on cue, the cannon boomed, and Danny tensed as shells fell around him.

CHAPTER ELEVEN

As shells fell among the troops, a shudder of fear swept the regiment, but Blair lifted a hand. "Steady, men. Follow me."

As if his words held a charm, the men steadied as they marched shoulder to shoulder toward the ridge. The cannon rounds started to fall harmlessly behind the advancing regiments, and Danny felt the men's spirits bolster. But the cannon crew adjusted their range, and the shells continued to blast gaps among the rows of marching men, bellows of cannon mingling with screams of the wounded.

Danny's ears rang as he moved forward, attempting to ignore the cries of horses and men falling all around him. Ahead, the ridge above the meadows seemed to bristle with rifle barrels as the rebels peered down the hill at the approaching blue horde.

In the regiment beside their own, the young lieutenant in the front suddenly screamed and fell to his knees, clutching his throat. Behind him, a cannon round exploded, scattering the first two ranks in a flurry of flying bodies and dirt.

"Steady, men," Corporal Hewitt called from beside Blair. The sergeant glanced over his shoulder at his men and Danny saw the resolution on his countenance. Blair seemed determined, and Danny steeled himself, willing himself to stick with the sergeant.

When another cannon blast tore a ragged hole in the rear rank of their regiment, a few men turned and ran. "Hold, hold," Blair called after them, willing his men to follow him forward.

For a brief moment, a deep terror filled Danny. He almost turned and fled the field with the infantrymen, but then he recalled his motivation. *Danny Mason doesn't run.*

"Stay with me, boy," Nelson said, as if sensing Danny's faltering tenacity.

"I'm with you," Danny growled from between clenched teeth. Whatever happened, he must stand. This was his moment. There was nothing else for him.

Finally, the shattered blue lines arrived below the ridge, the low hills humped above the wide meadow, their serenity destroyed from battle. A jumble of granite boulders marked the edge of the field. Danny wondered if he'd be a coward to fire at the enemy from the protection of these big rocks, but he stayed beside Nelson and moved steadily up the hill.

"Charge!" Blair bellowed as he pushed a flag bearer forward.

Together, the pair raced up the knoll. With a shout, the entire platoon lunged after Sergeant Blair.

Danny gripped his rifle so hard his knuckles ached. He leaped over a fallen comrade only to be knocked backward by the concussion of a cannon blast. Ears ringing, he pushed himself up from the ground, trying to clear his blurred vision. When his sight cleared, he glanced at his feet where he recognized Roland, the young soldier he'd joined the scout platoon with, staring up at him with unseeing eyes.

With a shriek, Danny pointed his Henry rifle up the hill. A soldier in a gray jacket took aim at him and Danny fired. First one man and then another, his shots thinning the ranks of rebels firing down upon the hapless Yankees. Abruptly, a hand gripped his shoulder.

"Come on, boy," Nelson shouted above the din of battle. "Charge!"

As if his heels were on fire, Danny pushed himself erect and raced after the old hunter, still firing as he ran. Slowly, the pair worked their way up the hillside, shooting Confederates who showed themselves above their earthen fortifications. At one point, Danny halted to reload as Nelson shot a man beside a cannon.

"They must be low on ammunition," Nelson observed as he shoved the ramrod down his rifle barrel, tamping another round into place. "Not as many shots as before."

Danny slapped the final round into the chamber before lifting his rifle to his shoulder. He fired once, twice before replying. "Go, Nelson, take us to the trenches."

With a lunge, the old trapper scrambled up the steep hillside. From the corner of Danny's eye, he saw other blue-clad soldiers leaning into the knoll, struggling up the incline to where the Confederates hid behind their defenses. There was no turning back now. He'd be shot in the back if he ran for the rear. He shoved aside the fleeting consideration, and Danny knew his life would end here, on this grassy hillside.

Four men lifted rifles from the trenches ahead and fired down on them. Danny cringed when he saw Nelson stagger and turn, his jacket suddenly red from blood. Danny shot two of the defenders before a man grabbed his shoulder, spinning him around.

"Help me, Mason!" Sergeant Blair shouted, grabbing one of Nelson's arms.

Together, they dragged the old trapper down the hill to the mound of granite boulders, bullets hailing around them like rain. Behind the rocks, they propped Nelson against a huge stone.

Danny watched as Blair stuffed torn shirt material into the hunter's bullet holes. All around them, men screamed, but Blair worked mechanically, as if unaware of the bullets whistling overhead. Beside Nelson, a young soldier sat, his head leaning to one side, eyes closed. At the end of the line of rocks, a third soldier lay prone, firing from behind the corner of a boulder, a bloody rag tied around one leg.

"Come on." The sergeant finished his ministrations and led the way back up the hill, racing toward the trenches.

Out of the clouds of smoke and noise, a few men joined their mad rush up the knoll. Danny recognized Hewitt and Hamilton as they plowed their way to the earthen breastworks. With a shout, the Union soldiers leaped over the fortifications and fired their rifles. In an instant, they grappled with soldiers in gray rags, men fighting with bayonets and clubs. Dead men lay all about, but Danny stood atop the dirt mound and fired at every rebel soldier he could see. His rifle heated in his hands, still he fired, halting to reload before firing again, felling countless rebel soldiers.

Hamilton went down, and Danny shot his attacker. Vaguely, behind the rebel trenches, he heard the bugle call for reinforcements. Something struck a wicked blow to his shoulder, but Danny ignored the red-hot sting, still finding targets with his rifle. Then Blair staggered, and Danny heard Hewitt bellow like a bull. As if in slow motion, Danny took aim on the gray-clad soldier who thrust a bayonet into the sergeant's chest, then Danny fired. With a swing of his empty rifle, Corporal Hewitt struck the head of another attacker who aimed a pistol at the wounded sergeant.

"Mason!" Hewitt shouted, a river of blood streaming down the side of his face. He picked up the fallen pistol and fired at the few remaining rebels before throwing the empty gun at another. With a gesture to Danny, the corporal indicated he help carry the injured sergeant from the muddy trench. Still clutching the Henry rifle, Danny reached for the sergeant's shoulder and grasped the blue jacket. Without ceremony, they dragged Blair down the hill to join Nelson behind the boulders at the foot of the knoll.

Now, the limited space behind the big rocks was filled with wounded men, as if the small space had become a hospital staging area, crammed full of injured and dead men. Nelson still sat where he'd been left, but Danny grimaced when he saw the old hunter's eyes were closed. Men pleaded for water or help, but Danny propped Sergeant Blair between two dead soldiers and gripped the bayonet that protruded from his blood-soaked jacket.

"No, no," Blair insisted, stilling Danny's hand. A bloody froth appeared at the corner of his mouth, and the sergeant's scar seemed to brighten against his pale cheeks.

Danny felt his eyes widen as he shot a worried glance to Hewitt where the corporal knelt before Blair, but the sergeant shook his head, as if understanding the concerned look that passed between his two soldiers.

"I'm all right," he mumbled as more blood spilled from his mouth.

Danny had seen too many chest wounds to not recognize a lung injury.

"Jesus waits," the young sergeant whispered. With a trembling hand, he pulled his coat open and withdrew a pair of black books. Pressing them into Danny's hands, he smiled, his gray eyes glazing. "Dream. Dream."

The shining eyes stared hard into Danny's and then their gleam faded. Blair's gaze shifted and he stilled, as if he'd become like the rocks around him.

CHAPTER TWELVE

Danny crouched beside the dead man for another moment, looking down at Blair's peaceful face. Then, slowly, he looked up. Corporal Hewitt glowered, as if Danny had somehow been responsible. In the distance, Danny observed a tight cluster of mounted officers, eyes riveted on the battle before them. Their nervous horses sidestepped with every blast of the cannons atop the ridge. He blinked when he heard the bugler beside the fat major sound retreat.

"We need him," Hewitt said in a low voice, laced with bitterness. "We need Sergeant Blair."

A sharp pang pierced Danny's chest, as if he'd been the one stabbed with a bayonet. He stuffed the black books into his jacket as he rose. "Come on. We don't need Blair. We know what to do."

Corporal Hewitt poked Danny's shoulder with a finger. "You've been shot."

Danny stared at the red stain on his jacket, a small hole telling him where the round had gone through. Around them, Union soldiers fled the field. Hobbling soldiers leaned on others as the blue-clad soldiers retreated.

"I'm all right," he said, suddenly shocked he'd just heard Sergeant Blair mutter these same words. "Bind it up, Hewitt."

Taking a rag from his pocket, Danny handed the bandanna to the corporal. Hewitt bound the wound quickly, then looked about. "Lost my rifle up there," he explained as he searched the wounded and dead men that sprawled behind the boulders. Picking up a rifle, he checked the load before snatching ammunition from a dead soldier. "Let's go," he said.

This time, rather than joining the fray, they raced across the field toward the forest behind them. The tide of battle had swayed, and the rebel soldiers were creeping from their trenches. With the premature attack of the Union infantry, the Confederates routed them, forcing Sherman's Army from the field.

At first, the Federalist troops held an organized retreat, but the rebels seemed frenzied. Lack of food and supplies drove them down the hill to tear packs and weapons from the dead soldiers that lay everywhere.

In the headlong flight from the battle, Danny helped limping soldiers or wounded men barely able to escape the rebel counterattack. To fall into the Confederate hands was a fate worse than death. Everyone had heard of the deplorable and inhumane conditions of the Southern prisoner of war camps.

Shocked, Danny slowed to a walk when he reached the defensive lines the Union had hastily formed a few miles behind the battle. Hewitt was nowhere in sight. Everyone else from the scout platoon was probably dead. Feeling a sense of dejection, Danny wandered the front lines. Finally, an officer noticed his bandaged shoulder and directed him to a field hospital.

He didn't remember the orderly cleaning and binding his wound. Thoughts of Blair and Nelson filled his mind. Even Roland and Hamilton held a place in his memories, and he hated himself for allowing the scout platoon to break down his reserve. He'd worked so hard to stay alone, to remain isolated from others, only to succumb at last to Sergeant Blair's encouragement. What journey did Danny find himself on now?

With a sneer, he realized Blair had been wrong. There was no message in life, no meaning other than to live strong and then die. Honor meant everything, yet he'd fled the battlefield, and his ideals stumbled once more. He'd fought bravely, but despite his best efforts, he'd survived the battle. Guiltily, Danny recalled the rout from Four Oaks. The Battle of Bentonville would always stain Danny Mason's reputation, at least in his mind.

Later that night, he found himself in a wagon loaded with wounded, bound farther to the rear. As the wagon jostled over the rutted road he'd walked only that morning, he gazed up at the silent stars that watched his passage. He grimaced as he gripped his injured shoulder. What was the meaning of meeting Blair? What wisdom could he glean from knowing Nelson?

★★★

The next day, Danny was seen again by an army doctor. Three weeks later, just when he was ready to return to the fight, General Lee surrendered to Grant. Two weeks after that, Johnston's Army surrendered to Sherman after eluding Union forces for almost a month. Depleted by countless deserters, the ragged Confederate troops finally abandoned any hope of success. The Battle of Bentonville proved to be the final engagement between Sherman's men and the Confederacy. Old Joe's surrender brought an end to the war.

Danny recuperated at the tent hospital, eager to rejoin his platoon. However, with all the troop movements and surrenders, no one knew where Danny's comrades were located. As he prepared to search for his platoon, the army released soldiers from active duty, eager to have them return home and to some level of normalcy.

Lincoln's assassination on the heels of the Confederate surrender stunned an already grieving nation. The tall president who had won the war was now dead.

Danny made his way to Philadelphia. Although he had nowhere else to go, the city no longer seemed like home. The long war was over, yet it was the death of the president that pervaded the dark atmosphere of the northern cities. Despite men returning from the battles, a somber shroud descended upon the land, as if this final blow were more than a weary nation could endure.

As the wound in Danny's shoulder healed, he considered his next move. Life must go on. He took a room at a lodging house, determined to pick himself up and carry on. He was Danny Mason, a courageous man, he reminded himself stubbornly. Yet his guilt rankled. While Sergeant Blair had raced over the battlefield, saving men and fighting bravely, Danny had done nothing remarkable. He'd fought the only way he knew how. But at a time when few wanted to be reminded of the past four years, Blair's memory lingered, refusing to let Danny forget.

Not only had the sergeant fought like a lion, he believed he now resided in heaven. What more could any man wish for? Obsessed, Danny looked for work while he mulled over his military career, unable to escape its impact.

He was Danny Mason, so he became a stoneworker. Perhaps his name had meaning after all, he reasoned as he learned to stack brick and form rock walls. The nation had suffered too great a cost with the interminable war, and no one seemed to care he was a veteran. Too many veterans, too many wounded missing a limb or an eye.

Keep moving, he urged himself, anxious to recapture a sense of identity or purpose. He'd not died in the war as he believed was inevitable. He'd always fought bravely, but now there was no one to impress. Danny found himself more alone, more a nobody than ever.

Yet, as America tried to put the dreaded war behind her, Danny could think of nothing else. By day, he worked harder than Joe or Nick on the stonemason crew. Desperately, he wanted to tire himself out so he could fall asleep at night, too exhausted to think. But each night, remembered faces of soldiers drifted before his mind's eye, reminding him of wide grassy fields where hundreds perished. Dimly, in the recesses of his memory, he could hear the roar of cannons where the artillery hunkered beneath trees at the edge of the battles.

But as spring blended into summer, Danny discovered he could not escape these ghosts. Always a man alone, he became even more alone.

Other men visited the saloons or taverns each night, relishing companionship or a means to dull their restless minds, but Danny could not make himself waste his precious wages on drink. The hard school of poverty had indelibly impressed on him the wisdom of frugal living. He hoarded his wages for what he knew not.

After twelve-hour days of placing bricks and carrying buckets of mortar, he would tumble into bed, only to find the darkness of his small room could not conceal the troubling thoughts that tormented him. By candlelight, he dressed each morning, often not returning until the familiar darkness filled every corner of his drab dwelling. He took his meals at a tavern near his work, eager to leave his room each day, reluctant to return each evening.

Despite openings in many professions, Danny preferred his job as a mason. Many men did not return from the war—opportunities abounded for hard-working men. Yet, he couldn't escape the desire to find meaning. The brick and rock mason who reported to work each day provided a focused countenance to the world. With determination, Danny threw himself into his work. He ached as his back and arms bulged with new muscle. Even his injured shoulder caused him discomfort at first, but he ignored the pain and improved daily as a bricklayer. It wasn't long before Joe, the supervisor, put Danny on the most difficult tasks, beating out the more experienced Nick. Danny wasn't afraid to lean far over the busy city streets from a shaky scaffolding, balancing on a narrow beam as he scooped mortar from a bucket.

As if driven, he strove daily to push himself. To place more brick, to lay more stone, to carry heavier buckets of mortar, these efforts consumed his waking thoughts. But still, his sleep refused to provide rest.

Hot days filled the long summer months, but Danny kept to his work, yearning for something he couldn't understand. In his heart, he felt the longing, a longing for something unnamed. His goal before the war had been to fight bravely, to die in such a way that his borrowed name might possess true merit. Men would remember his valor. Now, he wanted to forget his years in the army. Day after day, his memories swirled, not allowing him to erase those empty objectives.

***

Lifting the trowel, he worked another brick into place. Above, the July sun beat mercilessly upon the Philadelphia streets, yet he gloried in the sweat and familiar ache in his arms as the walls went ever higher. His wound barely bothered him anymore, and by next week, this building would be complete. Joe reported they would next move to repair the rock wall near the convent.

In the afternoon, Joe would whistle, calling Danny and Nick to a short lunch break. But Danny often worked on, refusing to take the respite his body screamed for. Although fire burned in his weary muscles, he remained perched atop the tall scaffolding, pushing himself even harder. If he could tire himself out, he might at last enjoy one restful night.

As he lifted another trowel with mortar heaped along one edge, he glanced at the street below where Joe and Nick conversed in the shade of a canvas awning, enjoying their lunch break. The shade covering made him think of the ramshackle hovel where he'd lived last winter beside the harbor in Savannah. Memories surged, crashing around him, reminding him of the war and the dead men he'd known.

Far below, he saw a man round a corner, his gait reminding Danny of someone. The man's companion laughed, and the pair walked beneath the scaffolding, temporarily out of his sight. When they emerged farther down the street, Danny stared after them, his skin prickling with a niggling sensation.

He squinted, ignoring the heavy trowel he held. That man, that walk, he *knew* him. And as the man rounded the far corner, he turned to his companion and spoke, his countenance visible from Danny's high perch. With a start, he recognized Corporal Hewitt.

CHAPTER THIRTEEN

Danny dropped his trowel and clambered down the tall scaffolding. In his haste, he slipped and nearly fell. Hand over hand, he worked his way down the high structure until his feet scrambled on the sidewalk. A knot formed in his belly and anticipation bubbled, making him feel as if everything hinged on speaking with Hewitt. He caught Joe and Nick's curious glance, but ignored them as he raced around the corner, skidding to a halt when he lost Hewitt in the crowded street. Peering frantically about, he searched for a glimpse of the two men. Nothing.

A trolley car rang its bell and moved away. There, behind the brightly painted car, was Hewitt and his companion. Dressed in a tailored suit, the corporal was almost unrecognizable. But his characteristic walk reassured Danny as he skittered across the dirt street in pursuit.

As the pair halted before a newspaper stand, Danny stood back at arm's length, studying the former corporal. Yes, it was Hewitt, no mistake. Danny's heart raced with his efforts to descend the scaffold and pursue the two men, but now he drew breath and ran a hand through his hair, uncertain how to proceed.

He cleared his throat, and Hewitt glanced at him. For a moment, their gaze locked and then Hewitt's brows bunched, as if struggling to place him. "Mason?" he whispered, his eyes squinting even more.

Danny nodded and stepped closer. Should they shake hands? An embrace seemed too awkward, yet they'd endured battle, privation, and loss together. Corporal Hewitt had never liked him, Danny remembered abruptly, but they had shared much. And they both knew Sergeant Blair.

"Corporal Hewitt," Danny began. His voice sounded weak to his ears and difficult to form. A sudden lump lodged in Danny's throat, and he could not say anything more.

Hewitt's companion stepped forward. "Hewitt, you know this man?"

The corporal nodded. "I know him. Give me a minute, Jimmy."

Jimmy glanced at Danny again before turning to the rack of newspapers once more. Danny stared at Hewitt. As if reluctant yet compelled, Hewitt stuck out his hand and they shook, squeezing fiercely. For a long moment, neither spoke.

"Corporal Hewitt," Danny began again.

"Mason, I can't believe it's you. I've tried to get in touch with the old platoon but couldn't find anyone. Then, the war was over, and everyone mustered out."

Danny nodded. "Last time I saw you, blood poured from a head wound."

Hewitt's hand went to his temple. "Only a gash. I'm fine." He gestured to Danny's shoulder. "You were shot."

"I'm fine," Danny said hurriedly, feigning indifference, his minor wound insignificant to those who never came back. "I never saw the old unit again."

They paused, memories flooding over Danny as he considered his next words. "I saw Roland go down. And Hamilton died in the trenches. Nelson—"

"Stop," Hewitt barked, holding up his hand. "Please don't say anymore."

Danny shifted on his feet. He wanted to say more. He hadn't even mentioned Sergeant Blair.

"Don't," Hewitt repeated in a strangled voice. "I was in the field hospital three days before reuniting to our regiment. Most of our platoon was killed at Bentonville, so I was reassigned to the regular infantry."

His grin seemed lopsided as he attempted to smile, but Danny saw the tremble on his lips and his eyes clouded. "No more need for a scout platoon. We'd located the enemy." He looked away and swallowed, his throat working. He blinked when he looked at Danny again. "We chased Old Joe for a few weeks. Heard about Lee's surrender, and then Johnston followed suit."

Again, Danny nodded, as if there was nothing more to tell. The war had ended. Yet he longed to talk to someone he knew, who knew him.

"Look, I have to get back to the office. Perhaps we could get together some time, for a drink," Hewitt said in such a way that Danny knew they'd never get together. Perhaps his former corporal felt haunted too.

Feeling depressed, Danny turned to go when Hewitt stopped him. "Whatever happened with Blair's journals?"

Danny knew what he meant. The sergeant's Bible and journal sat on the top of his dresser, tucked far back in the shadows when the dim candlelight burned in Danny's small room. They belonged to him now, and Danny decided he would not share them with Corporal Hewitt.

But Hewitt pressed. "I saw him study both books plenty during the two years I knew him." At Danny's silence, Hewitt shrugged. "Guess he wasn't so lucky after all," he mumbled as he turned to his companion.

Heat seemed to flood Danny's veins, and he felt his eyes widen with the shock of Hewitt's words. With a hand of steel, he grasped the corporal's shoulder and spun him around.

"What did you say?" Danny felt his stomach tighten as Hewitt sputtered.

"Let go, Mason. Blair was just a man, nothing special. I was wrong. He had no charmed life."

Danny punched him, blood spurting from Hewitt's nose as he stumbled backward. Jimmy leaped between them, holding out his arms. "What's this? Stop, stop!"

Danny held his fists up for another blow, but Hewitt straightened and wiped his face with a linen handkerchief, glowering at Danny. "You're crazy, Mason. What's gotten into you?"

But Danny couldn't speak, and Jimmy propelled Hewitt away, pushing through the crowd that had gathered to watch the altercation. The mob thinned when the fight ended, and Danny stood alone on the busy street, angry at Hewitt and himself.

He glanced around at the crowded street, everyone busy to get somewhere. But Danny seemed overwhelmed at the sensation he was going nowhere.

Slowly, he made his way around the corner to the job he worked with Joe and Nick. Ignoring their curious glances, he worked the afternoon, quiet and thoughtful. If Sergeant Blair wasn't special, what hope did Danny have of finding purpose or satisfaction? Blair was the kindest man Danny ever knew. The sergeant cared for his men and died bravely, much the way Danny had longed for.

He knew what he must do. As assuredly as he knew he'd never see Hewitt again, Danny knew he must look at the sergeant's books tonight. Until now, the books represented a connection to his past, one he longed to forget. But Sergeant Blair should never be forgotten.

His thoughts whirling, Danny returned to work. As he worked, he felt lonelier than ever before. Despite attempting to remain isolated during the war, his comrades had shared something personal, something remarkable. They'd fought in battles together, they'd served beside one another. Every engagement and every troop movement had left scars and memories that now worked inside his head, never allowing him to forget. Yet Hewitt had dismissed the best man Danny could recall.

Hewitt had not wanted to be reminded of their connection, yet the chance meeting had only made Danny want to look at things more clearly. The mention of Blair's books filled him with an eagerness he rarely experienced, except when he marched into battle. Abruptly, he couldn't wait to see the black books that lay on his small dresser.

When the workday finished, they'd completed the brick wall. The hot sun leaned far west of the city. The smells of rotting rubbish and discarded refuse filled the air, and the even fouler stench of animal excrement lingered along the docks where the blood drained from the slaughterhouse. Everywhere, people moved along the crowded streets. Businessman and ladies in fine dresses frequented the nicer part of town, while men in dirty workmen's clothes and women in soiled dresses thronged the narrow avenues of the older part of Philadelphia. Children raced through the crowds, shouting as they chased one another.

But tonight, Danny ignored it all. He could imagine the pair of books stacked neatly atop one another at the back of his dresser. He wanted to see them, to hold them. He *needed* to see them.

"We're done here," Joe remarked as Nick gathered their tools. "Tomorrow, we'll start the job at the convent," the supervisor called when Danny turned to go.

After waving to Nick, he hurried the several blocks to the tenement house where he had a room. He took the stairs two at a time, refusing to allow his weariness to slow him down as he climbed to his small chamber. He didn't stop at the tavern for dinner tonight. His hand trembled as he worked his key into the lock. With his shoulder, he pushed into the tiny room, fumbling for the matches beside the door.

When the match flared, Danny held the glowing stick high, checking to make sure the long untouched books still occupied the dresser top. From the corner of his eye, he saw the Henry rifle leaning in the corner. While other soldiers had turned in their assigned rifles before leaving the army, he'd kept the special weapon that had been purchased with private funds. Not distracted by the rifle he hadn't touched in months, he reached for the black books.

In the candlelight, he cradled the books, softly caressing them. When he'd first called to Hewitt near the newspaper stand, the corporal had seemed happy to see him, right? Danny frowned, not sure. Regardless, they had never been close. The connection they shared had passed with the disbanding of the scout platoon.

Yet Sergeant Blair's journal and Bible offered something else.

Slowly, he lifted the cover on the slender journal. He read a few pages describing the land around a frontier town in Colorado Territory. Trinidad had boomed with the discovery of coal. According to Blair, a few cattle ranches dotted the plains around town, but only freight wagons visited the desolate range. And a stagecoach.

Danny scowled as he read Blair's report of the infrequent stage that stopped at Trinidad en route to distant destinations. The location of the mines near the Santa Fe Trail made prosperity a possibility for investors and workmen alike. Heavily laden wagons carried the precious mineral to urban centers, but Blair's interest in the coal industry seemed to stop there. The stagecoach appeared to hold special interest for Sergeant Blair, and Danny scanned every page of the journal as he read about the land and its ore deposits deep underground. Yet, something drew the sergeant's speculation further on. His one surviving relative was his sister, left behind when Blair joined the eastern conflict. Apparently, she wasn't keen on his leaving her alone in the frontier town, but his convictions had governed his decision to forestall his dreams and join the war.

Danny turned the page. The next few entries were about Blair arriving east and enlisting in the Union Army. His first post had been to an infantry regiment, but soon his skills of stealth and marksmanship made him a perfect candidate for scout. Soon, he worked with a platoon of men with similar talents, scouting far afield, obtaining valuable information about enemy troop locations and movements. Where the cavalry was confined to roads, Blair and his platoon often traveled overland, unimpeded by fences or rivers.

After the platoon leader was killed, Blair made sergeant, and his superiors never searched for a replacement officer. The next year, Danny joined Blair's scout platoon.

Danny peered around the dimly lit room. When had he dropped onto his narrow cot? Through the small open window, heat wafted with the strong stink of the overcrowded city. A piano played at one of the nearby taverns. A woman laughed, sharp and distinct above the dull din of talking men at the drinking houses that lined the streets below. He knew nothing of women and wondered briefly at the laughing woman in the tavern.

He turned back a few pages to the description of the land around Trinidad. Blair had included such detailed descriptions. Once, when Blair had saved an old Indian from a beating in town, the grateful man had shared the secret location of a spring in the desert to the east of Trinidad.

Danny traced a finger on the meticulously drawn map of the region that filled two pages in the journal. A line at the top of the pages indicated where the Arkansas River ran to the east from the Rocky Mountains, stretching across the plains and into Kansas. The freight trail that followed the mighty river was described with a dotted line, turning south along the Purgatory River where Trinidad was situated. The trail continued south, over the Raton Pass and into New Mexico Territory, making its way to Santa Fe. In the empty expanse east of Trinidad, a lone X marked the location of the hidden spring, the only sign of anything in the desolate lands between the Raton Range and the Arkansas River.

The history of the old trail was not lost on Danny. Although the western lands remained much of a mystery to the people of Philadelphia, many had heard of the Santa Fe Trail that connected the United States with Old Mexico.

His scowl deepened as he wondered at Blair's interest. The sergeant had gone into great detail about the land, the rough stage route along the Arkansas and up the Purgatory to Trinidad, but Danny couldn't understand why.

His grip tightened on the thin book when he read the next entry.

About thirty miles east of town, along the northern edge of the Raton Range, a cut in the bluff reveals where the spring trickles down the rock face, disappearing into a hole at the bottom of the escarpment. If I can purchase this parcel of land, I hope to construct a stage station that would allow the stagecoach to avoid the more rigorous route along the Purgatory. If I could develop a shortcut from Old Bent's Fort to Trinidad, through the empty land, I could provide a good living for Jenny. God willing, I plan on building something that lasts.

Danny squinted, as if seeing the unknown landscape in his mind. Blair's idea was to build a wonderful oasis in the desert, where travelers would receive delicious meals and care for the stage stock. The place would ensure the future and security of his only sister.

Danny lifted his gaze from the pages and stared out the window into the darkness. While engrossed in the book, the sun had long since vanished. Usually, Danny would be asleep by now, exhausted from the day's toil, but tonight, he couldn't disregard the excitement he felt at reading Sergeant Blair's journal.

He didn't try and comprehend the significance he attributed to the thin little book. Danny always had selfish goals, to obtain some kind of recognition for his borrowed name. He never wanted to help others or improve a situation. Something spoke to him from the pages the sergeant had written. Danny sensed something deep about the information he'd read. But what did these words have to do with him?

As if laying aside a pile of gold, he placed the journal back on the dresser and reached for Blair's Bible. For a long moment, he studied the cover of the thick book, feeling its weight. Something mysterious lay inside, Danny knew. He'd heard of God, even heard the name of Jesus, but he had no idea what the Bible would say to him. He only knew Blair had been a great man, courageous in battle and thoughtful to his men. Without knowing, Danny had come to idolize the intentionality of the young sergeant. Blair knew what he wanted, where he was going. Surely, his death surprised Danny. He'd had his whole life ahead of him. Blair had a plan. What did Danny have?

He stared at the Bible in his hands. Something about this book, or God, made Blair different. Danny wondered at the distinction.

Taking a deep breath, he opened the book to the middle, gently fingering the incredibly thin pages as he thumbed toward the back of the book. Stopping when he read bold words, he peered closer, blinking as he read. Book of John. He blinked again and wondered if God were real. Would the Almighty be looking down on him as he examined the Holy Book?

"God," he whispered to the empty room. "I've never had account to speak with you before. I guess you know why I fought so hard in the war. You know everything, right? Well, I didn't die. Sometimes, I think of reaching too far on the scaffolding, reaching so far that I fall. But something holds me back. Are you watching me?"

He paused, his voice lowering further. "Sergeant Blair showed me another way. Somehow, his life spoke to me. I guess I want to know about Jesus. Can you work in me like you did him?"

He paused again and glanced around the shadowy room, his eyes widening. "Are you here right now?"

CHAPTER FOURTEEN

When Danny's crew began work on the convent the next day, he still couldn't forget the words he'd read the previous night. Since seeing Corporal Hewitt, Danny felt eager to study the two black books, as if by learning what Blair might've known, something about the sergeant still lived. Twice, he'd hefted the thicker book but wondered if he'd be able to understand its meaning. Yet he pondered God, wondering what the Lord might want with him.

"Needs new mortar," Joe explained, kicking at the pile of debris that had fallen from the crumbling wall around the convent. Danny stood back, watching the black robed priest as Joe gave the cleric a lesson in masonry. "We'll need to tear the wall down to the base and then rebuild. Should last another hundred years."

The little priest nodded. "I will want you to hurry, if possible. The nuns do not like being exposed. This garden is for their personal reflection. Privacy is paramount."

"Of course, Father McKay," Joe promised. He gestured to Nick and Danny to begin.

As Danny pried the stones from the decaying mortar, he piled them for later use. While Nick worked in one direction, Danny worked away from him, wanting to ponder his swirling thoughts.

What was God doing with him? Why would God want anything from him?

Danny wanted to know more. For the first time in his life, he felt intrigued by a mystery he couldn't solve. Nelson and Blair had been Christians. Both men had seemed confident in ways Danny couldn't appreciate. All the men of the scout platoon were good with guns and moved cautiously, but the Christians stood apart somehow, as if they possessed something more, an understanding of deep, unseen things.

"Well, God," Danny chuckled as he tore the garden wall down, revealing the gravel paths and benches of the little copse. Shrubs and flowers lined each walkway, with a young stand of elms near one wall, shaded and welcoming. "I didn't think I'd ever get so lonely I'd talk to you." His laughter died away. "I am lonely, aren't I?"

His whispered inquiries worried him. He'd always been a loner, even at the orphanage. Different boys came and went. The army had proven a good place to find companions, but then they too might disappear at any moment. Some had, in fact.

Sergeant Blair and Nelson had circumvented the impregnable fortress Danny had built around himself. They were gone now, and yet their memory lingered, teasing at the edges of his mind.

"Why would you do that to me?" Danny muttered as he worked the rough stones, poking at the rotten cement between each rock. "If you know me so well, you know I don't have any friends."

★★★

After tearing the walls down, the men labored meticulously to rebuild. Slowly, the walls went up. By the end of that first day, the base was laid.

Day after day, the high walls climbed. The busy street alongside the convent was ever filled with horse-drawn carts or heavy wagons of materials going up town to the many businesses that fronted the Delaware River. Men called to one another in the street, and a ceaseless din filled the air beside the small chapel and convent grounds.

The nuns never came outside to inspect the construction. Although occasionally, hooded figures peered at Danny from shadowed windows of the old convent.

The quiet and serene buildings seemed to watch him, making him wary as he wondered about God. Had Blair ever wondered at God's purpose for his life? A week ago, Danny hadn't cared, but now he began to see how his loneliness was making him bitter. Sergeant Blair had plans for his life, good plans. Danny had none. Why had he survived when the sergeant died? God didn't make sense, yet Danny's curiosity grew.

While the men built the wall, the elusive nuns stayed hidden. Only Father McKay braved Joe's incessant education on his trade. Danny tuned out the endless chatter from his boss, but something about the priest made him want to converse. The war still haunted his nights, and his isolation had become a companion he loathed. He yearned for the exhaustion that would allow him rest. Or for some kind of knowledge he didn't possess.

That afternoon, when Father McKay paused beside him, Danny didn't look up from his work. He tensed when the black robed priest didn't walk on, watching Danny as he placed each stone carefully.

"It's warm in the sun," the priest said with a smile. "Can I fetch you a drink, my son?"

Danny shook his head before glancing up at the older man, then blinked. Here was his chance. This man might know. "You work here, right?"

The priest chuckled. "I guess you can say that. Yes, I work here, at the chapel over there." He indicated the nearby little church. "I also live here. I serve the people of these streets." Together, the two men gazed at the avenues and tenement houses that ringed the convent.

Danny glanced to where Joe and Nick worked, farther along the wall. He brushed fragments of rock and mortar from his hands as he slowly stood, stretching the kinks from his back. "You read the Bible?"

"Yes," the priest whispered, matching Danny's low, guarded tone.

"What's it all about?" Danny shifted. "I mean, I've opened the book and seen the different sections. Some I can make sense of. Kings, Judges, a lot of men's names. But some worry me. Ecclesiastes, Lamentations," he said, stumbling over their pronunciations.

"I see what you mean," Father McKay grinned, the afternoon sun glinting off his bald head. He studied Danny. "You're interested in God?"

Danny shrugged. "Sure, I guess. I knew men who loved God. Good men. In the war. I figure if they took the time to know about the Lord, maybe I should too." He thought of Sergeant Blair and Nelson, wondering if this were how they first connected with the Almighty. "I can pay if need be."

"No, no, not necessary," the priest said hurriedly. "God's gift of grace is a free gift. He forgives us of our sins if we call on his Son's name. Jesus is free, my son, although salvation is priceless."

"Salvation?" Danny tilted his head, recalling Nelson had mentioned the unknown word.

"We'll take this slowly. Do you have time to speak with me after work?"

Danny nodded, wiped his filthy hands on his pants, and held one to the priest. "Danny Mason." He hesitated for only a moment after speaking his name. "I get off at six." He felt an unfamiliar excitement, unable to conceal the note of eagerness in his voice. "Can we talk about God then?"

Father McKay grinned again. "It would be my pleasure."

The pair met after work at a nearby tavern, and Father McKay began by telling Danny about a baby born in a manger. The boy was named Jesus, and he came to save sinners. He died on a cross to pay our debt before a Holy God and then rose again. Danny learned about the Bible and how the various books are ordered. More importantly, he learned about God's plan for redemption. Accepting Christ begins the adventure of a lifetime, discovering God's purpose for his people.

"But if each believer has a God-given purpose, why did Sergeant Blair die? He was so young. Surely, he didn't fulfill his purpose," Danny wondered aloud, his gaze lifting from the earnest priest to the rafters above their table in the main room of the tavern. Around them, loud men drank beer and discussed their day with coworkers, while Danny and Father McKay explored deeper issues.

The bald priest stroked his chin. "Well, God is faithful, so we know the sergeant completed whatever task the Lord wished him to accomplish. A certain mission, perhaps experiencing a situation that impacted those around him. Life is full of purpose, even when we don't see every aspect of a believer's time on earth."

Danny nodded, still uncertain. Yet his curiosity demanded answers, and the priest complied, talking to Danny until the tavern closed for the night.

The next day at work, Danny searched for Father McKay and arranged another session with the kindly priest. Danny's interest in spiritual matters seemed unquenchable, as if Sergeant Blair's memory instilled in him this quest for truth. The sergeant had never seemed lonely or pursuing personal glory, so different from Danny. And that difference now fueled an unexpected curiosity within him.

Two weeks passed. After the convent wall was completed, the crew moved to another brick building. But Danny continued to meet with Father McKay, studying the Bible and learning about the Lord's intent.

"I still can't understand why the sergeant died so young," Danny said one evening as they sat at their regular table in the tavern. "He was the best man I've ever known. And he loved Jesus."

Father McKay nodded. "There is a passage in Isaiah 57 that discusses this very idea. Be comforted, Danny, that today Sergeant Blair is with Christ in heaven. He experiences more joy than we can comprehend. The sergeant was sent here to do something, to say something significant someone needed to hear."

He peered thoughtfully at Danny before surveying the crowded room. "We are all here for a reason," Father McKay muttered. "Most have to work for many years to comprehend what the Lord sent them to do. Faith takes time to develop, often a lifetime."

Danny thought of the journal back in his small room. Blair's dream was unfulfilled. Did his life matter if he didn't accomplish what he desired most?

"He had a dream," Danny said tentatively. "There was something left undone."

"Then it will be completed by another," Father McKay said with a terse nod of his head. "Whatever the Lord wills, it will be done. Nothing can stop God's plan."

Not even death? Danny mused over this difficult lesson. Was God whispering to him, gently tugging on his heart? Did he have a purpose, like Sergeant Blair? How could he accomplish what was expected of him when he knew so little of the Lord?

"I'm such a broken man," Danny confessed softly, glancing around the smoky tavern. "I was selfish, pursuing what I believed would bring me happiness. I was such a fool."

"God is in the business of rebuilding lives. This," the priest tapped his Bible, "will unlock God's will for your life, perhaps point to a direction you are to take."

"Can you teach me all about the Bible—how it speaks to believers and guides their steps? How to listen to the Holy Spirit?"

Father McKay laughed as he sat back on the bench. "I can teach you what I know. But a man can study the Scriptures for a lifetime and still discover new lessons between their pages." He paused, a slow grin coming to his face. "You have taken the first step into a larger world, one of knowledge, but also one of spiritual sensitivity. From now on, you will learn with your head, your heart, and your soul."

For a long moment, neither spoke, and Danny remembered Blair and Nelson speaking of God's family. Would Jesus adopt him? With all he'd done in the war, would the Lord forgive him, welcome him? He felt intrigued, and he refused to allow the possibility to pass him by.

Danny squinted across the rough planks of the long table. "I'm ready," he whispered.

★★★

About a month later, the convent job done, and the trio having moved to another job, Danny sat in the shade of a building on the other side of town, eating his meager meal. Joe and Nick sat a short distance from him, talking casually of work, their families, and the aftermath of the war. Danny didn't want to join them, engrossed in his own thoughts. Yet he'd come to realize his habit of seclusion had been a mistake. While he craved connection with others, another sensation warned him he was on the brink of something big. His discussions with Father McKay—which had been ongoing since that first meeting so many weeks ago— had made him feel unnerved, as if he were about to learn something significant, something that would change his life forever.

"My brother moved west eight years ago," Joe said, a catch in his voice that Danny couldn't ignore. He leaned back, suddenly interested in their conversation. "Yesterday, I got a letter from his widow. Those wild Indians killed him and took off his hair."

Danny glanced over his shoulder in time to catch the stunned look on Joe's face, sweat beading his sunburned brow. He caught Danny's eye and scowled. "Oh, now, you're interested in us, are you?"

Danny winced at the cutting remark as the heat stole up his neck. "I'm sorry. I never wanted to intrude. And I thought I wanted to be alone."

Joe's features softened and he shifted, gesturing to a shady place beside Nick.

"Join us, mate," Nick welcomed. "We all have sorrows, we have."

Danny scrambled to move closer.

An awkward silence descended upon the trio until Nick offered up part of his tale. "Well, my sister married a man who moved west, and they are doing well. Have themselves a nice farm and a house full of kids. She says she's happy to get out of the city."

The pair stared at Danny, as if waiting for his response or possibly a contribution. He nodded. "I'm sorry to hear about your brother," he said to Joe, then turned to Nick. "Where did your sister settle?"

"Kansas," Nick replied, then took another bite of his sandwich.

Danny had read the newspapers about the far-reaching western lands, but they made little sense to him. *Where was Kansas?* The vast prairies seemed a magical, mythical place, far beyond the Appalachians, stretching even farther than the Mississippi River.

In his mind, Danny imagined the states where the war had played out. But the lands to the west intrigued him with their mysterious quality. Texas and the Great Plains, the towering peaks of the Rocky Mountains, and the deserts beyond to the Pacific Ocean where gold had been discovered more than a dozen years ago. Where had Nelson said Blair was from?

Danny's own geographic understanding had been expanded during the war, reaching far beyond the limits of the dirty city where he'd been born, to the pine tree-covered Carolinas and other Southern states. He'd never truly cared much about those lands, though, until recently. Now, Danny wanted to learn more.

CHAPTER FIFTEEN

After lessons with Father McKay every day after work, Danny would make his way to the tavern near his lodgings for a late supper. Tonight, he'd peppered the priest with questions about the West. In Danny's mind, he worked to form a map of the frontier. Wide regions stared back at him, empty and unknown, stretching far beyond the Mississippi. Father McKay shared what information he possessed but admitted his limited knowledge. He suggested perhaps Danny should visit the Philadelphia library.

Danny shouldered his way to the bar, laid Blair's Bible on the stained planks, and tried to catch the bartender's eye. He could sit at a small table and wait for one of the serving girls to take his order, but he wished to hurry to his room. Another workday loomed, and he felt eager for sleep.

His ears pricked as the man beside him whispered loudly to his companion, his words thick with drink. "Well, you didn't hear this from me. It's all very hush-hush at the Wells Fargo office, you know."

The fellow peered over his shoulder as if to catch unseen ears listening in on his conversation, but only Danny seemed to hear. "The rumor is Wells Fargo will soon buy out the Holladay Overland Stage Company. It is a smaller company than our own, but it operates some significant routes through the West that are key to Wells Fargo's expansion."

The bartender approached, and Danny placed his order for soup and a slice of bread. The two men beside him were served refills and drifted away, allowing Danny to mull over his newfound interest in the distant lands that seemed to come alive the more he learned of them. After studying Blair's journal a second time, he returned to the library for another peek at the frontier map and memorized Colorado Territory, wondering what the unknown land must truly look like.

He found himself restless back in his city now, as if eager to step out once more like he'd done in the war. Although he never wished to fight again, an interest in seeing new places filled him. But not just any land, he realized as he made his way up the dark, narrow stairs to his room. He wanted to know more about the West.

Behind his closed and locked door, he lighted a candle. A lantern was far too expensive, although he could afford one a hundred times over. Living in a rundown, cheap tenement house while squirreling every penny away he could, he'd amassed a small pile of wrinkled bills and coins. By the dim candlelight, he went over the evening's lesson he'd shared with Father McKay. In the Book of Ephesians, Danny read where believers are God's workmanship, created to walk with Christ in the good works he prepared for them to do.

He lifted his gaze from the thick book and stared at the wall. What good works had God created for him to perform? Clearly, according to Father McKay, Sergeant Blair had completed his tasks early in life. But what particular job did Jesus have for Danny?

The priest had informed Danny that whatever the Lord requested of his people, he would first equip them for the task. How was Danny being prepared for his particular purpose? Did he possess any specific talents?

He wondered what Christ might whisper to him in the shadowed chamber of the boarding house. His eyes darted around the room. "Are you with me?" His whispered query made him feel silly. Could he talk with God?

"Father McKay says a man can stand with confidence before the Lord when he accepts Christ. I submit to you, Lord."

Danny arched an eyebrow. Did Jesus hear him?

"I know you are God, and I'm nobody, but I need you. I need a Savior to save me from my selfishness. I only think of myself."

He paused and drew a deep breath. "You took Blair home to heaven when he finished what you had for him. I tried to die, and you let me live. You must have something for me to do. What is it, Jesus?"

Danny's roving gaze settled upon the black journal that sat upon the dresser. He tilted his head, wondering at the contents of the small book. Sergeant Blair's dream was unfinished. Danny believed that dream had died with him, but perhaps dreams never died. Perhaps they lay dormant for the next person to complete the unfinished work. Perhaps dreams always came true eventually, somehow, for someone. Maybe the work was just to be done by another as Father McKay had indicated.

Placing the Bible on the bed beside him, Danny reached for the journal. He settled himself upon the woolen blankets and thumbed the thin book. Blair's life, his faith, his ideas were penned here. Blair was dead, but maybe his desires were not.

Was Danny's destiny somehow connected to Sergeant Blair? A shiver snaked down his back, and he felt not as alone. Again, his gaze searched the darkened corners. "Is this from you, Lord? Do you have a message here for me?" He tapped the black journal. "Does Blair's dream concern me?"

As if grasping at a rope tossed to a drowning man, Danny saw clearly. He had nothing here in Philadelphia. No real home, no friends, nothing to hold him. Yet Blair's journal beckoned, urging him west. An unfamiliar sensation encouraged him to go soon, to find what he longed for.

A frown knitted his brow. What *did* he long for? Formerly, his isolation and self-absorption had skewed his direction, misguiding him into selfish goals. Now, because of Sergeant Blair's influence, Danny wanted to do things right. But he shook his head, too tired to consider further. It'd been a long day, and he felt exhausted. Much too exhausted to figure out this murky puzzle tonight. Placing the pair of books on the dresser, he stretched out on the bed.

"Lord, if you want something from me, if you want me to think about moving west, you'll have to do something more than just plant an idea in my head. I'm new to this Christian life. Although Father McKay has told me to listen for your voice, I'm not sure what the prompting of the Holy Spirit feels or sounds like. You're going to have to make your wishes for me obvious."

With a final glance up at the ceiling, Danny closed his eyes, hoping for more clarity in the morning.

***

The next day, Danny walked to work, feeling silly at his prayer of the previous evening. Who was he to tell God what to do? The Creator of the universe surely had more on his mind than to consider a mere stonemason in Philadelphia. The president had been shot just as the war ended, throwing an already reeling nation into further confusion and shock. It seemed the whole country faced an uncertain future. Now, months later, Danny wondered where he belonged.

With his time in the army finished, he found himself a lonely man working with stone, not certain where he should be. Finding the Lord and giving his heart to Jesus had filled him with a newfound desire to seek God's guidance for his life, but nothing truly exciting or remarkable had transpired. Maybe God didn't care about someone alone and insignificant like Danny.

As he rounded a corner and approached the work site, he saw a tall, lanky kid standing near Joe and Nick, their three heads drawn close in low conversation. The trio quieted as Danny drew near, and he could tell they'd been speaking about him.

"Nick, show Anthony the bricks we use on this job," Joe gestured, indicating the piles of red brick at the end of the partially constructed building. With a furtive glance at Danny, Nick led the young boy away.

"Who's he?" Danny pointed at the boy with his chin.

Joe shifted, stole a glance at the retreating pair, and turned to face Danny with a sigh.

"Look, he's my sister's kid. His pa never came home from the war, and they need him to step up, bring home wages. I had to hire him. Do you see?"

"Of course." Danny nodded amiably. "Everyone needs work."

Joe licked his lips. "What I mean to say is, I don't need more than three men working this job."

It took Danny a moment to realize what Joe meant. With recognition came clarity, and Danny lifted his chin, amazed how quickly and clearly the Lord had addressed his prayer. Philadelphia no longer contained anything to hold him back. A slow grin creased his face.

"Do you know what I'm saying?" Joe shifted again, squinting at Danny and shoving his hands in his pockets. "I hate to let a good man go, but I can't afford a fourth man on the job. Barely enough work for three."

"I understand, Joe," Danny said as he rubbed his hands, unable to conceal his excitement. "You have to let me go, I get it."

"Then what are you grinning at?" Joe demanded.

"Nothing." Danny laughed. "But can you tell me where a man can learn to ride a horse?"

★★★

For the next three days, Danny paid for riding lessons at the park near the river before purchasing a stagecoach ticket to Pittsburgh. From there, he'd take a steamboat to St. Louis and then to Westport Landing. Another stage would ferry him to Colorado Territory.

His next visit to the library paid off when he discovered a map of the West, and he kept the details in his head. He had a rough idea which places he needed to go through to land him near the Rocky Mountains, near Trinidad. With a thrill, he realized he'd soon see where Sergeant Blair had come from.

A week later, he felt ready to go.

"Are you still reading your Bible?" Father McKay stood beside him in front of the stage station. Inside the building, Danny recognized the clerk he'd overheard at the tavern more than a month earlier, the one explaining about the intended Wells Fargo takeover of distant stage routes.

"Yes, Father." Danny gripped his satchel, the Henry rifle slung over one shoulder. Inside the scarred and stained valise he'd bought at a secondhand store, Sergeant Blair's black books lay nestled between Danny's few articles of clothing.

The priest stepped closer, studying Danny. "You think this is what the Lord wants from you? You're certain?"

"He answered me clearly." Danny nodded. "I have no life here, but the sergeant's dream is unfinished. I plan on completing his goal. I owe him that."

"You owe the man nothing," McKay said softly. "This must be for you, directed by God. Don't do this for a dead man."

"He saved my life." Danny checked the time on the clock in the bank across the street and anxiously peered up the dusty avenue. The stage should arrive soon. "But more than that, the Lord has opened this door."

The priest sighed. "Trust God. Always." He made the sign of the cross and laid a hand on Danny's shoulder. "He who began a good work in you will carry it to completion. Believe that and write to me. I will look forward to hearing of your adventure."

A clatter of hooves sounded farther down the street, and the stagecoach rumbled to a halt before the two men, a cloud of dust enveloping them. Liverymen worked hastily to exchange the tired teams with fresh horses. Danny glanced at Father McKay when the driver resumed his seat on the high bench, gathering the long leather reins.

"Thank you for everything, Father." Danny wrung the priest's hand. Excitement swept through him, as if unseen wings carried him from Philadelphia. "I feel I'm embarking on a grand journey, one I'm supposed to make."

"Then the Lord rides with you," the priest replied.

Danny hurried to step into the coach, one of the liverymen closing the door behind him. "So long, Father," Danny called from the coach window as the teams strained in their harness.

"Goodbye, my son, and remember to write."

The kindly priest waved and soon disappeared from view as the coach made the next corner. Danny leaned back in his seat. Only two men in suits occupied the coach with him, both men lifting newspapers as they settled for the ride to Pittsburgh.

Danny glanced up, studying the darkened underside of the roof. "Well, Jesus, here we go," he muttered quietly. "I hope I'm doing your will. Guard me on this expedition. I'm here to serve you, to finish what Sergeant Blair started."

He paused, considering the war, meeting Nelson and Blair, and finally coming to know Christ. What adventures lay out west for him?

CHAPTER SIXTEEN

"Good luck, young man," the friendly farmer had called as he drove away, leaving Danny standing alone near the boardwalk in front of the Wells Fargo Office. "I wish you the best on the frontier."

Danny's gaze shifted to take in the dusty streets of Westport Landing. *Frontier?* He pondered this word as he scanned the crowded town, seeking the stagecoach that was to take him farther west.

Beside the small Wells Fargo building, a massive structure towered, a mercantile the farmer reported supplied the freight outfits that traveled across the plains to Santa Fe. While on the steamer from Pittsburgh, Danny had heard more than one man suggest a railroad would soon cross the prairies west of the Missouri River. Could this be true? He knew so little of transportation and the settling of the frontier. He'd been consumed with the war and finding notoriety on the battlefield, a reputation that would erase the shame he felt at borrowing another man's name. For the hundredth time, he realized how foolish he'd been, how foolish his thoughts had been.

He sighed and allowed his gaze to linger on the café down the street, feeling the hunger pangs gnaw at him.

What was he doing here? He'd never traveled outside Philadelphia before the war. Then he'd seen Tennessee and Georgia and the Carolinas, but now he stood on the edge of the frontier. Was he crazy?

A scowl descended, pinching his countenance. "Am I crazy, Lord? Am I crazy to think you guide me? Did you really nudge me west, or did my sense of responsibility make me take this trip? Am I hearing you right?"

Only the low hum of the busy street came back to him. He glanced up at the sky, wishing for a sign.

"Jesus, are you with me?" he whispered, hoping he'd discerned God correctly.

The clerk in the stage office assured Danny he had another four hours before the next stage arrived. He was told the route would follow the old Santa Fe Trail across the prairie to eventually connect with the Arkansas River and follow the watercourse to the Rocky Mountains.

Leaving his pack at the station, Danny slung the Henry over one shoulder and made his way to the café. He'd dug the two books from his gear and spent a couple pleasant hours reading both again, enjoying more coffee than he needed after his meal as an attentive waitress kept his cup full. He couldn't help but notice her bright eyes as she visited him time and again, as if she were trying to convey something. But her flagrant advances went unappreciated. Surely the pretty girl never gave him a second thought, he mused, lifting his sixth cup of coffee to his lips. What did he know of women or their ways? She might just be kind.

When he returned to the station, he found a bench near the mercantile and waited. On the southern horizon, a dark cloud appeared, slowly growing as the afternoon advanced. Two hours later, he checked with the clerk who told him the stage often missed its scheduled run if something untoward happened. "Maybe the last station couldn't provide fresh horses," the indifferent clerk replied to Danny's query. "He'll get here when he gets here."

Frustrated, Danny resumed his seat on the bench before the large emporium. Late afternoon turned into evening as the wind began to bluster. Across the prairie, the white clouds of earlier had been replaced with ominous black ones, massing into a bulk of pent ferocity. The sun vanished into the billowing storm and a dim, muted light covered the land.

Danny wondered if the station would remain open for him to evade the coming tempest, but as he considered asking the clerk for a quiet corner to wait for the stage, the very vehicle turned the corner at the end of the street and came clattering up the dusty road. With a pull on the reins, the driver brought the running teams to a halt, horses heaving as he leaped to the ground.

The man leaned heavily on his knees, gasping until he caught his breath. When he looked up at Danny, the driver grinned, his smile barely visible through the thick beard that covered most of his leathery face. His unbuttoned coat revealed the handle of a pistol shoved into his belt and sweat glistened across his forehead when the driver removed his hat.

"That was a race, I'm telling you." He gestured behind him, indicating the dark clouds hovering on the far horizon. "I could see that storm building all afternoon, but we made it."

He whooped merrily, as if he'd beaten a monster in a foot race. When the liverymen appeared and reached for the harness, the driver waved. "Swap them, Frank. They did their job today. Hitch up the fresh teams while I get some coffee, and we'll be on our way."

With a wave to the clerk who retrieved the canvas mail bag from the boot, the driver stiffly walked down the street to the café. As Danny waited beside the coach, a few drops of rain splattered on his face. A moment later, the driver returned, gripping a steaming mug, the young waitress from the café beside him.

The driver grinned between sips, his gaze darting between the pretty girl and Danny. "Meg here is my daughter. She says you spent a long time in the café this afternoon." His eyes twinkled mischievously, but Meg interrupted.

"Pa, don't go telling stories of what I said. I merely made the observation this young gentleman drinks a lot of coffee." She held a hand to her wafting apron and another to her hair as she smiled shyly at Danny. Hastily, the liverymen harnessed the fresh horses.

The driver handed his empty mug to his daughter and scrambled up the wagon wheel to his perch on the high bench. Unwrapping the long reins from the brake handle, he motioned for Danny to climb aboard.

"Get in, young man. You're my only passenger going west, and that storm is heading this way. We'll get our shirt tails wet tonight if I don't miss my guess." He looked down at the waitress where she stood holding his mug. "Meg, you'll be finding no husband this day."

He chortled as Danny hurried to board the stage, the driver's laugh ringing in his ears. The wagon jostled roughly as he clambered in. Was the young miss flirting with him? He couldn't tell.

"Get up, boys," the driver shouted above the wind that gusted across the plains. With a lurch, the stage moved, and Danny caught only a glimpse of the waitress watching their departure, her hair blowing in the sporadic rain.

Danny settled back in his seat after staring out the window for another hour. Tired, he pulled the canvas window coverings tight as the fading light of dusk vanished from the evening sky. What had he gotten himself into? He closed his eyes, allowing his muscles to relax as fatigue washed over him. He was here to finish a project Sergeant Blair had begun, nothing more. Certainly, a pretty girl had nothing to do with his journey west.

Yet he couldn't ignore the sensations that whirled within him. He'd been lonely for so long. What would a wife and family be like? He shook his head, grinning at his wanderings. "No, Jesus, I will not stray from my task, don't worry. I'm here for you, Lord."

He almost laughed at the humorous way the kind stage driver had teased him. But Danny knew nothing of women and vowed to be more careful in the future. He felt he was on a mission.

When the storm finally struck, the stagecoach had already passed Lawrence, a stopover on the Oregon Trail. The powerful wind lessened as the rain pounded continuously. Progress slowed as the wagon covered miles on the muddy trails. Somewhere in the night, they angled to the southwest, striking for Council Grove.

As dawn broke over the eastern prairie, Danny peeked out the window. Rocked by the constant moving of the stagecoach, he'd endured a fitful night's sleep. Gray clouds tinged with pink hovered along the horizon, the rising sun reflected on the pregnant clouds. Not a breath of air moved across the brown prairie grass.

Danny marveled at the unfamiliar sight. He'd known only forests and the edge of the vast eastern sea. He'd never imagined there could be so much empty land in all of America as these endless plains that stretched in every direction.

At a shout, his gaze shifted forward, eyes widening as the coach entered a small village. Rolling to a halt before a low, squat building, he could see they'd arrived before most of the residents had arisen. Eager to finally be almost to his destination, he climbed stiffly from the coach. Danny frowned at the weary driver's disappointing greeting.

"Morning, young man, and welcome to Council Grove. You still have a long way to go, but this is the end of my section. The Hays House is the best place to eat," he suggested, indicating the eating house with his whip. "We'll be here at least an hour, swapping horses and eating. Then you'll head on west with Old Crawford."

Not bothering to ask who Old Crawford might be, Danny strode into the eating house, grateful to be out of the coach, although anxious at still being so far from Trinidad. They'd driven mostly west of the storm, although Danny recalled hearing rain pound the stage for a few hours last night.

Feeling grimy and not truly rested, he took a seat at a long table with benches on either side. A young girl with pigtails poured coffee into a tin mug before taking his order. While he waited for his venison and eggs with potatoes to arrive, he looked around, enjoying the empty room and the warm surroundings of the frontier restaurant. Danny wondered when he might eat so well again. Farther out on the prairie, were there other such eating places? What did Trinidad have to offer?

Placing a coin on the table, he left the dining room and made his way back to the wagon. For a long time, Danny paced beside the coach, hoping to keep his limbs from becoming too stiff. The replacement driver was nowhere to be seen, and Danny's anxiety grew, wondering if he'd ever arrive at Sergeant Blair's hometown. Eventually, he watched as an old man slowly climbed the wagon wheel to the driver's seat. A battered brown hat pulled low shaded his features, but piercing eyes above a scraggly beard studied Danny. Four fresh horses were harnessed in place, stamping impatient hooves. Like Danny, the horses were ready to go.

"Well, sonny, you'll be the only passenger again," the grizzled driver called to him. "Lots of mail and freight, though."

Without a word, Danny climbed into the stage. Boxes and canvas covered parcels littered the interior, but there was plenty of room for him. He heard the driver shout as the teams pulled the wagon from town.

For hours, Danny sat alone with his emotions. He stared out the window as prairie once again stretched out before him. Excitement surged in his chest when he saw a herd of buffalo grazing, and he whooped when he saw a bunch of frightened antelope race away from the coach, their striped tails vanishing over a low hill. He considered taking a shot at them with his rifle but dismissed the idea immediately. He'd never hunted before.

To their left, the Arkansas River could be seen through the scrub thickets and occasional cottonwoods lining the low banks. Danny knew from the map he had memorized they'd follow the river for many miles before turning south along the Purgatory River. The stage stopped only briefly at watering holes and outposts for fresh horses.

Fort Dodge was the next town reached after Council Grove. The blue-clad soldiers stationed at the tiny frontier outpost reminded Danny of his former days during the war. His stomach tightened, but he gripped his rifle to him as workmen removed cargo from the coach and loaded new bundles. Danny had stepped from the stagecoach, wanting to stretch his legs. He walked up and down the dusty street for a minute before stopping beside the stage driver. Old Crawford offered Danny a cracker before stuffing one into his own mouth.

"Are the soldiers here to protect passage on the Santa Fe Trail?" Danny watched as the hostler pushed the final team into position, draping the eager horses with leather harnesses.

The driver nodded, still chewing. "Indians and outlaws haunt the trail. Usually, freight wagons bound for Santa Fe travel in large numbers for protection. Stages like ours are always in danger, but we're pretty quick, hard to catch."

Soon, the coach was ready for departure, and Danny resumed his seat inside the loaded vehicle, although he remained the single passenger. Old Crawford called to his newly harnessed horses and the coach left Fort Dodge, Danny's final view of the soiled tents and sod buildings reminding him briefly of his military service.

Still following the Arkansas River, the stage continued to move west. Danny felt his experience held some historical significance as he covered the plains toward his destination. These were the Great Plains of America, vast and untamed. Would big cities ever fill this endless expanse? The small outposts of civilization nestled among huge herds of animals that grazed upon the endless prairies made him feel he was on a grand adventure. Surely there could not be another such place in all the world.

The enormity of the open plains grew upon Danny as each mile passed. The crowded cities of the east and the farms and dense forests contrasted sharply to this vast emptiness in which Danny now found himself. Low hills covered with blowing grass was all he could see for miles in every direction. A few isolated trees marked the nearby river, but none lifted from the prairie. Heat filled the interior of the coach, reminding Danny summer lingered upon the stark landscape. He'd removed his coat long ago, but now he rolled up his sleeves.

He sensed a kinship with the land, lonely like him, yet Danny loved it. A sense of anticipation surged within him, promising something exciting ahead. "Do you have something special for me, Lord? Are there other reasons I'm here?"

Danny knew God had prompted him to begin this trip, to complete something a friend had already started. But now, as the stage rolled across the endless miles, he wondered if Jesus had a specific purpose for him in the West, and not only to complete another man's goal.

Did the prairies hold his destiny?

At Bent's Fort, the stage drew to a halt.

"Climb out, sonny," Crawford called as the driver stepped from the coach. He gestured to a lightning-struck tree along a small stream. "Gather wood for a fire. We'll have coffee while the horses take a breather."

Danny stepped from the coach as a cloud of trailing dust covered the entire stage and the four heaving horses. He glanced at the abandoned, quiet fort, wondering at its tumbled walls and burned logs before hastening to comply with Crawford's instructions, eager to have a task outside of the jostling stagecoach.

Within minutes a fire blazed. Soon, the pair of men held steaming tin cups, their gaze locked on the uplands to the west.

"There." Crawford pointed with his mug at the dilapidated trading post a short distance away. "That's where Bent had his trading post. Burned it down when he abandoned it. Along over there"—he shifted his mug to include the empty expanse to the south of the Arkansas

River flowing nearby— "that desert would take us almost direct to Trinidad, but we need to stay close to water." His mug shifted again, pointing to the west, along the river. "We have to follow the river, stay where the horses can drink."

Danny's ears perked, and he stared to the south where a line of mountains rose in the distance. He felt certain those high peaks must be the Raton Range. "You mean there is no water out there?"

Crawford sipped his coffee and shook his head. "None anyone knows of. We'll follow the Arkansas to the Purgatory, go south toward Raton Pass. Just this side of the pass is Trinidad."

Danny squinted, something stirring in his chest. Sergeant Blair knew of water in that desert. Was it real? Was Danny on a wild goose chase or was this God's plan?

"Those mountains there?" Danny pointed to the distant peaks with his own cup, indicating the line of high ridges to the south.

"The Raton Range," Crawford corroborated as he refilled their mugs and kicked dirt over the small fire. "Runs east to west, to the Rockies yonder."

Danny allowed his gaze to drift all over the region, drinking in the massive Rockies to the west and the smaller range to the south. Carefully, he noted his surroundings, checking each landmark with the map in his head. Somewhere out there was a piece of land he would soon settle. What would it look like? Were there trees, land to be cultivated into fields, rocks for building material? Or was the land desolate, worthless as many believed? He glanced at Crawford. Certainly, this old man believed the desert held nothing promising. And wouldn't he know better than anyone? Danny wondered if the aged stage driver knew more than Sergeant Blair. Was the secret spring in the desert a myth?

A shudder raced down Danny's back as doubts assailed him, but he clenched his teeth, determining to believe he'd come west for a purpose.

"Why haven't we seen any freight caravans to Santa Fe? Don't they use this same road?"

Crawford scowled at Danny's question and led the way back to the coach. The horses had been watered and the old man busied with their harness. "Well, sonny, it's not yet winter. Could be some late season traffic, but no caravan wants to be caught out in the prairie in winter. All traffic on this trail will slow soon. They will start up again come spring," he explained.

"How come we haven't been attacked by Indians? Aren't they all around us?" Danny glanced over his shoulder for emphasis.

"The Indians out here are all different. Most don't like to fight in the cold. The ones south of us in the Indian Nation are those the government sent from their lands in the east. Some here in Kansas are the same. But out here west of Dodge, you still have Indians that live off the buffalo. The Kiowa, the Comanche, the Wichita, the Arapahoe, and others roam the plains for the buffalo. Down in New Mexico Territory, the Apache have risen up against the army while the troopers were back in the east fighting the Civil War."

"Do I really need to carry my rifle everywhere I go? Is it truly as dangerous as they say?" Danny helped drape the harness into place and run the lines through their traces to the coach.

Crawford said nothing for a long minute as he buckled the horses into position. Then he straightened and pointed to the burned down trading post. "Old Bent's Fort," the driver said in a mild tone. "He burned it himself when he left, not wanting the Indians to have it. I've helped bury more than one man who was caught unprepared out here." He walked to the stage and opened the door for Danny. "There are a thousand ways to die on the frontier, young man. Always be prepared."

CHAPTER SEVENTEEN

A dust devil whirled down the main street of Trinidad when the stage rolled into town. Chilled winds gusted from the higher elevations, the towering peaks of the Rockies peering down on him as Danny stepped from the creaking stagecoach. He walked in a circle, allowing blood to circulate in his stiff legs as Old Crawford climbed from the high seat. Without a word, the pair moved to the boardwalk where a man stood in front of a general store, watching them intently. Danny tried to ignore the curious man's gaze when it locked on him.

Danny turned when he stepped onto the boardwalk and studied the nearby Raton Range angling to the east, looming high above the small settlement. A thick coating of evergreen trees and snow blanketed its ramparts. On the other side of these mountains lay New Mexico Territory.

His scrutiny shifted once more to the busy street before the general store. Miners smeared with coal dust mingled with ranchers. The men and few women who walked along the small town's main street appeared intent to get where they needed to be and out of the cold wind that blew down from the mountains around them.

"No snow yet, Crawford." The older man in front of the store spoke to the stage driver as Crawford slowly mounted the stairs to stand beside Danny.

"No," the driver reported. "There weren't no weather to speak of except cold nights. And a rainstorm chased the stage out of Westport. We was lucky," he commented as he reached for a bucket near a watering trough. He carried the bucket in turn to each of the four animals, allowing them to drink before refilling and moving to the next one. "Where's Edmonds? He hasn't been on his duty this whole summer. I shouldn't have to water my stock when I come to Trinidad."

The storekeeper grinned, a blush creeping up his neck. "Michael has been sore ever since I married Lil last month. The fool hostler thought he had a chance with the lady."

Crawford laughed. "Well, I surely enjoyed watching the way the pack of you pursued her. Lil is a looker, I'll say that for her. And you're lucky to land her, Carl."

The storekeeper nodded. "Carl Hanson doesn't let any grass grow under his boots," he said with a chuckle. "We all had our chance. Even Bill down at the café threw his hat in the ring. But she chose me, and Michael needs to get over it."

"Yes, he does," Crawford growled as he sat the empty bucket on the edge of the porch. "I'm hired to drive the stage, not feed and water the teams unless I'm out where there ain't a livery."

"I know, I know," Carl said with a slap to Crawford's shoulder before turning to glance at Danny. "Are you here to work in the mines?"

Before Danny could reply, Crawford moved to the stagecoach. "I'll be saying my goodbyes, Carl, and congratulations. Tell Edmonds he needs to be here when I next come through," The old driver mumbled as he mounted his coach.

Danny stepped forward. "Thanks for the ride." He paused, wondering how to move along in his mission. "Probably would shave time off your run if there were a station northeast of Trinidad."

The old driver settled on the high seat as he grasped the long leather reins. "Nothing out there but snakes, horned toads, and cactus. No water."

"But the trail along the Purgatory is very rough," Danny goaded, hoping to hear even more complaints of the current stage route.

"Worst stretch of road in Colorado," the old man agreed as he nodded to the storekeeper. "Be seeing you, Hanson."

With a crack of his whip, Old Crawford called to the teams. The quartet of horses leaped in their harness and raced down the street, dust rolling behind them. Danny turned to Hanson.

"You think there should be another stage route, one not so rough?"

The storekeeper shook his head. "Doesn't matter what I think. Besides, I heard the stage was selling to a bigger company soon. No telling what changes the new company might make. They might even cancel this line to Trinidad. Nothing but miners and cattle ranchers out here. Not a lot of business for the stage."

He turned to enter the store behind him, a bell ringing as he walked through the door. Danny followed, intrigued by the simple rock walls of the massive building. Using native stone, someone had built the mercantile with crude skill. He opened his mouth to ask about the building when a welcome wave of heat enveloped him, and he stopped to bask in the warmth. Danny halted inside the door, the middle room spreading out before him. He scanned the interior of the mercantile while his aching bones came back to life.

Three spacious rooms made up the whole of the store, each room with a potbellied stove. Winter was still far off down here on the plateau, but in the nearby mountains, white-capped peaks shone brightly in the glaring sun. Still, cool autumn breezes forewarned what would soon come to this lonely corner of Colorado Territory.

Taking two more steps into the mercantile, Danny could see two bigger rooms extended to right and left. Ahead of him, a long counter ran along the back wall of this center room. Shelves lined every wall, sagging with the weight of clothing, dry goods, and household items. The room to his right seemed filled with ropes, guns, leather goods, and sacks of grain. The room on the left overflowed with brightly colored dress goods in rolls of fabric surrounding a large cutting table. The air smelled delicious, scented with licorice, leather, and rich aromatic coffee.

Finally, he peered at the back counter where Carl Hanson tugged an apron over his head and tied it behind him. Stuffing a pencil into his front pocket, the storekeeper nodded to Danny, as if he were now ready for business.

As Danny approached, his steps faltered when he saw Hanson's assistant. Beside the storekeeper, a young girl waited on customers, her brown hair and slim nose reminding him of someone. Her gray eyes, too, seemed familiar somehow, just now lively and intelligent as she served the patron. But her round face held a note of sadness Danny couldn't disregard, clouding her attractive features.

Mr. Hanson chuckled when he caught Danny staring at the pretty girl. As the customer turned away, she looked up and their eyes locked.

Something stirred within him, images flashed across his mind of blue uniforms and heavy rifles, of the boom of cannon and the smells of gunpowder and blood.

"Well, young man," Mr. Hanson boomed. "Off the stage for two minutes and already hunting girls." He glanced at the young woman beside him and grinned. "Be careful, Jenny, or this fellow will give Reggie a run for his money."

As if not comprehending the storekeeper's teasing, Danny continued to stare. The girl's sorrowful look turned into a deep scowl.

"Can I help you with something?" Her courteous query lacked civility.

Danny shook his head and then nodded. "I'm sorry, miss. You look like someone I used to know."

Mr. Hanson chuckled again. "Hear that, Jenny Blair? You have a twin somewhere."

Danny felt his eyes widen. "What is your name?" His words came out barely above a whisper, and Danny felt his chest tighten.

She crossed her arms over her chest. "I'm Jenny Blair. And don't act like you didn't know I worked here. You're the third miner to come in here today and ask me to the dance."

"Dance?" Danny frowned. "I will not be going to any dance. But your name." He narrowed his eyes as he studied her high cheek bones, the same curve of her lips, the same gray eyes.

"Sergeant Blair," he whispered, and a lump rose to his throat.

Jenny shot Mr. Hanson a pained glance before she leaned forward, her hands dropping to the countertop. Her eyes gleamed with a fierce light, and suddenly Danny felt they were alone, only the two of them in the busy store. "You knew Patrick?"

Danny never heard the sergeant's given name, but could this girl be related? Didn't the journal make mention of a sister in Trinidad? How could Danny have forgotten that piece of information?

"We were both in the scout platoon, ahead of Sherman's Army. Georgia and then the Carolinas." His comment was as much a statement as a question.

Jenny nodded. "Yes, he was a scout, under General Sherman." Her brows furrowed deeper. "He—he's dead then, right?"

"Weren't you informed?" Danny remembered dragging the wounded sergeant from the side of the hill, watching him die as Blair handed him the black books. He gulped, trying to dislodge the constriction in his throat.

Tears brimmed in her gray eyes. "After so many officers had been killed, his platoon never received another. Patrick assumed command, although he waited for another officer to take charge. At the end of the war, there seemed to be so much confusion. I assumed he got lost in the muddle."

Danny pressed his lips into a thin line, recalling the sudden collapse of the Confederacy, their surrender, and the end of the war. *What a mess.* "I'm sorry. Yes, he's dead. I was with him."

She glanced once more at the stricken storekeeper before the tears flowed unchecked. Sobbing, she fled to the back room. Danny watched her go, then faced Mr. Hanson. "I had no idea the army never notified his kin."

"She sensed his death last spring," Mr. Hanson said softly, "when his letters stopped coming. We all kind of knew he wouldn't come home. He was the type of man who would throw himself into harm's way to help someone else." He peered sharply at Danny. "No doubt you knew him as a brave man."

There was no question in the storekeeper's remark. Danny nodded, remembering even more of the courageous sergeant, always willing to serve.

"I have to go, but I'll be back to buy supplies," he said abruptly as he turned to stride swiftly for the door.

Outside, a cool breeze buffeted him, blowing down from the heights as Danny made his way blindly down the street. He didn't know where he was going, and he didn't care.

What was he doing out here? He gritted his teeth and gripped his satchel tight. He didn't remember slinging the Henry rifle over his shoulder, yet its familiar weight comforted him somehow, allowing him to find his bearings. His steps slowed, and he stepped from the dusty street just as a buckboard passed him, almost grazing his arm. He glowered at the unaware driver and slouched against a building, out of traffic. Mindless of his presence, riders rode down the street, wagons stopped before businesses, and passerby ignored him. He was nobody. They didn't see him, didn't know him. His life seemed so small, so insignificant. For the thousandth time, he wished he'd died in Sergeant Blair's place.

His gaze lifted from the dirty street to the majestic mountains rising in the west, their white coverings glistening in the late afternoon sun. "You brought me here. I am nobody, but to you I'm somebody. A child of God, a new creation in Christ. Work in me, use me for your glory, but give me the strength. I want to finish this task. I need your strength, Jesus."

The mission. He was here on a mission. Danny nodded, feeling his lungs fill with the crisp air. He could do this. With God's help.

"I can't do this without you," he muttered, his gaze roving over the high peaks. An eagle screamed, drawing his attention. The hunting bird soared so gracefully, so effortlessly.

"Yes, Lord, I understand," he went on. "This is easy for you. But I don't want to hurt anyone along the way. Not the sergeant's sister, and not me."

In the street, a gust of wind swirled and enveloped a passing wagon. The frightened horses plunged wildly as the driver struggled to hold them. After a fierce ordeal, the driver regained control. Danny grinned.

"All right, I'm in a different war, one with different battles, and it might not be without challenges. Let me trust you, Father. Grow my faith."

He pushed away from the clapboard building and continued down the street, finally turning into the livery. A tall man in a dirty coat stepped from the shadows, a pitchfork in hand.

CHAPTER EIGHTEEN

"Are you Mr. Edmonds?" Danny hunkered into his coat, trying not to allow the chilled wind annoy him.

The hostler nodded at his query, taking him in from head to toe with a measuring glance. "I'm Edmonds. What can I do for you?"

"I heard at the mercantile you have horses. Any for sale?"

Edmonds peered up the street to the stone mercantile. "Hanson sent you here?"

"I'm here on my own accord. I need a horse."

An hour later, Danny sat astride a gelding as the hostler patted the horse's flank. Dusk had settled over the frontier town, and yellow lantern light glowed from several buildings along the main street. On the nearby mountains, final rays of sunlight glimmered, casting folds between the peaks into deep shadow.

"He's not old, but he's not young," Edmonds explained as he reached to scratch the gelding's ears. "He's gentle. Lot of years left in him."

"Let me buy you dinner," Danny suggested as he dismounted.

Danny's goal was to create a stage station in the middle of the desert, but he'd never been good at building friendships. Perhaps that time had come. He'd met Old Crawford and Carl Hanson, men he figured held positions of standing in the community. Now he would try to make friends everywhere he went.

They worked together to unsaddle the horse and stow Danny's gear before the two men trooped up the darkening street to Bill's Café. With the disappearing sun, the temperature had dropped significantly. Along the river at the edge of town, colorful leaves fluttered in the evening breeze, the vibrant trees clearly visible among the dark green conifers. At the opposite end of town, he could hear the shift change at the mine. Miners in clean clothes milled, waiting to begin work, as others streamed home, weary and filthy.

Edmonds and Danny stepped to the boardwalk, the hostler reaching for the café door handle. Warmth washed over them as they entered. Danny felt grateful for his coat, placing his rifle in the corner of the dining hall.

"Evening, Michael," the fat cook mumbled as he approached their table.

"Evening, Bill. Are you waitress tonight?" Mr. Edmonds reached for the coffeepot the man placed on the plank table.

Bill gestured over his shoulder. "She's washing dishes. I'll take your order and get started while she finishes."

They gave their order and then the hostler introduced Danny. "Young man just bought a horse from me." He glanced sharply at Danny. "Didn't catch your name, stranger."

"Danny Mason." He hoped these kindly men didn't ask him any questions. He wasn't ready to share. But folks in a small town are curious.

"Come in on the stage?" Bill persisted.

Danny nodded, squeezing his coffee mug.

"Did Crawford water his own horses?" The cook glanced at Edmonds. "You know Crawford isn't going to allow that much longer."

"Hanson stole Lil from me," the hostler snapped as a plump woman approached the table, drying her hands on her apron. She brushed Bill's shoulder in a familiar way, but Danny tried to ignore the comfortable gesture.

"I'll get their order started, Bill, if you want to talk."

"Thanks, Gertie." Bill relayed the two men's orders and grinned at Edmonds as she headed for the kitchen. "See, Michael, you need to let that go. There's other fish in the river."

"I wanted Lil," the hostler grumbled, crossing his arms over his chest.

"Too late." Bill laughed as he turned to follow Gertie to the kitchen. "Didn't I have an eye on Lil myself? Time to move on, like me."

When he vanished into the back room, Edmonds glared at Danny. "Women. Can't trust them. I could've sworn Lil liked me best, even danced with me at the sawmill. Now she's married to Hanson, my former best friend."

Danny shrugged and lifted his steaming mug, pleased the attention had shifted away from him. "I don't know anything about women."

They discussed the weather turning colder, the ending of summer, and the amount of snow already accumulated on the high peaks.

"It snows early at the higher elevations," the hostler confirmed.

Danny listened attentively, trying to learn all he could about the region.

After their meal, Edmonds allowed Danny to sleep in the loft above the livery. "This isn't a hotel, and you'll have to be out tomorrow," Edmonds explained as he lighted a lantern and showed Danny the ladder to the loft.

"Thanks, Mr. Edmonds. I'll make my purchases in the morning and head out of town."

Danny shoved his bag beneath his arm and pushed his rifle sling higher on his shoulder as he put a foot on the bottom rung. In the dark stalls around them, horses munched softly. A hen cackled from the end of the barn.

"You are a miner?"

Danny stepped up another rung before he replied. "No, sir." He hurried the remaining rungs up to the dark loft, hoping Edmonds wouldn't press further.

"Goodnight, Danny," Edmonds called, the lantern dimming as the hostler walked away.

Relieved, Danny tiptoed to a corner, then reclined in the hay fully dressed, draping a blanket over him. Mice scurried through the hay. Familiar feelings of loneliness surrounded him, but a sensation of not being alone warmed him. The Lord was with him, Danny could feel his presence.

"Thanks, Jesus, for not making me do this all by myself. I've been alone for so long, and I guess I've gotten tired of my own company. It's good to have a friend."

He was about to launch into his laundry list of concerns he wanted to share with God when a step on the ladder made him still. Heavy breathing and a grunt sounded nearby as a man climbed to the haymow. The vague outline of a man's head and shoulders rose above the edge of the loft.

Danny reached for his rifle. At the sound of the hammer pulled back, the man on the ladder stopped. "I'm sleeping up here," Danny said conversationally.

The man grunted. "Well, there's room for me too," he said. "You don't need that gun, mister. Just looking for a place to sleep."

Danny eased the hammer down. "Come up slow. And go to the other corner." The visitor scrambled up the ladder and moved away from Danny, eventually settling in the darkness.

"Does Edmonds know you're up here?" Danny felt honored to have the hostler's permission, wondering if drifters stayed here often.

"Michael knows me," the newcomer mumbled.

Danny noticed his inquiry went unanswered. A pause followed before the tramp spoke again.

"Why are you up here? If you're with the mine, the company has bunks available."

"I'm not with the mine," Danny said tersely, too weary to explain. Days of travel where he sat on a hard bench in a bumpy coach made him yearn for real sleep. He'd thought long and hard about this journey, this adventure he'd embarked on. Now he wanted rest to prepare for tomorrow when he hoped to see the place Blair located in the desert.

"I'm done with the mine," the stranger said. "I quit today. Can't stomach working underground. I need the sun and the wind."

Danny's ears pricked. He'd need help. Perhaps this was God's way of bringing it to him. "What can you do?"

"Oh, most anything I put my hand to. My grandpa taught me to trap and hunt, and I've worked for the Bloomberg ranch, although I can't say I enjoy working cattle." He sighed loudly as the man formed a nest in the loose hay, shaping a bed, trying to get comfortable. "But beggars can't be choosers. I guess I'll do anything until I find a job I like."

"Can you build, work with stone or wood?"

The newcomer chuckled in the darkness. "I'm not bragging when I say I build the best stone fireplaces you've ever seen. Draw air perfectly. No smoky chimneys."

A thought nagged, and Danny pondered. *Is Jesus already at work?* Was this man sent specifically for him? He drew a deep breath, amazed how quickly the Lord heard his prayers. "What'd you say your name is?"

Another chuckle came from across the loft. "I didn't."

"Well, if you don't have a better offer, I'd like to talk with you over breakfast in the morning," Danny called through the gloom.

From the other side of the loft, another pause and then, "I'm Luke."

CHAPTER NINETEEN

The next morning, Bill nodded a greeting when he saw Danny and Luke enter the café and find a table in the corner. Gertie approached them, a friendly smile plastered on her rosy cheeks.

"Morning, boys. What'll it be?" The portly waitress poured coffee into two mugs as she listened to their orders. When Luke ordered antelope, she shook her head. "A hunter delivered a fat elk yesterday, fat and flavorful. The herds are coming down from the high mountains. Winter coming."

Luke grinned. "I'll have the elk."

After the waitress retreated to the kitchen, Danny eyed Luke over the rim of his mug. He'd shared his name with the former miner, but nothing about his purpose in Trinidad.

Luke seemed about his own age, but Danny couldn't be certain. His darker complexion spoke of Indian blood, especially since he'd been working in the mine and not spending time in the sun. Danny tried not to stare at the man's short hair.

Luke grinned at him from across the table. "Are you regretting asking me to breakfast?"

Danny shook his head. "No. Why do you say that?"

"I'm Indian, part Delaware."

"Delaware? Out here?" Danny couldn't conceal his surprise.

"Some of our tribe moved west many years ago. My grandpa turned to trapping. He knew Bridger and Fitzpatrick and Carson. We've had to adjust to different surroundings, different lands." His gaze met Danny's, his grin gone. "It's not been easy."

Danny sipped his coffee. He wanted to tell Luke of being an orphan in a rat infested, drafty building, never having enough to eat, but he held his tongue. "Life is tough for everyone," he said instead.

Luke nodded. "I know." He narrowed his eyes as he sipped his own drink. "What kind of building are you considering? I've worked with the big timbers in the mine and planks for shoring the tunnels, but I've never built a house."

"I want to build a stage station," Danny said, glancing around the room to see if anyone could hear him. He leaned toward Luke before saying, "In the desert, about thirty miles east of Trinidad."

Luke sat up straighter. "I knew only one man who found water out there. He kept the location secret, never telling anyone as far I recall."

"He told Patrick Blair."

Luke stared. "That's right," he whispered, almost to himself. "How do you know Patrick Blair?"

"We served in the war together." He didn't want to explain the entire story of how the sergeant died in his arms, handing his books to Danny with blood-covered hands. "He had a dream of building a station in the desert. I'm here to finish what he started."

The grin reappeared on Luke's face. "Does Jenny Blair know you're doing this?"

"You know Jenny?" He remembered the attractive girl, her silken brown hair, and the way the light gleamed in her gray eyes. A blush creeped up Danny's neck and he lifted his mug again, hoping Luke wouldn't notice.

Luke shrugged. "Prettiest girl in the region. Everyone knows Jenny. And she's Reggie Bloomberg's girl."

It was Danny's turn to shrug. "I have no interest in Jenny Blair," he retorted quickly. A little too quickly.

"Reggie doesn't look favorably on any man showing too much interest. They plan to marry one day."

"What does she have to do with the stage station?" Danny felt nettled as the conversation had drifted to the girl who worked at Hanson's General Store.

"Only that it's no secret Blair wished to develop a business where he and his sister could work together, beholden to no one." Luke's eyes darted around the room as he leaned closer. "If you ask me, I don't think Patrick cared all that much for Reggie Bloomberg." He leaned back on the bench. "Neither do I. He fired me from their ranch when he thought I was too friendly with Jenny."

Danny felt his eyebrows arch. "Were you?"

Luke grinned. "No, of course not. Jenny's kind, that's all. She would talk with me when I ran errands to town. Word got back to Reggie I was making up to his girl."

For reasons he couldn't identify, Danny felt pleased Luke didn't have designs on Jenny Blair. "Well, no matter," he went on as Gertie delivered their breakfast. "I plan on homesteading the land Blair chose, then building a station. Those were his intentions, and I aim to see it through."

"You'll need help," Luke said as he lifted his fork.

"I can only give you room and board. I will need help with the building. After that, I'm not certain what I'll do." How could he share he had no idea what the Lord wanted after building the station? Danny figured God would address those deficits in time.

"I need the work," Luke said around a mouth full of pancakes. "When are we going to the site? Even I don't know its exact location. No one goes out that way. Nothing out there."

"I want to order supplies and stake my claim," Danny explained as he shoveled potatoes with his fork. "Perhaps we could head that way this afternoon."

Later, at Hanson's spacious mercantile, Danny ordered enough food for two men, carefully counting his money before tucking his wallet back into his coat. He'd spent a lot on the trip west, and now he'd spent more on necessary supplies. Along with the price of the homestead claim, he'd made a sizable dent in his carefully hoarded funds.

Although Danny kept one eye out for any sign of Jenny Blair, he felt disappointed only Mr. Hanson filled his order. When the bell jingled over the front door, the three men turned to watch a woman enter, her gaze scanning the list she held before lifting to the countless shelves on every wall.

The storekeeper scowled. "Lil should be here soon," he muttered, sitting a large bag of flour on the counter.

"I have time, Mr. Hanson," Danny said. "Help the lady, please."

Hanson smiled his thanks as he scurried away to assist the woman. Luke sighed. "We'll never get out of here in time to start today. You haven't even filed your claim yet."

"No one's leaving town today," Mr. Hanson chuckled as he passed the two men, his arms full of items for the shopper. "The dance is tonight."

Luke and Danny exchanged indifferent glances. "I don't think we'll be attending the dance," Luke called after the shopkeeper.

A middle-aged woman entered the store from the back room. Hanson waved to her. "Lil, over here." Danny watched as she hastened toward the storekeeper.

"Lil Hanson," Luke whispered. "Got married only a few months ago." He paused and then added, "They seem real happy."

Danny watched the elegant woman join her husband, wondering what it would be like to have a companion who fostered happiness. He frowned at the unexpected thought and turned so Luke couldn't see his face. "Sorry, Lord, I'm not trying to get distracted. Help me stay focused. I have a job to do," he muttered in a low voice.

Soon, his purchases piled on the counter, Mr. Hanson faced Danny. "Luke mentioned a land parcel. You wish to file a claim?"

Danny reached for the journal in his pocket. As he drew the black book out, Jenny appeared from the back room. Danny forgot the book in his hand as he watched the slender girl approach.

"Morning, Jenny," Luke called merrily.

She smiled. "Good morning. Why aren't you in the mines?"

The young man hooked a thumb in Danny's direction. "I'm working for Danny now. Going to build a station in the desert."

Her steps faltered, and a pained look leaped into her startled eyes. "A station?" Her gaze swiveled to Danny.

He nodded, thumbing the pages until he located the proper entry. "Your brother wanted this station built."

She halted before him. "That's his journal," she whispered, eyeing the book in Danny's hand.

He froze, not sure how to proceed. Should he share details about his personal faith journey, how he sensed Jesus directed his footsteps west? He blinked, unsure.

Jenny held up her hand. "Never mind. I have a new direction, one that seems more secure." Without waiting for a reply, she spun on her heel and sped away, including herself with Lil Hanson as the women helped various customers.

Danny sensed he'd angered her, but Mr. Hanson placed a hand on his shoulder. "Don't let it bother you. She's been sad ever since Patrick went into the army. They were supposed to build that place together. His going upset her more than she can say."

"It is not my intention to interfere," Danny told him. "I thought—well, I thought this was what I should do." He tapped the black book in his hand. "I never wanted to cause any hard feelings."

The bell jingled again over the front door, and Mr. Hanson frowned. "Look, Danny, I'd like to help you file your claim, but the town is full because of the dance tonight. Perhaps later," he called over his shoulder as he made his way to intercept the throng of customers streaming into the mercantile.

Luke laid a hand on Danny's shoulder. "We'll have time this afternoon when folks go to supper and dress for the dance. Come on." He helped Danny carry his supplies to the livery.

As they trudged down the street, Danny couldn't help but notice the increased traffic in town. As if by magic, the quiet frontier metropolis burst with noisy visitors and countless vehicles in from the surrounding region. He huffed impatiently, knowing he'd not be able to leave town today. Despite his eagerness to see the land the sergeant had chosen for the station site, he knew he'd have to wait another day.

After stowing their gear, the two men walked to a dilapidated shack on the outskirts of town. A lone horse stood in a small corral behind the adobe structure, the walls crumbling and cracked from years in the weather.

Luke let down the bars and scratched the pinto's nose. "I bunked here with a few other miners, but I lost my place when I quit the mine."

"You said the company provided bunks for their miners."

"Yes." Luke grinned. "But you're paid more if you have your own place to stay."

They led his horse to the livery and made arrangements with Mr. Edmonds. The hostler seemed agitated and curt as he pointed to an empty stall. "Just for tonight, Luke."

"What's got you in such a fuss?" Luke led the mare into the stall as Danny leaned in the barn doorway.

Edmonds bristled, a dark look crossing his bearded face. "I never wanted a wife until I met Lil last spring. Now, all I can think of is getting married. I've never seen Carl so happy. Any chance I have of meeting a woman is tonight, this dance at the sawmill."

Danny tilted his head, unsympathetic. He'd never given marriage a thought. Surely there was no woman out there for the likes of him. He felt grateful the Lord had smiled on him, called him to an adventure he'd never expected. But even with this new promise of a better life, a wife hadn't crossed his mind.

Luke chuckled as he came from the stall. "Every female in a fifty-mile circle will be here tonight," he agreed.

The three men stepped to the front door and looked out on the busy town, the street thronged with folks moving every direction in their haste to prepare for the evening's festive event. Men, children, and a few women mingled along the boardwalk, filling the atmosphere with a sense of charged electricity.

"Even the sawmill knocked off early today to have time to clean the floors," Edmonds grumbled.

"I wish you luck," Luke said as he slapped the hostler on the shoulder. "Of course, you'll have to hurry if you want to look your best for tonight. The ladies will have high expectations."

"Expectations?" Edmonds glanced at Luke.

Luke winked at Danny. "Well, sure. No woman wants to dance with a dirty, hairy man. Let alone consider marriage to him."

The liveryman's eyes widened with comprehension as he stroked his unruly beard. "Yes, yes, of course," he mumbled before turning and disappearing into the barn.

Luke chuckled. "He'll be busy for hours, leaving us alone. What business do we have this afternoon, boss, after we file our claim?" The Indian arched his eyebrows as he studied Danny. "You weren't planning on going to the dance?"

"Me?" Danny laughed. "I have no desire to make a fool of myself. Nor do I suspect any girl would want to dance with me." He didn't elaborate he'd never danced in his life.

Luke squinted. "I don't know, boss. A handsome galoot like you might trap a girl, if you tried."

Danny laughed again. "Come on. Let's grab an early supper before the café fills with all these newcomers."

He led the way to Bill's where Gertie took their order. After their meal, they lounged outside the mercantile until the crowds thinned, people hastening to their lodgings to prepare for the evening dance.

As the sun tipped far to the west, the two men entered the general store, the bell ringing merrily above their heads.

Mr. Hanson stood in the center of the spacious room, his features lined with fatigue. "Oh, I'm glad it's just you boys. The women have all raced away after shopping all day. Even Jenny and Lil have gone to the house to clean up and change dresses."

The storekeeper led the way to the wide table used for cutting fabric. After Danny told him roughly where the station was to be, Mr. Hanson rolled out a scroll of paper with a detailed map of the region. Luke added details he remembered his grandfather telling about the site as Danny searched the sergeant's journal. Soon, they all agreed with the place the shopkeeper indicated on the map, and Danny paid the fee from his carefully collected funds.

"If you determine the boundaries are not right, come back in and I can adjust. No one's been interested in that land, not even Bloomberg."

"Bloomberg, the rancher?" Danny stuffed his wallet back into his coat.

"He's the biggest rancher in the area. He will be your closest neighbor, although he claims more than he legally holds," Hanson explained as he made notes in a ledger and then stowed the map.

"I thought Bloomberg had an eye on Jenny." Danny enjoyed how her name rolled off his tongue, like a pleasant melody he'd never heard before.

"Jeremy Bloomberg is the father. It's young Reggie, his son, who shows interest in Jenny." A scowl crossed Hanson's features. "Although you wouldn't think so if you saw the way he flirted with some of the young ladies who came to town today."

"Well, don't ask me about Reggie Bloomberg. I don't feel I can be fair," Luke said as he moved toward the front door. Darkness had fallen outside, and dusk loitered faintly, only a brief suggestion of the vanished sun lingering in the twilight. "He fired me off his ranch, and I don't like him for such a fine girl as Jenny."

The two young men stepped onto the boardwalk as Mr. Hanson turned the sign in the window over to closed. "Will I see you two at the dance?"

Luke glanced hopefully at Danny, but he shook his head. "I want to get an early start tomorrow morning. We'll be turning in soon. Mr. Edmonds said he wants us out of the barn. He's no hotel."

The three men chuckled.

"Michael can be gruff, but he's a good man," Carl Hanson stated. He shook hands with Danny and Luke. "Drop by when you come to town next." He locked the door and hurried into the night.

CHAPTER TWENTY

Danny found a seat in the loft, then tossed his blankets across his legs. He pondered his mission as he listened to Luke prowling below, speaking in low tones to the horses in their stalls. Only an occasional rumble of a passing wagon drifted to Danny's ears from the street beyond. Probably late folks hurrying to the dance.

Trinidad seemed quiet. Even Bill's Café had closed early, and only a single saloon remained open. But attendance must be low, Danny thought, not hearing the piano music from the drinking house as he normally did at this time of night.

As he contemplated the journey west, his thoughts lingered on each point. He recalled Philadelphia where he'd been struck with the idea to fulfill the sergeant's dream. Something niggled in Danny's mind now, reminding him of the small bit of information he'd overheard at the tavern where he took his meals. The stage companies might be changing hands, but how did that affect him?

He shook his head and remembered Pittsburgh and then the steamer on the Ohio River. St. Louis and Westport Landing. Then the stage west, across the plains and along the Santa Fe Trail, so famous that even Danny had heard of the well-regarded route.

At the burned down and abandoned Bent's Fort, Old Crawford had mentioned a new stage company might soon take over. Danny frowned and stuck a piece of hay between his teeth, chewing thoughtfully. Did an opportunity lurk here, in the shadows, just out of his reach?

"Lord, are you telling me something?" His whispered inquiry went unanswered, and Danny shook his head again. What was God doing with him? He'd only come to know Jesus a few short months ago. Already, he knew he loved God and the Holy Word found in Scripture. The Bible seemed so alive, speaking, whispering, pointing. Danny longed to understand the deeper meaning embedded in the writing. He knew God spoke to him, but did Danny hear correctly?

He sighed. "I'm new at this, Jesus. You have to give me a little slack. I pray my trust grow as I learn to recognize your hand in my life. I pray your Spirit speaks to me."

He paused, letting his eyes search the darkened corners of the haymow. "I know you're with me. Guide me, allow me to serve you. I believe you brought me here for a purpose. To fulfill Blair's dream, I suspect. But whatever the reason, may I cling to you throughout this adventure."

His prayer ended abruptly at someone banging on the barn door and Luke's reply. Danny reached for his Henry rifle but relaxed when he recognized Mr. Hanson's voice. Pushing the rifle away, Danny scrambled down the ladder.

"What's happened, Mr. Hanson?" Luke asked as Danny stepped into the halo of light cast from the lantern hanging on a hook.

The storekeeper wrung his hands, his gaze locking on Danny. "It's Jenny. Reggie came to the dance smelling of whiskey. When she told him she wouldn't dance with him, he went crazy and shouted he'd see any man fired who danced with his girl. None of the miners dare go against him. The Bloomberg's provide the beef for the miner's meals. And no rancher's son will dare brook the Bloombergs."

"Why not simply go home?" Danny suggested, not comprehending the depth of the situation.

"Jenny would be disgraced," the storekeeper explained.

"Pride," Danny growled in an accusing tone. Then he recalled how his misplaced pride had carried him across countless battlefields. Where would he be now if Sergeant Blair had not been patient with him? Still, he didn't see how he could help.

He held his hands wide. "So what? Why does this involve me?"

"You were friends with her brother," Mr. Hanson said swiftly. "Surely, her honor demands a champion. Patrick Blair would want you to stand up for her, dance with her, show she is not the property of Reggie Bloomberg."

Danny glanced at Luke. "None of my affair. I'm here to do right by Sergeant Blair, but that doesn't include dancing with his sister."

Mr. Hanson scowled. "Why, that's exactly what it means. Don't you want to save her from—well, I mean, Reggie Bloomberg doesn't own this town. They're not married. He has no hold on her."

Danny shrugged. "I'm sorry, Mr. Hanson, but this seems out of my hands." He glanced at Luke for support.

"Don't look at me," the young Indian said. "Bloomberg would make it difficult for my family too. We still have to make a living."

"That's true," the storekeeper corroborated. "Bloomberg holds a lot of power in the area."

"Well, it doesn't concern me," Danny glared at the storekeeper. "And why don't you ask her to dance, if it's so important?"

"We did. Me and Michael and Bill. But she said no, we were old friends, not young men," Mr. Hanson swiped his hand across his mouth.

"Well, I'm sorry," Danny said as he reached for the ladder to the loft. "She sounds spoiled. Perhaps she deserves this Reggie Bloomberg. Again, none of my business."

"Be brave, lad," Hanson called as Danny's hand touched the rung.

He froze, recalling the power of those words. With bravery, he'd marched with Sergeant Blair, hoping to die gallantly. But it was Blair who'd died bravely, racing around the battlefield to save wounded men and fight valiantly.

Slowly, Danny turned his head, glowering at Hanson. "What did you say?"

"Be brave, Danny. This is a moment in time, a moment to help Jenny maintain her honor. She is not Reggie's yet, and he can't tell her what to do. Or tell others they can't dance with her. You must do this. Show her the respect she deserves."

Danny paused, his grip on the rung tightening. Sergeant Blair had been so brave, braver than Danny. The sergeant had given him the books, a new lease on life. The Bible, the journal ... they both spoke of a fresh start, an exciting prospect. He owed Sergeant Blair.

He drew a deep breath as he turned to face Mr. Hanson and Luke. "Show me the way."

Beyond the edge of town, music drifted from the doors and windows of the sprawling sawmill, but a pregnant feeling hovered over the dance, as if a storm brewed. Danny followed Luke and the storekeeper toward the building, slowing as Luke indicated dark figures of men gathered around a bonfire in the clearing. They chortled among themselves, passing a bottle between them.

"That's Reggie Bloomberg," Luke whispered.

Danny could not make out any characteristics of the young rancher, but he fumed inwardly at the cowardice of the man.

Inside, a few dancers glided over the smooth wooden floors. Lanterns hung from almost every rafter, brightening the room with a glow of warmth that seemed lacking at the moment. Vivid bunches of fall leaves clustered around each beam of the building, lending a festive note to the event. Around the room, men and women stood in small groups, whispering as they stole furtive glances at a silent figure sitting alone on a bench.

"There," Hanson pointed, identifying the lone figure as Jenny Blair. She sat with bowed head, her shoulders shaking.

"Perhaps she should leave." Danny frowned at her pathetic posture. Yet her resolve whispered to something within him.

"Would you retreat from battle, soldier?"

Hanson's words cut into Danny's heart. With a sharp glance all around the brightly lit room, he marched across the dance floor. He'd performed braver deeds before, but this time they were not for him.

He halted in front of the quiet girl, feeling every eye in the place on him. "Miss Blair, may I have this dance?"

She glanced up quickly, startled at his unexpected presence. Then her eyes cooled when she recognized him. "Oh, it's you. I thought—well, I thought—"

"You thought your lousy boyfriend would come calling," Danny finished for her. "He didn't, but I'm here. Want to dance?"

She dabbed at her nose and eyes as she shook her head. "No, not with you. I should hate you for your purpose in town. But now, I can't. But I also can't dance with you."

He looked down on her for a long moment. Around the room, people chuckled as they guessed her response to his request. "Your brother was a brave man. I'd hoped it might run in the family."

Jenny gasped, then squinted at him. "Are you calling me a coward?"

"No. I'm asking you to be brave like your brother. Don't let anyone push you around, Jenny."

She swiped at her eyes once more and stood, extending a slim hand to Danny. She followed him onto the dance floor as the music continued. "Perhaps you are the brave one, Mr. Danny Mason. Reggie has threatened any man who dances with me."

Danny grinned as he turned to face her. "He is the least of my worries. I can't dance."

Her eyebrows arched. "Indeed, you are brave." She blinked, surveying him sharply. "Hold this hand," she instructed with a wave. "And place your other hand on my waist."

"Like this?" Danny hesitantly held her slender form. A thrill raced through him, and he realized she was the first woman he'd ever touched.

She nodded and placed one hand on his shoulder. "Now, rock back and forth, barely lifting each boot off the floor as we move." In a moment, they found their rhythm, the pair gently swaying to the music.

"Like this?" Danny repeated.

"Yes, you're doing wonderfully." Jenny smiled. "And no one can say I cowed to Reggie's bullying."

"Or that we were a graceful couple on the dance floor," Danny smiled back, actually enjoying the nearness of the young girl. Before, he would've kept his distance out of indifference. Now a kinship brewed he couldn't deny. Together, they'd thwarted Reggie Bloomberg and his drunken demands. After all, Jenny Blair was the sergeant's sister.

They rocked gently, never leaving their small square on the sawmill floor as other couples glided around them. Holding her made him aware of emotions he'd never considered. Shaking his head to remove the troubling thoughts, he vowed to ponder them later.

He stared at her finely chiseled features, her pale cheeks smeared with spent tears. Her gray eyes appeared extremely large, shooting glances around the room to gauge the crowd's reaction.

"What do you think?"

She nodded slightly at Danny's question. "My honor has been satisfied. Reggie will be angry when he hears, but I don't care." Her gaze locked on his own. "Why did you ask me to dance?"

"Mr. Hanson said it was the thing to do. I guess he doesn't like the way Reggie treats you."

She sighed. "I know, but a single woman has limited options."

Danny frowned, still rocking to the fiddler's tune. "I don't understand."

"No, you wouldn't," she replied quickly. "You're a man, you can do what you want, go where you want. I had only Patrick, and he promised to take care of me. I felt so excited when Luke's grandpa told him about the secret water in the desert."

"Luke's grandpa?" Danny pieced the puzzle together. "So, Blair saved Luke's grandpa from a beating."

"Rowdy, drunken miners picked on the old man. Patrick saved him. He told where the spring was located."

"And Blair thought he'd build a stage station, create a shortcut across the desert the stage couldn't refuse."

Jenny nodded. "It would mean our success, my independence. With Patrick gone, I have few choices than to assent to the questionable charms of the richest rancher in the area."

"You have a job at the mercantile," Danny offered.

"Yes, but with Lil marrying Mr. Hanson, my hours have been cut back. Occasionally, I pick up a shift at Bill's Café. But there is little in Trinidad a single woman can do."

As the tune drew to a close, Jenny smiled and then dropped her hands to her side, stepping from his grasp. Danny felt a little sad the dreaded dance had ended so swiftly.

"Thank you, Mr. Mason," Jenny said softly, her eyes glowing as she peered up at him. Danny nodded, unable to speak. His chest tightened as he stared down at the pretty girl. Then he found his voice.

"Call me Danny."

She nodded, her smile widening before she turned and fled.

CHAPTER TWENTY-ONE

The next morning, Danny and Luke took the road out of Trinidad that led to the Bloomberg ranch. A wide, clearly defined track showed the way, and Danny followed Luke, allowing the native to lead.

Only their horse's hoofbeats broke the silence of the early morning, the sun still not above the eastern horizon. Danny felt his warm breath on his cheeks behind his scarf. From the north, a breeze gently buffeted, merely making a cold morning a bit colder. No sign of a storm showed.

The two men remained quiet as they passed the hours, first coming to the Bloomberg ranch before launching into the desert beyond, only a vague trail indicating Blair's previous presence. The sun lifted before them, giving Danny his first glimpse of the bleak plains east of Trinidad. The stagecoach had followed the Purgatory from the Arkansas River, not venturing anywhere near this desolate range. He thrilled at the unfamiliar landscape. As they rode, the breeze increased, and a cluster of gray clouds massed to the north. Autumn had only begun, but Danny heard of the western winters striking early and fiercely. Would winter be upon them before they built shelters at the spring?

Another hour passed before Luke gestured to the darkening clouds. "We're in for a storm."

"Will we make it to the spring before it hits?" Danny peered far ahead, searching for any indication of the secret watering hole.

As if on cue, the wind gusted even harder, small slivers of sleet pelting the riders' exposed cheeks. Danny tugged his collar higher.

"I doubt it," Luke replied as he led the way deeper into the desert.

Behind them, Danny could no longer see any sign of the distant ranch house they'd passed hours before. To the south, the bulk of the Raton Range heaved, stretching another seventy miles to the east. Behind them, the massive ramparts of the Rocky Mountains loomed, almost unseen now as the sleet augmented.

"If we can't find the spring before the storm hits, what's your plan?"

Luke turned in his saddle to address Danny. "We ride until a better solution presents itself. We cannot stop on the side of the trail and make camp. Better to just ride on if the weather doesn't worsen. If we find a good place to camp, we camp and wait out the storm."

Although the weather threatened, Danny felt excited. Anticipation simmered within him as they approached the spring. This was what he'd come west for, right? An image of Jenny Blair darted across his mind, and he shook his head, clearing his thoughts.

He was here because of God, because of the work Sergeant Blair left unfinished. The Lord guided Danny's destiny, he reminded himself stubbornly. Yet a sense of delight coursed through him when he recalled the feel of the slender girl last night at the dance.

He scowled into the gathering storm. "Sorry, Lord. I am here for you, nothing else. Give me strength to serve you with my heart. Let me complete the task Patrick Blair began."

At a shout from Luke, Danny squinted through the sleet to where the Indian pointed. A huge boulder, bigger than a house, loomed out of the gathering gloom. With eagerness, the two men dismounted behind the giant rock.

Luke grabbed his shoulder and leaned close to be heard above the wind. "Make camp."

Danny nodded. Working the canvas water bags free from his pack with clumsy fingers, he filled the bucket they'd brought. Each horse drank a little as Danny held the bucket while Luke unsaddled, tossing their gear behind the rock, out of the wind.

Soon, they'd gathered mesquite wood and started a small blaze, the fire ringed with stones. Heads down, the horses stood against the massive boulder, blankets tied over their backs to keep them warm.

"Will this last?" Danny gestured to the blustering wind.

"Can't say." Luke shrugged. "We have plenty of food and the temperature isn't dropping. I doubt if it'll snow." He wrapped a ground sheet around his shoulders and hunkered near the flames.

Danny glanced all around, amazed to find himself on the plains of Colorado, in the desert east of Trinidad. Only a few weeks ago, he'd been in Philadelphia. He grimaced when he remembered how lonely he'd been, a stonemason with no prospects. Would he work and die there if he'd stayed? Did life hold any purpose for him if he'd remained in the crowded city where memories haunted him?

He lifted his gaze to the mountains in the south. The Raton Range sprawled nearby, but the white caps of the higher Rockies were not visible here. Only dark swaths of evergreen trees blanketed these smaller mountains, winter still holding off its snowy mantle.

A bitter wind whipped across the prairie, curling icy fingers around the giant stone they huddled behind. Sleet seemed to fly over them, and if not for the gray sky and intense cold, their location wasn't bad.

He glanced to where Luke squatted beside the fire. As if by magic, he'd met so many interesting folks on his journey west. Danny was not alone anymore. And despite the inclement weather, he felt he was having the time of his life. Truly an adventure, like Father McKay had predicted. He wondered at the information he'd heard about the different stage companies, but he wouldn't worry about that now. The Lord guided him, right? Those details seemed like God's problems, not Danny's.

"We're on Bloomberg land," Luke said suddenly, breaking the prolonged silence. He shifted and pulled his covers higher. "Well, not legally correct. They own their house and the land nearby, but this is free range. They claim it for their cattle to graze, but no one properly owns this land."

"Is this good grazing land?" Danny knew nothing of cattle and little about horses.

"Part of the year, yes. But this corner of the territory is dry, with little grass. High desert." He gestured to the north. "That way is the Arkansas River and wonderful prairie. Good grazing."

"Will we have trouble with the Bloombergs because I've claimed land out here?"

Luke shook his head. "I don't see why you should. You're not running cattle, and your station shouldn't be any threat to their holdings." He grinned at Danny. "Except maybe Reggie's holdings on Jenny Blair."

Heat stole up Danny's neck at mention of the pretty girl. "What does that mean?"

Luke shifted again. "It means she ain't married yet. Reggie better have an eye on his girl if he wants to keep her."

Did Luke have designs on Jenny? It was none of his affair, yet he felt his stomach coil into knots. "You've known her a long time," Danny ventured, probing.

"A few years, I guess. I never knew her brother, though. He was always working somewhere, trying to make ends meet for the two of them. He vanished into the desert, searching for the secret spring, before going east to join the war." Luke tugged his canvas sheet around him. "I saw the way you looked at her last night. And I'm sure everyone else saw it too."

Danny gaped, eyes wide. "What—what—the way I looked at her? I don't know what you mean," he stammered.

Luke chuckled but didn't reply. Danny tossed more wood on the small blaze and wrapped his blankets around him more snugly, as if protecting himself from something frightening.

"I am here for you, Jesus," he whispered so Luke couldn't hear. "Let me complete the stage station and fulfill Sergeant Blair's dream."

Danny drew in a deep breath, angry he'd allowed his mind to wander to insignificant thoughts. He was on a mission, he reminded himself sternly.

Yet he couldn't deny he enjoyed the adventure. The West felt so big, endless. Everywhere he looked, he found picturesque landscapes, towering mountains, vast plains. He thrilled at the notion God had given him a special task to perform. Surely this purpose merited a significance Danny could barely comprehend. The Creator of the world guided his footsteps.

***

Danny awoke to blue skies. With frozen fingers, he pushed the covers away from his face and peered all around. Not a trace of the sleet storm remained.

He'd not removed his clothing the night before. Already dressed, he stood and foraged more wood, hastening to build a fire to warm himself.

Luke stirred when Danny shoved the coffeepot into the flames. The Indian grinned when he saw the small blaze crackling merrily. "You'll do, Danny. A man learns to appreciate fire on the open range." He nodded his thanks as Danny handed him a steaming mug of coffee.

Together they sipped their drinks and stared at the white peaks of the Rockies, the heights glistening with new snow in the morning glare. Danny used his mug to point at the tall mountains.

"Is this winter?"

"Not yet, I think. At least not down here." Luke took another sip. "We should have weeks of fine weather before the snow flies."

"Good," Danny said. "I want to raise the walls of the station before it gets too cold."

Luke nodded. "We'll have time, if I don't miss my guess."

It took little time to pack their gear. The horses didn't want to get moving at first, warm beneath their cozy blankets, but when saddled and packed, the tiny cavalcade walked to the east.

The sun shone brightly, almost too brightly as Danny squinted into the crisp air. When had he ever felt such fresh air? He filled his lungs, his body tingling at the chill.

Impatient to arrive at their destination, Danny wanted to ask Luke how close they were to the spring. But he held his tongue, not wishing to appear over eager and spoil the charm of the early morning ride across the desert.

Mesquite thickets and manzanita bushes sprawled everywhere, the plants unfamiliar to Danny until Luke pointed them out. Rocks of all dimension and patches of scant grass and bare soil carpeted the ground. Only an occasional stunted cottonwood tree or dense thicket of brush appeared in ravines where water clearly raced during flash floods, the deep washes etched by signs of erosion.

As they rode, the sun lifted above the plains. Danny recalled those boundless grasslands he'd crossed with Old Crawford. He'd seen buffalo and antelope, huge elk with massive racks of antlers, and black bears. Countless prairie wolves and even a panther that slunk through the grass. His adventure unfolded around him, and Danny lifted his face to the warming sunlight.

"Thank you, Lord," he breathed softly, enjoying the unfamiliar environment.

When the sun stood directly overhead, Luke stopped and pointed to a rent in the nearby bluff. "I've never been here, but Grandpa told me to look for the notch in the hills."

Danny nodded, recalling Blair's description of the spring listed in the journal. His heart seemed to pound more loudly, anticipation enveloping him. He kicked his horse into motion. "Come on," he called over his shoulder, taking the lead for the first time.

At the opening of the gap carved into the bluff, Danny reined his mount again. The two men sat their horses, peering all around, the silence loud in their ears. Were they in the right place? Danny squinted at the walls of the gap, the spot where the water should be. Yet no green bushes marked any sign of water.

"Look," Luke called, pointing to a hawk sailing lazily overhead, circling lower. As they watched, the bird descended to vanish into the notch. The two riders quickly dismounted.

Slipping quietly across the uneven ground, they made their way to the high walls of the gap, peering everywhere for the elusive water.

"Blair says the spring is on the wall, near the opening," Danny called as he scanned the cluttered stones at the base of the bluff.

Another step into the jumbled rocks of the opening to the small canyon and the hawk gave flight, its wings flapping with force as the heavy bird drew skyward. But not before giving away the location of the secret spring.

"It came from there." Luke pointed to a place on the wall beside the gap, mounds of fallen stones piled beneath the bluff.

Scrambling up the rough ascent to the rock wall, the two men burst upon a ledge. Carved into the wall, beneath a protective overhang, the sheen of cascading water colored the cliff face.

About four feet above the heap of stones, a fissure ran across the rock wall, two feet in length, a dozen rivulets dribbling from the deep gash. The water followed tiny gullies etched in the stone, all leading to another crevice at the base of the wall where the water vanished beneath the cliff.

Danny leaned forward to taste the magical, life-giving water. He placed his hands on either side of the gleaming flow and drank from the biggest channel. With a grin, he turned to Luke.

"It's here," he said, as if he'd considered otherwise. "We'll have to find a way to get it down to the level, but there's water here."

Luke chuckled as he reached to touch the wet surface of the cliff face. "I trusted Grandpa. He's never been wrong about a spring or stream. He's hunted and trapped these mountains for many years."

"How can we get it down there?" Danny gestured to where they'd left their horses.

"I didn't work in a mine for nothing," Luke said, his grin widening. "We can pound a pipe into this crack and the water will flow down to the level. Simple."

Danny frowned. "I don't have much money left. Is pipe expensive?"

"There's a junk pile of discarded materials near the blacksmith shop at the mine," Luke explained as he led the way back to their horses. "I'll check there first, see if I can get some old pipe cheap."

By the end of that first afternoon, they'd dug a small ditch through the heap of stones at the base of the cliff to a basin near the mouth of the gap. Luke leaned on the shovel they'd bought at Hanson's mercantile, studying the makeshift water trough as the channel of water slowly filled the depression. He waved at the swelling puddle. "Here's the beginning of your station."

Danny shook his head as he delivered another stack of firewood to their camp. "Nope, not my station." He wiped the bark from his hands as he stared up at the bluff, a few scattered conifers perching high on the mountain. He thought of Sergeant Blair and Father McKay, of learning about Christ's sacrifice on the cross, and the purposeful life of a believer. His chest swelled as he pondered the amazing twists and turns of life an orphan boy from Philadelphia experienced out here on the prairies of Colorado. Is adventure for everyone who knows Jesus? Danny's gaze took in the rocky desert and majestic peaks of the higher

Rockies and felt his heart swell with exhilaration. He'd arrived. He'd come to where Sergeant Blair dreamed.

Far to the north, he knew the Arkansas River ran, threading a course across the plains to the Mississippi River. Could he develop this empty land into a stage station, one Old Crawford might consider changing his current route for? And did the old stagecoach driver have any say in routes and trails? Was Danny wasting his time?

"Lord, guide me," Danny prayed aloud, mindless of Luke's presence. He glanced at the Indian where he stood with the shovel perched on one shoulder. Luke looked down at his shoes, not meeting Danny's gaze as he spoke with Jesus. Danny grinned, speculating there might be many reasons for his coming west.

"Lord," he went on. "Tell me what to do. I promise to do my best, to build a solid station. But the rest is up to you. If the stage is to divert routes, you will have to interfere. That's out of my hands."

At the silence that followed his simple plea, Luke lifted his eyes, meeting Danny's stare. Danny grinned at his friend as a sense of significance swept through him, as if he were launching something momentous. "Let's build."

CHAPTER TWENTY-TWO

The next day, they explored deeper into the notch, taking time to search the depths of the grassy glens between the bluffs. Excellent grazing carpeted the box canyon. There would be pastures of luxuriant feed for stage horses, Danny thought as he worked with Luke to build a temporary stone wall across the opening of the notch.

As the two horses roamed the grassy recesses of the chasm, the two men carried stones. Piling the building blocks near the chosen site of the station, the heaps soon grew.

Danny wiped his hands on his pants. "We'll need lumber." He eyed the pile of rocks with satisfaction, but he wanted more. "Tonight, I'll put together a list for Mr. Hanson. I assume he can order lumber."

Luke dropped the heavy rock he carried and nodded. "Yes. I can deliver your order whenever you want and take the time to check the junk pile near the mine. I'm sure I can find some odd pieces of pipe."

Danny studied the cleared, level space they'd picked for the station. "Three rooms, one front door, one back door. A window in each room. Two fireplaces, one for heat, one for cooking."

"And lumber for door frames, windows, and the roof," Luke added.

"Don't forget the plank door," Danny said, feeling excited every time the two men discussed plans for the building. He'd come west for this, he felt certain, yet his guilt loomed every time he considered his new friends. Would he settle in the West? Would the Hanson's, Luke, Mr. Edmonds, and Old Crawford become better friends?

What of Jenny Blair? He blushed when he thought of the pretty girl. Was she his friend too? Danny shook his head, disturbed at how easily her image flew to his mind.

★★★

Barely seen above the tall peaks of the Rocky Mountains, the dull autumn sun loitered, its light valiantly lingering upon the plains below. Soon, it would be too dark to work.

Around their campfire that evening, Danny held Blair's journal in one hand, feeling the weight of the small book. The words printed within had such an impact on his life. He'd already memorized every word that described the location and building suggestions for the station, so he tucked the journal into his pack and retrieved the Bible.

This book he gripped, sensing the import, the difference between Blair's two black books. Here was the Word of God.

Luke tossed another stick on the fire, sparks lifting to the heavens. He sat back, staring across the leaping flames at Danny. "You set store on that book."

Danny grinned, excited to share. "It's truth. And it's changed my life. I never knew God. I'd never heard anything useful about him, his desires, his hopes for his people. Then I met Sergeant Blair."

Luke was silent for a moment before he spoke. "God has hopes for his people?"

Danny nodded. "Sure. He loves us. He wants to see each of us grow to maturity. He is eager to see our faith develop, to watch our love for him blossom."

Luke pointed at the book in Danny's hand. "You read all that in there?"

A smile crept across Danny's features. "Oh, yes. God's love, his desire for me to live a purposeful life, and the way he wants me to think of others."

"Live for God?" Luke persisted.

"For him, for his glory, and for my enrichment," Danny explained. His tone changed as his smile faded. "It's not easy, though. To put aside your own desires for those of the Lord is very difficult. I wrestle him daily, my wants tangling with what he knows is best for me."

Luke laughed. "You wrestle God?"

"I do, I'm sorry to confess."

"Who wins?"

"Some days, I think I do, which means I lose. His ways are better than my ways. I wish I could just obey him and not have to struggle so much, but I realize that's how he's shaping me, molding me into the man of God I should become."

He cringed when he recalled the lethargy that enveloped him after the war. Despair and hopelessness had thrust him into a dark place he didn't ever want to return to. Since knowing Christ, he'd felt the Lord's guiding hand, leading him into the unexpected adventure that brought him west.

A shiver of anticipation coursed through him, and Danny knew he was where he should be.

Luke tilted his head, staring intently at Danny. "You intrigue me." He paused and then shrugged. "I'd like to hear more, if that's all right."

Danny's grin returned. "My pleasure."

***

The next day, Luke rode early from camp. Danny had been pleased how well the road from Trinidad to the spring was defined and easy to locate. With a little more work, the track would be suitable for wagon travel. Sergeant Blair's preliminary work showed.

Danny had risen before the sun to see Luke off. "You have enough money for all these supplies and the lumber?"

Luke's question worried Danny. His money supply was dwindling, but he hoped he'd have enough. Perhaps Mr. Hanson would give them credit until the station was up and running. Danny hoped that day would not be far off.

"Let's get started and see how the Lord answers my prayer. I need to have faith, Luke, if I'm going to make this work. God is with me, I'm certain."

Luke swung into the saddle and looked down at Danny, arching an eyebrow. "I hope you're right."

"Trust God," Danny called after him as he rode from camp.

For the reminder of the day, Danny worked with pick and shovel to dig the foundation of the rectangular building. He stopped occasionally to remind himself Patrick Blair had stood right here, in this isolated corner of the desert. He stared across the prairie, knowing the sergeant had observed this very scenery.

Carefully, Danny measured the length of each wall, trenching the space in equal depth. By late afternoon, the trenching was almost complete.

Taking a break beside the basin of water that served as a horse trough, Danny looked up when he heard the clatter of hooves, a group of horsemen riding toward his camp.

The quartet of dark riders came swiftly upon him, but Danny only glanced at his Henry rifle where the weapon leaned against a nearby boulder. The pound of hooves on hard ground stilled as they reined their horses near the site for the station. They seemed engrossed in the construction as Danny strode forward.

An older man nodded cordially when he saw Danny. "Howdy, young man. You'll be Danny Mason."

"I'm Mason," Danny called as the four riders faced him.

"Luke used to ride for me. I'm Jeremy Bloomberg. We spoke to him when he passed our house, and we figured to ride out here and see for ourselves." He hooked a thumb at the man beside him. "This is my son, Reggie."

Danny could see the family resemblance, although the handsome younger man held a sullen expression Danny distrusted. He decided to ignore the icy stab to his guts at meeting Jenny's suitor.

"Well, you can see what I'm doing. I filed on the land at Hanson's, and hope to have the building up before snow flies."

The senior Bloomberg pushed his hat back. "Stage station?"

Danny nodded, then exhaled. If they were going to be neighbors, he should be more considerate. He took another step closer. "Get down, Mr. Bloomberg, and water your horses. Let me show you what I want to do."

For the next half hour, Danny showed the rancher around, explaining about the chasm between the bluff that served as pasture and corral, and the spring he hoped would eventually flow into a proper water trough. When they stood beside the trenches he'd dug, Danny indicated where each wall would stand, each door, each window.

"And you will run no cattle out here?"

Danny smiled at the rancher's inquiry, suddenly understanding their unexpected visit. "There is not enough water for cattle. I own only this section of land and have no stock other than my horse." He turned to gesture toward the tiny spring issuing from the crack in the cliff wall. "Not enough water for anything other than a stage station. I am no threat to your operation, Mr. Bloomberg."

The rancher nodded. "I see that, Mason." He smiled as he moved toward his horse, stepping into the saddle before speaking again. "Not enough grass out here to tempt my stock drifting this way," he said as his gaze surveyed the desert beyond the notch in the bluff, then looked back at Danny. "I hope you won't mind if my riders stop by here occasionally for water, when they come this way."

"They will be welcome," Danny said.

Bloomberg nodded and tugged on his reins. "Thank you, young man, and I wish you luck."

As the rancher turned to go, followed by his two cowboys, Reggie lingered, his cold eyes on Danny. "I'll catch up, Pa," he called as his father trotted from the camp. With a belligerent glower, he scanned the construction site. "I hear you danced with my girl after I told everyone to stay away."

Danny tensed, wondering how safe he truly was with this angry man. He glanced over his shoulder to where the rifle leaned. "Not very gentlemanly of you to ruin a lady's evening, especially a lady you intend to marry."

"You're new here, stranger. None of your affair. And keep away from Jenny, or there'll be trouble between us. Trouble you won't be able to handle."

Danny lifted his chin, a silent challenge to the young rancher. He wasn't afraid of this peacock, but Danny had a task to complete. He reminded himself he was here to fulfill Blair's wishes, not get involved in a lover's quarrel. What did he know of Jenny Blair? She'd told him she was to marry the richest rancher in the region. Perhaps Danny's involvement was not wanted.

With a jerk on the reins, Reggie turned his horse and rode from camp, spurring the animal cruelly to catch the retreating riders. Danny watched him go, a sick feeling settling into his stomach. His gaze shifted to the few clouds that hovered to the north.

"Lord, I thought you brought me here to build with stone, something I'm familiar with. But I feel like I'm dangling from a cliff, my boots not touching ground. I don't like this sensation of not being in control."

He grunted, drawing in a deep breath of the clean air as he shoved his hands into his pockets. "Maybe you're teaching me I'm not in control, and I need to let you work. Well, Jesus, you know what you're doing, right?"

CHAPTER TWENTY-THREE

Danny discovered the second spring the next morning. Sergeant Blair's directions to the notch cut into the mountains had been exact, leading Danny directly to the desired location for the desert station. He felt annoyed he'd doubted God's guiding hand. Surely the Lord brought him west, Danny surmised as he scouted further into the small box canyon where his horse grazed contentedly.

At first, he wouldn't believe what his eyes told him when he stared at the hummingbirds darting between two rocks. Upon closer inspection, he found the tiny seep where the small birds had drunk. As he crouched beside the jumbled rocks, he scanned the scant grass around him, evidently sub irrigated. There must be more water in this unknown oasis than he first believed.

He walked to the overhang where they'd dropped their gear. The shallow cave served as a temporary camp, but Danny felt eager to begin building. But he would curb his impatience, wanting Luke's help so the construction went well. Now that they'd discovered water, they could afford to take a little time and build correctly.

Squatting beside the glowing coals of his dying fire, Danny lifted the new coffeepot he'd picked up in Trinidad.

He wasn't used to camp gear, especially new gear. He'd always made do with whatever was at hand, usually others' castoffs. Especially at the orphanage. He'd never worn new clothes until he'd joined the army.

As he filled a tin mug, he thought of the war and the men he'd known. Blowing the steam from the rim, he sipped his hot drink, his thoughts lingering on Nelson and Sergeant Blair. They were the first Christian men who made an impression on him. He'd always shied away from the Bible-wavers he'd heard in camp those early days of the war, uncertain of their faith as all the men prepared for death. All manner of men died in battle, Christian or not.

But now, Danny realized his fledgling faith had more to do with how he lived than how he died. Sergeant Blair had been a man of character. Brave, thoughtful, kind, a servant. Danny had been brave, but for all the wrong reasons. Was he a good man, like Nelson and Blair? He wanted to be.

His brow furrowed when he wondered what the sergeant's reaction might be to Danny dancing with his sister.

He leaned back on his heels, his gaze taking in the narrow chasm between the bluffs before lifting to the sun just tipping the eastern rim of the natural bowl he camped in. "Lord, you know me, but I'm only just getting to know you. I'm so new at this, Jesus. What kind of man do you want me to become? I think I'm brave, and I know how to build with stone, but other than that, I have nothing to offer."

He took another sip and snuggled deeper into his coat. These autumn days on the desert chilled him every morning, heralding the coming winter. But he still had much work to do before snow slowed his progress.

"I need to trust you, God. You chose me for this job. Out of all the folks you know, you picked me. Let me trust you made a good choice. Use me, with all of my faults and shortcomings, to complete the work you have for me."

An image of Jenny Blair darted into his mind, and Danny tensed, her lithe figure and lovely features igniting an unfamiliar fire in his heart. "Forgive me, Father, when my mind wanders. I'm here for you, to do your work, but sometimes my mind gets away from me. I've never known a girl before, and I guess I'm naturally curious. But don't worry. I've always been a lonely man, and that's probably why you chose me for this job. I'm used to getting a job done alone."

He spent the morning building rock walls around their camp in the shallow cave. When the station was complete, and the men moved indoors, this makeshift shelter would make an ideal stable, protection for the horses from bitter winds and intense cold.

After a meager meal at noon, he continued gathering stones for the main building. Earlier, when he'd been searching for firewood, he'd discovered a sun-bleached tree trunk in a nearby ravine, probably washed down from the heights above during a storm. Using the ax, he'd shaped the length of wood into a crude sled. Harnessing the horse to the toboggan, he loaded the sled with heavy stones and dragged them to the work site. By late afternoon, weary and hungry from work, he washed in the primitive trough and prepared supper. He reached for the Henry rifle when he heard a lone horse approach at twilight. He emerged from the cavern when he recognized Luke's call.

In the dim evening light, Danny watched as Luke dismounted, a bundle of supplies held in his arms along with additional bundles tied behind his saddle.

"Take this," he said as he handed the pack to Danny. "Whew! That was a long ride," the Indian reported as he untied the packs behind his saddle. "I brought what I could carry. Mr. Hanson promised to deliver the rest."

"Deliver?" Danny's brows knitted together. "He'd bring a wagon out here?"

"It's a stage road, right?" Luke threw the heavy canvas covered bundle over his shoulder and led the way to the shelter beneath the cliff overhang. He whistled when he saw the newly built rock wall of the dwelling.

"No one can say grass grows under your feet," he chuckled, letting the supplies slip to the ground.

Danny lowered his own pack and gestured to the stable walls. "I built these this morning. Easy enough. Then I gathered more stones for the station. I'll be ready to begin construction in the morning."

Luke moved toward the doorway, his form shrouded by the gathering gloom outside. "Let me unsaddle my tired horse and then you can explain your ideas about tomorrow." He nudged the coffeepot with his boot. "Have coffee ready when I get back."

For an hour, Danny explained his plans for building the station walls as Luke ate hungrily.

"Breakfast at Bill's seems a long time ago," the young man declared as he devoured another bowl of soup.

Danny leaned against the cave wall and cradled his third cup of coffee. "Everything went well? The lumber order? All of our supplies?"

Luke nodded. "I tried my best to refuse their help. But they ganged up on me and forced me to take more than you ordered."

Danny narrowed his eyes. "Who's they?"

"Why, Mr. Hanson and Jenny, of course." Luke beamed. "As I told them what you wanted, Jenny would shake her head and add more, saying you had no idea how much was enough out here. She said a tenderfoot like you needed help from folks who knew better."

Ignoring Luke's jesting words, Danny felt himself bristle. He was in charge of this construction, wasn't he? Hadn't the Lord directed his path here? Danny felt uneasy accepting assistance from others, especially the sergeant's little sister.

"Well, you know how much money I have," Danny grumbled. "You didn't accept their suggestions, did you?"

Luke grinned and held his hands wide, palms up. "What could I do? I couldn't say no to Jenny. And then Mr. Hanson said he'd back you, as you were here to finish Patrick Blair's work."

Danny's scowl deepened. "I'm the one building this station. Why would they throw in with us, help me this way? What do they hope to gain?"

The smile vanished from Luke's bronzed face. He eyed Danny over the rim of his cup as he sipped coffee. "Danny, maybe you don't savvy us western folks. Jenny and Mr. Hanson don't want anything from you. They're trying to help, that's all."

Danny sat back again, not realizing he'd leaned forward in his agitation. "Well, I'm sorry," he muttered as he hid behind his mug, feigning another sip, then lowered his cup. "I'm not used to others thinking of me. I've always been on my own."

Luke nodded. "I get it. But out here, life works better with friends. Don't look a gift horse in the mouth. Be grateful."

"Yes, yes," Danny went on, "But *why* would they help me?"

A long moment passed before Luke shrugged. "Maybe because Patrick Blair didn't come home, but you did. Maybe

Mr. Hanson looks on Jenny as a daughter, and she wants to see her brother's work finished."

Danny pursed his lips, feeling reprimanded. He should be more grateful.

"Or ..." Luke glanced at Danny from the corner of his eye.

"Or what?" Danny prompted when the man hesitated.

"Or Jenny wants to help you for other reasons."

"Other reasons?"

"You danced with her when everyone else was afraid of the Bloomberg's power. You helped her hold her head high."

The fire brightened as a log folded, sparks fluttering upward. Danny gazed into the dancing flames. Jenny Blair. He shouldn't think of her. He looked up abruptly, remembering.

"The Bloombergs came by."

"Here?" Luke's eyebrows arched.

Danny nodded. "Mr. Bloomberg wished me luck. Said I'm no threat to their ranch."

"No, you're not, but that's mighty big of them. I never had any trouble with the old man, but Reggie can be pigheaded." He peered at Danny sharply. "He came out here too?"

"Said I was to keep away from Jenny."

Loud laughter erupted from Luke. "Well, he doesn't like anyone standing up to him. And Jenny does it all the time. She won't marry him if he doesn't change."

"Why *would* she marry him? He seems like such an idiot."

Luke filled his cup again and replaced the pot into the coals when Danny refused another. The Indian sat back, warming his hands with his hot mug.

"I didn't know Patrick and Jenny Blair until recently. He was always working odd jobs around town, trying to take care of his kid sister after their parents died of fever. They lived in a shack near the river, and Jenny took in sewing after Patrick went to work in the mines. I learned more about him when he saved Grandpa from a beating. Those drunken miners weren't happy when Patrick stopped them, and one was a shift manager. They fired Patrick."

Danny could read the tension in Luke's features as he spoke. He studied the fire for a minute before resuming. "The Blairs had a real hard go of it then. Grandpa told Patrick about this place, and he decided to build a station in the desert. Jenny was all for it. She got a part-time job in the mercantile while Patrick scouted out here and made plans to build. Then the war started. At first, he felt responsible for Jenny, but then something happened, and he enlisted. Jenny was furious."

"You don't know what made him enter the army later in the war?"

Luke shook his head. "At first, Blair said 'twas none of his business. A year and a half later, he joined up."

Danny pondered, recalling the intentional sergeant. Patrick Blair must've been very young when he went to work in the mines. He was very young to be a sergeant.

So, what had prompted Blair to join the war?

CHAPTER TWENTY-FOUR

The October day dawned a brilliant blue, the clear sky brightening with promise. Danny wanted to watch the sunrise alone. He took his cup of coffee to the building site and faced east. As if the crisp desert air radiated color, he marveled at the vibrant azure, so clear that he believed he could see a hundred miles to the horizon. Across the plains, he watched as shadows receded, the sun slowly climbing, revealing the vast emptiness of the boundless prairie.

Nothing stirred. Not even a hint of a breeze or a buffalo or an antelope. Sometimes, over the past week, Danny would catch a glimpse of an elk or deer, descending the mountains before the coming winter. They would always move away from his lonely camp, toward distant water and lower grazing pastures.

When a bird whistled, breaking the deep silence, Danny turned his head to catch the piercing melody. He filled his lungs with the evergreen-scented air, and his gaze lifted to the dark ramparts of the nearby heights. How had he come to love this forlorn vastness so quickly? He'd left the war and the crowded city only recently, and already the West claimed his heart. No matter what happened at this desert station, he knew he would never return to the urban centers of the Atlantic Seaboard.

With a deep melancholy, he thought of the men he'd fought beside in the war, remembering each of them with a salute of memory. Would he ever forget those difficult days? In his head, he heard the clash of arms, the roar of cannons, the battering of men struggling to survive as he'd survived. Combat etched scars into his being, never to be forgotten. But maybe alleviated? Could this empty place help heal his haunted soul? He pondered this idea as he continued to scan the sky, the colors changing slowly, holding his rapt attention. Only a single star lingered, hovering above the horizon, fading fast.

"Beautiful, isn't it?" Luke's boots crunched gravel as he disturbed Danny's solitary vigil.

Danny sighed, saddened to see the private moment pass, yet glad for the company of this new friend. His heart warmed at the thought he might belong somewhere, anywhere, for the first time.

"Look there." Luke pointed behind them at the bulk of the Rocky Mountains.

Forests of dark green conifers blanketed the distant parapets, their lofty crags crowned with glistening snow in the morning sunlight.

Danny wanted to say something, to give validation of his emotions as he surveyed the distant peaks. No words came to him, however, and he continued to stare, mesmerized by their grandeur.

Finally, he shifted. "How do you take in all this beauty? The only word that comes to mind is majesty."

Luke glanced at him. "Majesty?"

"Sure." Danny nodded. "I never used to see God's hand. Now I see it everywhere I look. He made this. His creativity is limitless."

Luke puckered his lips, thoughtful as he stared up at the massive mountains. "I think I know what you mean. Sometimes, when I study the stars at night, I feel *something*, you know? Like someone is calling to me, telling me this is made by ... someone."

"God," Danny agreed.

Luke shrugged, but Danny continued. "The heavens declare the glory of God. They have no speech, yet they tell of his presence." He shook his head. "I read Psalm 19 yesterday, but of course, I can't remember the words just right. The Bible speaks of God's creation calling to us." He turned to face Luke. "Calling to you."

The young man shrugged again. "Let's get started. How do we build a stage station?"

For the next two days, the two men labored to raise the stone walls, stopping only to stir additional mortar. They only went as high as the bottom of each window, having to wait for framing material to arrive with the lumber Mr. Hanson would deliver. They spent the third day forming the fireplaces.

At the end of the day, Luke pointed to the west. A wagon lumbered along the dim trail, two figures riding the bench.

"Who is that?" Danny squinted into the fading sunlight, trying to determine Mr. Hanson's passenger.

"It's Jenny," Luke whispered.

With a shout, he waved at the oncoming wagon, but Danny froze, startled at the unexpected sense of excitement that filled him. Just the young girl's name sent a thrill over him.

Danny shook his head, forcing himself forward to meet his guests. As Luke called a greeting to Jenny and shook hands with the storekeeper, Danny hastened to help the pretty girl down from the wagon. Without waiting for assistance, Jenny stepped to the wheel rim and dropped to the ground in front of him. When she smiled, he could only stare, stammering his welcome before turning away.

★★★

Mr. Hanson and Danny unloaded the wagon as Luke showed Jenny around the rustic campsite. As they worked, the storekeeper related information about the various supplies and pieces of lumber he'd delivered. But Danny couldn't keep his gaze from following Jenny Blair.

The sun dropped behind the Rockies as the two men finished stacking the last of the supplies near the new structure. A pleasant glow emerged from the rock stable beneath the overhang, and Danny led the way to the gap in the bluff. After washing up at the sunken trough, Danny gestured the storekeeper take lead upon entering the cramped quarters of the rock shelter.

"I watered your team, Mr. Hanson, and picketed them with our horses," Luke reported as they found seats near the bright blaze. Danny forced himself to not stare at Jenny as she scooped bowls of soup and passed them out. For the next few minutes, silence reigned as the hungry quartet ate.

Once, Danny caught her eye across the dancing flames, but Jenny averted her gaze swiftly, as if looking elsewhere.

He felt the color creep to his cheeks, feeling silly and awkward in the presence of the sergeant's sister. Why was she here?

As if reading his mind, she settled back upon a canvas pack after gathering the dirty dishes. "I'll do these later, but first, I wanted to say something."

"I will do the dishes," Danny said hurrying to rise.

"No, I'll do them, boss," Luke interjected, also coming to his feet.

Jenny held up a hand. "Stop. I need to tell you something." She spoke generally, as if speaking to everyone present, but her gaze fixed on Danny. "Patrick was my brother. It was his idea to create a shortcut across the desert the stage company couldn't refuse. But I supported him. The dream was both of ours."

Luke shifted. "So?"

"So, I wanted to come out here and see the progress."

Mr. Hanson laughed. "You mean you demanded."

Jenny shrugged, still watching Danny. "Call it what you will. I have a vested interest in the station. I knew of it before any of you."

Silence fell as she stood, gathering the dishes once more. As she turned away, Danny peered up to the black bulk of the distant mountains, their peaks outlined against the darker blue of the night sky. Stars glimmered, reminding him of the Lord's guidance. He thought of Jenny and Patrick Blair, alone against the world, only counting on one another. Danny could relate, and he felt a connection with the beautiful girl. Not long ago, he'd been alone too. Now, he felt he belonged out here, in the desert, with the mountains towering all around.

Jenny shifted the dishes in her arms, bringing Danny from his reverie. He'd thought she'd left the campfire. "This must be strange to you, a city boy." She smiled as she indicated the quiet beyond the firelight with her chin.

"If someone had told me I'd love the prairie, I'd have called them a liar." A slow grin spread across his features. "I love this land. I feel called here."

"Called?" Jenny narrowed her eyes at him, but Danny caught Mr. Hanson and Luke studying him too.

He drew a deep breath, then nodded. "Yes. Called."

Jenny tilted her head as a look of curiosity passed over her face. But Luke laughed, rising to relieve half the dishes from her. "Watch out, Jenny. This one's canny," Luke said as he led the way toward the spring. "And I've caught him talking to God."

As the pair vanished into the darkness, Danny caught the gleam of Jenny's eyes as she glanced at him over her shoulder.

Later, while Luke shifted packs to make room for the quartet in the stone stable, Danny retreated to the half-constructed station. He studied the stars glimmering across the sky, the heavenly bodies shining like brilliant lights.

"You made this, Father," he murmured as he worshipped. "You are the Creator of all, and yet you have time for me and my small life. Praise you, Jesus, for what you do, what you've done, and what you will do in this corner of Colorado. I know you brought me out here for something. To build a station in the desert? To share my faith with Luke? Or was it to help me escape a dead-end existence in the city?"

He dropped his gaze from the night sky when he heard gravel crunching. He tensed when he recognized Jenny Blair coming up beside him.

For a long moment, they stood in the silence, each absorbed with unshared thoughts. For Danny, he could see the way her hair tumbled loose down her back, framing her oval face, her cheeks gleaming pale in the moonlight. Her nearness uneased him.

"I love the desert," she breathed softly. "After Ma and Pa died, Patrick used to bring me out here."

Danny felt his eyes widen. "You've been here before?"

A low chuckle escaped her. "Oh, yes. I've been here a few times. We'd build a little fire in a hole so no one could detect our presence. Tales of marauding Indians always frightened me, but Patrick said we were safe. Still, he humored me, digging a hole in the sand for our campfire. He was like that, thoughtful of my feelings. A good brother."

Danny nodded, although he knew she couldn't see him in the darkness. Sergeant Blair was all of that, and more. Danny would never forget the courageous sergeant he'd known for such a short time and yet had made an unquestionable impact on his life.

"You miss him."

She nodded at his comment, her dark form barely discerned in the dim light. "You have no idea," she whispered huskily. He was startled at her sudden laugh. "We argued at the end."

The laughter broke off into a sob, and Danny reached for her hand. He couldn't say what prompted such a brash reaction to her sorrow. Yet she squeezed his hand in return.

"I'm sorry," she mumbled, not bothering to pull her hand free.

"I think I understand a little." He gave her hand another squeeze. "I only learned to feel after meeting your brother. He was kind to everyone, even an insignificant orphan from Philadelphia. Yet he taught me many things."

"Like what?"

He could feel her gaze upon him, and Danny smiled into the gloom. For an instant, he considered speaking again of Sergeant Blair's kindness, his willingness to do more than his share, his courage under fire, his care for the platoon. Instead, his voice dropped even lower, thick with meaning. "He was my friend."

"He was a fool," she said, her whispered words laced with anger.

Danny stared at her, trying to penetrate the darkness to perceive her meaning. "How can you say that? He was the best man I've ever known."

"He left me when I needed him most," she replied bitterly. "I told him not to enlist, and at first, he listened to me. But I saw the restlessness in him. As each month passed, I could see he wanted to join up. And as each month passed, I tried to hold him back, yet I knew what was coming."

"Why hold back such a brave man? His position in the scout platoon probably saved countless lives." Danny couldn't understand why a life of purpose should be restricted. Blair had certainly touched his life.

"I needed him here," Jenny snapped. "After our parents died, he was all I had left." She tugged her hand free and wrapped herself with her arms. For a long moment, neither spoke.

Finally, Danny cleared his throat. "He saved my life."

"Great. He's dead, but you're alive. He was a fool," she repeated.

Something surged within him, a desire to defend the man who'd given Danny a new lease on life. He faced Jenny. "You're more alike than you know. His honor would not allow him to stay out of a fight where he believed he could do some good, and your honor wouldn't allow you to leave a dance when you felt slighted. Retreat was not an option for you or him. But his bravery mattered."

She gasped. "I—I—" she sputtered with indignation.

"He was my friend," Danny repeated with a stern note to his words.

Whirling, Jenny fled into the night.

CHAPTER TWENTY-FIVE

Only the intense chill drove Danny into the stone stable hours later that night. A bed of coals glowed, revealing the three motionless figures. The smallest sleeping form shifted as he stretched in his blankets, and he stilled, squinting at where he believed Jenny slept. Did she struggle with remorse, or did the heat of anger still burn in her veins? Blair had become his hero, and not even Patrick's pert sister could affect Danny's loyalty. His faith, his ideals, and even his future had been impacted by knowing the Christian sergeant.

He rolled over and punched his coat into a pillow. Lying back, Danny stared at the underside of the overhang, dancing shadows from the dying fire revealing crevices in the stone.

The coals hissed, reminding him of the cold he'd endured outside, attempting to keep his distance from the pretty girl. Jenny Blair was an irritation, casting disparaging comments on Sergeant Blair. What did she know of the countless sacrifices her brother made for the men of the scout platoon?

With a grunt, he stretched a hand from beneath his blankets and pushed more fuel into the red coals. A minute later, yellow flames leaped, hungrily licking at the wood. Heat filtered over him, and Danny lay back once more.

Why was he out here? Would the stage company even consider an alternate route, one untried and new? If Jesus didn't intervene—

"You're driving me crazy," he whispered as he studied the leaping shadows upon the cavern ceiling. "You brought me out here, right? Am I impatient? My plans are progressing, but there's no guarantees any of this will work out. Is your goal to stretch my faith through a wasted effort? Why am I building an unknown station in the desert?"

Danny bit his lip. Did God test him? Surely the Lord didn't make mistakes. There must be a reason why Danny felt compelled to come west, yet doubts assailed him.

The sergeant's final words played in his mind, recalling the ghastly look on the dying man's face as he reminded Danny of his dream.

"I'm trying to fulfill Patrick Blair's wish," he muttered. "I'm here to complete this task, this mission."

But another thought darted across his muddled mind. Did the sergeant want Danny to dream? Blair knew the lonely orphan from Philadelphia had never allowed personal desires to clutter his intentions. His goal had always been to die bravely, to honor his borrowed name. But he'd never considered future plans. There was no room for empty fantasies in Danny's life.

He closed his eyes, clearing his thoughts. He would stay the course. He was here for a specific purpose, nothing more.

He drew a deep breath as he opened his eyes once more, listening to the crackling firewood. "I will trust you, Jesus. You know what you are doing, even when I don't. Your will be done, not mine. I give you a willing heart. Do what you want with me. Use me for your glory."

His prayer made him relax, his tense shoulders loosening beneath the covers. A moment later, he fell asleep.

***

In the morning, he awoke to the rich smell of simmering coffee. When he opened his eyes, he found Jenny attending the fire, feeding small sticks to the cheerful blaze. Their gaze met over the merry flames, but she turned away quickly, a look of grief etched into her soft features.

Within a minute, he'd pulled on his boots and shrugged into his coat. Jenny Blair would have no effect on his plans, he vowed as he accepted the steaming cup she thrust into his hands. He nodded his thanks, neither of them speaking before he stepped into the glorious morning air, crisp and filled with a promise.

He strolled to the construction site, listening to Luke and Mr. Hanson moving about in the stable. Danny studied the half-built wall as he sipped the hot drink. Why did Jenny Blair have to be so difficult? Her brother had been his hero, impacting Danny in ways he was still discovering. He wished she weren't so harsh about Sergeant Blair's decisions. He shook his head, reminding himself he had a task to complete. When he returned to the stone stable, he ate hurriedly, unwilling to let the other men start work before him.

As the day passed, Danny grew more excited. Every stone, each rock he lifted into position, moved the sergeant's dream closer to fruition. He'd come west to finish Patrick's goal, right? This was the mission the Lord had given him. Danny would obey God.

Mr. Hanson shaped the window frames and wooden shutters, fitting them tight over each opening as the walls rose. His sawing whirred softly as the men worked. Luke handed Danny stones as the mason carefully crafted each rock into position, making sure they fit precisely. Mr. Hanson moved from the windows to the plank doors while Jenny darted about, offering suggestions or handing a man a tool or fetching water. Occasionally, she stepped in front of Luke and handed Danny stones, his fingers tingling when their hands touched. He found it difficult to ignore her, but he tried valiantly, maintaining his focus.

By early afternoon, the walls were complete to Danny's high standards. "No wind or cold will get through these walls," Danny said proudly, surveying his handiwork as the other two men stood beside him. Jenny nudged his elbow, handing him a steaming mug. Did she smile at him? Did she feel as miserable as he did about last night's disagreement? Danny frowned as he sipped coffee, watching her as she retreated to the rock stable to prepare supper.

"Windows done, walls done, doors should be finished by this evening." Mr. Hanson nodded his thanks after Jenny handed him a tin cup.

"The roof will take time," Luke commented, eyeing clouds banking on the northern horizon. "Maybe a storm tomorrow."

"Come on," Danny growled as he moved toward the stack of lumber at the end of the station. "We're wasting daylight."

With a concerned eye to the gathering clouds, the men hurried to place the beams for the roof. When the sun dipped behind the high peaks of the western mountains, Danny felt pleased at the day's progress.

Gathering before the front door, the three men peered at the near finished station while shadows stretched across the clearing. Danny gloried in the familiar ache in his shoulders from a hard day's work.

"Such a wonderful rock house in the desert," Luke marveled, his eyes glowing.

Mr. Hanson gripped Danny's shoulder. "Patrick would be proud of you."

A lump rose in Danny's throat as he surveyed the stone station. Not long ago, he'd been a mason in Philadelphia, lost, wondering what to do next, hopeless. With the war over, he hadn't been sure where he fit.

His thoughts turned to Sergeant Blair's Bible and the spiritual discussions he'd enjoyed with Father McKay. Was his time in the army to play a part now, guiding him toward his destiny?

"I'd like to say a prayer, if you don't mind."

Luke frowned at Danny's request, but Mr. Hanson grinned. "Definitely," the storekeeper agreed.

The three men bowed their heads as Jenny approached. Mr. Hanson grasped her hand and pulled her close, including her in the small circle of workmen. Danny pursed his lips at her nearness, but then closed his eyes and concentrated.

"Jesus, you've done this. You brought each of us to this place, for today. May this building always provide welcome and comfort to travelers, in your name. May this station be a place where your name is spoken freely, with reverence and love."

He paused, the emotion welling within him, his heart full. This was what God wanted, right? Didn't Father McKay say something about the Lord bringing to completion every good work begun in Christ?

He gritted his teeth, knowing the task wasn't complete yet. They still didn't have a stage contract for the station.

Jenny cleared her throat. "God, do mighty things here. We love you."

Danny opened one eye, glancing at her. She'd ended his prayer with simplicity, with the words he couldn't find. Abruptly, he felt grateful at her presence.

"Look," Jenny said, pointing to the northern horizon.

The final rays of the departing sun lingered overhead, a glowing intensity brimming the western edge of the massive bank of clouds.

Luke glanced at Danny. "God's painting the sky? Just for us?"

Danny nodded. "Just for us. He's with us, Luke."

At supper around the campfire, Jenny and the men ate quietly, too tired to speak of the day's work. All of them turned in early, the darkness outside preventing other options.

As Danny lay in his blankets, a low moan whispered in the notch between the bluffs, the wind forming staccato shrieks, scuttling the flames of the fire. The horses were securely picketed, Danny knew, having checked their tethers himself before turning in. Yet something made him feel restless, something unfinished.

Across the blaze in the deeper shadows at the back of the cavern, Mr. Hanson snored. Luke lay motionless, but Danny wondered if Jenny slept, tucked near the old storekeeper. Danny had caught her eyes upon him more than once today, making him feel a mixture of dread and anticipation. Why did he care what she thought of him? She was nothing to Danny. The little cross-grained girl seemed to always have an opinion on things that nettled him. Her presence made him uneasy.

The next morning dawned with a wind that blustered across the desert, carrying the scent of pine and sage. A gray sky stretched like a canopy above, threatening as they worked. By the time they finished the roof and moved their belongings into the completed station, large raindrops splattered the ground.

With the last load of gear, Danny kicked the front door shut as the rain fell in earnest. He glanced at Luke where the Indian knelt to light the kindling in the big fireplace, the spacious center room acting as parlor and dining room. To the left, he saw where Jenny's bedding littered the one bedroom. On the other end of the station, a door led into the kitchen, where Jenny worked to brew coffee.

"Just in time," Mr. Hanson remarked as he watched the storm from the narrow window beside the fireplace. He grinned at Danny over his shoulder and barred the shutters, drowning out the roar of the rainstorm.

"Good thing we didn't start for home today. I'm glad we helped finish the roof. The Lord knew we'd be better off here than on the road to town."

The storekeeper shot a meaningful glance at Jenny, but only Danny saw the covert look.

Shadows crouched all around the vacant room, yet slowly the firelight stretched to the farthest corner. Danny sat against the wall and nursed his steaming cup as Jenny poured drinks for the others.

"Snow maybe?" Luke slid down the wall beside Danny.

Mr. Hanson shook his head, his gaze fixed on Jenny as she leaned in the kitchen doorway, a pensive look creasing her features. "Don't worry, lass. Not cold enough for snow. I can get us home tomorrow. Lil can handle the store until then."

Jenny sipped her coffee and stole a quick glance at Danny over the rim of her mug. "I'm not worried," she said softly in a voice that made Danny's ears tingle. Was her comment for his benefit? He hated how much he hoped so.

"I think Indian summer will last," Mr. Hanson went on. "I'm eager to see Lil again, and I don't foresee any difficulty in returning to town after this rain."

"The trail will be all right?" Jenny's question held a note of regret.

"I think so. You boys should take advantage of this wet ground to work the trail, shape the road for stagecoaches."

Danny nodded, not replying. His gaze surveyed the rock walls and the cheerful fire crackling in the large fireplace. He'd done this, he'd built Patrick Blair's stage station. He eyed Jenny and moved on swiftly, not allowing his scrutiny to linger on the lovely girl.

He'd come west to finish a project, and now he drew a deep breath, satisfied with the results. Of course, the road needed to be cleared and the stage company must somehow be notified about the shortcut across the desert the station provided. But something still made Danny restless, like he hadn't completed the work the Lord brought him here for. Despite the strongly built rock building, something still felt undone within him.

CHAPTER TWENTY-SIX

Mr. Hanson was right, and the weather cleared, Indian summer settling warm and drowsy over the plains east of the Rockies. With the departure of Jenny and the storekeeper the next morning, Danny had turned his attention to developing the grassland pasture behind the gap in the bluff.

"What about the road, like Mr. Hanson suggested?" Luke dropped the heavy rock he carried at Danny's feet and wiped his hands on his pants.

Danny gestured to the narrow trench he'd dug in the damp earth. The rectangular shape should be just right for a water trough. "After this. The horses need a proper trough."

The three-foot-tall water trough was finished by sundown.

"In a day or two, we'll pound that pipe into the spring and see how this works," Danny said, indicating the section of bent pipe Luke had retrieved from the scrap heap near the mine.

"We'll have to build a fence across this opening," Luke said.

The two men gazed deeper into the narrow box canyon. Rocks of every size lay strewn across the uneven ground.

Danny knew they would have to clear pastureland of the stones, fearing the horses might break a leg. And perhaps the seep he'd discovered in the far reaches of the chasm could be developed into a water source, perhaps irrigating a garden plot.

Ideas swirled in his mind, and he smiled, enjoying the task of creating something out of nothing. The Lord had uniquely gifted him for this mission, and Danny enjoyed the challenge.

"We can do that when winter really comes, and we're stuck close to home. In the meantime, let's tackle that road."

Home? He pondered his choice of words as Luke brought the horses to the station to pack. While they loaded the animals with necessary tools and supplies, he wondered if the station would truly become his home. He'd never had a real home, never experienced a settled sensation. Would he ever find his place in the world? Did he belong anywhere?

When Luke closed the plank door to the station and grasped his horse's lead rope, Danny nodded. There was still much work to do, he reminded himself. The Lord gave him a responsibility, but God was ultimately responsible for the outcome. As long as Danny was faithful and diligent toward the job Jesus had given him, the results were up to God.

"Let's go," he said, leading the way from the clearing and taking the trail toward Trinidad.

For the next three days, they walked the trail to the west. Moving rocks and leveling hillocks, filling depressions and removing thick vegetation, they carved a road for a stagecoach to follow.

Danny felt amazed this portion of the trail seemed easy to shape. When he shared his opinion with Luke, the Indian nodded.

"Patrick had already done some work this way," he explained, pointing to a boulder that'd been shoved from their path. "Jenny told me he intended to connect with the Bloomberg's road from town."

"Yes, that would make sense. A few miles of road are already done."

As Luke halted the horses to wrestle another large rock from their path, Danny peered ahead, trying to catch a glimpse of the biggest ranch in the region. Thoughts of Reggie Bloomberg made him bristle.

Only the brown grass blowing in the chilled breeze met his searching gaze. In the distance, the Rocky Mountains loomed large, massive on the western horizon. To the south, the smaller Raton Range extended from the Rockies to the east, passing behind the stage station. Luke had reported he'd found a way to the top of the mesa above the station. Lots of cedar trees and a few other varieties blanketed the high desert, but few pines. Higher on the slopes of the mountains, vast forests of pine trees extended as far as the eye could see.

While Luke dug around the base of the big rock with his shovel, Danny glanced over his shoulder to scan the vast plains, stretching toward the east like an endless sea. Memories flooded his mind as he studied the lonely prairie. Philadelphia, the war, the orphanage, Father McKay, and meeting Christ for the first time. The Lord had done this, brought him here to the solace of the desert. But he'd found no solace yet. He sensed the potential, though, as if peace awaited him when he finished what he was supposed to do. Was it only to complete the stage station?

Danny scowled, feeling uneasy, as if the Lord spoke to him in riddles.

"What is it?" Luke leaned on his shovel, watching him.

Danny grunted and swung his pick, dislodging loose soil from the base of the rock at his feet. "I'm not sure," he admitted, taking another swing. "I feel ... well, I feel ... I don't know what I feel. But something isn't right. Something I can't put my finger on."

Luke grinned. "My old grandma says a wandering, restless spirit is expected in young men."

"Yeah," Danny corroborated as he dropped to his knees to scoop dirt from beneath the big rock. "That's probably it. I'm a restless man, that's all, looking for a place to belong. I wonder if Trinidad will become home for me."

Luke's grin widened. "Grandma also says a young man can't understand his restless heart alone."

Danny leaned his shoulder against the rock and pushed. The stone shifted. He scrambled to his feet and looked at Luke. "Well, I guess the Lord is teaching me about myself. I feel I'm on a journey out here, learning to connect with God while discovering more about my heart along the way."

Together, the two men grasped the huge rock and shoved it to the side of the trail. Using pick and shovel, they graded the loose soil into a wide path for a wagon to follow. When they'd finished the section of new road, Luke handed Danny a canteen.

His friend tilted his head as Danny drank thirstily. "I don't think Grandma was talking about God."

Danny wiped his mouth with the back of his hand before passing the canteen to Luke. "Who then?"

Luke grinned again. "You will have to learn that for yourself. Part of that journey you spoke of."

★★★

Short grass, juniper trees, mesquite, and rocks showed in every direction. To the north, the Arkansas River remained unseen, its tree-lined banks still too distant for Danny to see from here. Yet he searched the horizon often, wanting to familiarize himself with the terrain and landmarks.

He walked beside Luke, his shovel leaning on one shoulder as his rifle had done in the war. Without speaking, the two men would push stones from the trail or dig up manzanita bushes that blocked their way. He and Luke had become friends. Once, he'd repelled any effort to make friends, fearing they would leave or die. But after meeting Sergeant Blair and Nelson, Danny realized how much he wanted people around him. As if God were teaching him the importance of community, Danny understood that life without friends felt empty. To be alone allowed him to never grieve the loss of someone he cared about, but that kind of life now seemed so desolate.

He peered at the lonely desert around him and nodded, appreciating the Lord's guiding hand. "You brought me to this desert to show me what my life looked like before," he whispered. "Thank you, Jesus, for your methods of teaching me in ways that speak to me."

Luke straightened from the rock he'd removed. "What are you mumbling?"

Danny shrugged and pried a rock from the dirt with his pick. "Talking to Jesus," he muttered, not wishing his conversation with the Creator be disturbed.

Luke stared. "Does he speak back to you?"

They halted in the dull afternoon sunlight. Although Indian summer remained, a chill draft wafted from the heights, and Danny smelled the tangy scent of pine on the breeze. He believed they were more than halfway to Trinidad, the roadwork going well. He looked forward to a hot meal at Bill's Café, a cup of coffee he didn't brew over a campfire. Only a few more of the canvas water sacks remained, and the horses would drink most of that. His back felt sore from sleeping on the ground, and the image of soft hay in Mr. Edmond's loft made him eager to finish this section of road. Luke assured him this would be the easiest part of the road, the section northeast of the station to connect with the Arkansas River would take much longer.

Danny took a deep breath and peered up at the highest peaks of the nearby mountains. "Yes, God speaks. In the Bible, through his handiwork," he gestured to the white-capped summits. "And through his Spirit, guiding me as I navigate open doors, opportunities he brings to me."

"Sounds difficult," Luke grumbled, clearly not pleased with Danny's response.

A chuckle erupted from Danny as he stepped forward, back to work. "Sounds like an adventure to me," he said as he kicked a pumpkin-sized rock from their path. "He speaks, he prompts, he provides. I've never felt so alive in my life. He promises to be with me, wherever I go. I am never alone with Jesus by my side."

Luke grabbed his arm, stopping him once more. "What does he tell you right now?"

Danny arched an eyebrow. "Right now? He tells me you think of him. The Spirit tells me you want to know more."

Luke's eyes widened in surprise. "How can you know that?" His whisper was barely audible above the ceaseless wind.

Danny resumed walking. "I read in the Bible that the Word of God does not return empty handed. He is working on your heart, as he does on mine. In time, you will have to make a decision."

"What decision?" Luke hurried to catch up.

Danny halted again, and Luke almost bumped into him. "You will have to decide what to do with God. He is real, and he's calling to you. Will you worship him, will you accept the love he offers? Or will you ignore him and live only for yourself?"

From the corner of his eyes, Danny watched as Luke pondered his words. They worked in silence for a long while before his friend spoke.

"I think I know what you mean. Patrick told Grandpa similar words when Blair saved him from the miners. He told Grandpa about Jesus and living for God."

"The Lord offers grace, a free gift to all who accept him."

Luke didn't say anything further, and the day passed with another mile shaped and smoothed. That evening, as they sat around their little blaze, watching the flames dance as they sipped their coffee, Danny asked, "How far are we from Trinidad?"

Luke chuckled. "You ask this each night. I figure we're about ten miles from town, but only six or seven from Bloomberg's ranch."

Danny sat up, not realizing they were so close to finishing this section of the road. He tugged his collar higher against the raw wind blustering over the prairie, the flames fluttering as the gust passed.

"Maybe a couple more days and we'll be in town," Luke added, studying Danny intently.

Danny shrugged. "Good," he answered indifferently, hoping Luke couldn't see his excitement at nearing Trinidad. And Jenny Blair.

He thrust a stick into the fire, sparks fluttering skyward as Danny scowled. He'd tried to ignore the pretty girl, to not allow his mind to conjure her image as they cleared the road, but somehow the sergeant's sister wouldn't depart from his thoughts.

"You look suddenly mad, as if something is bothering you," Luke observed, rolling in his blankets.

"I'm all right," Danny growled, angry at his lack of focus.

He pushed a log into the fire and stretched in his blankets. Staring up at the night sky, he marveled at the countless stars twinkling above. He considered his presence on the plains, how Jesus maneuvered his path to intersect others the Lord wished him to impact, and the purpose of his coming west. Why was he here? Was it merely to complete Sergeant Blair's station? Or did God have something else in mind?

CHAPTER TWENTY-SEVEN

The Bloomberg ranch house sat on a low knoll a few miles from Trinidad. The two men had connected their crude stage route with the well-defined road that led past the fine house. Danny squinted at the lavish layout of the huge ranch, the impressive barns and numerous corrals. Reggie Bloomberg was wealthy, he reminded himself bitterly, turning away as he led the loaded horse up the road toward town.

"We could stay here tonight," Luke said, a hint of hope in his voice.

Shadows filled the folds of the tall mountains, the sun already vanished behind the crest. The temperature would surely drop with the sun, but Danny had no intention of staying at the Bloomberg house. He was about to say so when he halted in the deepening dusk, something in Luke's voice making him hesitate.

"You were fired from this ranch, but you'd stay the night?"

Luke shrugged. "Everyone knows it was Reggie, not Mr. Bloomberg or because of my performance. They'd let me stay for the night." He paused and then added, "The cook liked me. If I cut firewood or fetch water, he'll feed me."

"I'd rather make the trek to town," Danny muttered. "It's not far now."

Luke shifted in the gathering gloom. "Well, boss, my family is camping nearby. If I stay here tonight, I can find them in the morning. I'd like to take a few days to visit while you get supplies at Mr. Hanson's."

"Oh," Danny said, deflated. He would not stay in the same house with Reggie Bloomberg. "Of course, see your family. I'll see you at the station in a few days, Luke."

He reached into his pocket and withdrew some crumpled bills.

"We agreed I'd work for room and board," Luke protested as Danny pressed the bills into his gloved hand.

"Take it." Danny walked on, tugging on his horse's lead rope. "I wish I could give you more. See you in a few days," he repeated as the darkness swallowed him. In another minute, he couldn't hear Luke's boots crunching the gravel toward the sprawling ranch house.

Danny peered up at the countless stars that hung overhead, creating a canopy of shining lights that illuminated the road to town. He started walking, grateful he didn't have to clear rocks from this completed section of road. The shimmering lights above shone upon the compact gravel and dirt, revealing a well-trodden path. Despite the cold, the night was beautiful, brilliant in magnificence.

"You did this, Lord," he whispered as he strode toward Trinidad. His great fatigue subsided as he worshipped. "This land is yours, the work of your hand. Your splendor amazes me, and I praise you. Praise you for bringing me here ... to see your hand."

As if in a cathedral of immense proportions, Danny felt an awe—a reverence—surround him as he made his way to town. He'd never gone to church or sang songs or learned hymns, yet his soul yearned to speak, to connect with Jesus. His chest swelled as he felt the Spirit's presence.

The dull roar of the nearby river made him lift his gaze from the dark trail. He couldn't believe he'd arrived in town until the lantern light from a few stores indicated they were still open. He halted his horse and stared down the dusty street toward the big livery. No light showed in Mr. Hanson's mercantile, and many other places were dark, but yellow shafts of light stretched from the few saloons farther down the street, near the mine.

He walked on, leading his horse to the livery. Surely Mr. Edmonds would allow him to sleep in the loft. Danny grinned as he thought of the taciturn hostler, telling him the barn was no hotel, but relenting all the same.

He considered visiting one of the saloons to see if he could obtain a meal when he saw lanterns glowing in Bill's Café. Danny picked up his step, eager to settle his horse before returning for a late meal.

Mr. Edmonds was nowhere to be seen when he reached the barn, but Danny spent only a little time unsaddling his horse and pitching hay to the tired animal. Taking only an additional few minutes, he removed his coat and filthy, sweat-soaked shirt to bathe in the pump water beside the livery.

Shivering from the cold water, he pulled on a clean shirt from his pack and shrugged into his coat before striding toward the café, his stomach growling fiercely. As he entered the dining hall, he felt startled to see Mr. Hanson, a handsome older woman, Mr. Edmonds, and Jenny Blair seated at a table.

He hesitated, not wanting to intrude, when the storekeeper waved him over. Danny leaned his Henry rifle in the corner before removing his hat as Mr. Hanson greeted him with a firm handshake. "Danny, my boy, you know Michael Edmonds and Jenny, but I want you to meet my wife, Lil Hanson."

He nodded cordially to the hostler and arched an eyebrow when he nodded to Jenny. He wondered what she thought of his sudden appearance at the café, and then wondered if he were a fool. Surely, she thought nothing of him.

He smiled when he greeted Mrs. Hanson. The woman possessed an air of elegance and charm Danny immediately liked. "A pleasure meeting you, ma'am. And thank you for lending your husband last week to build the station. We couldn't have done it without him."

"Or me," Jenny interjected. "I was there too—working beside all you men."

Danny grinned at her, recalling her scraped hands as she handed stones to him to place in the wall. She also kept the workmen fed, preparing every meal so they could continue the labor.

"I appreciate all you did, Miss Blair." He stepped away, heading for an empty table, when Mr. Edmonds stood.

"Sit here, boy. I need to get back to the barn."

Danny hesitated only an instant before accepting the invitation. He felt pleased he'd taken the time to clean up a bit before coming to supper.

"By the way, I'll be sleeping in the loft, if you don't mind," Danny whispered as the liveryman moved for the door.

"'Tis not a hotel," Mr. Edmonds called over his shoulder as Danny took his vacant chair.

"And we'll be taking our leave too," Mr. Hanson said. He glanced meaningfully at Danny as he helped his wife to her feet. He shifted his glance to Jenny as he led Mrs. Hanson to the door. "You'll be all right until Reggie arrives?"

"Danny will keep me company." She waved to the older couple as they stepped into the night.

Startled to be left alone with Jenny, Danny feigned a confidence he didn't feel. He leaned back in his chair, hoping she didn't see the tremor in his hands as he reached for the coffeepot. "So, you're to meet Reggie Bloomberg here?" Steam rose as he poured, obscuring his view, but he stole a glance at her nonetheless.

She stiffened, a frown puckering her lips. "And why not? We're to be married."

"So I've heard." He raised the hot mug and blew softly, still watching her. "But I don't know why."

Danny felt his eyebrows climb. Where had that come from? He had no business asking such personal questions or making rude comments. The sergeant's sister was none of his concern.

"Is that any of your affair?" she asked in a flat tone, her chin rising.

He took another sip of his coffee. "Well, if I had a sister—"

"Which you don't," she hurriedly interjected.

Danny nodded. "Which I don't. But if I did, I'd want my friends keeping an eye on her in my absence."

"Oh, well, now," she countered as her eyebrows lifted. "I didn't realize my brother told you to keep an eye on me."

He shifted, his chair scraping the wooden floor. "He didn't," Danny confessed. "But I'm certain he would want me to, if he could've warned me before I came west."

Jenny's gaze narrowed as she leaned forward. "Warn you about what?"

She'd lowered her voice, and Danny remembered it wasn't healthy to say too much about Reggie Bloomberg in town. He was a wealthy rancher, and Danny was nobody.

"Is Reggie the sort of man your brother would approve of?"

Jenny smiled, lips tight, eyes brimming. "Patrick didn't like Reggie. But he doesn't have a say now, does he? He left me after I pleaded with him not to go."

She swiped at her eyes with her napkin. "I told him to stay, to help me. We were going to build the stage station. God guided Patrick to that water in the desert. But his honor demanded he fight injustice. He left me in the shack near the river, alone, frightened, cold, and starving."

"He didn't take care of you?" Danny scowled at this report of Sergeant Blair.

"At first, he did, sending his army pay every month. But the mail was unreliable from the front lines. Some months, his pay never reached me. I did without, and eventually Mr. Hanson gave me a job in his store, although I'm little needed now with Lil helping out."

She blew her nose and dabbed her eyes once more. Danny felt miserable he'd made her cry.

"You see? I've become a charity case, someone to pity. When Reggie Bloomberg asked me to walk out with him, I enjoyed his attention. I leaped at his suggestion we get married one day."

Danny's scowl deepened. "You don't love him. Your fear makes you accept his offer. But I know you value honor and bravery as much as your brother did. I saw that at the dance."

Her face paled as she glowered at him across the table, but Danny couldn't stop himself from continuing. "You were frightened, your brother died, you needed help. But enough to marry a man you don't love?"

"I vowed to never be hungry again," she snapped, leaning back in her chair, eyeing him intently. "I know what you must think of me, but I don't care. I was alone, scared, and Reggie offered me security."

The front door opened, and Danny turned. Reggie Bloomberg stood in the doorway, his wide grin slipping when he saw Jenny and Danny seated together. He hurried to their table.

"Jenny, I'm sorry I'm late." He studied the silent girl. "You've been crying," he accused, and his gaze turned to Danny. "I'll kill you if you butt in where you're not wanted, Mason," the young rancher growled.

Danny smelled liquor on his breath.

"We were just talking about you, Reggie," Danny said as he rose to his feet. He noticed the pistol holstered at the rancher's belt, and Danny glanced at where his rifle leaned in the corner. Jenny stood hurriedly.

"Come away, Reggie." She grasped his arm and dragged him toward the door.

"Stay out of my way, Mason," Bloomberg shouted as Jenny propelled him around the tables. Reggie stumbled but quickly regained his balance. "I'm warning you to stay away from Jenny Blair."

CHAPTER TWENTY-EIGHT

Reggie's final words lingered in the dining hall after he and Jenny disappeared into the night. Danny sat alone in the quiet café, pondering his brief encounter with the sergeant's sister, wishing he could go back in time and start this evening over again.

Gertie approached his table, hesitating with a glance toward the door before nodding at Danny. "Kitchen's closed, but we still have a pot of chili on the stove."

"Chili is fine," Danny mumbled, attempting to hide behind his coffee cup as he took another sip. But Gertie dawdled, wiping his table with a damp rag. When she caught his eye, she smiled.

"I think Jenny Blair puts on a bold front, but I think she feels very alone."

"She has Reggie." Danny couldn't keep the bitter sting from his voice. "She's not alone anymore."

Gertie shook her head. "You're wrong, young man. Look past the surface." She scurried back to the kitchen.

While Danny ate his chili, he mused over the plump woman's words. Could Jenny be lonely like Danny? He'd been lonely all his life, even in an orphanage full of boys.

Even during the war, keeping his distance from the other soldiers. Somehow, Patrick Blair had slipped past his defenses and made an impact.

A grin touched his lips as he recalled the sergeant and the old trapper, Nelson, being more of an example than Danny had realized. They were two good men, dead now, but not forgotten.

"They inspired me to learn more about you, Christ," he whispered over his dinner. "What am I to do with their memory? Did they teach me anything I can pass on to others?"

Nothing came to him, no soft whisper in the vacant room. Only the gentle banter between Bill and Gertie drifted from the kitchen where they cleaned.

With a sigh, he heaved to his feet, tossing a coin on the table. "Thanks." He waved through the window to the back room as he lifted his rifle and left the café.

Bill called goodnight in return, and then Danny stood in the darkness, fewer lights now shining along the main street. He made his way thoughtfully to the livery where he climbed into the loft and tried to go to sleep, turning restlessly despite his fatigue.

Morning came too soon, and Danny didn't hurry to crawl from his blankets. He and Luke had worked hard building a road in the cold—the wind never ceasing from the snow-covered heights above. Yet, they'd accomplished a great deal. True, they'd followed a marked trail. Again, he worried about the unknown piece of land beyond the station.

What now? He felt the most difficult aspects of this ordeal remained. He didn't have a contract with the stage company, and the longer piece of land to the Arkansas River still needed to be cleared. Perhaps that land was too challenging to build a road across. He felt foolish he'd made decisions without scouting the entire route before beginning construction. Perhaps he'd wasted his time coming west to finish Sergeant Blair's dream.

He scowled as he threw back his covers and tugged on his boots, doubts flooding over him. No. The Lord brought him here, he reminded himself stubbornly. Keep the faith, he coaxed, fussing over his horse for an hour before walking to Bill's Café.

Inside, he nodded to Old Crawford, the stage driver who delivered Danny to Trinidad many weeks ago. The grizzled codger nodded in return, and Danny located a corner table, wanting to be alone with his thoughts.

"Hot cakes and venison," Gertie welcomed him as she placed a coffeepot on his table. He nodded his thanks and poured coffee. As the waitress disappeared into the kitchen, a man in a dark suit entered the dining hall. Danny watched as the stranger surveyed the room before his face brightened, and he made a beeline for Danny's table.

"Mr. Mason?" The stranger removed his hat and reached for a chair. "May I sit with you?"

Danny squinted but nodded, intrigued.

The man sat and leaned forward. "I understand you're building a road, a shortcut across the desert."

Danny blinked. "Well, uh, yes, I am."

The man beamed. "Excellent. I'm Hennessey, mine manager. Few secrets remain hidden in a small town like Trinidad, Mr. Mason, and I wanted to talk business with you. I'm in charge of shipping ore to Westport Landing."

Danny nudged an empty cup toward Mr. Hennessey. "Go on."

The mine manager filled his own mug. He blew the steam away and tasted the coffee before continuing. "The section of road from Trinidad down the Purgatory to the Arkansas and then to Old Bent's Fort is the worst section of road on the Santa Fe Trail. If you've found water on the desert—"

"I have," Danny inserted.

"Good, well, if you've found water and can cut a trail across the desert, you would shorten the amount of time it takes my freighters to deliver coal."

Hennessey paused, as if waiting for Danny's response. Over the mine manager's shoulder, he saw Old Crawford straining to hear their conversation.

"I have developed a spring about halfway from town to Bent's burned-out fort. The station is almost complete and will provide water to freight animals, although I'd hoped to land a contract with the stage company."

Hennessey shook his head. "I have to admit I care little about the stage. What about the road? Have you blazed a trail across the prairie?"

"I have a passable road from town to the station, but I haven't begun the route farther on," Danny admitted as Gertie placed a plate before him.

She smiled at the mine manager. "Good morning, Mr. Hennessey. We don't see much of you around here, what with the mine having their own mess kitchen for the miners. I guess you realize where the best food is served." Her sly grin made Hennessey laugh.

"I know Bill is the best cook in town, no argument from me." He sipped his coffee.

"Did you want breakfast, sir?"

"No, no, thanks, Gertie. I had breakfast hours ago. Coffee will do." Hennessey turned back to Danny when the waitress retreated. "Well?"

Danny frowned. "Well what?"

"Well, when will the other section of road be complete? I am eager to send my freighters the shorter route if the road is better."

"So, you'll pay for water?" Danny had never negotiated with businessmen, and he wondered if he was doing things right. But Mr. Hennessey seemed sincere.

"I'll pay a dollar a wagon, regardless of livestock, when you get the road open."

"Regardless of livestock?" Danny felt out of his element.

Mr. Hennessey smiled. "That means you get a dollar for every wagon I send through your station, regardless of the number of horses or oxen or mules pulling each wagon."

Danny nodded, understanding finally dawning. Then he shrugged. "But I have to complete the road first. And winter is fast coming."

"That's right." The mine manager drained his cup and stood. "Let me know when the job is done. I want to send ore that way as soon as possible." He replaced his hat and hurried to the door.

Before Danny could consider the mine manager's words, Old Crawford stood beside his table, peering down at Danny with shrewd eyes. "I don't know anything about stage contracts or the like, but I heard a rumor the Holladay company might be selling to Wells Fargo."

"I heard the same rumor." Danny lifted his fork, hoping to take a bite before his food grew cold.

"Well, I know when companies change hands, they often send new drivers for me to train. I haven't seen one yet."

"So, I have time." Danny guessed the cryptic message from the stage driver.

Crawford turned to go. "Good luck, sonny. I'd rather go a different way than following the Purgatory River. Too rough, too hard on my teams."

After finishing his breakfast, Danny made his way to the general store. He'd penned a note to Father McKay and wanted to pick up a few more supplies. When he entered the mercantile, Jenny saw him first, glaring at him before she flounced to a far corner of the store.

Mr. Hanson chuckled as he greeted him. "I don't know what you said to her last night after we left you at the café, but she isn't overly excited to see you today."

"No, she's not," Danny muttered as he handed the storekeeper the letter to Father McKay and his order. He vowed to ignore Jenny Blair as much as she ignored him. She was none of his business, the sergeant's sister or not. But the road through the desert was.

"I'll need these supplies, Mr. Hanson." As the older man surveyed the items on the list, Danny shifted. "I see Mr. Edmonds has forgiven you for stealing his girl."

Mr. Hanson lifted his gaze from the note and grinned. "Michael is my best friend, but between you and me, he never had a chance with Lilian." He chuckled and nudged Danny with an elbow. "Don't tell him that."

"No, sir, I won't," Danny promised.

Hanson's eyes narrowed, studying Danny. "Sometimes a man gets an idea in his head that a girl might belong to him, but well, he could be wrong."

At Danny's confused look, Hanson went on. "Take Reggie Bloomberg, for instance."

When Danny continued to frown, the storekeeper sighed and walked away, beginning to gather items from the shelves.

Danny's gaze roamed the crowded store until he located Jenny near the bolts of brightly colored cloth in the far section of the mercantile. Heat stole up his neck when he realized he'd searched for her. He turned away swiftly before she caught his stare, but he saw Mr. Hanson watching him.

The storekeeper moved closer, leaning in as he spoke. "She's spoken for, or so she says. But I don't see a ring on her finger." He nudged Danny again. "You knew her brother, and I can vouch for her character. She can be feisty, make no mistake, but she's a good girl and very dear to me and Lil."

Danny felt his eyes widen. "Mr. Hanson, I don't know what you mean," he sputtered, taking a step backward. He bumped into a stack of blankets, which tumbled to the floor. Danny scurried to pick them up, folding them clumsily as he tried to tame his whirling thoughts.

Mr. Hanson laughed loudly, attracting Jenny's attention and horrifying Danny further. "Don't worry, son. Your secret is safe with me," the storekeeper said as he patted Danny's shoulder.

For the next hour, Danny hovered in the farthest corner from Jenny, trying to keep his distance from the keenly observant storekeeper as well.

Later that day, he pondered Mr. Hanson's curious remarks all the way back to the station.

CHAPTER TWENTY-NINE

For two days, Danny worked around the station, enjoying the silence. Loneliness suited him, he told himself as he moved rocks in the narrow notch between the bluffs, clearing pasture for horses to graze without tripping over cumbersome stones.

When he'd first arrived at the vacant station, he'd found tracks around the makeshift water trough pressed into the mud. Deer, mountain sheep, a coyote, and even a mountain lion had left prints, visiting the spring to drink the precious water. He vowed to leave access for wildlife, even after the station was operational.

As the familiar quiet bore down on him, he recalled how much he felt comfortable being alone. He was a loner, he mused, an island. And he liked things that way, quiet and peaceful. No one to bother him, no one to interrupt his life.

The problem was, he knew he lied.

He blamed Sergeant Blair. The kind Christian had easily sidestepped Danny's defenses. Despite his best efforts, Danny realized the sergeant had impressed him with his noble character and tireless zeal to serve others. Bravery and courage were rolled together in the sergeant's makeup, forcing Danny to consider his own character. With Christ's help, Danny felt he was growing, learning what God desired. And he loved it.

Thrown into an adventure he never anticipated, Danny found himself on the frontier, forging something out of nothing. Like him, the empty desert was being transformed—into a home, a stage station he'd built with his own hands. Also, he had new friends in Colorado Territory. He felt involved, active, a part of a community like he never felt in Philadelphia. Yet, nothing was going as predicted.

The stage station might very well become a stopover watering place for freight wagons carrying coal. If ore wagons came here, perhaps in time, other freight might pass through his homestead. Sergeant Blair's dream was coming to fruition—kind of. Perhaps it was developing into something else, like Danny.

He bent to remove another rock from the canyon floor. Jenny Blair darted into his mind, and he pushed her image away, irritated he couldn't keep her from his thoughts. The pretty girl annoyed him, Danny told himself over and over. Her admirable spunk contrasted with her willingness to unite with such a jerk as Reggie Bloomberg. Could wealth and security really be worth sacrificing her self-respect, her true self?

He shook his head and kicked at another embedded stone. His boot struck the immobile rock and he winced, angry at his rash attempt.

Why did he waste effort contemplating her issues? Certainly, the sergeant's little sister was none of his concern. Little sister? Hardly, Danny mused, remembering how she looked the night of the dance, the lantern light on her long hair, the way she felt in his arms.

He shook his head again with a reprimanding wobble.

Giving up on clearing more stones from the box canyon, Danny walked to the gap, halting beside the empty stone water trough. A gentle breeze wafted across the plains as he scanned the horizon. He craned his neck, searching the road from the west for signs of Luke. He should've been back by now. He couldn't wait to thrust the bent pipe into a crack in the back wall of the shallow cavern that concealed the hidden spring. Little by little, the desert station was coming together, but he needed Luke's help to complete things.

Danny drew a deep breath as he gazed over the silent land around him. "What are you doing with me, Jesus? Where's the peace I read about in your Word? I feel anxious, unsettled, as if something is going on I don't understand."

He squinted, searching for answers among the scrub oaks and mesquite that lined the shallow gullies. The wind rustled tumbleweed across the clearing where the rock station stood, and Danny frowned, feeling forlorn and wretched. What if Luke didn't return? Besides not being able to continue work alone, Danny missed his new friend.

"Two steps forward, one step back," he mumbled into the silence. "I came west, homesteaded this land, built the station, and shaped a passable road to town. But I have no stage contract, the longer road across the desert to the Arkansas isn't even started, and I'm upset with Jenny."

He felt like the Hebrews after they left Egypt. After watching God work in amazing ways, they swiftly turned to complaints and doubts. Hadn't God carried him through the war? Hadn't the Lord brought him from an empty life in Philadelphia? Did God bring him here only to forsake him now?

He drew another deep breath of the crisp air. "Don't let my faith waver so quickly, Lord. Let me trust you brought me here for a purpose, an elusive goal you are working through. Help me be patient."

But as the third day passed since he'd returned to the station, Danny's anxiety mounted. With no one to help, Danny struggled to add to the stone fences they'd begun in the gap between the bluffs. In frustration, he abandoned the project and started cutting firewood, knowing an endless supply of fuel would be necessary to heat the station through the winter. From the nearby mountains, cold wind gusted, reminding him winter was at hand. Already the towering peaks were crowned with thick snow.

"You drive me crazy, Lord. What am I doing out here? I can't complete this mission. What was I thinking? You've asked too much of me. I'm not cut out for this mission. You should've asked someone else to finish Sergeant Blair's station."

He dropped his gaze to study his boots, feeling despair creep over him like a fog. Had Jesus fooled him, brought him out here on a whim? Was Danny on a wild goose chase?

In the distance, he heard a horse's whinny. Danny lifted his eyes to peer west, following the Trinidad road. His brow bunched when he saw a cluster of Indians moving toward him, some mounted on ragged horses, others walking. He glanced to where his Henry rifle leaned close by, then lifted a hand to shield his eyes from the descending sun as the group advanced. As they neared, a young man waved. Relief washed over Danny when he recognized Luke.

"Sorry I'm late, boss," Luke greeted as the tired travelers bunched beside the stone station. An old man stepped forward, extending a hand. "This is my grandpa, Peter Walking Stick," Luke introduced as Danny met the old man's firm grip.

"You knew Patrick Blair." Danny studied the old Indian as Peter studied him in return.

"A good man," Peter said in a gruff voice. "Luke tells me he did not return."

Danny nodded, feeling nostalgic for his military comrades. Emotion surged, filling him with memories he didn't want to revisit. Not now. Now, Christ was with him. Right? He hoped so, hating his doubts held power to sway his fledgling faith.

He said nothing as the Indians began to set up camp. Mostly children and a few women, the group contained three teenage boys.

Luke grinned. "I would've been here sooner except Grandpa insisted the family come along. He has a proposition for you."

Danny felt his brows lift. "For me?"

Peter nodded. "First, I must help my people settle. These were long days of travel for the little ones. Let us set up camp, and then we will talk." He pointed to the stone station. "Perhaps you will invite me in tonight for coffee."

Curiosity coursed through Danny. "Sure. Coffee tonight, after you've settled. And welcome." He gestured all around the clearing and the gap in the bluff that led to the chasm of grasslands he'd recently cleared. "And let your horses graze in the box canyon."

Luke and Peter nodded before returning to assist with the camp chores. As the sun dipped behind the Rocky Mountains, a small cooking fire brightened the desert where the Indians set up camp. Fur-covered lodges soon appeared, as if nomadic life was not unfamiliar to this small group of Indians.

Danny watered his horse at the dugout trough before tethering him on a likely patch of grass in the canyon. He watched as his visitors made themselves at home, watering their few horses and carrying water to their campsite. He ate a meager meal of dried venison and stale bread he'd picked up at the café when he was in town. Stoking the fire inside the station, he shoved the filled coffeepot into the coals, anticipation mounting as he prepared for Peter's visit.

He looked up when the door opened. Luke and Peter came in from the darkness and sat at the table and benches Mr. Hanson had fashioned with remnants of lumber. The storekeeper had also built a sideboard in the kitchen.

As Danny poured coffee into mugs, he watched the two Indians from the corner of his eyes. They didn't wear bright beads or feathers, nor did they have long hair. Dressed in flannel shirts and workmen's pants, they seemed more modern than Danny would've guessed Indians on the frontier might be.

Peter grinned as Danny handed him a steaming mug. "Thank you, Danny. Luke tells me you are here to complete what Patrick wanted."

Danny sat at one end of the table, nodding as he sipped his hot drink, waiting.

"Luke also tells me you are from Philadelphia." At Danny's surprised look, the old man chuckled. "I am a Delaware, from the same region. I came west over forty years ago to trap the high mountains. But now I'm old, and I ponder more than I work. We have almost everything we need, for the land provides. We go into the mountains each spring but return to the prairie each winter. The snow is too deep higher up, and the cold lingers in my bones."

He sipped coffee as his gaze roamed the stone building before turning to his grandson. "You helped build this?"

Luke smiled proudly.

"Patrick Blair saved me from a beating, perhaps saved my life," Peter added with a sharp glance at Danny.

"He saved my life too," Danny said quietly. "On the battlefield."

"Ah? So, you feel you owe him, like I do." Peter grinned. "We have more in common than just where we are from."

No one spoke for a long moment as the three men drank coffee. Inside the large stone fireplace, the fire crackled merrily. Outside, the cold wind whipped around the station like a hungry wolf, trying to get in.

"Like I said, we come down from the mountains to locate a place to winter, to sit out the cold months. Luke says you need help building a road. Pushing rocks from the trail and working the dirt with shovels and picks."

Danny tilted his head. "Road work is hard work, especially in winter. It will be very cold."

"But you will feed us? If we build your road, you will provide food?"

Doubts assailed Danny as he narrowed his eyes, evaluating the old man and his family. "This is hard work," Danny reiterated. "Maybe too hard for such young helpers." He gestured to the Indian encampment beyond the stone walls.

Peter and Luke exchanged a sly grin. "Have no fear of our abilities," Peter said with another chuckle. "We are a tough people, used to difficult ways. We can surely shape a road across the desert. Difficult tasks shape boys into men." His laughter died away, and he grew serious, an eagerness shining in his dark eyes as he leaned forward, lowering his voice. "Luke also says God speaks to you."

Danny frowned before he glanced at his friend. Luke squirmed on the bench. "Well, yes, I said that. But I meant the Lord speaks to me through the Bible and through the works of his hand. The beautiful mountains and the solitude of the desert, the emptiness of the vast plains, they speak to me of God's presence."

Peter nodded, laid a hand on his grandson's shoulder, and peered at Danny with a stoic look etched into his lined features. "Yes, yes, I see what Luke meant. You think in deep ways, like me. Patrick told me similar things. Your troubles and your pain, the sorrow you've felt, speak to your heart, helping you search for meaning."

He held his empty cup up and Danny hastened to fill the mug. His gaze locked with the old man, and he wondered at the significance of this unexpected meeting.

Peter sipped his hot coffee, watching Danny over the rim of his cup. "You know God."

Again, Danny nodded, feeling unsure and yet strangely confident, as if this moment had been ordained.

Peter slapped the table with the palm of his hand, making Danny jump. "Then we will build your road this winter, and you will feed us." A light gleamed in his old eyes. "And you will tell us about God."

CHAPTER THIRTY

Danny sat his horse, pulled on his gloves, then drew his collar higher. With a wave to the Indians, he turned his mount toward town. It was a long ride, and he hoped to reach Trinidad by early afternoon.

A bitter wind rustled across the plains, but he focused more on walking his horse, the rested animal eager to run. "Not yet, boy." He patted the gelding's neck.

He shot a final glance over his shoulder before the road led around a corner of the bluff, cutting off the station from his view. On the road beyond the station, he saw the small crew of five Indians, heading to the east. Peter, Luke, and the three teenage boys marched along, shovels and picks over their shoulders. A pair of horses walked with them, strong harnesses and several canvas water sacks strapped to the animals' backs. The long strap had proven essential for pulling stubborn stones from the trail.

When he faced forward once more, Danny forced himself to relax, to enjoy the break from his ever-vigilant companions. For the past week, they'd watched him intently, listening attentively each evening as he read from the Bible. They hadn't peppered him with questions he couldn't answer, much to his relief. Yet they'd leaned toward him each night, on the edge of their seats, as if he held the secrets to the mysteries of life.

"Lord, what have I gotten myself into?" Danny nudged the gelding into a trot, hoping to warm them both on the morning ride. He squinted as he felt the dull sunlight on his shoulders. "What have *you* gotten me into?"

In a week's time, they'd covered the two major portions of the Bible, Old and New Testament, and the introduction and exit of Christ in the Gospel of John. Then the coming of the Holy Spirit.

Danny shook his head. "Too much, Jesus. I don't know what I'm doing. I've only been a Christian half a year. What do I know of the Scriptures?"

His complaint went unanswered, but Danny settled into the saddle, content to have time to consider. Only a week had passed since he felt alone, abandoned by God, filled with anxiety. Then, Luke and his family had appeared, eager to work. His nervousness had been for nothing. Danny couldn't ignore how the Lord provided a team to help with the road construction. But now he had the added load of additional mouths to feed. And Peter Walking Stick's family could eat a lot of food. Gratefully, the women had taken over cooking duties. But they'd plowed through his meager supplies in a week. He'd have to hurry and return before the remnant of rations were consumed.

He eased the strap of his rifle on his shoulder before tugging his hat brim low. The cold wind stung his cheeks and nose, and he promised himself a scarf would be among his order of supplies. He'd given his to one of the young boys. Gloves and scarves for all the Indians too.

Would he see Jenny? Danny blinked, not wishing to think of the sergeant's sister. But thoughts of Jenny Blair seemed too strong to so easily be ignored. With a sigh, he allowed himself a moment of reflection on the pretty girl.

Her pert nose reminded him of Sergeant Blair, but a scattering of freckles across her cheeks and the way her gray eyes flashed when he said something she didn't like made him grin. He respected her sense of independence, although he felt annoyed she'd cast it away so easily for the likes of Reggie Bloomberg.

He wondered why she often wore her hair in a tight bun, severe and austere. An image of her the night of the dance dashed across his mind, and he grinned, recalling the delicate curl of her long tresses. He'd almost tucked a loose strand behind her ear, stunned at the impulsive desire. Or at the mercantile, when he saw her hair woven into a single braid, thick and lustrous, hanging down her back. He enjoyed looking at her chiseled features and slim figure, but he had to admit it was her eyes that captivated him.

Danny shook his head, clearing his wandering thoughts. "Forgive me, Christ. I like Jenny, nothing more. She is the sergeant's sister. As I try to honor his memory, show me how to serve her as well. She's an orphan, like me. I can't understand her grief at losing a brother, but I understand sorrow. Use me, as you see fit."

He peered at the finished road beneath him. They'd done well, he and Luke, to shape the trail into a usable wagon path. He stared as he passed the campsite the Indians had used when coming to the station, a ring of blackened stones revealing where their fire had been.

Anxiety filled him at thought of the spiritually inquisitive Indians. They thought he knew more than he did. He recalled the way Jesus had delivered the sergeant's journal into his hands, the way Danny had pondered a purposeful life, and the way God had brought him to Father McKay.

The kindly priest had shared details of the Christian faith Danny cherished. The Lord had touched his heart, drawn him to God. But he still knew so little. How could he impart his small measure of knowledge without embarrassing himself?

He grinned as his gaze rose to the lofty heights before him, the towering peaks blanketed in glistening white splendor. "Lord, you brought me here. This is all your doing. I want to obey you, share what I know with others, but I'm no preacher."

He hoped his candor might persuade God to give him a pass. Instead, Danny sensed the Lord wanted more from him. "Jesus, I'm telling you I can't. I don't know much about you or the Bible. How can I share with Peter's family what I don't know?"

Again, a feeling of encouragement flooded over him, as if urging him to press on. Danny chuckled. "Persistent, aren't you? Well, I lay the responsibility at your feet. If you want me to speak with the Indians, you must give me the words."

As his gaze dropped to the road once more, he felt surprised to catch sight of the Bloomberg ranch. He was only a few miles from Trinidad now—the day had passed swiftly while he wrestled countless thoughts and ideas. The familiar feeling of loneliness had never reached him today, and he felt he'd spent quality time with a good friend.

"Thanks, Jesus, for riding with me," he whispered as he trotted past the Bloomberg house.

He frowned as he studied the wide porch and the spacious house, the numerous barns and corrals. Why wouldn't Jenny be impressed by the Bloomberg wealth? Danny was. She would be mistress of this fine ranch one day. Knots coiled in his guts at the thought.

When he trotted into town an hour later, the dusty street stretched quietly in the dull afternoon sunlight. Only a few wagons stood in front of the mercantile or the café. Past the livery barn, a couple of horses stood hitched to the rail before a saloon, closer to the mine.

Danny glanced into the mercantile when he passed, then felt irritated when he realized he searched for Jenny through the front window. His stomach growled as he passed Bill's Café, and he promised himself a good meal after putting up his horse at the livery.

"Hello, Danny," Mr. Edmonds greeted when the hostler came from the shadows of the big barn, a pitchfork in one hand. "You're getting to be a regular visitor in town."

There seemed to be an implied question in his tone, but Danny ignored the unspoken inquiry and handed the older man his reins. "I hope to be in town only overnight. A little grain would be appreciated."

Mr. Edmonds nodded, his gaze following Danny as the young man started for the café. "I guess you'll want the loft."

"Thanks, Mr. Edmonds," Danny called over his shoulder, picking up his pace.

The cold wind blustered down the main street, kicking up dust devils that swirled and vanished.

It took almost an entire pot of coffee before Danny felt thawed. Gertie was an attentive waitress, keeping his cup filled. As he ate his meal, he listened to the friendly banter between the plump woman and the portly cook. They seemed happy, and Danny wondered if he might ever take a wife—someone to share conversation and life with.

His fork paused in midair, and Danny narrowed his eyes. Why would he think such thoughts? He wasn't here for himself. He had important duties to perform.

After his meal, he strode to Mr. Hanson's General Store, a sense of anticipation swelling as he neared the big rock building. The bell jingled overhead as he pushed through the door, his gaze roaming for signs of Jenny. He stilled when he caught sight of her.

As Mr. Hanson weaved a path around barrels and stacks of dry goods, Danny couldn't tear his eyes from the slender girl where she helped a woman cutting fabric. Her brown hair hung down her back, the afternoon sunlight gleaming on the long braid. Danny caught his breath, mesmerized.

"Danny, my boy." The cheerful storekeeper slapped him on the shoulder and grinned. "How goes the road building? Weren't you here only a week ago?"

Danny tore his gaze away, feeling his ears tingle. "Luke's family has joined me. I need more supplies," he explained hastily, fumbling in his pocket for his list. "I'll need more supplies, Mr. Hanson," he repeated absently as his eyes went to Jenny once more.

Annoyed, he looked away again, trying to find something else to occupy his sight. Remembering his reason in town, he settled on the storekeeper.

"I'll need to discuss credit with you."

"You're new in town. Mr. Hanson doesn't extend credit to people we don't know."

Jenny's unexpected presence at his elbow made him jump. He peered at her, drinking in her loveliness before glancing away. He shifted again, feeling the heat rise to his cheeks.

Mr. Hanson nodded, eyes shining. "A wonderful suggestion, Jenny. We don't extend credit to strangers. Danny, you'll have to come to dinner tonight, to our home. This is a perfect opportunity to get better acquainted. Say ... six-thirty?"

Without waiting for a reply, the storekeeper moved to help another customer. Danny looked at Jenny, seeing the same surprise he felt reflected in her features.

"That's not what I had in mind," she grumbled in a low voice.

Danny grinned, suddenly feeling excited. "I'll look forward to tonight, Miss Blair."

She glowered, her smooth face pinching. "I will not, Danny Mason. You've made a mess of things between me and Reggie." She squinted even more, her lips pursing into a thin line, as if she wanted to say more but couldn't think of the proper words. "I wish you'd never come to Trinidad," she finally snarled. With a twirl of her dress, she fled.

CHAPTER THIRTY-ONE

For the remainder of the day, Danny kept his distance from the mercantile. He'd spent the late afternoon hours helping Mr. Edmonds around the livery instead.

"I appreciate your help, Danny," the hostler said more than once. However, mucking out the stalls and pitching hay from the loft to the horses below allowed Danny the time he craved to ponder his surmounting responsibilities, his entanglement with Jenny Blair, and his blossoming faith.

He stilled, resting the end of the pitchfork on the toe of his boot. A cold zephyr raced from the mountains, a gray sky heralding severe weather. Would the storm hold off long enough for his return to the station? The Indians would need his supplies, but not for a few days.

He speared the fork into the pile of hay. "I feel over my head," he muttered, letting his thoughts flow as he spoke with God. "The station was easy. I get that. But building a road across the desert? And now sharing my faith with Luke's family? You have me in deep water, Jesus, more than I signed up for. "

He felt vindicated throwing that tidbit onto the Lord's shoulders. He could build with stone but telling others about God seemed beyond him.

"And I never saw the coal mine wanting to use the spring. I feel you are introducing unexpected situations, events I never anticipated."

As he worked, he began to grin. "Oh, I see. You are in control, I'm not. I don't need to anticipate any of this. You will handle things in your ways, right?"

His grin faded as he recalled Jenny. Danny stopped tossing hay and lifted his gaze to the highest peak of the barn, the apex shrouded in shadow. "And you know I know nothing about girls. What are you doing with my heart? I feel—I mean, I think—" He shook his head. "I don't know what I feel."

★★★

When Danny knocked on the Hanson's door later that evening, his chest tightened. Despite the cold, his hands felt moist, and he thrust them into his pockets as the door opened. Lil Hanson ushered him into a brightly lit parlor, where he was instructed to take a seat.

After the hostess had retreated to the kitchen, where he overheard Mr. Hanson arguing with Jenny in loud whispers, he sat with his hands griping his knees, his gaze surveying the small, comfortable room.

It had not been difficult to locate the Hanson's house, perched atop a small rise overlooking the Purgatory River. He wondered if the shack the Blairs had lived in was nearby.

A frown creased his features when he realized this was quite possibly the nicest home he'd ever visited. He looked up as Jenny entered the sitting room. She wore a light green dress, her long hair arranged in intricate fashion, cascading down her back, but her gray eyes seemed to crackle and spark as she stared at him.

"Good evening, Mr. Mason," she stated crisply. "Carl, er, Mr. Hanson requested I keep you company while supper is prepared."

Danny stood. "Suggested or demanded?" He gestured to a seat on the settee.

Jenny seemed to relax as she took the proffered seat, smoothing out her skirts. She dropped her gaze, not meeting his as he resumed his seat. "I guess you heard our row in the kitchen."

He snorted. "I think half the town heard your row."

She looked up quickly, eyes flashing, then cooled when she saw his grin. "Well, I admit I can get my back up. I don't like to be told what to do."

"Who does?" Danny shrugged. "I know I like things my way, but that doesn't mean there isn't a better way. Sometimes it's hard for me to remember that."

Jenny tilted her head, as if surprised by his reply. "Yes, yes, me too." She paused, studying him intently. "Not the answer I expected," she added softly.

He chuckled and leaned back. "I thought that was the intent of this evening's gathering, Miss Blair. To get to know one another better."

Before she could say anything, Mr. Hanson appeared in the doorway. "Quite right, young man. We're here to get better acquainted." He peered pointedly at Jenny before adding, "Supper is ready. Let's all move into the dining room."

Danny stood and allowed Jenny to go first as the storekeeper led the way down a short hallway to a dining room set with finely painted plates, two lanterns glowing brightly at either end of the table.

Mr. Hanson indicated a chair for Danny across from Jenny, and the trio sat as Lil delivered steaming platters from the kitchen.

"I should be helping," Jenny protested as she scooted from the table.

"No, no, dear," Lil corrected with a glance at her husband. "Remain seated." The older woman scurried to the kitchen for more dishes, while Jenny shot Danny a confused look, and Carl beamed.

"Everything smells delicious, Lil," he declared when his wife returned, arms loaded again.

"Thank you, Carl." She smiled as she stood beside her husband, surveying the lavish meal.

Danny had never seen so many dishes.

"Take your seat, Lil, and I'll say grace." Carl bowed his head as the others followed suit. "Lord, thank you for bringing Danny to our town and to our table. We're certain you have something significant for his presence among us." He paused for a moment. "And thank you for this wonderful meal. Amen."

Everyone said amen as faces lifted, but Danny thought maybe he was the only one who caught the curious look Jenny gave Mr. Hanson.

"So, Danny, tell us a little about yourself." Lil handed a dish to her husband. Carl served himself a mound of potatoes before passing to Danny.

"Well, Mrs. Hanson, not much to tell. I was raised in an orphanage in Philadelphia. When the war broke out, I waited until I was of age to enlist. I served in the same regiment as Patrick Blair."

He glanced at Jenny, but she stared at her plate.

"And were you with Patrick when he passed?" Her somber question seemed to make everyone still, a silence filling the room as Danny nodded.

"Yes, ma'am. He handed me his Bible and his journal before—well, before he died." He glanced again at Jenny, but she still wouldn't look at him.

"And what brings you to Trinidad?"

Carl's inquiry made Danny frown, his fork poised above his plate. Surely, they all knew he had read the sergeant's journal and felt compelled to travel west to finish the Blair dream. The stage station in the desert certainly wasn't his idea.

Jenny's silverware clunked to the table. All eyes turned at the sound.

"He is here because he has no life of his own." Her clipped words fell like freezing sleet.

Danny laughed, all eyes turning to him. "A truer statement has never been uttered," he said. "The Lord knew I had nothing but a talent with building stone structures. I had no life in Philadelphia, no family, no future. With the sergeant's journal and his Bible, I felt led here, like you said. But I never expected the way things are unfolding."

Carl leaned his elbows on the table. "Tell us, Danny, what do you mean?"

For the next half hour, he shared his concerns and how the Lord seemed to be answering them, bringing provision while, at the same time, introducing more complexity into the situation he faced.

Carl Hanson laughed, eyes bright. "He is like that, isn't he, Lil? Just when you think you know what the Lord is doing, he does something else, keeps you on your toes."

"'Tis true, Carl," Lil said as she nodded. "My own life is a testimony of God's clever plans to move someone where they didn't expect to go."

"I would love to hear of your own journey with Christ," Danny said after wiping his mouth with his napkin. He couldn't remember a more scrumptious meal. He lifted his coffee mug, sipping as he studied the Hansons over the rim of his cup. His gaze shifted to include Jenny, but she remained quiet, as if reluctant to join the conversation.

Lil cleared her throat, drawing Danny's gaze from Jenny. He felt his cheeks heat as he glimpsed his hostess exchange a knowing grin with her husband, as if they'd detected Danny's interest in Jenny.

"My introduction to Trinidad is an exciting tale, no doubt. Jesus works in miraculous ways. But tonight is to get to know *you* better. Tell us about Danny Mason."

Danny straightened, suddenly uneasy. He didn't like being in the spotlight. "Well, not much to tell. Joined the army, met Sergeant Blair, and here I am. You know most of the other details. His dream has become my purpose, my mission."

"Yes, but what of your dreams?" Lil's persistence unsettled Danny, and he shifted.

"My dreams?"

"Yes, dear," Lil pressed. "What do you want from life?"

Danny stared, uncertain how to respond. He'd never had dreams for himself. He'd expected to be dead long ago. What could he say now to placate his curious hostess? He considered explaining how he'd never imagined a future for himself. Dreams were for other people. Only with Christ had the doors opened for him to see beyond the shortsighted goal he'd followed in the war.

However, lately, thoughts had niggled within him, unexpected thoughts.

He tensed as his gaze darted again to Jenny. She watched him closely, as if truly interested in his reply. A heavy atmosphere descended upon the room, threatening to dispel the enjoyable evening as he grappled with his emotions.

Carl pushed back from the table, then began clearing dishes. "Perhaps that story is for another time, Lil, but I would enjoy telling Danny how you came to Trinidad last winter and the merry chase you led me on before I captured you for myself, dear."

Lil stood to help. "Captured my heart, you mean," she murmured as she carried an armload of dishes from the room.

When Jenny rose to assist, Lil shook her head. "No, dear, entertain our guest. I'll bring more coffee."

"But I want to help," Jenny complained as Lil vanished into the kitchen.

"Not tonight, Jenny," Carl said as he tagged after his wife.

"Oh," she growled when she was left alone with Danny. "They are forcing me to sit with you."

He stood quickly. "Then I will take my leave."

Jenny scowled but then motioned he sit down. "No, please don't go." At the confused look on his face, she went on. "I did not want your visit tonight, but the more I thought about your coming, the more I wanted to hear about Patrick." She shot a glance toward the kitchen and lowered her voice before continuing. "Besides, Carl and Lil would be cross with me if I chased you away."

She sat back in her chair, watching as Danny slowly took his seat once more. "You already know how angry I felt when he left me here alone. Struggling to survive. By God's grace, the Hansons and others showed me kindness I could never repay."

Her eyes drifted around the comfortable dining room. "They invited me to live with them, helping me escape the miserable shack near the river."

Danny lifted his mug and sipped. "What do you want to know?"

Jenny bit her lip. "I miss Patrick so much," she whispered. "Tell me what you remember, what you learned about him."

As Danny talked about the scout platoon and the march to the sea, he shared what he recalled about her brother's character, his intentionality, his strong presence among the soldiers. Patrick Blair's faith had come alive in the way he served his men.

When he told how the sergeant's manner had so intrigued Danny, made him curious about Blair's faith in Jesus, Jenny cried.

CHAPTER THIRTY-TWO

As Danny loaded the supplies on the horse's back, he glanced worriedly at the lowering sky. Since his meal with Jenny and the Hansons last evening, he'd struggled to keep his mind attentive on today's trip to the station. With impending weather hovering on the horizon, he needed to stay focused.

"You can return the pack animals on your next visit to town," Mr. Edmonds said as he slapped the rump of one of the additional horses.

Danny's fingers worked swiftly to tighten the ropes around the packs, despite the mounting cold. He dearly wanted his gloves back on, but he needed to secure the knots correctly. These supplies were essential for the work crew at the station.

His thoughts darted to the Indians. How had Luke's family fared? Danny felt chagrined at not thinking more of them since arriving in Trinidad. With a grin, he realized he'd thought too much of a captivating girl with gray eyes.

He completed the packing, the final knots secure, and he slapped another of the horses on the rump as he moved to his own mount. He stepped into the saddle and lifted a gloved hand to the hostler as a single snowflake drifted from the leaden sky.

"Maybe you should consider staying in town until the storm passes," Mr. Edmonds suggested, watching the snowflake multiply into a dozen more.

Danny shook his head and pulled his scarf over his face. "Luke's family will need these supplies." He nudged his horse forward. "See you, Mr. Edmonds, and thanks for letting me sleep in the loft."

He didn't hear the hostler's reply as he and the three pack animals moved toward the trail, the steel gray sky churning even more snow. Muted shapes outlined the familiar buildings Danny knew, but already the snow obscured Trinidad.

He reminded himself he'd marched in winter, worked in Philadelphia's snow, and endured freezing temperatures before. Could a prairie storm be any worse?

By the time he'd passed the Bloomberg ranch, he was wondering if Michael Edmonds might have been right. The snow fell in waves, blanketing the plains in a white cover that concealed familiar landmarks. Yet the outline of the new road indicated he was still moving in the right direction, and his horse seemed indifferent, plodding on faithfully.

He made another three miles before he topped a rise and allowed the horses to take a breather as he surveyed the countryside. He could see little beyond the immediate range of vision, the snow falling faster.

"Well, Lord, am I stupid? I sense I'm to go on. Luke's family will surely need these supplies, but I want to be wise. Should I turn back?"

A gust of wind whipped past him, making him snuggle deeper into his coat. He thought the horses seemed game, the cold not as bitter as before, but the snow fell thick and wet. Perfect snowman weather, Danny thought with a grin behind his scarf, recalling the wet snow of Philadelphia when he was younger.

"Another twenty miles, I figure," he mused and tugged his gloves on tighter. "Stay with me, Christ. I'll need your company."

For the next three hours, he made fair time, not losing his way once. The road had been clearly marked, big rocks shoved to the side, indicating the right trail. He stopped when he rounded a knoll, startled at the dozen head of buffalo shielded in the lee of the low hill. The shaggy beasts stood with heads down, backs to the wind as snow piled along their spines. Danny calmed the nervous horses and went on, marveling at how closely he could inspect the silent buffalo.

The frontier amazed him, impressed him, with its countless varieties of wildlife and breathtaking landscapes. He felt a warm glow in his chest when he thought of Jenny Blair, the most breathtaking view he'd ever encountered.

He shook his head. "Focus. You're risking everything on a feeling. Keep your eyes fixed on Jesus. Don't forget you have a job to complete."

He peered up at the falling snow. "I'm with you, Lord. You brought me here for something, a purpose you have special for me. Let me finish the task. Ride with me, Jesus. I need you."

Bolstered, he plunged on, straining to find the indications revealing the trail before him. When another two hours passed, he wondered if he'd lost his way, inadvertently passing the stone station and the notch in the bluff. After another hour, he felt certain he'd lost his way in the storm.

Panic surged, and he considered turning back to search for the elusive station. As he prayed, straining to see through the snow, a dull glow pierced the storm. Danny squinted, not trusting his blurred vision. Yes, the light remained. As he walked closer, he made out the dark bulk of the stone station, a lantern perched in the open window.

At his shout, a dozen people streamed from the building, all talking at once as they pulled him from the saddle and dragged his frozen body inside.

"Get some coffee into him," Luke ordered as he and Peter pulled on their gloves. "We'll take care of his animals."

Seated before a blazing fire, Danny sipped coffee while the women hurried to wait on him, tugging his boots off to place his ice-like feet onto heated rocks wrapped in burlap. In his absence, the Indians had vacated their camp and moved inside the station, filling the three rooms with their belongings. For a long moment, the Indians all stared at Danny, stealing sidelong glances at one another as the fire crackled in the fireplace. He grinned up at the two men when they burst through the door.

"What's wrong with you?" he asked when he realized they stared at him as if he weren't real. "I'm all right, only a bit cold." He paused, yet still no one spoke. "I want to thank whoever placed the lantern in the window. I'll bet that let in a lot of cold, but it surely helped me find the station in the storm."

Luke moved forward until he lowered himself to a bench, eyes fixed on Danny.

"What is it, Luke?" Danny sensed the Indian's unease.

The young man glanced at his grandfather before he spoke. "We were out of food when the storm hit. I figured you would wait it out in town. I've been hungry before, but we worried about the children. Grandpa said we should pray, like the Bible says. We argued, not sure."

Danny frowned, confused. "Not sure about what?"

Luke shrugged. "Your God is not ours. But Grandpa says you know God, and so we prayed."

Danny stilled, sensing significance in the telling. "So you prayed. I'm here now, safe."

Peter stepped forward. "Danny, we wondered if God would hear us. He made the mountains and the endless prairie. He makes snow melt into the rivers, and he grows the trees to the sky. He makes the stars shine at night." He paused, studying Danny before he lowered his voice. "He heard our prayer. He brought you safely here. God hears us."

***

December passed into January. Danny didn't realize he'd missed Christmas until his next trip to town.

"Two weeks," Mr. Edmonds said as he helped stable the borrowed pack animals. "I wondered when I'd see you again." He glanced at Danny as he led his saddle horse into a stall and removed the tack.

Danny leaned against the wall, grateful to step from the saddle and out of the wind. The snow of the last storm had mostly melted, except in shaded spots, but the cold persisted, impeding road construction as the Indians slowly cleared the trail across the desert.

"What's new in town?"

He peered through the open doors to the fading sunlight, the street filling with men as the shift changed at the mine. A dozen wagons with canvas tarps tied over their loads thundered past the barn, the teamsters dressed in thick coats and scarves over their faces. Mr. Edmonds stepped beside him in time to see the wagons pass.

"Coal wagons, heading across the plains to Westport."

"In the winter?" Danny watched the last of the wagons rumble noisily over the bridge at the edge of town and turn into the old trail, following the river to the Arkansas. Briefly, he wondered if the desert road he built would ever open.

The hostler shrugged. "Hennessey got a new contract from a steamboat company, providing coal. They can pick up right on the Missouri River."

A frown touched Danny's mouth, but he waved aside his impatience. God brought him here. If Danny were to complete the shortcut across the plains, he'd have to trust the Lord had a purpose in everything, even the slow progress of the road.

Mr. Edmonds nudged Danny with an elbow. "You asked what's new?" He grinned. "You missed the caroling on Christmas Eve. Everyone was there. Bill served coffee and hot cider while the town celebrated the holiday. I never saw so many happy couples."

"Including Mr. and Mrs. Hanson?"

Still grinning, Mr. Edmonds shrugged. "Lil made her choice. And after me, Carl is the best choice. My day will come." He gestured to the café farther down the street. "Look, even Bill found Gertie. I need to be patient. A handsome man like me will find someone soon enough."

Danny laughed and slapped the hostler on the shoulder as he stepped into the street. "I'm heading that way now. I'm starved."

Mr. Edmonds returned to the stables as Danny made his way down the street. Only the café and the saloons seemed open, the other businesses already closed. He passed Hanson's General Store with a thoughtful glance into the darkened emporium. Where would Jenny be right now?

Shaking his head, he stepped onto the boardwalk. Jenny Blair was none of his affair, he reminded himself as he entered the dining hall. With a jolt, he froze, his gaze locked on the small table across the room where Jenny sat with Mr. Hanson. The storekeeper waved him over when he saw Danny. Warily, he weaved through the partially crowded room to stand before them.

"Sit with us, my boy." The storekeeper indicated a chair. "Just arrive in town? You smell like horses. No matter, welcome. Good to see you."

Danny lowered to a seat while he watched Jenny from the corner of his eye. She appeared not to notice his presence, her cheeks stained a rosy pink as she stared across the room.

"More supplies?" Mr. Hanson went on as he gestured for Gertie. Danny had no opportunity to answer as the waitress handed him the clean mug and took his order.

He nodded his thanks after Mr. Hanson filled his cup. "Yes, just rode into town. Cold, but the road work continues."

Mr. Hanson glanced at Jenny before leaning forward. "Well, I feel I didn't get a chance to talk much with you when you came to dinner."

"That's because you abandoned me with him as you cleared dishes," Jenny mumbled, still not meeting Danny's look.

"So I did, so I did." Mr. Hanson agreed, eyes twinkling beneath bushy brows. "Mrs. Hanson is busy on a baby blanket for a miner's wife. Told us to get our own dinner. Jenny and I have been busy all day in the store, no time for making supper. So here we are."

Danny nodded and sipped coffee, pretending to ignore Jenny as she clearly ignored him.

Mr. Hanson shifted. "Well, since we're together now, suppose you tell us how things are going at your station."

Jenny abruptly faced him, eyes flashing. "Yes, tell us how things are going at *your* station."

A scowl creased his features. So, she was angry at his presence where she believed her brother should be. Danny nodded, understanding grief. Why had he returned from the war when Patrick Blair couldn't?

"It's not my station," he began hesitantly. "I feel I've been commissioned to complete another man's dream."

His remark seemed to take the fight out of Jenny as the silent trio contemplated.

Finally, Jenny broke the awkward silence. "That is noble of you, Danny."

He shook his head. "Not noble at all. I was overwhelmed with loneliness after the war, needing direction, a purpose. I feel the Lord brought this project to me. I appreciate Christ thinking of me."

Mr. Hanson laughed. "God is always thinking of us."

"But I'd not thought of him," Danny confessed. "I only grew curious about Jesus because of Sergeant Blair. Now, I can't imagine living without God in my life."

Jenny looked away, her chin quivering. "I love God and look where that's gotten me."

Danny arched an eyebrow. "You're engaged to one of the richest men in the region. Your future looks bright."

She shrugged, still not meeting his eyes. "Because I'm pretty," she murmured.

Danny chuckled, and her head jerked, her eyes widening as she faced him. "What's so funny?" she demanded.

He gestured with his coffee mug. "Just that, what you said. That's what I'm talking about. God doesn't love me because I have everything in order, because my heart is clean and pure, a beautiful thing. I'm broken, filled with anxiety and sorrow, with deep scars. And yet he loves me. I feel I have so much to learn about the Lord and his plans for such a mess as me."

Mr. Hanson leaned back while Jenny leaned forward, her gaze intent upon Danny, searching. Her eyes softened as she studied him, and he felt a kinship with her for the first time, as if maybe they understood one another.

"Perhaps you have more in common than you realized," Mr. Hanson said softly, his gaze darting between the two young people.

Again, the uneasy quiet surrounded them. Danny pursed his lips. Had he shared too much? The door opened, and Danny looked up. Reggie Bloomberg stood in the doorway, letting cold air in while he scanned the room.

"Reggie, here," Jenny called, waving with a smile stretched across her face.

Danny felt his frown return as the rancher made his way to their table.

CHAPTER THIRTY-THREE

Jenny patted an empty chair, and the young rancher dropped into the seat.

Mr. Hanson cleared his throat. "Good evening, Reggie. Just come to town?"

The rancher nodded, fixing his gaze on Jenny. "Pa sent me in for a box of nails, but I see the store is closed."

"I can open for you," Jenny suggested with a note of eagerness in her words that nettled Danny.

"Reggie, have you met Danny Mason?"

At Mr. Hanson's introduction, the rancher shrugged, barely taking notice of him. "Yeah, we met. You have that spring on the base of the Raton's, right?"

"Danny's building the stage station my brother was going to build," Jenny blurted.

Reggie waved a dismissive hand. "Waste of time. Not enough water there for cattle. And there's already a stage road along the river."

Danny felt his irritation mount, but Mr. Hanson gave him an almost imperceptible nod, and he choked on his retort.

"Where have you been, Reggie?" Jenny placed a hand on his arm. Danny felt his irritation ratchet up a notch. "I haven't seen you since the Christmas caroling." She pouted.

"Been busy," he growled. "Ranching is hard work. I was going to grab a drink in the saloon when I saw you through the window."

"I don't like it when you go to the saloon," Jenny said in a reproving voice.

Bloomberg glowered. "I came in here, didn't I?"

"Well, let me get your nails for you." Jenny stood quickly, sidestepping the altercation Danny expected. The three men rose to their feet. As Jenny dragged the young rancher away, Mr. Hanson and Danny watched them go before resuming their seats.

Danny lifted his cup of coffee. "They make an interesting couple."

A frown hovered around the storekeeper's countenance. "She was almost starved when we found her, freezing in that little shack beside the river. I gave her a part-time job in the mercantile and insisted she move into our home. Neither Lil nor I ever had children. Jenny is like a daughter to us."

"She told me Patrick's army pay wasn't reaching her there at the last," Danny reported quietly.

"I suspect she was desperate when we found her. Lil believes Jenny was about to look for work in the saloons." Mr. Hanson's face purpled.

"But to accept Reggie Bloomberg? Surely there are other good men in Trinidad?" Danny couldn't keep the ring of scorn from his words.

The storekeeper shrugged. "She swore never to starve again. And other men wouldn't approach her now with Reggie on her trail."

The sad and tormented look he'd seen on Jenny's face when she spoke of her ordeal made his chest tighten. Danny shook his head once more. "What would Sergeant Blair say?"

"Patrick didn't like Reggie." Mr. Hanson chuckled humorlessly. "Thought he was arrogant." He sighed. "Patrick always said Jenny could do better than Reggie. That's why he set so much store on the stage station in the desert. He thought she'd never look at Bloomberg if she had her own business."

"Speaking of business," Danny said, sensing an opportunity to ask his question. "Mr. Hennessey at the mine has spoken to me about payments if I can open the shortcut to the Arkansas. With that in mind, I'll need additional credit at the mercantile. With Peter Walking Stick's help, I believe I can open sooner than I expected, but they eat a lot of food. I'm good for the advance."

Mr. Hanson smiled and raised his mug. "You don't need Mr. Hennessey's recommendation, Danny. I like you. Of course, you can have more supplies."

***

Wind moaned across the vacant street as Danny made his way to the livery barn. He tugged his collar higher and thrust his hands deep into his pockets, unwilling to pull on his gloves for the short trip down the street. A glance to the high peaks in the west revealed the moon shining brightly, perched atop the crest of the Rockies. He sighed, sensing the Lord's presence as he ducked into the dark barn and fumbled for the ladder to the loft.

With slow steps, he mounted each rung until he stood on the edge of the upper floor. Arms reaching into the darkness, he searched until he located the pile of bedding he'd tossed up earlier.

As he stretched in his blankets, waiting for them to warm, he shivered contentedly. Although he'd offered for one of the Indians to retrieve supplies from Trinidad, he felt secretly pleased Peter and Luke insisted he go, allowing the family construction crew to work together.

"The young ones need my guidance," Peter had assured Danny. He wondered if he would benefit from the old Indian's wisdom as well.

"I can fight and build with rock," he muttered, still wondering about his presence on the frontier. "I haven't landed a contract with the stage company or completed a road across the desert, but you are with me, aren't you?"

He didn't hear a response from the night, but Danny enjoyed trusting God. Life held purpose, much more purpose than Danny had ever realized before. As the Lord moved him from selfish desires that served only himself, he comprehended the Lord's hand in his life, building his faith, developing his character. He was growing in Christ while the Lord led him through challenging situations, unexpected situations. Ones beyond his abilities, ones that demanded he trust Jesus for the outcome.

His grin slipped when he thought of Jenny Blair. Like him, she was an orphan. Alone, she'd worried and feared for her future. Danny never worried about his future because he didn't think he'd have one. But now, he found himself on the frontier, and the sergeant's little sister had crossed his path. Was there purpose in this too?

He drew a deep breath, drinking in the crisp air thickly scented with hay. "You are God, I am not. Let me trust you. You did this. You brought me here. Now, let me get out of your way and watch you work. Show me what you want me to learn. May I change and grow to be more like your Son, Jesus. And—" He paused, drawing another deep breath. "—Speak to me in a way I can hear. I confess I need affirmation, encouragement that I am where you want me.

I want to do things right, for you, and I feel so inadequate. I fear you ask too much of me, Lord."

He thought of Moses who was instructed by God to speak to Pharaoh. The reluctant man had given so many excuses why he couldn't, all of which the Lord refuted. In the end, Moses had proven to be the right man for the assignment.

After another long pause, Danny whispered, "Are you sure you have the right man for this job?"

CHAPTER THIRTY-FOUR

When Danny stepped into the morning sunlight, he felt refreshed, although more than a little nervous at running into Jenny. He hated how annoyed he felt at seeing her with Reggie Bloomberg at the café. She was none of his business, he reminded himself for the hundredth time, yet he felt Sergeant Blair would want him to do something. But what?

He washed up in the trough beside the livery, spluttering in the freezing cold water. He took a moment to study the workmanship of the plank trough, comparing it with the bigger stone one he'd built for the desert station. Luke had inserted the bent pipe into the crack in the rock and water flowed smoothly into the receptacle, tumbling like a tiny waterfall. He figured the water might freeze if temperatures dropped. But the sun seemed to linger on the protected spring, water flowing despite the advent of winter. In addition, with the help of the willing work crew, it had taken little time to construct fences across the gap of the box canyon. Additional corrals would be added in the spring when more time allowed. He felt pleased at how the station was evolving.

When Danny left for town every couple of weeks to pick up supplies, the Indians continued to work the road. He always felt excited with their progress upon his return, always impressed at the distance they carved across the frozen desert. Working with picks, shovels, and the horse for pulling stubborn stones from their path, the crew had cleared miles of rocky terrain. Despite the frigid temperatures and bitter winds, the road lengthened toward the Arkansas River.

After bundling his gear near his horse, he walked to the café, his Henry rifle riding easy on his shoulder. He didn't feel like he needed the weapon, yet its nearness comforted him.

As he walked, he passed sleepy-looking miners trudging toward the mine, the morning shift reporting to work. Although Danny felt he would do anything he had to, he was grateful he didn't have to go underground. The stone station promised a position he thought he would enjoy. The wide-open plains, the immense sky, and the towering mountains whispered to him, telling him he belonged in the West. Would his future include Trinidad?

When he neared the café, his gaze lingered on the ramparts looming over the small town. Shadows between the clefts receded as the sun tipped above the plains behind him. He'd never seen such a magnificent sight, as if God were revealing his glory especially for him.

"Thank you, God," he said softly as he stepped onto the boardwalk and reached for the café door. "Thanks for bringing me here."

Before he could grasp the handle, the door swung wide, almost toppling him from the stoop. Danny stepped back swiftly, barely avoiding the door.

"Oh, Danny," Jenny said as she stepped onto the boardwalk, her cheeks pinking. "I didn't see you."

She wore a pale-yellow dress and her hair shone in the morning light, her bonnet still gripped in one hand. Her gray eyes held a note of anxiety, and Danny wondered if her concern was truly for him.

"Miss Blair," he mumbled with a nod. "What brings you out early on this chilly morning?"

She frowned, as if reluctant to share. Her glance darted up the street, and her annoyance seemed to increase. "I was supposed to meet someone, if you must know."

Taking a stab in the dark, Danny grinned. "Reggie didn't show, huh?"

She scowled at him, her eyes narrowing to slits. "Something delayed him, that's all. Ranchers are busy men. You couldn't understand."

Now, Danny felt annoyed. His boots shifted on the wooden sidewalk as he reached once more for the door handle. "I have no desire to understand Reggie Bloomberg."

But Jenny didn't move aside, effectively blocking the door. She crossed her arms over her chest and glowered at Danny. "The Bloombergs are big men in this country."

"And I am not? Well, you are right. I am nobody, but I am here to complete your brother's unfinished task."

Her rosy cheeks paled, and her eyes flashed wide, as if his words had stung her. Her arms fell to her side as she stepped back.

Danny said nothing more as he entered the café and made his way to an empty table. He nodded his thanks to Gertie when the waitress poured coffee, but his gaze went to the front window where he watched Jenny stomp toward the mercantile, her back as stiff as a board.

"She's a headstrong filly," Gertie said softly, drawing Danny's attention.

He shifted on the bench. "I don't know what you mean," he mumbled as he reached for his steaming cup.

She chortled as she moved away. "Oh, I think you know exactly what I mean," she called over her shoulder.

Later, he picked up his supplies at the general store, grateful at Jenny's absence. He told Mr. Hanson to put the things on his tab, then he carried the food stuffs to his waiting horses. Although a cool breeze wafted from the nearby heights, the sun shone brightly, giving a false sense of spring in the air. Winter would persist for another couple months, but for now, a respite from the bitter cold would allow progress to continue on the road across the desert. He felt eager to return to the station with his supplies.

"How is Luke's family working out?" The storekeeper followed Danny to the boardwalk, watching him pack.

"Fantastic. I couldn't wish for better workers," Danny reported. He added with a chuckle, "But they sure can eat a lot of food."

"Hard work, carving a trail across the land," Mr. Hanson offered.

Danny tugged the knot he'd tied. "Peter Walking Stick seems to have an instinctive ability to locate the best route. If they don't eat me out of house and home first, I predict a shortcut to the Arkansas by spring."

"So soon?" A worried look came to the older man's features.

"I'm working as quickly as I can," Danny replied, somewhat surprised by the storekeeper's alarmed response.

Mr. Hanson scrubbed a hand across his face and glanced toward his house on the knoll. "Yes, yes, I'm sure you are," he mumbled. Then he brightened. "But surely there is no real need for haste. When will you be back to town?"

Danny stepped into the saddle. "Probably a couple of weeks. I'd like to push during this mild weather. You know it won't last."

"Good luck, then." Mr. Hanson waved as Danny rode down the main street, the three pack animals trailing.

With a good road to follow, he made the distance to the station in under five hours. He felt pleased to find the station empty when he arrived, the Indians apparently camping on the trail as they worked to the northeast, toward the river. Danny unpacked the supplies and hurried to locate his friends before dark overtook him.

★★★

For the next two weeks, Danny and the Indians worked like mad to extend the road across the plains. Each night, around the campfire, he read from the Bible. Although he wanted to introduce the Indians to his faith in Christ, Danny found the nightly Scripture reading encouraged his own beliefs. Every day, he looked forward to the special time.

"How far have we come from the station?" Danny leaned on a shovel, peering to the north, still not able to see the line of trees that marked the Arkansas River.

Peter rested his pick on his boot and followed Danny's gaze. Around them, Luke and the three teenage boys pushed stone from the chosen route and dug rocks from the ground.

The women lingered a mile behind, tending to camp chores, gathering firewood, and preparing meals.

"About twenty miles," Peter finally said, still gazing to the north. Off to their right, the endless prairies stretched to the horizon, a gray sky lowering as cool wind blew in their faces.

Danny lifted his scarf from around his neck, shielding his cheeks. "I smell like sweat and wood smoke," he grumbled and then chuckled, remembering his army days. "I could use a bath."

Peter gestured to the east. "Storm coming. We'll return to the station tomorrow. Good time for you to go to Trinidad for supplies while we regroup." He gestured to the three younger boys. "The children and women would benefit from a rest."

Danny nodded, appreciating the old man's wisdom and leadership. "Time for more supplies anyway. I think we could all use a break."

That night, the wind howled across the plains. Danny worried they'd be caught on the naked prairie, exposed to the storm. But they reached the protection of the station late the next afternoon.

A reluctance filled Danny, and he turned to finishing work around the homestead. He completed the stone walls of the stable in the box canyon and reinforced the rock wall across the gap of the box canyon. He even made a short trip to the top of the bluff to collect precious firewood.

"Danny, you're stalling," Peter accused the next morning.

Luke grinned as the two Indians faced Danny in the windswept clearing. A curl of blue smoke lifted from the stone chimney. His workmen were safe within the station, yet he felt hesitant to go to town.

"We need supplies," Luke added. "Running out of food."

"Then you go," Danny growled at his friend. He desperately wished to see Jenny and yet feared the encounter. Every time they met, sparks flew. Besides, she was spoken for. Reggie Bloomberg claimed her as his own, like a piece of property, which grated on Danny's nerves.

Luke shook his head, still grinning. "Oh, no. I don't feel comfortable in town. Besides, I sense there is a reason you should go and not me."

Danny opened his mouth to retort when Peter laid a hand on his shoulder. "Luke is right, young man. There is a reason you should go, and I think you know that."

A tremor passed through Danny, and he stared at his friends. Despite his trepidation, he suddenly realized they were both right.

CHAPTER THIRTY-FIVE

God was with him, right? Danny hated how his doubts resurfaced when least expected. He'd come west to complete Sergeant Blair's goal, and the task was advancing nicely. The station was built, and the road should be complete sometime this spring, Lord willing. Even if he didn't land a contract with the stage company, he thought Mr. Hennessey's proposal should allow the station to prove a success. Yet something rankled in him as Danny paused for a breather between two hills, keeping from the cold wind.

He patted his horse's neck and glanced at the three pack animals. He felt everything was progressing well, according to schedule. However, his doubts simmered just beneath the surface, making him pensive. He never foresaw he'd be sharing his faith with new friends. He narrowed his eyes, wondering at the Lord's intent for his presence on the frontier.

His gaze shifted to the bleak landscape around him. "I didn't think of coming west. This land was a mystery to me, nothing I cared to know. And yet, now I cannot imagine leaving. You have met me here in ways I never could imagine."

His gaze lifted to the towering peaks above him. Blanketed in endless white, dull sunlight glimmered across the mountains, making Danny shiver. He tugged his collar higher and nudged his horse forward.

Danny forced his animals to a trot, keeping them warm as they made their way to Trinidad. Even with the bath he'd taken this morning and delaying his departure to town, he still arrived as the sun vanished behind the Rocky Mountains. A bonfire ringed by town folks drew his attention as he rode onto the main street, and he hurried to stable his horses before leaving the barn, eager to warm himself at the huge fire near Hanson's General Store.

Harsh laughter rang out as he passed a saloon, and Danny peered in, not surprised when he glimpsed Reggie Bloomberg at the bar. Anger burned in Danny's guts. He sensed something sinister in the young rancher, and wished better for Jenny Blair, but he pushed his annoyance aside. How Jenny liked this man, he had no idea, but women were beyond his understanding. Besides, he had more important business to attend to.

He hadn't seen Mr. Edmonds at the livery and suspected the hostler was at the café for his evening meal. Danny felt very hungry, but supper could wait until he thawed near the cheerful blaze.

He passed people in small clusters, all enjoying the town bonfire. As he stretched his hands to the heat, he glanced around, noticing couples and individuals standing in the bright glow cast from the giant fire. He wondered if the bonfire were a normal occurrence.

"What is this?" Danny gestured to the leaping flames and asked a young couple huddling nearby.

"Every now and then, the sawmill up on the hill puts together a bonfire to burn scraps, pieces trimmed from the lumber." The man pointed to a heap of various shaped lengths of wood, some still wearing bark. "This is a chance for folks to gather in the cold and spend time together."

Danny nodded, his gaze surveying the crowd. He smiled when he saw Bill and Gertie standing across from him, and he wondered who was manning the café. His smile grew when he caught sight of Mr. and Mrs. Hanson, a blanket draped over their shoulders as they stomped cold feet.

His roving gaze stilled when he saw Jenny standing alone, hovering on the outer edge of the gathering, and his incredible hunger was forgotten. As he peered at her, she looked down the darkened street, as if searching for someone.

"She could use a friend."

Danny jumped at Carl Hanson's whisper, the older man sneaking up on him.

"Who—who do you mean?" Danny stammered as he faced the storekeeper.

Mr. Hanson grinned. "Lil and I are going in. Take my blanket." He shoved the woolen cover into Danny's hands. "See you tomorrow."

Without another word, Lil and Carl disappeared into the gloom. Danny hesitated only an instant before making his way around the circle of onlookers to stand before Jenny. His heart thumped wildly in his chest and despite the cold, he felt his palms moisten.

"Miss Blair," he greeted.

"Oh, Danny, 'tis you," she said in a startled tone. "I was looking for—"

"For Reggie Bloomberg? Well, then we'll wait together. You look like you're freezing." Without waiting for a reply, he pressed his shoulder against hers as he draped the blanket around the both of them.

"Thank you," she murmured, and Danny felt her shiver.

He held his breath. How was it that in a twinkling of an eye, he stood under a shared blanket with Jenny Blair? He licked dry lips and tried to slow his racing heart, amazed at his sudden bravery.

They were silent for a long moment as they stared into the bright bonfire, but Danny's thoughts whirled. What was he doing? He wanted to shout, to congratulate himself on approaching the beautiful girl, but he stood riveted in place, afraid if he spoke or moved, the magic moment would disappear like smoke in the breeze. Yet shivers raced down his back, and he knew the trembles were not from the cold. He glanced at her profile from the corner of his eye, watching the ruddy glow of the immense bonfire cast dancing shadows on her cheeks.

"Are you in town for supplies?"

Her innocent inquiry helped him relax, and he nodded as he focused on the big fire, grateful to talk about something easy.

"Yes. We need food. We're working hard to shape the road across the plains, but my work force eats a lot." He chuckled softly, realizing how much he enjoyed her nearness. Jenny had annoyed him, irritated him, and then intrigued him. Danny wasn't sure what was happening, only that he wanted more.

Jenny smiled up at him, and then her smile fled as she glanced uptown once more. "You know he doesn't like you."

Danny grinned, feeling better. "I'm all right with that. I knew I didn't like him the day he told me he had the fastest horse in the region and the prettiest girl."

She pursed her lips. "Things. Possessions."

"Yes," Danny agreed.

A frown creased her features, and she shifted. Slowly, her chin lifted. "I think I'm done waiting, Danny." She glanced at him from the corner of her eyes. "Will you please walk me home?"

"Of course." He stepped from the blanket and wrapped the edges around her. "Here. I'm used to the cold."

They moved around the crowd, stepping from the firelight into the deeper shadows. Gravel crunched beneath their tread as Danny pointed at the shimmering stars above.

"The Bible says God counted the stars and calls them each by name."

She tugged the blanket around her more securely. "You read the Bible?"

"Almost every day," he said with a laugh. "Luke's family insists I read to them. We all enjoy the Gospels."

Jenny's laugh rang out, warming Danny's heart at the merry sound, rich and thrilling. He thought it might've been the first time he'd heard her laugh.

"They want to hear you read Scripture?"

He nodded. "They seem interested in knowing Christ. I must confess, I'm surprised at what the Lord asks of me. I feel so inadequate." He paused and then added, "I only became interested in Jesus after I met your brother."

They stopped in a dark patch a little way from the Hanson house. A lantern glowed in the storekeeper's kitchen window.

"Patrick loved the Lord," she whispered, her voice sounding more husky than before.

"Everyone could see that. He didn't hide his faith. His connection to Christ governed his every action. His courage seemed from above, as if he were guided by Jesus."

Jenny turned and smiled at him. He felt dizzy as he stared into her eyes. His heart beat even faster, and he tensed, sensing something niggling within him, prodding him on.

"You respected him, didn't you?"

Danny smiled. "He was the best man I've ever known. I felt God in him, calling to me, urging me to come to Christ. I had no idea how powerful the Holy Spirit can be."

"And God used Patrick to call men to Christ?"

She seemed so small, her oval face pale in the starlight. Danny licked his lips again and wondered what she was thinking. Did she remember her brother the same way he remembered Sergeant Blair?

"He lived his faith every day. He went to war because he was brave. He valued justice and doing the right thing, although he couldn't have known how you might suffer in his absence."

She wrinkled her nose. "I know that. At first, I was angry at him, as things got worse for me. But I know he's not to blame." She tilted her head, studying him in the darkness. "Why did you go to war?"

He tensed again, then decided to be honest. "I had nothing else. I found myself in a dark place, lonely and hungry. If you can believe it, I longed for the security the army offered."

"While men were shooting at you?"

Danny shrugged. "I wasn't worried about that. I had nothing except a name I borrowed from a traveling pugilist. Stupidly, I hoped someone would remember me if I fought and died courageously."

She stared at him in the dim light, and he worried she could read his thoughts as she shifted. "You thought only of yourself," she accused, but he didn't feel he had to defend himself.

He nodded, still staring at her.

"The way Patrick died. I wonder ... would you have come west if Patrick hadn't died? What would you be doing now if you stayed in Philadelphia?"

The smile fled from Danny as images of his life flashed before his mind's eye. The horrible orphanage, the even more horrible war, and then the unendurable loneliness that overwhelmed him. Grief, an endless ache in his heart, deep sadness. Jesus had called him to the frontier, offering him significance and purpose. He knew he'd never go back, wouldn't leave this rich land. He never expected to be carving a road across the plains or sharing his faith with new friends, but he felt the Lord guided him and leaving Philadelphia had saved his life. And he never could've anticipated the way he'd fall in love with Jenny Blair.

The unexpected awareness fell into place like the final piece of a challenging jigsaw puzzle. His heart swelled, the unfamiliar sensation filling him with warmth.

On his ride to town, he wondered what more he could do for Christ. He never considered there'd be something more Jesus would do for him. Danny's purpose was to build the stage station, but perhaps God had another purpose for bringing Danny west. Was there a future for him on these desolate plains? He'd never loved before, except when he'd opened his heart to Jesus. And now the Lord revealed Danny's true feelings for the sergeant's little sister.

He stepped close, peering intently into her face. He couldn't read her gray eyes in the vague light, but the stars shone on her pale skin, smooth and lovely. With his fingers, he brushed her soft cheek before lifting her chin, studying her features. "I left Philadelphia to fulfill your brother's dream. But God has opened my eyes, revealing other reasons for bringing me here."

"What reasons?" Her whispered inquiry seemed to bolster him, encouraging him to go on.

"In the desert, I've learned to seek the Lord, to look for his hand, and to wait for his guidance. I believe he has guided me to you."

Her eyes widened, but she didn't pull away from his gentle touch.

"We both have scarred hearts, you and me. We both have known tough times, and we both know Christ. I came out here to serve the Lord, but he is rebuilding me, growing my faith in ways I never expected." He paused as he lowered his face, drawing closer to her as he dropped his voice. "And I've fallen in love with you, Jenny Blair."

He pressed his lips to hers. As they kissed, Danny thought he felt the blanket slip from her shoulders to tumble around their feet while her strong arms encircled his neck, but he couldn't be sure.

He stepped back swiftly, his brashness startling him. He wanted to apologize for his sudden boldness, but he knew he wasn't sorry. He stared at her as moonlight shimmered around them, a stunned look on her face he well understood. With a lunge, he stalked into the night.

CHAPTER THIRTY-SIX

Danny squinted into the gloom as he stumbled away. What had he done?

His boots sounded loud on the gravel as he made his way back to the center of town. The huge bonfire still burned brightly, although there seemed to be fewer figures grouped around. Without pausing to warm his hands or identify anyone, he strode on, eager to retreat to the dark of the big livery barn.

Had he really kissed Jenny? He'd sensed a startled look on her pretty face before he kissed her soft lips. Was she angry at him for his imprudent action? How could she not be?

More raucous laughter from one of the saloons drew his gaze, and Danny chuckled when he recognized Reggie Bloomberg once more. Danny walked on, excitement crowding out his worries. The young rancher had allowed an opportunity Danny would not soon forget. Danny laughed as he reached the barn. Slowing his rapid gait, he moved into the darkened livery. The sound of horses munching hay came to his straining ears, but he didn't hear Mr. Edmonds or anyone else. He was alone.

Danny lifted a boot to climb the ladder to the loft, then froze. There was no way he could sleep now. Dropping his boot to the ground, he paced, walking up and down the length of the barn.

What had he done? What had compelled him to kiss Jenny Blair? He pulled his hat off and dragged a hand through his hair.

"Oh, Lord, am I crazy? What was I thinking? I've made a mess of things now."

For what seemed like hours, he walked his somber vigil. One moment, he felt like crowing jubilantly into the night— the next, he felt heavy weights on his shoulders, pressing him down. Finally, worn out from anxiety and exhilaration, he found his way to the loft and rolled in his blankets. He didn't fall asleep until just before dawn.

A rooster's call awoke him. Danny stared up at the underside of the barn roof, instantly vigilant. Dull sunlight filtered across the barn floor, and he glanced over the rim of the loft, seeing the morning was further advanced than his normal wont of rising. He laid back on the hay and grinned. He'd kissed Jenny Blair.

His sense of satisfaction seemed short lived when he rose and washed at the water pump beside the barn. How could he face Jenny today? He still needed to visit the mercantile for supplies.

Maybe he didn't need to go to the general store. Danny shook his head. The Indians needed these supplies. The road work needed to be completed. The Lord had brought him here for a task.

"Oh, Jesus, what have I done?" He glanced around the quiet barn, only the horses' swishing tails disturbing the silence.

He shook his head again as he walked to the café. Miners passed him on the street, filthy from a night underground as they dragged themselves home, but Danny could only think of his predicament. How could he meet Jenny in the light of day? How could he speak with Mr. Hanson, his friend and Jenny's surrogate father?

Gertie only smiled at him as he ate, as if the waitress guessed the reason for his unease. She grinned wider when he pushed his empty plate back and accepted another cup of coffee.

"Saw you talking with Jenny last night at the bonfire," she whispered as steam rose from his mug. "I also saw Reggie Bloomberg in the saloon." She winked before she turned to go. "His loss," she said over her shoulder as she moved among the tables, pouring refills.

Danny gripped his hot cup. So, others suspected his interest in the sergeant's sister. He scowled at the unexpected idea. How could anyone guess his attraction to Jenny when he'd only just discovered the fact for himself?

The dilemma followed him after he paid his bill and walked to the café door. He'd have to brave the store and fetch supplies for the Indians. The stage station was what brought him to the frontier. The work must go through.

As he stepped onto the boardwalk and let the door close behind him, he saw Old Crawford stalking toward the café. Danny paused, grateful to not charge to the mercantile just yet. A cold wind drifted from the nearby mountains, and Danny thrust his hands into his pockets, waiting.

The aged stage driver seemed not to see Danny as he reached for the café door. Danny stepped closer. "Mr. Crawford, I wondered if you've heard anything new about the stage company?"

Crawford hesitated, seeming to study Danny with arched eyebrows. "It'll cost you a cup of coffee," the driver growled as he pulled the door open and entered.

Danny heaved a sigh of relief.

"Back so soon?" Gertie winked again as she poured coffee for the two men. "I know you had breakfast," she said with a glance at Danny. "What'll you have, Mr. Crawford?"

In a raspy voice, the stage driver gave his order. He watched Gertie retreat to the kitchen before studying Danny over the rim of his cup as he sipped coffee. "You still working on that stage stop in the desert? You really found water?"

Danny nodded. "I hope to finish this spring." He blew on his coffee before going on. "Any word from the company?"

Crawford nodded. "Rumors are flying. Probably not just rumors anymore. But no one wants to come out and say for sure. Definitely not a good time to ask for a change of route."

Danny frowned. "You mean I might get this road completed for nothing?"

"Who knows?" Crawford shrugged. "Wells Fargo might listen to a proposal—after the deal closes. Holladay Stage Line is over as far as I understand things. You will not get anywhere with them right now."

Danny pushed his still full cup away and stood. Tossing a coin on the table, he nodded to the weathered driver. "Thanks anyway," he mumbled as he made his way to the door once more.

At the mercantile, the bell jingled merrily as Danny pushed into the store. Outside, the crisp morning air held a bittersweet tang, as if everything good and everything bad collided on the streets of Trinidad. The haunting memory of Jenny in the starlight warred with the discouraging news from Old Crawford. What would he do if he couldn't get a stage contract?

His gaze darted across the store, searching each crowded aisle where dry goods piled in tall stacks.

"She's not here, young man," Mr. Hanson called from behind the back counter.

Danny sighed as he made his way toward the storekeeper. "Am I that obvious?" Danny pulled his list of supplies from his pocket, feeling the heat rise above his collar.

Mr. Hanson grinned and tugged an apron around his neck. He tied the strings behind him as he nodded. "Only to people who love her, like Lil and me."

Lil stepped from the back room and patted Danny's arm. "We called her to breakfast this morning, but she wouldn't come out of her room. Says she's ill. She's ill, all right. Lovesick." The older woman smiled, and Danny thought he detected a gleam in her shrewd eyes.

"But I'm nobody," Danny grumbled as Mr. Hanson took his list. "Reggie Bloomberg has a big ranch and lots of money and power. He can give her a life I can't."

Lil and Carl exchanged glances, and the older couple chuckled. Danny frowned at their merriment.

"It's not funny to me," he snapped as the storekeepers gathered supplies from the shelves and piled them on the counter.

"I think it's entertaining," Lil said then put her hands on her hips and faced him. "I suspect Ezekiel's valley of dry bones brought you west. If I don't miss my guess, you feel a great adventure led you here, with the Lord prodding you along the way?"

Danny felt his eyes widen again. "How can you know that?"

Lil nodded to her husband. "Thought so. I never knew Patrick Blair, but I know Jesus. His adventures always include more than meets the eye. Mine did. Carl tells me you came to Trinidad to complete a project Patrick wanted.

I'll bet God has more in store for you than merely building a station in the desert, young man."

She moved away, retrieving more items from Danny's list as he glanced at Mr. Hanson. "Ezekiel's valley?"

The storekeeper nodded. "In the Bible. Read it. I think you'll understand. The Lord is rebuilding you, bringing you back to life. It's no accident you're in Trinidad. And he has a land for you, a special land all your own." The storekeeper winked at Danny. "Jesus is doing more than you know. Lil's right. You're not here only to build Patrick's station."

★★★

When Danny walked to the livery to fetch his pack animals, he stole a glance toward the Hanson's house, perched atop the low knoll beside the Purgatory River. Jenny was there, hiding in her room. Did she think of their kiss? Was she as confused as he felt? He'd always thought he was brave and unafraid, always willing to throw himself into any task. To build, to accomplish, to conquer.

Now, for the first time, he felt he wasn't supposed to do things on his own.

"Lord, is there something more you want from me?" Danny blinked in the bright sunlight. He peered up at the mountains, wondering, seeking guidance. Deep snow glistened on the ramparts. Although winter maintained a tight grasp on the eastern Colorado landscape, hints of spring fooled him, as if nature taunted Danny with these mild days, heralding warmer ones to come.

He stepped into the barn and hurried to the stalls. If he could pack soon, he might make the station before nightfall. He smiled when he thought of the good road they'd shaped.

He tossed pack saddles on the animals before saddling his own horse. His fingers stilled when he recalled Lil

Hanson's reference. Hurriedly, he rummaged his saddle bags until he located his Bible, the black book Patrick Blair handed him on the battlefield. It took only a minute to find Ezekiel.

He scanned each chapter, seeking mention of a valley. He thought he'd have to look later when he finally found the passage.

He sank onto a grain sack as he read the words. His chest tightened when he read about new flesh bringing the dry bones to life. When breath entered the carcasses, Danny gasped, seeing a connection with his own story. And when God brought these people to a land of their own, he stilled, sensing the Lord speaking directly to him.

Thoughts whirling, Danny staggered to his feet. He thrust the book back into his pack and rode to the mercantile, unable to focus on the task before him. How could he load supplies while he felt God speaking to him in such a personal way?

Mr. Hanson helped load the supplies, not suspecting the turmoil Danny suffered. Was God doing something greater with him than just using his construction talents? Was there a personal message for him in the Scriptures?

Danny waved at the kindly storekeeper before trotting out of town, eager to gain some distance before the emotions that coursed through him overcame his sensibilities.

As if traveling in a fog, Danny led the way down the road, past the Bloomberg ranch, to the edge of the desert, where the grassy plains mingled with the rocks and scrubs of the arid lands.

"Are you telling me something?" His whispered prayer choked in his throat, a lump rising as he scanned the sky. "I felt grateful to have something to do, a direction when I came west. I'm pleased to fulfill Sergeant Blair's dream, but is there something more you haven't told me? Do you want me to discover joy out here? I deserve nothing, Jesus, yet you've allowed me to feel something for Jenny I never thought possible. Even if I never experience love in return, thank you for opening my heart and letting me know what love feels like."

His words cut off as his vision blurred. He'd often been alone, felt loneliness acutely, never experiencing this deep yearning for another. And yet, here in the West, love had surprised him.

Danny bent his head and gripped the reins tighter, allowing the horses to find their own way as he wrestled with himself, the Lord, and his overwhelming emotions.

He chuckled humorlessly when he lifted his face to the faded sunlight. "Am I a different person? Why would you give Danny Mason anything? I'm nobody, have nothing, yet you love me. I've come to need you, Jesus, like the grasses need the sun. Does the God who made the mountains want to live in my heart?"

His laughter rolled louder, as if he finally accepted the generous gift.

For miles, Danny prayed, at first wondering why God should cherish him, and then basking in the Lord's grace. He stopped on a rise to allow the horses to take a breather. Danny's gaze surveyed the lonely land, realizing his own loneliness had dissipated with his coming to Trinidad.

"If I could sing, Jesus, my song would be you," he whispered so only God would hear. "Show me how to love Jenny in the right way. I'm new to this, and you created love. Let me learn from you."

As the sun dropped behind the Rocky Mountains, an exhausted Danny rode into the clearing before the station. Spent from the draining trek from town, he slumped in his saddle, surveying the quiet station and the empty land around him. But he wasn't alone.

Danny peered up at the outline of the Rocky Mountains, the sun long since dropping behind the towering peaks. "Thank you, Christ, for showing me you have more in store for me," he whispered into the desert wind. "I'm not here only to serve you, I'm here to interact with you, to experience your blessings." He paused as he blinked away the sting in his eyes. "I love you, Jesus."

CHAPTER THIRTY-SEVEN

For the next two weeks, Danny threw himself into road construction. With the frozen ground, his crew often wrestled half-buried rocks, straining to extract them after digging deep trenches around the stones. The horses would pull on the ropes lashed to the rocks, tugging them free for the Indians to move to the side of the road. But the trail needed to be cleared if he hoped to attract the attention of the Holladay Stage Company, assuming they hadn't already handed control over to Wells Fargo, or Mr. Hennessey at the mine in Trinidad. Either way, Danny needed to finish what he'd started.

A brisk February wind roiled across the plains, blustering the intense cold, and making the crew snuggle deeper into their coats. Danny noticed their need for replacement gloves, the last ones he'd delivered already tattered and worn from the extreme labor. He promised to bring new gloves after his next visit to town. He longed to see Jenny again, yet anxiety worried at him like the bitter wind. Would she speak to him? Surely, she must comprehend his bewildering feelings better than he did.

Luke slapped his shoulder, bringing Danny back to the moment. He glanced at the grinning Indian as Peter strode to a nearby knoll, beckoning the pair to follow.

"What's wrong?" Luke walked to his grandfather as he kept an eye on Danny. "You've been out of sorts since the last trip to town, pushing the work as if hounds were on your heels. Anything you want to share?"

Danny glowered at his friend as they halted beside the old man, Peter scanning the intended road from the high vantage point. Before Danny could reply, Peter pointed along a low ridge, slowly tracing a line through the air.

"That way, along that ridge," Peter said in a low voice, as if thinking to himself. "There can't be more than a dozen miles to the Arkansas, to the Santa Fe Trail."

Danny's gaze followed the old man's finger, nodding as he envisioned the proposed route. Peter had a canny way of reading the land, of choosing the best path to follow. Danny had relinquished the lead on this project long ago, pleased at how the Walking Stick family proved to be expert road builders.

"Looks clear most of the way," Luke agreed. "Not a lot of ravines or ditches."

Danny said nothing, his thoughts far away. He imagined a pretty girl with a long brown braid draped down her back, gray eyes resting on him as he spoke to her about himself, the stars above, and the work God was doing in his life. He felt rebuilt, reborn, and sensed the Lord's hand on him. He gazed upon the desert and the bleak plains of southeastern Colorado. Beautiful, stark, quiet ... this place called to him. He'd found his land. Had he found his future?

His thoughts turned to Ezekiel and the valley of dry bones. God was with him, building him anew.

Luke laughed, and Danny narrowed his eyes, annoyed at being disturbed from his reverie. "What?"

"Grandpa asked you twice what you thought of his plan for the route."

Danny turned from Luke to the old man, feeling chagrined at not paying attention. "Sorry, Peter. Show me the route."

For the next few minutes, the old Indian indicated the proposed road, pointing out the most level place for a road to run. Danny nodded, impressed with Peter's ability to locate the best possible course for wheeled vehicles to travel across the plains. When he'd finished, Peter turned to study Danny with a penetrating look.

"What's on your mind, young man?"

Rather than reply, a frown teased the corner of Danny's mouth. He wouldn't share his personal feelings with this old man. God was doing something within him, but his spiritual journey still baffled him, still puzzled his practical nature. He'd thought his purpose here was clear. Yet something deeper seemed afoot. Even Lil Hanson sensed it. And Danny suspected Mr. Hanson and his Indian friends sensed something bothering him.

Dare he confess a woman plagued his thoughts? And what was Jesus doing with him? Ezekiel's valley seemed to speak directly to him, as if God's Holy Word was written to address his particular struggles.

Before Danny could think of something to say, Peter clapped him on the shoulder and grinned. "You have been a good friend to my family. You have read the Bible to us and explained many difficult things, although I suspect these lessons are difficult for you as well. Your time in the eastern war has troubled your heart, and I sense Jesus wants to heal you here on the desert. Our life journeys have crossed paths, and the Creator is using you in mighty ways to point to him, declare his greatness, but also to refresh you in some special way."

The old Indian paused, and Danny shivered in the cold. Below the knoll, the three younger Indian boys threw rocks at a distant outcropping, enjoying the delay in work. Danny looked at Peter once more when the old man squeezed his shoulder.

"I believe the Spirit whispers to you on the wind. He led you here, to the spring I told Patrick Blair about. You are doing a great thing in completing Patrick's goal, but you struggle to understand what God is building within you, the work he is performing within your heart."

Danny stared at Peter, amazed at the old Indian's insight. "What am I to do?" The wind whipped his whispered query, almost stealing his words away. But Peter nodded gravely.

"You have been called by Jesus, the Son of God. He will guide you. Do not let your fear take root like the oak tree. Let the Spirit have time to work. You are right where you are supposed to be. Trust God."

Luke laughed again and nudged Danny with an elbow, drawing his gaze from the old man. "Grandpa, I think Danny is speaking of something else. Or maybe *someone* else."

Peter crossed his arms over his chest and grunted. "So am I."

★★★

The final ten miles of plains before striking the Arkansas River seemed endless as winter dragged on. Although a downhill slant predominated over the land, the intense cold and unobstructed bitter winds proved more challenging than many of the longer stretches the work crew had cleared.

As February drew to a close, Danny and Peter's family retreated to the station, just ahead of another winter storm that promised to rage across the prairie. A canopy of steel gray clouds raced across the dull sky, pregnant with the threat of snow. Freezing wind pushed Danny and the Indians over the newly constructed road, recently cleared.

As they neared the rock station, Luke grabbed Danny's arm, halting the shuffling cavalcade. The women and teenage boys huddled around the smaller children as Peter joined Luke and Danny.

"Look." Luke pointed across the frozen desert at the station, still a half mile away. Danny squinted into the blustering wind and felt his chilled forehead furrow when he spied a wagon parked near the stone structure. Someone was at his station.

"Must be Mr. Hanson," Danny said above the gusts. "I've been going to town every couple weeks for supplies. I'm a few days late."

Luke grinned and slapped him on the back. "You think we haven't noticed you've been reluctant to go to town? Grandma swears a girl is responsible."

"That doesn't make sense. If I had a girl, wouldn't I be quick about visiting town?" Danny growled at his friend.

Peter shook his head as he stepped onto the trail, moving toward the station. "Sense has little to do with anything where a woman is concerned."

While the group made their way toward the station, Danny felt his eagerness to get out of the cold turn into apprehension. Surely Mr. Hanson had missed Danny's timely visits for supplies and thought to personally deliver them. But the thought that Jenny Blair might have accompanied the storekeeper made him pick up his pace only to drag his feet, unsure which response was warranted. What if she were angry at him? How could he explain the unexpected kiss had taken him by surprise as well? He'd never believed he'd find the courage to attempt such a brazen incident.

Peter instructed the women and children to hurry into the station while he and Danny looked after the stock. The horses that trailed the Indians needed water and shelter.

Luke led his family into the station as Danny stalked beside the old man, eager to settle the horses. He struggled with impatience and trepidation as they unpacked the animals and crowded them into the rock stable Danny had built months ago. His fear didn't dissipate when he recognized the storekeeper's team in the stalls, the pair munching grain while they watched the new arrivals shoulder their way out of the wind.

Had Jenny Blair come with Mr. Hanson? Why would she? What girl would endure such a frigid ride across the desert to deliver supplies? He was nobody, Danny reminded himself grimly. Although they'd shared a kiss, he was nothing to Sergeant Blair's little sister.

Danny took his time rubbing the chilled horses down, taking time to pamper the faithful animals that had worked to help clear the new road. Desperately he wanted to know if Mr. Hanson had come alone, and yet he wanted to delay finding out if the storekeeper had company on the long trip from Trinidad.

Finally, Peter nudged him as the old man jutted a chin toward the stone station. Danny nodded, knowing the time had come. Peter stepped to the stable doorway as the final muted rays of sunlight dulled across the clearing. Dusk fell quickly, the massive mountains to the west already shadowed in darkness.

"I'm coming, I'm coming," Danny muttered as he placed the curry brush on a ledge and turned to follow the old man. But Peter remained where he stood, his gaze studying the younger man.

"This is not the war. You do not have to prepare for battle." His somber words were softened when a faint grin touched the corners of his mouth.

Danny exhaled loudly and tucked his gloved hands into his armpits. "Am I so easy to read?"

Peter's grin widened. "Women affect men in deep ways. I am old, but not too old to forget how the flames of love would leap and dance. Now, those fires have turned to glowing coals, burning brightly in my heart, still warming me to my bones."

Danny cocked an eyebrow, not sure how to respond. But he smiled to himself when they entered the rock station, and Peter bent to kiss the wrinkled cheek of his wife.

Carl Hanson looked up from the blazing fire on the hearth when Danny stepped to him.

"Mr. Hanson, you didn't have to deliver supplies all the way out here," Danny said, reaching out his hand to shake.

Carl grabbed his hand, then glanced round the warm room appreciatively. "Well, I confess I worried about you, missing your every two-week visit. But I admit I wanted to see your place again. The water trough and the horse stable are new to me."

Before Danny could reply, Jenny came to the kitchen door, pink stains on her cheeks when she saw him. He felt his heart lurch at the sight of her and hurriedly removed his hat.

"Miss Blair."

She met his searching scrutiny for a brief instant before dropping her gaze. "Hello, Danny," she murmured.

A chorus of voices heralded the prepared meal, and the room broke into organized turmoil as the women and children crowded to the table while the men and older boys found seats along the walls. Peter's wife waved away any offers of help as she carried a heavy pot and ladled soup to each person. Silence fell upon the hungry bunch as everyone ate, but Danny stole covert glances at Jenny where the pretty girl sat with the Indian women at the table.

Luke nudged him, and Danny tore his gaze from Jenny. "Do you want more?"

Danny blinked, heat surging through him at the memory of the scrap lumber bonfire a few weeks ago.

Luke held his empty bowl up as his grandmother poured soup.

"Oh, more soup?" Danny nodded, relief flooding over him as he lifted his bowl for seconds.

As the old woman filled his bowl, he glanced to where Jenny sat, gray eyes glowing as she talked with the young girls at the table. Brown coils had escaped the bunched tresses above her nape and draped across her cheeks. She seemed so beautiful, so unattainable, so out of his reach. Why was he allowing himself to be tormented with thoughts of Jenny Blair? The kiss had meant nothing to her, he felt certain. Yet, he trembled with hope. Why had she accompanied Mr. Hanson if she didn't have feelings for him?

As if on a cloud, he allowed a secret thought to flourish. Could Jenny ever care for a man like him? His heart swelled with his clandestine wish.

A knock at the door made everyone turn. Peter hurried to open the door, and Danny felt his heart sink like a stone when Reggie Bloomberg stepped into the room.

CHAPTER THIRTY-EIGHT

Everyone in the station stared at the young rancher. Even the children grew quiet, as if sensing the adults' abrupt apprehension. Only the sound of the whistling wind could be heard above the blaze crackling in the big stone fireplace.

Reggie grinned when he saw Jenny sitting among the women and children at the long table, then closed the door behind him and faced the room. "Well, I went to town to see my girl, and imagine my surprise when Mrs. Hanson told me she'd gone delivering supplies to the desert." He took another step into the room and dropped his pack near the wall. "Right past my own house too, as if I'd not be willing to take this cold ride with her all the way out here."

Danny placed his bowl on the dirt floor and rose to his feet. He appreciated Luke standing beside him, not feeling alone as he carefully watched Reggie. Was the rancher drunk? Angry? Danny felt the tension mount when Jenny came to her feet.

"Reggie, I'm not hiding from you. It's no secret I came with Carl."

Before Reggie could reply, Peter motioned for his family to move into the kitchen where the cookfire still blazed.

Hastily, the women and children, along with the teenage boys, moved into the other room. Danny felt pleased when Mr. Hanson, Peter, and Luke remained with him.

Reggie shot Danny an annoyed glance before he went on. "But I guess that's what I'm curious about." He ignored the three men and strode to the fireplace, stretching his hands to the heat. "I'd like to talk with you private like, but if there're no secrets, I'll have my say."

Jenny slowly lowered herself to the bench beside the table, all eyes on the rancher. Danny saw the tip of a leather holster beneath the rancher's coat and knew he had a gun. He glanced above the front door where the Henry rifle hung on pegs.

Reggie turned his back to the fire and glowered at Jenny. Danny didn't like the way he looked at her but sensed this moment had to happen. He clenched his fists, taut like a bow string, ready to pounce at the first sign of danger to Jenny.

"We used to go to dances and Christmas caroling. We've been to scrap lumber bonfires together, but since the one I missed, I can't seem to get you alone." He paused, studying her intently before he lowered his voice. "Everyone knows we have an understanding."

Reggie's declaration felt like a punch to Danny's guts. He held his breath, wishing Jenny would refute the rancher's claim. Hadn't he kissed her? More importantly, hadn't she kissed him in return?

He scowled, not certain of his memory of that wonderful night. What had truly transpired the night of the bonfire? Had he tricked himself into imagining something that didn't exist? Suddenly, he felt like a fool. Sergeant Blair's sister was not for the likes of him, beyond his reach. He knew that. He'd always known that.

With a loud exhale, he drew everyone's gaze by stepping to the rancher and holding out his hand. "Reggie, welcome."

Reggie stared at the outstretched hand before slowly shaking.

"You've had a long ride in the cold, and you'll be staying the night. Let's see if we can rustle some soup. You must be hungry."

"I'll need to take care of my horse first," Reggie said as he moved to the table and sat down, his gaze never leaving Jenny's face.

She nodded to herself, as if coming to her senses. She called for Peter's wife and walked into the kitchen to retrieve a bowl of soup for Reggie.

"You haven't taken care of your horse?" Luke's query hinted of reprimand, but Reggie ignored him.

"Let's get your horse into the stable," Peter said, shrugging into his coat and tugging on gloves. "Danny, give me a hand?"

A silent signal passed between grandfather and grandson, and Luke nodded slightly. He sat across from Reggie, watching the young rancher like a man watches a rattlesnake.

"I'll help." Mr. Hanson hurried to put on his coat.

Reluctantly, Danny went to the row of pegs driven into the wall beside the door and pulled on his coat. He wanted to catch a glimpse of Jenny before he went with Peter to the stable, but the girl stayed hidden from view, as if she didn't want him to see her.

Peter tugged on his elbow. "Come on."

At Danny's continued hesitancy, the old Indian dragged the younger man from the warm room. Mr. Hanson closed the station door behind them, and the trio stood for a moment in the cold wind.

The chilled horse stamped an impatient hoof, and Peter reached for the reins looped around the hitching rail. Danny pursed his lips and thrust his hands into his pockets, his gaze lifting to the dark clouds drifting across the night sky. Few stars peeked between the ominous canopy.

As he searched for a connection, a snowflake fluttered from above, melting when it landed on his cheek.

"Where are you, Lord?" Danny whispered, yearning to feel God's nearness.

"That boy was lucky to find this place in the dark." Peter tugged his collar higher as he led the horse to the gap in the bluff.

Complete darkness surrounded them, cutting off any light from the dim stars. Danny wished he'd brought the lantern off the table.

Mr. Hanson chuckled humorlessly. "Good road. Hard to get lost."

What do you want from me, Jesus?

Peter led the way through the darkness to the water trough. Thankfully, the water wasn't frozen, and Danny listened as the horse drank thirstily. In the stable, a match flared. Mr. Hanson lit the stub of candle Peter indicated, and the stone room glowed dimly while the men unsaddled Reggie's cold horse.

As the old Indian rubbed the horse with a piece of grain sack, Mr. Hanson chuckled again. "He surely doesn't like you."

Danny leaned against the door frame, his mind on the events unfolding within the stone station. He glanced at the storekeeper, not really paying attention. "Who?"

"You, my friend," Peter explained as he checked each of the horse's hooves. "Young Mr. Bloomberg senses a rival in you."

Danny snorted. "Rival? I have nothing to rival Reggie Bloomberg with."

The two older men stared at Danny in the flickering candlelight. "Don't sell yourself short," Mr. Hanson cautioned. "You have more in common with Jenny than Reggie does."

Danny straightened and shook his head. "You're fooling yourself. She has no interest in me. Besides, what could we possibly have in common?"

Peter blew out the candle, plunging the stable into total darkness before brushing past him, leading the way back to the station. Danny tagged after the two men, hoping beyond hope there *was* something between him and the sergeant's sister.

"You knew Patrick Blair. You're both orphans. You've both struggled to find your place in the world," Carl stated in a matter-of-fact manner. "Lil is very sharp, and she says she can tell you've both been through Ezekiel's valley. The Lord is rebuilding the both of you, slowly bringing you back to life. But not just any life. You both love the Lord, and Lil says that will be your connection."

Danny halted, unaware of the cold wind that blustered from the mountain heights. In the distance, dark clouds massed across the sky, masking the towering peaks he'd grown accustomed to. He thought of the corpses in the valley of dry bones, and the way flesh encased their rotted bodies, rebuilding them into new creations. Was the Lord bringing him back to life, a life where dreams came true?

"Jesus," he whispered to the night, the name filled with reverence and a plea.

He'd come west to fulfill another man's dream, only to discover more simmered beneath the surface than met the eye. He'd never suspected he had dreams of his own, but Jesus did. Both Danny and Jenny were involved in the situation, the two of them learning how to depend on God while seeking a peace they'd never possessed. Or was Danny a fool, yearning for something beyond his reach?

He recalled Peter's words from earlier today and promised to trust God. Danny would not allow fear to take root. He needed to believe God brought him here for something. And although he didn't believe Peter and Mr. Hanson's assertion about Jenny, he appreciated their encouragement. He had friends.

Carl Hanson slapped him on the shoulder and reached for the door handle. "Come on. It's cold out here."

***

Later, in the rock station, the lantern had been extinguished and the building seemed still and quiet. The women and children—along with Jenny—slept in the kitchen while the three teenage boys huddled under blankets in the corner of the main room. Luke, Peter, and Mr. Hanson sat leaning against the far wall covered in blankets, shadowed firelight dancing across their faces. In moments, the room filled with the even breathing of sleeping men.

Danny glanced once more at the rifle hanging over the front door before he settled for the night against the remaining wall. Either by accident or design, he stretched out near Reggie, the young rancher dragging his pack to him as Danny draped a blanket over himself. He'd not bothered to remove his coat upon returning to the station, and now burrowed against the stone wall, seeking comfort he knew he wouldn't find.

Danny watched as Reggie covered his legs with blankets before pulling a brown bottle from his saddlebags. A cork popped and the bottle tilted, the rancher chugging greedily.

"Ahhhh," he sighed as he lowered the bottle. "That's to me, Mason. I'm celebrating my good fortune. Ever since the last scrap lumber bonfire, Jenny's been out of sorts, a little distant, like she doesn't know what she wants. But I think I've put her back on track."

Danny felt his stomach tighten. He squinted into the flickering flames in the big fireplace and watched the dull shadows darting across the rock walls of the spacious room. Jenny was in the next room. Did she sleep, or did she suffer the anxiety Danny felt? Again, he reminded himself to give his pensive mood to the Lord. He must allow the Spirit to work, like Peter suggested.

"So, you patched things with her?" Danny held his breath, not wanting to know the answer, while a desperation consumed him, forcing him to know.

"Well, not exactly, but I think I've got my rope around this filly again. She turned cold as ice the last few weeks. I'd forgotten our date and met some friends in the saloon. She just needs some time to forgive me."

He chuckled and shot Danny a sidelong glance. "I wondered if she'd found another man, but that's ridiculous. I'm the best man on this range. Women like to know they're thought of. She'll forgive me in time, and things will be right as rain."

Danny clenched his fists beneath his blanket. Patience, he told himself. He had a job to finish, a task to complete. The completed station was supposed to secure the future of the Blair family. But somewhere along the way, the unexpected had occurred. While Danny was seeking and serving Christ through the building of the stone station, Christ had been rebuilding Danny's life. A beautiful new land, new friends, and a sense of belonging filled him in surprising ways. Was Jenny part of this unfamiliar life? Was Jesus blessing him more than he could comprehend?

Danny grunted, drawing Reggie's gaze. "I walk with the Lord. He lifted me from the ashes and brought me west to discover something. I thought it was for me to build, but I've learned he is building me. God is here, speaking, guiding, telling me to trust him."

Reggie stared at him and then snorted, holding up the brown bottle. "Have you been drinking? What are you talking about?"

A grin creased Danny's features and he relaxed. "Nothing. Nothing you'd understand." He glanced around the rock-walled room, to the blanket-covered mounds that slept on the dirt floor. Perhaps one day he'd put in a flagstone floor, or possibly planks. With the sawmill in town, he could, in time, make improvements to the homestead. Sergeant Blair would like that.

CHAPTER THIRTY-NINE

In the morning, Danny awoke to find Peter folding his blankets before feeding sticks to the glowing embers in the fireplace. Mr. Hanson, Luke, and the three younger boys slept soundly while Reggie Bloomberg snored, the rancher's chin on his chest.

"I'll check on the stock," Danny whispered to Peter.

The old Indian handed him the empty coffeepot as he strode for the door. He stared at the kitchen door, wondering how Jenny had slept. He reached for the rifle above the door before quietly slipping outside into the crisp air of a high plains morning.

Danny stood there a moment, the blackened pot dangling from one hand, the rifle slung over one shoulder, as he scanned the eastern prairie. He snuggled deeper into his coat as the chill penetrated. But the storm that threatened yesterday had passed as if it had never existed. In its wake, a clear day dawned—only a scattering of clouds lingering to the north.

In the distance, he watched the morning star fade. The sun tipped the eastern horizon, bright rays shooting across the land as dark shadows hovered in the folds and clefts.

"You are with me, Jesus," he whispered to the sunrise. "I am yours, and you are mine. Take my heart, use me for your glory, and allow me to bring you joy. I praise you for your wonderful creation. The magnificent mountains, the endless plains, and the bright stars I see every night."

He paused, feeling a lump rise to his throat. His chest clenched, and Danny nodded, a sense of gratitude cascading over him.

"You brought me here. Use me. I know I have a purpose, but I'm sensing something more, as if you want me to experience more than I bargained for. As I encounter you, grow my faith."

His words drifted off, and he swallowed the lump before going on. "I love you. I give you a willing heart, although it's battered and bruised. But I expect you already knew that when you chose me for this project."

He pulled on his gloves as he made his way to the box canyon. With satisfaction, he saw a cloud reflected on the still surface of the water trough. No ice this morning, an encouraging note as Danny wondered how long until spring.

As he scrambled over the bars of the gate, he thought he heard the station door close. He straightened inside the corral and watched a figure stride across the clearing, her dress billowing slightly in the gentle breeze. His eyes widened when he recognized Jenny.

"Morning, Danny," she greeted merrily, as if her fiancé did not sleep in the nearby station.

For a moment, he couldn't speak. Danny stared at her rosy cheeks, pink from the chill or the stolen moment alone with him.

"Morning, Jenny. You're looking pert."

She lifted her chin, not breaking their eye contact. "And why not? Patrick's station is coming along fine. Isn't that what you came west for?"

He nodded, bewildered at her nearness, her beauty, and the possible hidden meaning in her remarks. What was her game? He felt the heat creep up his neck when he thought of the kiss they shared only a couple weeks ago.

As if sensing his thoughts, she glanced away, her cheeks growing even more rosy. "What are you doing out here? It's so early."

Danny held up the empty container. "Everyone will be wanting coffee. And I need to check on the stock."

She pointed at the pot. "Fill that, and I'll take it in. But wait for me. I'll go with you to check the stock."

Anticipation swirled in his stomach as he placed the empty coffeepot below the steel pipe. She didn't give him a clue as to her desire to accompany him to the stable when he handed her the container, water sloshing over the rim as she turned to take it to the station. He watched her open the door quietly and reappear a moment later, hurrying to join him near the opening to the gap. She ignored his offer to help her over the gate. Yet, she allowed him to hold her hand as she alighted on the other side, peering at one another.

He waited for a long moment, waited for her to pull her hands from his. But she smiled up at him, and his heart warmed.

"Aren't you going to check the horses?"

He nodded dumbly, confused at the pretty girl's question. Then he shook his head, remembering his chore. "Yes, yes, of course."

Their hands parted as they turned toward the notch between the bluffs. He leaned his rifle against a rock and joined Jenny where she watched a horse grazing, the gelding's tail swishing in the morning chill. Other horses came toward them, suspecting food. Danny went inside the stable for the grain.

"This split in the mountain surprises me," she said. "How did Peter ever discover the place?"

As he fed and watered each horse, Danny explained Peter's discovery of the spring so many years ago. "Apparently, the local Indians knew of the place, but they never developed it. The water sliding down the rock face of the bluff to disappear once more into the ground is not really suitable for travelers or animals. Only with the pipe can water be delivered to the water trough."

He gestured to the bent pipe protruding from the concealed spring. Jenny nodded, seeming interested, then licked her lips. "Patrick always wanted to make this our place, a place for the Blair family, where we owned something that could provide an income. Our family had always been poor, but he felt God wanted more for us."

She paused as he led the way deeper into the box canyon. Absently, she followed, apparently absorbed in her memories.

"Did you share his conviction?" he asked. "I mean, what if God doesn't want more for you? What if the Lord wants you to work hard, endure tough days, and wait on the Lord? What if Jesus has a plan you can't understand? Perhaps he has something else in store for you. Will you be faithful and watch him work?"

She stepped around a mound of rocks Danny had removed from the level grassy places, clearing the pasture for the horses to graze when spring returned. Along the west wall of the chasm, dirt piled where the men had deposited excess soil for a future garden.

"You've done a lot of work in here. This will provide plenty of grazing for stage teams when spring comes."

"You didn't answer my question," he accused softly, watching her intently.

The morning light had not filtered down into this notch in the bluff, and the chill deepened as they progressed deeper into the gap. Above, a blue sky brightened as the sun rose in the east.

Jenny looked up at him, and he caught his breath. "I don't know," she whispered. "Life is too difficult. I was so lonely when Patrick left for the war. He left me to fend for myself, alone. I vowed to do anything to never suffer again." She dropped her gaze, studying her shoes peeking from beneath her dress. "With Reggie, I will have everything. I'll never suffer again."

"Everything?" Danny lifted her chin with two fingers until their eyes met. "Everything?" he repeated in a soft voice.

"Don't, Danny." She retreated a step. "You confuse me. I promised myself I'd do anything to avoid difficulty. With Patrick gone, I'm alone again. With Reggie, I'll have a big house, servants, and all the new clothes I want. Am I wrong to want security?"

Danny didn't step closer, instead crossing his arms over his chest as he listened attentively. "I know the loneliness you speak of. I know the desperation you feel, thinking you're always going to be alone, that no one cares about you. I know despair, sorrow, the desire to give up. But then I met Jesus—"

"I know Jesus," she snapped, narrowing her eyes. "I prayed unceasingly to him, begging him for help." She shrugged. "He brought Reggie Bloomberg."

"You can't believe that." Scorn laced Danny's allegation. "God would not have you marry such a man." He took a step, closing the gap between them. "I know you are nothing but a prize to him. He doesn't really love you."

She raised both hands, palms out. "Stop. Stay back. I won't listen to you."

Danny nodded. "Fine, don't listen to me. But listen to the Lord. What is Jesus telling you?" He placed a hand on his chest and took another step closer. "What is he saying to your heart?"

"Stop," she cried and whirled, fleeing for the fence.

Danny gave chase, but she proved more nimble and scrambled over the rail fence before he could catch her. As she dropped on the other side, he caught her hand, halting her at last. She glowered at him over the top rail.

"Let go," she hissed, gray eyes blazing.

"Why did you come here?"

She only glared at his question.

"You know how I feel about you," he went on in a low voice as the station door opened and Peter stepped out. They both glanced at the old man, still too far away for him to hear their conversation. "Tell me what you feel for me."

Jenny tugged her hand free, walking backward as she locked eyes with him. She shook her head before she turned and marched into the station.

Peter watched the girl pass and then looked at Danny with an inquisitive tilt to his head. When Danny didn't explain, a wide grin spread across the old Indian's face. Eyes twinkling, he nodded slowly. "Coffee's ready."

★★★

After breakfast, Mr. Hanson and Jenny prepared to depart the station. The storekeeper shot Danny a searching glance but asked no questions about Jenny's sudden silence and aloof manner. She ignored Reggie too, barely giving the rancher a civil word.

The men gathered in the clearing as the pair mounted the high wagon seat. Reggie tried to assist Jenny, but she stepped onto the wheel and settled herself on the bench without his aid. The scowl on the rancher's face made Danny want to smile, but frustration clouded the small victory he felt.

"Thanks for bringing supplies," Luke offered after glancing at the taciturn Danny.

Mr. Hanson lifted the long reins as Jenny stared across the prairie. "I was worried for nothing, but now that I know you're busy with the final stretch of road, I'll not bother to deliver. You'll come to town when you need to." He surveyed the plains that stretched to the east before glancing at the mountain heights to the west, snowcapped and glistening in the morning sun. "Won't be spring for another month, I figure." He looked at Danny. "Mr. Hennessey asks about your road every few days. What'll I tell him?"

"Tell him I hope to be open for business by spring. We should finish the road by then." He peered at Peter, the old Indian nodding in agreement.

"Will do," Mr. Hanson said. He glanced at the fuming Jenny and then slapped the reins over the team. "Good luck," he called to the onlookers as the wagon lumbered from the clearing.

"Might as well scout the eastern range of the ranch, while I'm out here," Reggie said to no one in particular. "Wasted ride," he muttered as he strode to the stable to fetch his horse.

Peter, Luke, and Danny watched him go as the women and children trooped out of the station, readying for departure. Despite the cold, the road construction would go on.

Danny paused in his preparations a few minutes later to watch Reggie Bloomberg ride to the east, his horse loping over the newly fashioned trail. Luke slapped Danny on his shoulder, drawing his gaze away from the vanishing rider.

"He's spoiled and has issues, like many of us. But I don't think he turns to Christ for direction."

Danny drew a deep breath. "I remember when I thought I didn't need the Lord. I had no idea the adventure that awaited me. God understands me better than I know myself."

"And he knows what is best for you," Luke added with a gleam in his eye. "And who."

He turned to help his grandmother pack supplies before Danny could reply. His gaze shifted from the activity around him to the tall Rockies, the morning sun making the snow on the mountains shine as if polished.

"You know me," Danny said to the Lord with a confidence he'd come to rely on. "I want to serve you, finish Sergeant Blair's plan for this place. But then what?"

He waited, wanting an answer to boom from the sky or a giant hand drop from the clouds to show which way to turn.

"After I complete this task, what should I do?"

No answer came to him, no sensation or feeling filling his head.

"Am I not sensitive enough to hear the Holy Spirit?" His voice held a note of pleading. "Please, Jesus, talk to me. Tell me what to do next."

He thought of Jenny and hoped the Lord knew what he was trying to communicate. He'd never had feelings for a girl, any girl. She filled his mind and heart. Was that true love? He knew nothing of such things.

He shifted, pondering, and tried once more.

"What I mean is, I don't want to make a mistake. I want to obey you, follow your desires for me."

He felt his shoulders slump as the three teenage boys came from the stables, leading a large number of horses.

The work crew would ride double to the end of the road to continue the work, using the animals to drag large rocks from the route. The women and children would ride the remaining horses with the supplies. Ready or not, Danny knew they would leave in a few minutes. Yet he wasn't through praying.

He drew a deep breath and nodded. "All right, I'll take my own advice and wait on you. I think I love Jenny Blair, but I want to follow your will, not my desires. Guide me and speak in a way I understand. I trust you, Lord."

CHAPTER FORTY

Peter's insightful eye determined the path as the work on the road continued. The three teenage boys along with Danny and Luke proved to be an efficient crew, following the old Indian's directions as they moved ever closer toward the Arkansas River and connecting with the Santa Fe Trail.

Cold wind blustered across the prairie, ineffective at keeping the dedicated work force from their task. Foot by foot, mile after mile, the road grew.

Weary after each day's work, they returned to the camp the Indians had pitched beside a trio of huge rocks where the women prepared every meal. Chapped lips, wind burned cheeks, and numb fingers plagued the men and boys, but they worked on.

"It's not forever," Peter said one day in early March as they took a break behind a knoll, out of the wind. "When spring comes, we'll go back to the mountains."

Danny stared, stunned at the news. "I thought—well, I thought ..."

Luke grinned. "You thought they would stay down here on the plains?" He shook his head, his grin widening. "Grandpa used to trap the high valleys. He's not a flatlander."

Peter nodded. "I only agreed to help you so we would be fed." He looked up at the nearby mountains, a longing in his old eyes. "Come spring, we'll head back up."

A frown shadowed Danny's features. He hadn't thought about his newfound friends leaving when spring arrived. Somehow, he'd hoped they'd stay around the station, finding work that would enable them to remain close. Had he made friends only to lose them, like in his youth?

Peter seemed to sense his unease as a hawk circled in the gray sky. "We will see you again, Danny. We have shared campfires and coffee. We know one another, and you have become one of us. We will not forget you."

"Besides," Luke said with a punch to Danny's shoulder as he passed his friend. "You still have me."

Peter chuckled as he followed Luke. "I'm afraid you are stuck with my grandson."

But Danny remained in the lee of the low hill, watching the work crew return to their job. The abject loneliness that had driven him west seemed to shrink as the months passed. He'd found friends. He thought of Mr. Hanson and Luke ... Jenny. He felt his chest constrict. Was she more than a friend?

He missed Jenny, missed seeing her shining eyes and hearing her gentle voice. He felt lifted to the heights when she was near, and he longed to see her again. After only nine days since he'd seen her last, he announced he'd be going to Trinidad for supplies the next morning.

"But we're so close," Luke grumbled, pointing to where the line of trees bordering the Arkansas River stretched across the prairie. "I think we have enough supplies for a few more days."

Peter handed his wife a tin cup and waited for the refill before reclining beside Danny. He blew on the hot coffee, eyeing Danny over the rim before he spoke. "A storm is coming. Danny is right. We should go back to the station while he is in town." He gestured at the children huddled near the fire. "The little ones need a break from the cold."

Luke snorted as he surveyed the sky, dusk descending quickly over the plains, casting dark shadows everywhere. "I don't see any sign of a storm. What do you see that I don't?"

Peter winked at Danny and sipped his coffee. "You are young, Luke, and cannot see the signs. Old men like me are connected to the land and the sky. I can feel a storm coming—my bones tell me so."

Luke scowled but didn't argue with his grandfather. Danny silently thanked the old man with a slight grin.

The next day, the small cavalcade followed the newly cleared road to the west, over thirty miles, to the rock station. By nightfall, they'd reached the shelter of the stone building as freezing sleet pushed them the final mile.

"I told you so," Peter shouted to Luke above the roar of the wind.

Luke grumbled something Danny couldn't hear as the men unloaded the women and children at the door of the station. After stabling the stock, the three men hurried to join the others inside.

Leaping flames brightened the spacious room as the trio entered and removed coats, hurrying to the blaze to warm their hands as Luke's aunt handed them steaming mugs of coffee.

"None of you need thank me." Peter sipped his coffee. "I have become close to the Lord, and I believe he tells me things. I'll bet you are glad I listened. If not for me, we'd be freezing right now, camping on the prairie."

Luke glanced at Danny from the corner of his eye as he turned his back to the fire. "I thought our return to the station was because you wanted to see Jenny Blair."

Peter nodded gravely. "Ah, I remember when I was too young to realize the wisdom of my elders. But we all grow up, Luke."

Luke rolled his eyes, but Danny felt himself tense at the mention of Jenny. Did she ever think of him? He shook his head, clearing his muddled thoughts. He would try to be patient. God knew his situation, his frustration, and his excitement. Tomorrow he'd ride to Trinidad if the weather cooperated.

He tilted his head and peered at Peter. "Oh, wise one, will the storm pass tonight?"

Peter took another sip as the women delivered steaming pots to the long table in the center of the room. Danny's gaze locked on the old Indian as if Peter held the keys to whether a meeting with Jenny were possible. Around them, the air filled with a delicious aroma.

"I am confident the storm will pass when it should," the old man said as he found a seat on a bench.

For the next hour, Danny and the Indian family ate supper while the storm raged outside. As images of Jenny danced across his mind, Danny wondered if one didn't rage in his heart too.

"What will we do while Danny visits town?" Luke eyed his grandfather across the table.

"I have an idea, a project I've been considering," the old man said elusively, not meeting Danny's questioning gaze.

★★★

The noon hour had barely passed when Danny and his three packhorses rode up the quiet main street of Trinidad. He went directly to the livery, vowing to locate a bath before going to the mercantile. After stabling his cold animals, he went to the back door of Bill's Café where Gertie supplied him with buckets of hot water. He cleaned and filled an old grain bin at the livery before enjoying a hot bath, although he almost froze when he dried off with a burlap sack and hastened into clean clothes. Teeth chattering, he hurried to the café where he leaned his rifle in the corner before gripping a cup of coffee, sipping the hot drink until he warmed.

As he poured his third cup, Mr. Hennessey entered, and after scanning the dining hall, hurried to Danny's table.

The mine manager tugged gloves free and shook hands with Danny before sitting at the table, not waiting for an invitation. He waved to Gertie and waited while the plump waitress hurried over with a tin cup, steam rising as she poured.

"Thank you, Gertie," he mumbled, lifting the mug to his mouth. He stared intently at Danny when he lowered the cup. "Tell me everything. Is your road good for wagons? Have you connected to the Old Trail at the Arkansas River?"

Before Danny could reply, Mr. Hennessey rushed on after a quick sip from his cup. "My contract with the steamboat company is waiting on more shipments of coal. They say they can handle all I can deliver, the number of steamers on the rivers is booming with the war over. Business is brisk on the steamships as folks move west." He leaned forward, resting his elbows on the edge of the table. "The road along the Purgatory is only getting worse. My drivers report it's too rutted, too hilly, and too slow. My last shipment was delayed when two wagons broke wheels."

Danny sat back, pleased at this reception from the mine manager. If he could open the road across the desert, he'd have immediate income to finance the station. He calculated how much longer Peter and his crew would take to complete the task. And what was the secret project the old Indian had in mind?

He eyed the manager. "We're moving forward as quickly as we can. Not easy cutting road in the dead of winter."

"Of course, of course," Mr. Hennessey agreed quickly. "But business demands a swift response. Your shortcut should enable a quicker delivery time, perhaps cutting off as much as a few days."

Danny nodded, pondering the completion of the stage road. What would he do when the job was finished? Perhaps Luke would manage the station when Peter's family returned to the high mountains for another season. There would be no reason for Danny to remain—impossible for him to stay near and watch Jenny marry Reggie Bloomberg.

Taking a deep breath, he felt his chest swell as Gertie delivered platters piled high with pancakes and potatoes.

"No eggs this morning," she lamented as she wiped her hands on her apron. "The chickens didn't lay any last night." She hurried away to wait on other customers.

"When will you be ready for business?" Mr. Hennessey pressed, watching Danny closely.

He shrugged as he lifted his mug once more. "Another month, maybe sooner if the weather cooperates. Spring will be here soon enough."

"Not soon enough," the mine manager snapped. "I have contracts to honor, orders to fill. The mine is operating well, and the need for coal is growing. With a good road to Westport, we could have our best year yet."

The mine manager rose, waving as he headed for the door, not bothering to add a parting remark. Danny watched him go, thoughtfully considering Mr. Hennessey's impatience as he glanced at the ceiling. How would the Lord use all of this?

Later, as Danny made his way uptown, his thoughts strayed to his initial intent on coming west. Father McKay had promised an adventure while Danny had envisioned the fruition of Sergeant Blair's dream. He'd never considered another purpose for his shortcut across the desert. He'd expected one thing only to have the Lord fill him with other ideas.

He stepped onto the boardwalk in front of the mercantile, but stayed to one side of the door, not ready to enter. Images of Jenny danced across his mind, overwhelming him in ways he couldn't comprehend. What did he know of women?

His gaze lifted to the mountain heights to the west, snowcapped peaks glistening in the midday sun. A cold wind gusted along the main street, reminding him spring was still far off, but he longed for direction, yearned to know what Jesus wanted from him.

He blinked, trying to order his thoughts, then inhaled deeply of the crisp air. "I am here for you, Lord. Do with me as you will."

A strong wind propelled him to the door. The bell jingled merrily over his head as he stepped into the general store. Carl Hanson grinned at him across the counter, then pointed with his chin in the direction of the big table where bolts of fabric piled. He felt his heart clench when he spied Jenny.

Sunlight streamed through the big windows, making the gold strands in her brown hair gleam. He studied her bright cheeks as she helped the woman cut lengths of the colorful cloth, his breath catching when she lifted her face.

As if pulled by an unseen hand, she turned to him, her eyes widening. Her hands stilled, the scissors halfway through the fabric as their eyes locked across stacks of dry goods. For an instant, he couldn't breathe. Jenny's cheeks stained pinker before she dropped her gaze and continued her task.

"Careful, your hand is trembling," the customer warned as Jenny finished the cutting.

Danny stepped to the counter and handed Mr. Hanson his list. "I'm in for supplies."

The storekeeper took the slip of paper, his grin spreading. "Glad to see you, son. Too late to head back today. Lil would want me to invite you to supper."

Danny wanted to argue, to not accept the kind man's suggestion, but a thousand horses couldn't pull him from an opportunity to see Jenny tonight.

"I probably shouldn't, her spoken for and all," he muttered under his breath, his eyes darting to the pretty girl once more as he shifted the rifle sling on his shoulder.

Mr. Hanson snorted. "You'll be welcome company, young man." He shook the list Danny handed him. "I'll have this filled in a jiffy, then we'll see you at six-thirty."

Danny thanked the storekeeper and turned to the big table. Unable to resist, he made his way through the crowded aisles as Jenny wished the woman a good day, the customer hurrying to the counter to pay for her purchases.

Jenny straightened when she saw him approach, her arms crossing protectively over her chest. He thought he detected curiosity in her eyes before they narrowed.

"Good day, Miss Blair." Abruptly, his formal greeting sounded silly in his ears. He'd kissed this beautiful creature and sometimes wondered if she hadn't kissed him in return.

"Hello, Danny. Need more supplies?"

He nodded, watching her closely.

"Surely you're almost finished with the road. You'll be leaving soon, I figure, your reason for coming here finished as well."

He shifted and licked dry lips. "Perhaps I have a new reason for staying on, after the job is complete. Only God can tell."

Her eyebrows arched. "Oh, I couldn't imagine what could entice you to stay on the frontier. I should expect Philadelphia is beckoning you home."

He shook his head. "There's nothing for me back there. I've fallen in love with the frontier, and expect I'll stay."

Her gray eyes darkened. "Seems to me you've fallen in love with many things since coming west."

"Indeed, I have," he whispered. "And what about you? Who do you love?" His boldness surprised him, and he watched a scowl flash across her features.

"My feelings are none of your business. My future is secure. Soon, I expect to marry Reggie, and I'll have everything I've ever wanted. No more barely getting by for me."

Danny smiled but felt his heart sink at her words. "I'm happy for you, Jenny. I wish you the best. I've prayed for direction, which way Christ would have me go. My goal is to obey the Lord. How about you?"

Her gaze widened, and her cheeks paled. She said nothing, only staring at him, and the pain he read in her eyes almost made him regret his inquiry.

She glanced over his shoulder, as if searching for Mr. Hanson, before lowering her voice. "I've prayed until I'm blue in the face. God isn't speaking to me. With Lil here, I'm not needed at the store anymore." She looked away, her chin quivering as she went on. "Patrick's gone, and it's time I move on, find my own way."

Dread swept over Danny, filling him with a sense of loss. He wanted to argue, to explain his feelings for her, but he wanted the Lord to touch her heart first. With a nod, he turned and walked to the door, bowing his head to the bitter wind as he stepped onto the boardwalk.

CHAPTER FORTY-ONE

Carl Hanson helped load his supplies on the packhorses later that day, but still Danny wondered if he'd be wise to make a run for the station, braving the cold night rather than Jenny Blair's cold indifference. She wasn't interested in him, he felt certain. And like she'd threatened, she'd soon be married to Reggie.

He stowed the packs of supplies in the barn as he prayed. "I feel I'm trying, Lord. I want to fulfill the task you've given me. It was never my intent to become distracted by the sergeant's sister. But I can't deny my feelings for Jenny."

He paused, his hands stilling on the canvas sacks as he gazed up at the nearby mountains. "Am I doing right? I feel confused. Shouldn't you fill me with peace as I follow you?"

But the ache in his heart seemed only to swell as he thought of Jenny. Was this sensation love? What did he know of the unfamiliar sentiment?

"I have learned love from you, God. Help me live what I have learned."

In the end, he couldn't make himself leave town before seeing Jenny again. When he knocked at the storekeeper's house at six-thirty, he glanced at the place where he'd kissed

Jenny a month earlier, the nook burned in his memory for all time. Heat warmed him and he couldn't resist a smile.

When the door yanked open, she glowered at him. "Seems everyone knew you were invited to supper except me," she muttered as he stepped from the cold. When he leaned his rifle against the wall, she gestured to the weapon. "Do you carry that thing everywhere you go?"

He nodded. "Habit. Your brother learned to appreciate this rifle. He posted me on point of the scout platoon."

For a moment, Danny's thoughts drifted to the final days of the war and the battle in North Carolina where Patrick Blair was killed. Nelson had died there too, and Danny had been wounded. He glanced again at the leaning rifle before following Jenny into the dining room.

A long-suffering sigh escaped her as she dropped into the chair across from his. A row of candles glowed dimly down the center of the table. "I've been ordered to stay out of the kitchen. It seems a plot is afoot to force me to entertain you."

His grin felt good, and Danny realized how much he enjoyed being in her presence, despite her cynical manner. "My lucky day," he muttered as he reached for the glass of water before him.

"Is it?" She straightened in her chair. "I'm spoken for. I'm engaged to the most eligible bachelor in the region." Her gaze lifted to the ceiling, a dreamy look filling her features. "Mrs. Reggie Bloomberg." Her gaze dropped to rest upon Danny. "I wonder where we'll honeymoon. Denver? Chicago? Kansas City?"

Danny shrugged. "I think you're wise to consider everything. If you marry me, we'll probably not go to any of those cities."

Her eyes widened. "Marry you?"

He shrugged again before taking another sip of water, gripping the glass tightly to conceal the tremor that coursed through him. "You know how I feel about you. Your troubles are not with me."

He wanted to hold his tongue, listen to her without responding to her hurtful taunts. But his words seemed pulled from him, as if he couldn't help himself.

"Troubles?" Her whispered query made him grin.

"I sense your struggle. On one hand, Reggie can provide a good living, but you know the Lord would not have you marry him. On the other hand, I cannot give you all the things he can. Life with me will mean hard work and depending constantly on God for help. You feel the Lord urging you to think this over carefully. I'll bet you've had sleepless nights, praying a lot."

His confidence surprised him, his boldness unexpected.

She stared at him as if he'd looked into her soul and discovered her secret. She continued to watch him as the Hansons brought steaming bowls into the room.

They talked of the war back east, which had ended almost a year ago. They discussed opportunities in the West, folks moving to the frontier to try their hand at farming or opening a business. Gold and silver mining brought many more, and the occupations associated with towns. Saloons sprang up quickly, the need for churches hard on their heels.

Throughout the meal, Jenny remained quiet, as if deep in thought. Mrs. Hanson glanced repeatedly at the silent girl, but nothing seemed to compel her to join the discussion. After supper, the older couple insisted they clear dishes, leaving Danny and Jenny alone again at the table.

When she seemed determined to keep her silence, Danny stood. Her agitation seemed matched by his own, and despite his confident front, he feared his broken heart would force him to say things he would later regret.

"You seem quiet this evening, Miss Blair. And I need to get some sleep. Long ride tomorrow. Thank you for the meal, and I will take my leave."

She rose, not offering a protest to his escape. She walked with him to the front door, pausing only briefly for Danny to thank his hosts.

"You are always welcome here, young man," Lil Hanson said with a smile.

Carl nodded, his piercing gaze locked on Danny, as if trying to convey something unspoken.

"I'll see you in a couple weeks, when you return for supplies," the storekeeper said.

Danny nodded and continued to the door, Jenny following, while the older couple stayed behind. As he tugged on his coat, the sound of rattling dishes drifted from the kitchen. Jenny fidgeted as Danny reached for his rifle.

"You have a choice to make," he said in a soft voice.

Her gray eyes flashed as she studied him. "I've already made my choice."

"Yes, you have," he agreed as he grasped the door handle. "I hope for your sake it's the right one."

As her brow furrowed in consternation, he bent and pressed his lips to hers, not waiting for her to reply. When he pulled away, he watched her eyelids flutter open.

"Trust Jesus," he whispered as he stepped into the night, the cold enveloping him.

When he glanced over his shoulder, her pale face shone dully in the dim lantern light where she remained in the doorway. He was far away before he stole a second glance to find the door closed, windows glowing from the Hanson house.

CHAPTER FORTY-TWO

Dark clouds hovered ominously in the gray sky, mirroring Danny's dark mood as he made his way along the road east of Trinidad. He struggled to stay focused, his thoughts constantly returning to Jenny. She told him she'd made her choice. Why couldn't he accept her decision?

Sourly, he mulled over the previous night's dialogue with the pretty girl. She would marry Reggie, and Danny would have to leave the area when he finished the shortcut to the Arkansas River. He believed he was finishing the project for Sergeant Blair, a man he greatly admired. Now, Danny wanted to be done with the task and flee before his broken heart drove him crazy.

"Why, Lord?" He narrowed his eyes and studied the steel gray clouds as he rode, seeking answers. Why would God bring him here to suffer? He never wanted to fall in love, yet the image of the sergeant's sister was impossible to drive from his mind.

He dropped his gaze to the worn road and spied the Bloomberg ranch house, appearing grand and stately on its low knoll. He'd been content to have a direction, something to do. He'd cherished his time in the West, making new friends and experiencing the most amazing land he'd ever seen. Yet he couldn't help but wonder if his time on the frontier had come to an end. Surely, he couldn't stay near Trinidad if Jenny married Reggie.

"Forgive me, Lord," he muttered after passing the big ranch. His final words to Jenny last evening were for her to trust Jesus. Would he not take his own advice? "You don't make mistakes. You brought me here for something. I'll trust you. Although my heart aches, I'll keep my eyes on you."

As he prayed, his spirit relaxed, the icy grip of fear that wound cold fingers around his heart and mind letting loose their tight grasp. He nodded, realizing he was still on the prairie, still had a job to complete.

A sense of peace flooded him, embracing him. A slow grin stretched his cold cheeks as he rode east, the morning sun lifting bright over the endless plains. "You're still with me, Christ. Work in me and through me."

By the time he reached the stone station, a weariness filled him, not wholly from the long ride across the desert. Exhausted, he gratefully accepted Luke's offer to help him unpack when he rode into the clearing.

Yet an anticipation lingered when he thought of Jenny. Would she choose the safe security a marriage to Reggie Bloomberg offered, or would she allow her heart free rein?

"Grandpa says spring is in the air," Luke said as he threw a canvas pack over his shoulder and led the way toward the station. Danny followed suit, leaving the stable as dusk descended upon the plains. The wind had died down, but the gray sky remained, a few scattered clouds looming on the horizon.

"He doesn't think it'll snow?" Danny always deferred to Peter's uncanny insights when it came to weather.

Luke shrugged. "Who knows?" He waited a moment before adding, "Grandpa does seem to have a sense about these things."

Danny handed his rifle to Luke and stepped through the bars of the gate as the final dull rays of the sun vanished behind the western mountains, twilight descending. Adjusting their packs upon their shoulders, they walked to the station, Danny's gait slowing when he noticed something in the gathering darkness.

"What's this?" He indicated a tall sapling with bare branches near the front door.

Luke chuckled. "Grandpa's secret project. He had us move three young cottonwood trees he'd found. There's another one near the end of the station and one more beside the water trough."

Danny stared as a feeling of home slowly filled him.

His gaze lifted from the tall, leafless sapling to the bluffs concealing the narrow box canyon with shadows and then to the tall peaks to the west. He turned to study the endless prairie to the north and east, the folds in the land filling with deeper shadows as the final light of the day diminished. The tranquil desert sunset calmed him, spoke to him. Was he home?

He knew he'd never return to Philadelphia—the frontier had claimed his heart. But was he to live here?

He drew in a deep breath as Luke broke the comfortable silence. "We are a part of this land, my family. Grandpa came here over forty years ago to trap for furs in the mountains. This land is our home, will always be our home."

He turned to peer at Danny, his features shrouded in the deepening darkness. "We know you feel this too. You have become a part of this land, as we have." He gripped Danny's shoulder. "Now, you belong here too."

Emotion surged and a lump rose in Danny's throat. Did the Lord want him to remain here? And what about Jenny? Could he stay near the girl he loved if she married another?

He cleared his throat and dropped his pack to the ground. "I'll be right in, Luke. Give me a minute."

Luke opened the door and dragged both packs inside, squeals of delight coming from within before the door closed once more. Danny slung his rifle over his shoulder and watched the deepening blue of the night sky darken above the Rocky Mountains. A few scattered stars shone, peeking through the lowering clouds, but Danny didn't think of them as he turned to the Lord.

"I've almost finished Sergeant Blair's goal. You brought me here to fulfill his dream, but I think you had much more in mind for me to experience. I never expected you to work within me so thoroughly, so intensely."

He paused, his prayer catching in his throat. "Why do you love me so much?"

***

Danny helped load the supplies onto the horses, packing each bag around children riding double or women carrying gear. Canvas water sacks hung from every saddle, and the men held tools.

"I don't see why I can't go with you," Danny grumbled for the third time as he finished preparations. The sun barely tipped the eastern horizon, and the cold air stung his cheeks, yet the blue sky promised fine weather. Not a hint of storm lingered after yesterday's steely skies.

Peter exchanged glances with his grandson as they carried gear to the waiting horses. "We will need more water delivered before we reach the Arkansas River. I'll expect you in a few days with more water."

Luke caught his grandfather's cryptic glance and shuffled away, leaving Danny alone with the old man as the others began moving along the eastern road. Danny frowned as he watched them go.

"I still don't understand. Can't one of the women stay behind to deliver supplies? You'll need me for this last part of the clearing."

Peter shook his head and studied Danny. "I know I am right. The young ones need this time to learn from me. I will not be around forever. And I do not like having my family separated."

"I know, but—"

Peter laid a hand on Danny's arm, stopping his protestation. "You must trust me. I have connected with Christ and feel his Spirit within me. I sense he wants you to stay behind. We will expect you in a few days."

A frown stretched across Danny's features, but he nodded, wanting to respect the old man. "Well, I guess I can work on preparing the garden. And another rock wall in the box canyon would help manage the stock."

"Good," Peter said as he turned to follow his family. He glanced over his shoulder when he reached the edge of the clearing. "God willing, we'll see you soon," he repeated.

For a few minutes, Danny watched until the small cavalcade grew tiny in the distance. Inhaling sharply, he strode into the chasm in the bluff. There were a number of tasks he could work on, but he thought they could wait until the road was finished. He decided to make the best of a confusing situation and put himself to work clearing more stones from the canyon floor, making room for additional stock.

As his mind wandered while he worked, he appreciated the old man's wisdom. Danny felt he needed this time alone to process his bewildering feelings for Jenny. He didn't doubt he loved her, although he had no experience to draw from. But he didn't want his love for the pretty girl to distract from his relationship with Christ.

Yet as the day passed, he wavered between complete submission to the Lord and great anxiety. Was he to stay here?

He wrestled another stubborn rock loose. When the stone let go, Danny fell back, slamming hard against the ground. Panting, he stared up at the blue sky. Cold wind whipped across the plains but rarely penetrated this narrow cut into the bluff. A short distance away, the soft tumble of water from the steel pipe drifted across the small pasture. Come springtime, this little canyon would be filled with lush grass, perfect for feeding stage or freight stock. The station in the desert would soon be ready for business.

He turned to study the rock water trough, his rifle leaning nearby. From here, he could see all three cottonwoods the Indians had transplanted. He grinned when he imagined the shade they would provide in the hot summer months.

When the day was far advanced, he studied the large mound of stones he'd piled for the corral wall. One day soon, he'd build that wall, dividing the pasture into smaller parcels. He saw with satisfaction how the dark-tilled soil of the planned garden sprawled beneath the chilled sunlight. Would spring come soon, as Peter forecast?

With a quick movement, he reached for another stone at his feet as a bullet whizzed past his ear. Danny threw himself to the ground and scanned the edge of the bluff where the shot had come from. Nothing stirred, as if even the wind held its breath while Danny searched for his assailant.

"Hey, Mason. I'm going to kill you," an unseen voice drifted from above. Danny felt his stomach clench when he recognized Reggie Bloomberg's voice.

CHAPTER FORTY-THREE

Danny scrambled behind the mound of rocks he'd piled. Glancing around the heap, he looked to where his rifle leaned near the water trough. He gripped a fist-sized stone, his only weapon.

"I underestimated you," Reggie shouted from the canyon rim. "Just a drifter, down on your luck. You have nothing, and I couldn't believe she had any interest in you."

An arm lifted and another shot whined, ricocheting down the canyon. Across the narrow pasture, Danny heard his horse shift in the stable.

He leaped and raced for his rifle. A third shot blasted dirt from beneath his feet before he skidded beside the water trough. He peered around the corner as another shot echoed in the slim chasm.

"She's my girl, I tell you. No drifter is taking her from me," Reggie shouted again, his words slurring.

When another shot rang, Danny threw himself at his rifle, rolled once, and lay prone, the barrel trained on the edge of the canyon rim.

Despite the chill, Danny wiped damp palms on his pants. Memories of former battles raced across his mind, recalling the supposed bravery he'd touted. The empty motivation seemed so hollow now, so selfish. He'd wanted only to die with a little self-respect. He had nothing else.

Now, however, courage surged, real and powerful. He was a child of the living God, he loved Christ, and his life held significance. After giving his heart to Jesus, he'd been led into the wilderness where his faith seasoned, and hope blossomed. Like the dry bones in Ezekiel, he felt reborn.

A pistol shot went wide, howling across the canyon, and Danny fired at the crouching figure on the rim. Without a sound, Reggie stood and tottered before tumbling over the edge. Glass shattered as the figure fell atop a splinter of cliff before bouncing off a house-sized boulder. Finally, like a rag doll, the young rancher came to rest at the bottom of the canyon, his crumpled body collapsed like a wet sack.

Danny rose slowly, his weapon fixed on Reggie. He approached with caution but knew where his shot had landed, not wishing to seriously injure the rancher. Yet the fall from the thirty-foot-high wall might have done the young man in.

He picked up the fallen pistol, noticing the shards of brown glass scattered nearby before he knelt beside the limp form. Reggie groaned, and Danny pursed his lips as he glanced along his frame, searching for blood or obvious injury. Miraculously, the rancher seemed uninjured from his tumble, only the single bullet wound to his shoulder evident from the hasty examination.

"You're a fool," he muttered as he leaned his rifle against a rock and lifted the rancher in his arms. Was he a fool for treating his attacker, or was Reggie the fool for lamenting his loss of Jenny?

Danny froze, his thoughts making him ponder. Where had Reggie gotten the idea that Danny could take Jenny away from him?

As he carried the unconscious rancher to the station, hope bloomed anew within him. Did he have a chance with Jenny?

★★★

Danny bound the wound in Reggie's shoulder and laid him before the fire, covering him with blankets before retrieving his rifle and the few tools he'd left in the box canyon. He stowed the shovel and pick in the rock stable and scurried through the bars of the gate—just in time to catch the sunset in the west.

Darkness descended quickly as the final rays stretched faintly across the prairie. A coyote barked in the distance and a single star glittered in the deep blue expanse above. He wondered at the Lord's intent or involvement. Was a lesson to be gleaned from the rancher's unexpected attack? And had Peter guessed the incident?

When he heard the pound of hooves on the road from town, Danny squinted into the gathering gloom. His eyes widened when he recognized Jenny Blair astride a borrowed horse, windblown strands of hair tousled across her rosy cheeks.

"Did he come here?" she asked as she reined the horse beside him, not bothering to greet Danny as she studied him, demanding a reply.

His chest tightened at sight of her, and he glanced at the mountains, then back at her. "Why are you here?"

A scowl puckered her shadowed features, and a shiver passed through her—the cold ride catching up to her. Danny reached for her bridle.

"Let's get you into the station. You must be half frozen. I'll stable your horse."

He tied the animal to the hitching rail and waited for her dismount, but she stared down at him, shaking her head.

"No, no, Danny," she murmured. "I need to know. Did Reggie come here?"

He pointed to the rim of the bluff. "Fired a few shots at me from up there."

She blanched, and her eyes grew round. "Are you hurt?"

A slow grin came to him, and his heart warmed, afraid to hope. "Would you care?"

Her scowl deepened. "Are you hurt?" she demanded. When he simply stared up at her, she raced on. "After our last conversation, I couldn't sleep. Your challenge kept me up all night, praying, seeking answers, wanting to know the Lord's will for me. I think I already knew, but I wrestled with him anyway, refusing to give in. Then, this morning, I knew I couldn't marry Reggie. I broke off our engagement, although it wasn't a formal attachment at all. He'd never actually proposed. He told folks we'd marry, and I'd accepted his unspoken proposal. I felt excited at being a rich rancher's wife."

"You don't love him?" Danny rested his hands on either side of her, gripping the pommel and cantle as he studied her face in the darkness. Little light remained, except for a dim glow from a few scattered stars. The cold was forgotten.

She shook her head, the loose tendrils dancing across her cheeks. "No, Danny. I thought I did. But when you came to Trinidad—"

Her words choked off, and she lifted a foot from the stirrup. She slid to the ground, her back to the heaving horse, but she wouldn't meet Danny's searching gaze. But he lifted her chin, locking their gaze once more.

"Oh, no, you don't. You need to finish. Tell me."

She nodded at his forceful command. "Ever since you came to town, I sensed something about you. At first, I thought it was the connection we shared with Patrick. But every time we talked, I realized I enjoyed you, your feelings, your resolve. Where I was captivated by Reggie's wealth and what he could provide for me, I was captivated by your faith, your desire to serve God, and your dedication to Patrick's dream."

She paused, allowing her words to sink in, then drew a deep breath and continued. "You didn't know this was my dream too. For years, Patrick longed to develop this spring, to carve a station out of the desert. We planned for so long to build this place, to clear a road and open the stage station, make a home for the Blair family. I felt cheated when Patrick left for the war, his noble intentions clouding my selfish wants. Then when you came to complete his goal, our dream ... it was more than I could bear."

Danny grinned. "You didn't like me at first, did you?"

Her voice dropped to a whisper, and she glanced away. "Indeed no. But that's what the Lord revealed. I couldn't keep you from my mind. While trying to ignore you, you intrigued me with your yearning to build our station. At first, our lost dream rankled me, jealous as you worked out here. But then I began to see."

"See what?" Danny felt poised on the edge of a precipice. He longed to hear her words, her declaration, and understand how Jesus had worked on her heart as he had in Danny's own.

When she smiled, her white teeth flashed in the night. "I began to see the Lord's hand. Through Carl and Lil's kindness, I no longer needed the home Reggie offered. Then you worked with Peter Walking Stick and his family, the very man who told Patrick about this spring. It was you who shared Christ with them. And I saw the way Jesus worked on your faith, growing you through the adventure of coming west."

He nodded, encouraging her on.

Jenny licked her lips. "Don't you see? As God worked in your heart, he was working in mine too. Together, we've found hope. Ezekiel's dry bones spoke to me, and I know they spoke to you. Through everything." She waved to indicate the station, the road, and the spring. "Through everything, I see the Lord led you here to shape you and ..."

"And?" he urged when she hesitated.

"He led you here for me." Jenny finally slipped into his arms. Danny grasped her, pulling her close as the cold wind ruffled her loose hair. Her hands rested on his shoulders as she went on. "This morning, when I broke off our engagement—if you can even call it that—Reggie vowed he'd kill you. He thought you'd stolen me from him. I tried to reason with him, but he blamed you, nonetheless. He left town soon after, and I told Carl what had happened before following him, hoping to get here in time."

"You came to warn me?" Danny slid his hands around her slim waist, their faces close as he listened to her tale.

Jenny nodded, eyes shining in the dim starlight. "Yes. You said you loved me." She lifted his collar to ward off the cold. "Well, Danny Mason. I have fallen in love with you too."

God was so good to him. Danny saw it now. He pulled Jenny in and kissed her, pressing his mouth to hers as he held her tightly. She did not resist, and he was surprised when she responded in kind. He didn't deserve anything in life. He was an orphan with a borrowed name.

He pulled back from Jenny as doubts assailed him. He stared down at her, wishing he didn't have to reveal this.

"My name, Mason. You know I borrowed it from another man. No one at the orphanage knew my right name." He shared his secret tentatively, waiting to see her response. But he relaxed when she laughed lightly.

"Mason is a strong name, a good name. And we will share it proudly."

★★★

Hours later, he sat propped against the stones of the spacious room where a fire leaped on the hearth and shadows darted across the rough walls. Jenny had gone to sleep in the kitchen where a bed of blankets kept her warm before the cooking fire while Danny shared the big room with Reggie Bloomberg, the rancher still unmoving in the still room.

Although long past midnight, Danny couldn't sleep. Thoughts and memories swirled unbidden around his mind, reminding him of the orphanage, the terrible war, and the impetus that had brought him west. Patrick Blair, Nelson, and Father McKay seemed to hold center stage in his imaginary play, conjuring challenging feelings and emotions that welled within him, making his chest tighten and release in turn.

When Reggie stirred, Danny glanced over to where the wounded rancher lay, a bandage wrapped around his right shoulder. He didn't move when Reggie struggled to prop himself up, the wounded man's gaze locked on the low fire on the hearth.

"Mason?" He didn't bother to glance at Danny.

His garbled speech grated, and Danny shifted his gaze back to the flames in the big stone fireplace.

"Where am I?"

Danny drew a deep breath at the rancher's inquiry. He felt suddenly relieved to put his mental wanderings to rest, telling himself he'd have to watch those past reminiscences and not allow them too much leash.

"You're at the station I built. You paid me an unexpected visit today."

"Did you shoot me?"

Danny nodded before turning to face Reggie. "You caught me in the box canyon, almost killed me. I'm grateful I could get to my rifle."

Silence settled for a long moment. "I remember now," Reggie murmured, almost to himself. "Jenny told me she was breaking things off with me. I accused her of having another fellow. When she didn't deny it, I guessed you." Another pause. "I could see by the look on her face I'd guessed right," he whispered.

Danny closed his eyes, thanking God for bringing him to the frontier. A grin played at the corners of his mouth as he opened his eyes to study Reggie in the dim firelight.

"What now? You tried to kill me, said I stole your girl."

Reggie inhaled and then released the pent breath slowly. "Last time Pa and I went to Denver to meet a stock buyer, I met a girl. A real pretty girl."

Danny's grin faded. "We're done then?"

Reggie grunted, then shifted on the cold dirt floor. He glanced around the big room before his gaze settled on Danny. "I don't suppose you have a drop of whiskey in the place?"

CHAPTER FORTY-FOUR

Reggie seemed startled the next morning to find Jenny at the station, preparing coffee as if it were the most natural thing in the world. And despite her protests, he demanded Danny saddle his horse after one bracing cup.

"If you wait, I'll ride to town with you, or fetch you safely to your ranch," Jenny offered again as Danny brought the rancher's horse to the hitching rail.

"I'm fine," Reggie barked as he stepped into the saddle.

But his foot slipped in the stirrup, and Danny hastened to assist, the rancher grunting in pain when Danny knocked his wounded shoulder. After Reggie sat his saddle, he glowered down at the pair.

"I'll take my leave now, but I will not be wishing you good luck." He scowled at Jenny. "You made your choice, and you'll have to live with that now." He grimaced as he tucked his injured arm against his chest, gathering the reins with his other hand.

When Danny stepped beside Jenny and slid an arm around her slim waist, the rancher only grunted again before jerking the horse's head toward town. They watched him ride to the west, the early morning sun rising behind them.

Danny was first to break the comfortable silence. "Cold," he observed, puffs of steam coming from his mouth. When she turned to smile up at him, his heart melted.

"I feel warm," she said softly, eyes glowing. She draped her arms around his neck.

"What now?" He wanted to pull her into his arms and hold her all day. His eyebrows arched suggestively, and her smile widened as she pushed him away, stepping back.

"None of that, Danny Mason. We have work to do."

She led the way back into the station where she prepared breakfast while he packed his gear. He grinned as she called to him from the kitchen, enjoying her presence in the station he'd built.

"You'll join Peter and his family and complete this blasted road. Try and convince Luke to stay on after his relatives return to the mountains, to help around the place. It'll take a long time to make this place comfortable. With Mr. Hennessey's wagons from the mine and the stage coming through, we should have a decent income right off, God willing. Come springtime, we'll need to work the garden, and I want an orchard planted. Of course, you'll have to build Luke a house, what with us taking the station."

When Danny heard this, he stole behind her where she worked at the cooking fire and pulled her into his arms.

She frowned up at him. "I said none of that now, and I'm making breakfast." She glanced over her shoulder to where potatoes simmered in a skillet.

Danny studied her intently as his arms tightened around her. "I'm no hand at this, Jenny, but you know I love you. Will you marry me, share my life?"

Her frown softened into a playful grin. "I thought we already had that understanding. I'll quit my job at Hanson's, and we'll manage the station together. I'll want children," she said shyly, glancing away as a rosy stain lifted to her cheeks. When she looked at him again, she appeared all business. "This was always my dream, to work beside Patrick and run this station. And now the Lord brought you, the man who's stolen my heart. Perhaps dreams do come true, just not in the way you expect."

★★★

The miles slipped by swiftly as Danny rode the newly cleared route to the northeast, toward the Arkansas River. Across the plains, he saw where leafless thickets huddled beside shallow ditches, waiting for the spring rains that would bring life back to the prairie. As his horse trotted the easy path, Danny marveled at the faded blue sky, scattered clouds scuttling across the expanse. Was spring in the air as Peter suggested?

To the west, the high peaks glistened with deep snow, no sign of winter letting up. But he had to admit the temperature didn't seem as bitter as before, as if a hint of warmer days whispered in the wind.

He also marveled at the Lord's hand in his life. Had it merely been chance when he was placed in Sergeant Blair's regiment? Danny's love of God, his coming to Trinidad, and finding Jenny Blair could all be traced to that one fateful moment when he'd been assigned to Blair's scout platoon. Jesus had been working on him before Danny ever knew of Christ.

When he caught sight of the bare branched cottonwoods that lined the Arkansas River, he knew he'd come to the junction with the Old Trail. A tendril of smoke lifted from a campfire at the place he'd helped Crawford water the horses when the stage brought him west, so many months ago.

He reined in his horse when he rode into the wide, well-worn path that led from Santa Fe to the Kansas plains. Danny stared down at the dirt, wondering how many freight wagons, how many stagecoaches, and how many pioneers had traveled over this very spot. Something niggled in his stomach, reminding him with a thrill that he'd traveled this very road and now was a part of this magical frontier.

When he recognized Peter and Luke near the fire, he waved, eager to join his friends. "You finished the road," was his greeting as he stepped from the saddle, accepting a steaming mug from Luke.

Peter shook hands with Danny and lifted his gaze to the tall mountains. "This final section was the easiest part to shape. We have completed our task, and it is time to return to the forest."

Startled at the abrupt news, Danny felt his chest tighten. He wasn't ready for his friends to depart. He'd only just become engaged to Jenny, plans for their future swirling in his mind all morning. Were changes to come so quickly—before he had time to process?

"I'll stay with you, if that's all right," Luke said. "I'd like to continue at the station."

"And we will return next winter for a visit," Peter announced as he gestured to the Indian's piled packs where the women were preparing for departure. Down by the river, the three teenage boys skipped rocks across the shallow water.

"But it's not yet April," Danny protested, not ready to lose his friends so unexpectedly. He recalled the soldiers he'd known in the war, so many vanishing without warning. "Surely winter is not over."

Peter shrugged. "Only God can tell the mountains when winter is over. I feel the time is right to follow the river back to the forest." He locked eyes with Danny. "I want to thank you for telling us of Jesus. I long to know him more."

"Me too," Danny mumbled as one of the children shouted, pointing to the east. All heads turned to watch the plume of dust rise behind an approaching vehicle.

"Stagecoach," the sharp-eyed Luke confirmed as the wagon neared.

For a few minutes, no one spoke while the coach drew closer, yet Danny glanced at the opening to the newly completed road. Was this the time to try the new route?

He shot a quick prayer skyward as the driver hauled on his reins, bringing the heaving teams of horses to a halt before the small group. Danny grinned when he recognized Old Crawford on the high bench. Beside the driver, a man sat with a scarf across his face, his gaze riveted on Danny.

"Howdy, folks," Crawford sang out as he wrapped the long leather reins around the brake handle. "Sure hope you have coffee on."

"Help yourself, you old desert rat." Peter grinned at the stage driver as he stepped forward to help water the weary horses.

Crawford squinted at the old Indian. "Peter Walking Stick, I haven't seen you in a coon's age."

They shook hands as Danny watched the passenger on the high seat slowly remove his scarf. He felt his eyes widen when he saw the man's face.

"Howdy, Danny Mason," the old man said softly.

Danny gasped, not believing his sight. "Nelson." The two friends clasped hands after Nelson alighted. "I thought you were dead."

Nelson grinned, splitting the gray whiskers Danny remembered so well. "Almost," the old hunter chuckled. "Seems the rebs didn't want wounded prisoners, so I wound up in a Union hospital tent. By the time I healed, the war was over." He pointed to the rifle slung on Danny's shoulder. "I see you still have that fancy gun."

Danny's heart warmed at seeing his old friend. "Still comes in handy," he said, thinking of yesterday's events with Reggie Bloomberg.

Luke delivered a steaming cup to the former soldier. Nelson eyed Danny over the rim as he sipped the hot coffee. Behind them, Peter helped Crawford tend to the stock.

"Blair?"

Nelson's question didn't surprise Danny. He shook his head. "Died that day, after you were wounded. He gave me his journal."

Nelson glanced across the prairie, the gentle wind ruffling the ends of his red woolen scarf. "That explains why you're here." His gaze shifted to the faint outlines of the new road angling to the south. Nelson indicated the route with his tin cup. "Don't tell me you built this road. Blair's road across the desert?"

"I built his station at the spring." Danny gestured to the nearby Indian family. "We built the road, worked all winter."

Crawford stepped close. "You finished the shortcut across the desert?"

Danny straightened, feeling the significance of the moment, the moment he'd longed for. This was what he'd come west for. Now was the time to test Blair's shortcut. He pointed the way toward the unseen station. "About forty miles that way. Another thirty from there to Trinidad."

Crawford ran a hand across his grizzled chin. "I don't know. The Holladay stage line has been bought out, and I don't know how Wells Fargo will take to a new route, one not designated on the map. I'm supposed to be training a new driver." He indicated Nelson as he drained his cup and handed the empty mug to Peter.

"Good road, Crawford," the old Indian said as he stepped away from the coach, the watered horses ready for the next leg of the journey.

"If Danny Mason built a road, it's got to be good," Nelson alleged with a clap to Danny's shoulder. He climbed to the high seat beside Crawford as the driver reached for the reins.

Luke stepped forward. "I can show the way."

"Jump in, young man," Crawford nodded after a brief deliberation.

Luke hugged his family before scrambling aboard.

"Well, I trust Peter Walking Stick, and I trust Nelson here." Crawford peered at Danny from beneath his bushy eyebrows. "I guess I'll trust you too, young man. It's easier to ask for forgiveness than ask for permission." He shook the reins free and glanced once more down at Danny. "What's the name of your station?"

Danny grinned as he nodded to Nelson. "Blair Spring."

The old stage driver turned his teams into the new road.

"I guess I'll be seeing a lot of you, Nelson. Say hello to Blair's sister when you come to the station," Danny shouted after the coach, his old friend waving as Crawford lashed the reins, the horses shifting to a trot.

It took less than an hour for Danny to eat something and exchange his weary horse for a fresh mount. The Indians gathered around him, the younger children grasping his legs as he said his goodbyes.

After shaking hands with the three teenage boys, Danny grasped Peter's hand, their gazes locked. "Thank you for all you did, all of you," Danny said. "I couldn't have done any of this without you. Your family has come to mean a great deal to me."

Peter grinned. "Thank you for sharing Jesus, the greatest gift. And you are part of our family now."

Danny mounted his horse. "I'll see you this autumn," he called as he rode from their camp.

Peter's family waved and shouted until he was out of earshot. Tugging his hat low, Danny trotted in the afternoon sunlight, his heart warming as he followed the twin wheel tracks in the dirt.

Things were happening too swiftly for him to register. Reggie's attack, his engagement to Jenny, Peter's family departing for the mountains, and now a stage on the station road, bound for Trinidad. He'd worked so hard, planned so long. And now, the work was coming to fruition. Sergeant Blair's dream was coming true.

Almost a year ago, he'd fought his final battle, where Patrick Blair met his end, and he believed Nelson dead. Since then, Danny felt the lessons had mounted within him, drawing him nearer to God and to maturity. He felt much older now than the young boy who had joined the army at sixteen. While the war had stolen his youth, his time in a blue uniform had filled him with a lifetime of experiences and emotions he'd always remember. Was God using these lessons to grow his faith and color his future? With Christ by his side, Danny hoped he could take the sorrowful struggles of his past and impact his future with a more favorable outcome.

At his last, Sergeant Blair had challenged Danny to live, to dream. He hoped the sergeant would be pleased with the choices he'd made, coming west and falling in love with Patrick's sister. Something told him the sergeant would be delighted.

Danny's heart swelled as he rode across the desert, his thoughts filled with so many memories. He'd come west to serve God, to complete a mission the Lord had thrust upon him. He expected hard work and countless challenges, but he never expected to find new friends or discover love. As he gave his heart to the Lord, Jesus ministered to his soul, giving him the secret desires of his heart, desires Danny didn't even know he yearned for. From a broken man who searched for God, the Lord was rebuilding Danny, shaping him with challenges and blessings Danny could never have foreseen.

When he rode into the clearing, the sun leaned far west, perched atop the gleaming peaks of the Rockies. Danny reined in before the stone station and watched the sun slowly drop behind the tall ridge. He turned when the door opened and Jenny stepped out, a smile creasing her pretty face as she approached.

"Old Crawford said to tell you the road is wonderful. He sure was tickled when Luke showed him the water trough. He said he'd be sure and tell Mr. Hennessey at the mine."

Danny nodded, peering down at her as dusk's shadows shaded her cheeks. Slowly, wearily, he dropped from the saddle to take her hand. He grinned when she pinked at the familiar gesture.

"I'll put your pack near the fireplace. I'm sleeping in the kitchen tonight but tomorrow will return to town. Until we're married, I'll stay with Carl and Lil."

Danny nodded, eager to see that happy day arrive as soon as possible.

"There was a man with the stage, said he knew you and Patrick," Jenny added as an afterthought.

"Nelson," Danny said softly. "He's a good man."

Jenny peered up at him. "You're a good man, Danny Mason."

He drew her into his arms, suddenly struck at her heartfelt words, words he'd hoped someone might say over his dead body a year ago. His selfish ambition had failed, yet he'd become a man of significance in the eyes of Jesus, a more important goal. He studied Jenny's beautiful face as emotion rose in his throat, consuming him, filling him with a joy he'd never dared imagine. *God is so good*, he thought. Sergeant Blair's dream had not died with him that day on the battlefield. It had simply been lived by another man. By him, Danny Mason.

He turned to lead Jenny into the stone station and saw the young cottonwood sapling near the front door had budded. Danny smiled at the new life all around him, suddenly thinking of the dry bones in Ezekiel's valley and the way God rebuilds lives.